The Reign
of the
Favored
Women

The Reign

of the
Favored
Women

ANN CHAMBERLIN

FORGE®

A TOM DOHERTY ASSOCIATES BOOK
NEW YORK

THE REIGN OF THE FAVORED WOMEN

Copyright © 1998 by Ann Chamberlin

The excerpts appearing on pages 368–369 are from *The Honest Courtesan: Veronica Franco, Citizen and Writer in Sixteenth-Century Venice* by Margaret F. Rosenthal. Copyright © 1992 by Margaret F. Rosenthal. Reprinted by permission of University of Chicago Press.

This book is printed on acid-free paper.

A Forge Book
Published by Tom Doherty Associates, Inc.
175 Fifth Avenue
New York, NY 10010

Forge® is a registered trademark of Tom Doherty Associates, Inc.

Library of Congress Cataloging-in-Publication Data

Chamberlin, Ann.
    The reign of the favored women / Ann Chamberlin. — 1st ed.
        p.   cm.
    "A Tom Doherty Associates book."
    ISBN 0-312-86592-9 (alk. paper)
    1. Safiye, consort of Murad III, Sultan of the Turks, 1550–1605—
Fiction. 2. Mohammed III, Sultan of the Turks, d. 1603—Fiction.
3. Murad III, Sultan of the Turks, 1546–1595—Fiction. 4. Turkey—
History—1453–1683—Fiction.   I. Title.
PS3553.H2499R45   1998
813'.54—dc21   98-19412
                                                                        CIP

First Edition: September 1998

Printed in the United States of America

0 9 8 7 6 5 4 3 2 1

for

Cal and Jo Ann

ACKNOWLEDGMENTS

MUCH OF THE list is the same as for the first two volumes of this trilogy, but repetition should not indicate a lack of appreciation, rather the opposite.

I owe a great deal to the friendly people in Turkey, especially the guides at the Topkapi palace who hardly raised a brow as I went through the harem again and again. I'd like to thank my in-laws, Cal and Jo Ann Setzer—to whom this volume is dedicated—for their support, which allowed me to make that trip. And my husband and sons for their patience while my mind was elsewhere.

Kourkan Daglian, Ruth Mentley, Harriet Klausner, Alexis Bar-Lev, and Dr. James Kelly all unstintingly shared their expertise with me. Again I'd like to thank the Wasatch Mountain Fiction Writers Friday Morning Group for their support, patience, and friendship. Teddi Kachi and Leonard Chiarelli at the Marriott Library, as well as all the Whitmore and Holladay librarians—especially Hermione Bayas and Larraine Blamires—never stinted in their assistance. Early in the process, Debra Sandack and the book club offered their opinions. Near the end, Dave Willoughby, Marny Parkin, and others in the Life, the Universe, and Everything Symposium did so as well.

I'm afraid Gerry Pearce will still disagree with the decisions of orthography I have made. He—and any other person knowledgeable in these spheres—will appreciate the difficulties I've faced walking the line between Arabic, Persian, Turkish, both Ottoman and modern, and common English usage. Yes, I know I am still inconsistent from word to word but no longer—I hope—from one use of a single word to the next. At this point—and for the reader's ease—I'm not going to agonize any more. If you'd like, Gerry, we can try to thrash it out over dinner again. Your turn to buy.

There is another woman to whom I owe much but she didn't want her name mentioned. She knows who she is. She doesn't approve—except of good spelling and grammar.

Of course, there are my editor and dear friend Natalia Aponte, and Steve, Erin, Karla, and all the other folks at Tor/Forge.

And finally, Virginia Kidd, my agent.

Without these folks, *The Reign of the Favored Women* would have existed, but never in the light of day. None of them is to be blamed for the errors I've committed, only thanked for saving me from making more.

DRAMATIS PERSONAE

ABD AR-RAHMAN—Son of the deceased Mufti, eventually husband to Gul Ruh.

ABDULLAH—The narrator of the story, Esmikhan's eunuch guardian.

*AGOSTINO BARBARIGO—Andrea's father, *provveditore* of Venice.

*ANDREA BARBARIGO—Scion of a wealthy Venetian house, in this novel, lover to Safiye.

*ARAB PASHA—A protégé of Sokolli Pasha, governor of Cyprus and beloved of Gul Ruh.

*AYSHA SULTAN—Daughter of Murad and Safiye, sister to Muhammed.

BETULA—Daughter of the Mufti and Umm Kulthum, sister to Abd ar-Rahman.

*DJWERKHAN SULTAN—Daughter of Selim the Sot, half-sister to Murad and Esmikhan.

*ESMIKHAN SULTAN—Daughter of Selim and half-sister to Murad, the woman Abdullah must guard.

*ESPERANZA MALCHI—Safiye's Jewish Kira.

*FATIMA SULTAN—Daughter of Murad and Safiye, sister to Muhammed.

*FERHAD PASHA—Advanced first to Master of the Imperial Horse, later Agha of the Janissaries and Grand Vizier, in this novel, Esmikhan's lover.

*FERIDUN BEY—Secretary of Sokolli Pasha.

THE FIG—The midwife who apprentices to and later replaces the Quince.

FOSCARI—Andrea Barbarigo's father-in-law-to-be.

*GHAZANFER AGHA—Formerly Mihrimah's eunuch, now Safiye's, he eventually gains the post of *kapu aghasi*.

GIORGIO VENIERO—Abdullah's Italian name.

GIUSTINIANI—A sea captain, native of the island of Chios.

GUL RUH SULTAN—Esmikhan's daughter.

HUSAYN—A Syrian merchant and old family friend of Abdullah, later known as Hajji.

*JOSEPH NASSEY—Sultan Selim the Sot promised to give kingship of Cyprus to this Jewish companion.

*THE KIRA—Women, often Jewish, who brought bundles of goods in for the ladies of the harems to purchase and also served as messengers between secluded women and the outside world.

*MIHRIMAH SULTAN—Daughter of Suleiman, aunt of Esmikhan.

MITRA—A slave girl Safiye purchases and gives to Murad as a concubine. She is of Persian origin and a poet.

*MUFTI—The highest religious judge in Turkey, in this novel, Abd ur-Rahman's father.

*MUHAMMED III—Turkish Sultan from 1595–1603 C.E., son of Murad and Safiye.

*MURAD III—Turkish Sultan from 1574–1595 C.E., son of Selim and Nur Banu, lover of Safiye.

MUSLIM—As a personal name, it is Andrea Barbarigo's Turkish name.

*NUR BANU SULTAN—The woman who purchased Safiye, she is a former concubine of Selim, mother of Murad, and stepmother of Esmikhan.

*PIALE PASHA—The Kapudan Pasha, admiral of the Turkish navy.

THE QUINCE—Midwife to the Imperial harem.

*SAFIYE—Born the daughter of the Venetian governor of the is-
land of Corfu, she was captured by pirates and became the concubine of Murad III.

*SELIM II—Known as the Sot, Turkish Sultan from 1566–1574
C.E., father of Murad and Esmikhan, Nur Banu was his concubine.

*SOFIA BAFFO—Safiye's Venetian name.

*SOKOLLI PASHA—Muhammed Pasha Sokolli, Turkish Grand
Vizier, married to Esmikhan Sultan.

*SULEIMAN I—Known in the West as the Magnificent and in the
East as the Lawgiver, Turkish Sultan from 1520–1566 C.E., father of Selim and grandfather of Murad. He is already deceased
at the start of this novel.

UMM KULTHUM—Widow of the Mufti, mother of Abd ur-
Rahman, eventually mother-in-law to Gul Ruh.

*UWEIS—A rowdy native Turk, companion to Murad.

*Indicates documented historical character.

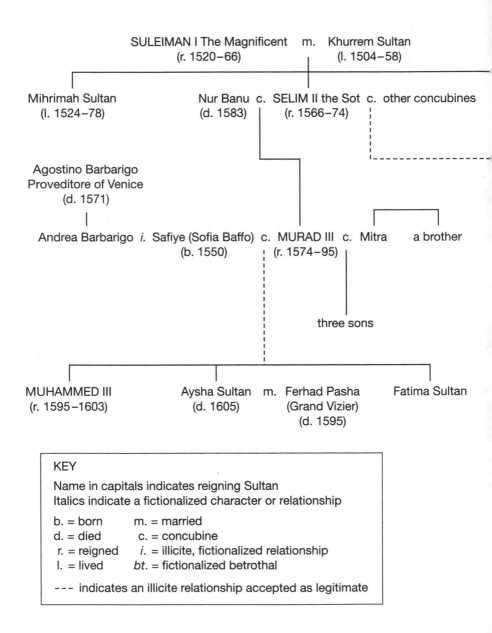

SULEIMAN I The Magnificent   m.   Khurrem Sultan
(r. 1520–66)   (l. 1504–58)

Mihrimah Sultan
(l. 1524–78)

Nur Banu c. SELIM II the Sot c. other concubines
(d. 1583)   (r. 1566–74)

Agostino Barbarigo
Proveditore of Venice
(d. 1571)

Andrea Barbarigo i. Safiye (Sofia Baffo) c. MURAD III c. Mitra   a brother
(b. 1550)   (r. 1574–95)

three sons

MUHAMMED III   Aysha Sultan m. Ferhad Pasha   Fatima Sultan
(r. 1595–1603)   (d. 1605)   (Grand Vizier)
(d. 1595)

KEY

Name in capitals indicates reigning Sultan
Italics indicate a fictionalized character or relationship

b. = born   m. = married
d. = died   c. = concubine
r. = reigned   i. = illicite, fictionalized relationship
l. = lived   bt. = fictionalized betrothal

--- indicates an illicite relationship accepted as legitimate

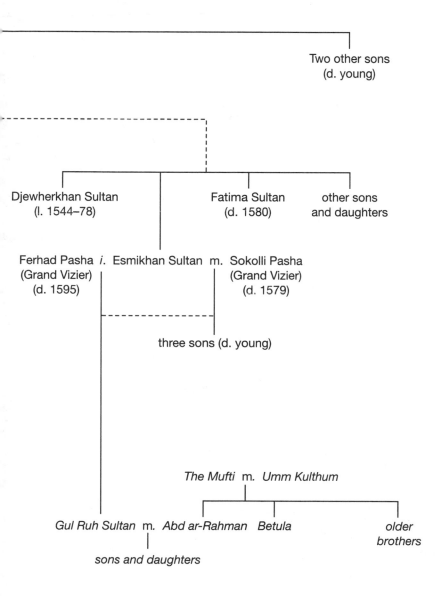

Two other sons
(d. young)

Djewherkhan Sultan
(l. 1544–78)

Fatima Sultan
(d. 1580)

other sons
and daughters

Ferhad Pasha *i.* Esmikhan Sultan m. Sokolli Pasha
(Grand Vizier)   (Grand Vizier)
(d. 1595)   (d. 1579)

three sons (d. young)

The Mufti m. *Umm Kulthum*

Gul Ruh Sultan m. *Abd ar-Rahman*   *Betula*   *older*
                                                               brothers

sons and daughters

Part I

Abdullah

I

AFTER THE VERY difficult birth of her daughter, my dear lady, Esmikhan Sultan, eventually learned to walk again with the aid of a cane. But she moved more like a duck than a woman and therefore preferred to be carried, either in her sedan or in a chair one of my assistant eunuchs and I would contrive by crossing our hands. She could sit for short periods without discomfort, but mostly she preferred to lie about in the harem, propped up with innumerable pillows.

Plump before, now inactivity and contentment made her fat.

To me Esmikhan was as dear as ever, but then, I had been forcibly removed from the realm where physicality was important. Huge breasts dominated her entire body. She nursed the child herself for four full years, and then it was Gul Ruh, teased by other youngsters for being a baby, who shook her head and said, "No, thank you, Mama," of her own accord.

This saucy weaning was as yet far in the future, however, one day of her daughter's first spring. The women of the imperial palace had invited a jeweler to display her wares, and my lady came, too. More than the jewels, she had wanted to show Baby Gul Ruh the gazelle fawns that always enlivened the Sultan's gardens at that time of year. Esmikhan caught my gaze over the child's delight, and the gentle love I read in my lady's round, gazelle-brown eyes was delight enough for me.

The day was so warm and bright however that we soon retreated inside with the rest of the harem as if the heat of summer were already upon us. Here, behind the bastion of the walls and playing fountains, we sank into the exquisite artifice that was harem reality.

Turkish women called their procurers Kira. Usually Jewish, always female, these were the wives or daughters of merchants who entered the harems to peddle their families' goods where men would not be allowed. This particular jeweler's wife was Esperanza Malchi. Her fathers had been expelled from Spain almost eighty years before, in 1492 as Christians tell the years, and had spent some years in Venice before finally ending their wanderings in Constantinople's jewelry *suq*.

And that particular day, as the culmination of her show, Esperanza Malchi produced a ruby necklace so magnificent it quite made the head reel.

"Come, ladies," she replied to the "oohs and ahs" with a purr that matched her black-cat features. "To truly appreciate the unique qualities of the major gem, you must view it in the light. Come to the window, if you please."

As if she were Moses and they the liberated Israelites, the Kira led all the women to the advantage of a high window on the other side of the room. Only my lady, her daughter, and I remained behind because Esmikhan had decided—wisely, I thought—that the pleasure of seeing a ruby in sunlight was not worth the trouble of getting up and moving to the window.

Because my lady was a married woman, not a slave, and a daughter of the Sultan besides, with an income of her own, the Kira had placed the display case right at her elbow, the better to tempt her. Most of the others could only look and sigh. Now, while they were all busy at the window, Esmikhan idly ran her fingers through the box's contents: the ransom of any European prince. But I think my lady fingered the gems from boredom.

If Esmikhan did look with interest, it was to consider trinkets for her daughter, who, at almost seven months old, lay nestled against her expansive breast. Esmikhan plucked out a pair of pendant earrings and held them up to the baby's ears: Was it too early to pierce that petal-like flesh?

I was more struck by the look of the father in the child. Remarkable, I mused, how the sunburnt features of a cavalry officer remolded themselves in plump pink baby skin. Surely my lady thought of her lover every time she looked at her daughter. Grief, loss, and guilt tainted each such thought, for Gul Ruh was not the Pasha's legitimate child. But only my lady and I must ever know that secret.

I sometimes wished I'd stopped the clandestine exchange of letters and gifts between the two lovers sooner—or more effectively. Those wordless missives of flowers and leaves that only the love-blind could read, how dangerous if discovered. And sometimes I knew the stab of my own jealousy, that the dashing Ferhad Pasha offered my lady something I could not. This wasn't the case with Sokolli Pasha, the old grey Grand Vizier to whom she was legitimately married.

I was never sorry I'd broken the master's trust to allow the single night's indiscretion. It had saved my lady from self-destructive heartbreak. It had produced this lovely dear rose to fill her childless arms. And yet, I couldn't be easy with the memory, nor with people's comments, given innocently enough, that "There's nothing of the Vizier in her, is there?" The very hint of adultery could not go well for a great man's wife in this land: even a Sultan's daughter could not hope to escape the death sentence if the charge were ever proven. Never mind how it would go for the eunuch entrusted with guarding her virtue. I tried, therefore, to shut the thought out of my mind.

Gul Ruh grabbed at the earrings, so my lady put them back, cooing all the while, and slipped a plain gold bangle on the fat little wrist instead. The child instantly took the bangle off and began to teethe on it. With the little hands and mouth safely occupied, Esmikhan introduced her daughter's eyes to the intricacies of a locket she fished out of the velvet-lined box. I noticed only briefly that the mosaic work above the clasp was Venetian. Then I closed my mind to all but the sense of contentment in the baby prattle that followed.

"I don't know what that is, sweetheart," was the next thing I was aware of my lady saying.

I idly glanced over to see what had caught her and the baby's attention. Esmikhan had found a scrap of paper concealed inside the locket. She opened the paper, looked at both sides, then shrugged and folded it again.

"My very sweet mountain stream, I think it is nothing. Only scribbling. Or it is a magic spell which, I pray Allah, you may never have need of."

Esmikhan quickly snapped the paper back in the locket lest uninitiated use of such magic cause bad luck. But before she had time to return the locket to the box, it was snatched a little too roughly from her—by the Kira.

"I'm sorry, most gracious Esmikhan Sultan," Esperanza Malchi said. "This particular piece is not for sale."

"I was only curious about what was inside . . ."

"It is nothing," the Kira said, and put the locket, instead of back into the box, into her bosom.

"There, see, I told you, honey blossom. It is nothing." These words gave the impression the world is really good, kind, and free from all intrigue. My lady lied.

The rest of the women had followed the Kira back to the divan and took up their places again. The ruby necklace, I discovered, had found its way around Safiye's neck.

I was not surprised. How to describe Safiye to those who never saw her? Lover to my lady's brother, Prince Murad, heir to the Ottoman throne. Mother of his only son to date, Muhammed, who was three years old. This mundane recital of functions falls far short. That she was the most beautiful woman in the world, even seven years after I first fell under her spell in a convent garden in Venice, I was not alone in believing. Brown eyes as cool as autumn leaves, a promiscuity of golden hair, skin as flawless and unchanging as marble. Tall and willowy, she had movements like a ribald song.

And beneath these features lay a soul with perfections of its own. Perfect in ambition, perfectly unflinching of either love or mercy to gain its own ends. Like demon-cold at midnight, she took the breath away.

The exorcism I had undergone to break her spell over me was hardly something I would recommend to the rest of her victims. What the tumble from Venetian seaman to harem eunuch had left me, I'd only just begun to call a life again.

Suffice it to say that Safiye—whom I'd once known as Sofia Baffo— got everything she wanted. My purpose was simply to see that what she got cost nothing more of me, nor more of those souls who, in spite of everything, had become so dear to me.

As far as I was concerned, Safiye could have the Kira's ruby necklace. It sat against the white flesh of her neck as if it had seeped there from the inside, as if alabaster could really bleed.

"Send the bill to Prince Murad, Magnesia," Safiye said, admiring herself in a mirror, "for I shall have this."

"How dare you!" Nur Banu was livid.

Nur Banu had been Sultan Selim's lover—once upon a time—and had produced Murad, his first-born son. As such, she was nominal head of the imperial harem. Her four hundred *ghrush* had bought the golden-haired Venetian beauty for her son's bed. Safiye, of course, had long ago outstripped the older woman's tutelage. Nur Banu was the only one who still attempted to contain the natural force she'd unwittingly loosed upon the world.

"How dare you demand such things of my son?" Nur Banu asked. "You refused to spend more than three months with him this winter. And half that time you were on the road."

Safiye smoothed the pearl-button closure of her *yelek* across her flat abdomen: the unconscious gesture I knew from my lady when she was with child. Was it possible Safiye had an additional reason to be smug about her trip to Magnesia?

She'd come through the birth of little Muhammed with beauty and power unscathed, the latter enhanced here in the East in ways she had not quite appreciated before. If one prince was a good thing, two must be twice as good. So such a condition was possible, even though my lady had no rumor of it yet and the tight, willowy figure didn't show.

I reminded myself I was a eunuch, with but abbreviated knowledge of such things. I returned my attention to the matter at hand.

Nur Banu was firing these words at her opponent: "I wonder my son doesn't sell you and spare himself considerable expense."

"He cannot sell the mother of his son." Did only my ears hear the echo in Safiye's voice that indicated, perhaps, two sons?

"Any more than he will marry her."

"But forgive me, gracious lady." Safiye's contrition was obviously a mockery. "Had I known you admired this necklace so much, I never would have presumed to speak for it first. Though Allah knows why it interests you. Against your dark and blotchy skin it would be lost. But—very well—each one is allowed her own taste." She reached behind her lovely neck for the clasp. "Please, Kira, send the bill to the Sultan himself and say, 'For his favorite.' "

This was followed by an awkward silence, for everyone, including the

Kira, knew that whoever Selim's present favorite was—and it was as likely to be a boy he bought rubies for as a girl—it was not Nur Banu. The mother of his eldest son, she had her food and household expenses paid for, but any extravagance was out of the question.

Dramatically, in the silence, Safiye slipped her hands forward and to her lap. The silence persisted. Safiye smiled. The insults were glossed like cheap plating on tinware. The rubies stayed on Safiye's neck.

Later, after we'd made our farewells, my lady pulled me close and whispered, "There was something written on that paper in the locket."

"Something?"

"I've been able to think of nothing else since I saw it."

"A Koranic verse, perhaps, to ward off the evil eye?"

"No, Abdullah. I have heard my fellow believers call Christian letters flowers because they cannot recognize them as writing. But you have opened my eyes to much, perhaps too much, since you taught me to read Dante."

"The note was in Italian?"

"Venetian, *ustadh,*" she teased with pretended formality.

I didn't need to ask whose hand. "What did she say?"

"Only two words. *Tomorrow.* And *afternoon.*"

"That was all it said?"

My lady nodded. "I fear I have much to learn in your language. I cannot fathom sense from just two words."

"No better than I," I said.

That was all the attention my lady chose to give to the matter, turning now to the ever-new delight of her daughter once she had placed the information in my hands.

So I was left alone to mull the message over. My mind raced. Close in the Kira's bosom, then, these two words were making their way out of the harem and to—where? I couldn't unravel that end of it, so I retreated to the other end again.

Only one hand could have written those words. I might have seen the feathery hand myself and recognized it as the same that had scribbled "Sì" in the stateroom aboard my dearly departed uncle's galley so long ago. Or from a love note I'd intercepted even before that on a fateful winter's night in Venice. Yes, only one writer, but there were thousands of possible recipients in Constantinople alone. And what, exactly, did those words mean?

Assuming no clandestine meeting could take place in the harem, the next afternoon I wandered on the off chance into the *suq* where the Kira and her husband had their shop.

II

THE CORBELED ROOF of Constantinople's Great Bazaar palled the shops with gloom. Every merchant gave his most dazzling wares place of pride beneath his open grille. Here the goods astonished the alley's steep incline between one bulging corner and the murk of the next. But in that light and in such quantities, gold and brass were revealed as yellow, cheap, and tarnished things compared to natural air and illumination.

And when I spied Safiye's eunuch Ghazanfer walking down the same street at the same time with my same pretended nonchalance, I knew it could not be coincidence. I dove into the shop next door to the Jews' and waited for him to pass.

"Yes, please?" The shopkeeper came forward to greet me with a bow.

"Uh—" I stammered clumsily, unsure of how to respond.

In that moment, I happened to look up on the man's wall and see a highly polished brass vase. It was set at such an angle that, reflected in it, I could see a good fifty paces up the street in the other direction. And whom should I see, slowly, coincidentally, making his way down the street, around the belly of the vase, but Andrea Barbarigo, the young Venetian attaché.

"This I simply must hear!" I exclaimed aloud and then turned instantly to the shopkeeper. "Has your shop a loft upstairs?"

"Yes," the man replied, but almost with a question. I didn't want to see any of his brass lavers or fine, encrusted goblets?

"Does it communicate with the shop next door?"

A slight smile came to his thin lips. I was not the first who had ever asked him that, but I had no time to demand particulars. "Yes," he said, smiling. "There used to be a door, actually, but——"

"Five *ghrush* to use that room for the next hour."

"My usual price is twenty-five."

"Twenty-five!" I exclaimed. "That's robbery!"

"It is a very good room," he insisted quietly, and laid a finger across his lips to indicate that discretion went into the bargain.

"I'll give you fifteen."

"This way, *ustadh,*" he said, and led me instantly upstairs.

The room was tiny, windowless, and cramped with dusty stock. There was hardly space for a man to sit. The arched doorway of which the shopkeeper had spoken was, like many such openings in the maze of old Constantinople, no more than chest high. It had been remodeled over centuries and finally boarded up, but more solidly at first than now. A difference in color told me that some boards had been recently removed. This led me to discover a cleverly camouflaged chink through which I had a perfect view of Ghazanfer and the Kira, who had just brought him a narghile to smoke.

I looked back at my host in amazement. His smile told me—if anything, for it was very tight-lipped—to recall that Italians were not the only ones who knew what a source of information Moshe and his wife were.

I handed the merchant his money, thinking I'd gotten the better of the deal. The man smiled, bowed, and left the room. Presently he returned with two glasses of sherbet and a cushion for me to sit on. He was so attentive that the scene that followed might have been played in public in the Divan, and I might have been legally, comfortably in attendance throughout.

Ghazanfer's name means bold lion, as odd a name for a eunuch as my Abdullah was. Our mistresses usually favor such atrocities as Hyacinth or—as my lady had wanted 'til I talked her out of it that first day of our acquaintance—Lulu.

Ghazanfer's size was due to fat rather than muscle. Still, he was as strong as an ox, a monster of a man grotesquely scarred by some history I did not know. His hands looked as if every finger had been tortured and crushed, though he could still crack walnuts between them. His broken nose (and maybe the cheekbones had gone in the same disaster), straggly hair, and sallow skin gave him a decidedly Mongolian appearance and recalled to mind some cruel aberration of the lithe, swift riders of the steppes. Because of the operation, Ghazanfer was as beardless as a girl, which not only added to his appearance as one from the Asian steppe, but was startling whenever one came upon him in a group of men.

Yet I knew he was not Mongolian. His hair under that tall white turban was lion-tawny, his eyes blue with hard chips of green. I heard he'd been born in Hungary. I suspected him of, among other things, fostering rebellion among the Hungarian troops on behalf of his lady's ambition.

The whitewash on the walls behind Ghazanfer was in need of reapplication. His eyes, however, were all too familiar with the space and allowed him to ignore the fact. His bulk filled the narrow room, furnished though it was with no more than the chair he occupied, his narghile, and a narrow rope-strung cot. There did not seem to be room for anybody else. Anything more than a quiet smoke, certainly an important meeting, seemed out of the question.

But Andrea Barbarigo entered the room almost immediately and the eunuch made space for him. Though I'd met both men before, it was only now that I was struck by the total contrast between them. Barbarigo was short and wiry. Whereas the eunuch was so obdurate as to make one imagine a swarm of mosquitoes could not force him to scratch, the attaché seemed to suffer eternally the torments of Io. Constantly the Venetian smoothed his beard, his hair, his hose, the end of his nose, cracked his knuckles, turned his rings around on his fingers, sniffed, coughed, and when he remembered himself after each act, he grinned sheepishly.

The eunuch was clean-faced as if every woman were a razor, and constant contact with them kept him smooth. The attaché, to continue the same image, had not seen the edge of female metal since I'd seen him last, just after Safiye's son was born and she'd sent me— Well, I thought she'd sent me for a priest. Not for the first time, I thought Venice should have seen their man married before they sent him here.

I'd first met Barbarigo long ago, in my Foscari uncle's reception hall in Venice. That was so far away I smiled to think how I'd imagined us mirror images of one another: same age, same height, same class, same future, if the Fates were kind. Then, he, as I, had been Venetian to the teeth. What had become of me was a tale not worth rehearsing, but now I noticed that he, although not completely Turkified, combined the styles.

Barbarigo wore a Turkish turban with a feather at an angle only an Italian would affect, hose and shoes, but his robe was of Eastern stuff, cut a bit short and sashed around the waist. It was the most foppish of both styles, the dignity of neither. And around his neck the young attaché was wearing the locket I recognized from the Kira's display box. He fingered it voraciously as he made his salaams to the eunuch.

"So tell me, tell me, how fares your lady?" Barbarigo asked, out of breath. "How fares Sofia Baffo?"

I had not known such words existed in Turkish. It was a question only an Italian would think or dare to ask of a eunuch and, as the conversation continued, I remarked to myself that, though he took on Turkish syllables, Barbarigo's inflections and ideas remained pure Italian. He hadn't a Turkish thought or value in his brain.

Ghazanfer forgave the man his lack of manners. It seemed he had done so before and Safiye must have assured him that if he would please her, he must continue to do so in the future. The eunuch's reply, though prefaced with a half smile, refused to be moved by Barbarigo's passion. But then Ghazanfer rose and, with his monstrous hands, began to palm the young attaché.

"By Jesu and Maria!"

The Italian came out of Barbarigo in such a groan of anticipation at Ghazanfer's first touch that I had to echo the sentiment in my own mind. By Jesu and Maria! What sordid thing am I going to witness here?

"You know I only do this to satisfy myself," the eunuch said in his flutelike, feminine tones.

"I know you do, *khadim*." My countryman groaned another reply.

Panting with the heartbeat of his desire, Barbarigo began to help the eunuch peel through layers of costume. The attaché's turban tumbled off and collapsed to its natural, formless self on the floor. His bare head revealed a very un-Turkish tumble of curls—so like a eunuch's in this Eastern world.

So like mine.

I couldn't say that there hadn't been rumors circulating about the strange tastes of Safiye's head *khadim,* but I'd learned never to believe a tenth of the things a harem whispers. Now?

Off came the shoes, the sash— I was about to turn away in disgust when suddenly the eunuch reached his satisfaction. Ghazanfer stepped away from Barbarigo, as calm as ever, and nodded. I saw now that, while the great Hungarian didn't balk at allowing strange men into his lady's presence, he did consider searching such men for concealed weapons a part of his duties. This was the satisfaction he had sought—and gained. No more. No weapons were concealed on this man, or none that Ghazanfer could remove without a castrator's skill. The eunuch bowed and exited.

But the attaché's frenzy continued to climb. He was down to mere hose when the door to the Kira's back room opened once again to admit the silent bundle of veils and wrappers that is a Turkish woman in public.

But then she wasn't in public any longer.

If I hadn't guessed before, I knew at the first whiff of jasmine through broken slats who this woman was. I never saw her face, for though veils flew like waves parting before a ship's prow, Barbarigo devoured her features in his hunger. I saw clearly the frantic collapse onto the room's narrow cot. The ropes creaked dangerously under their double burden.

Then I heard the all-too-familiar woman's crescendo of her lover's name, her *"Caro mios,"* her *"Amorosos".* Her yellow kidskin slippers were just a rotted board's distance from me as they kicked for purchase in her climax.

Desires I thought had been cut from me rose staggering from the dead. With no place to go, they festered within. I thought I was going to be sick.

III

AN HOUR LATER, I was waiting for him in the niche between two shops when he left the Jews' with his latest orders from the hell-born witch. My dagger was drawn, bejeweled and ceremonial though it was. Hadn't Ghazanfer done me the *khadim*ly favor of showing me my quarry was unarmed?

"Barbarigo." I stated his name.

My adversary wheeled, still drunk with love. I have known I must fight him since we first came face-to-face, I thought, face-to-face again. Duel him, duel him. The demands of seven years drummed in my head. Mask to mask at Carnival in Foscari's hall I had confronted him. Sofia Baffo had hardly been able to choose between us. Fate had chosen then; today it would again.

Barbarigo dropped his hands from their postcoital fussing with sash and codpiece. By God, I would have him dead. He stared at the come-on wink of my dagger as if with long-lost recognition.

"What?" he said, then stopped. He knew; every man recognizes death's angel.

He bolted suddenly. I'd fully expected him to. Though weighted down by my eunuch's skirts, I was upon him in a moment. I caught him by the sash and flung him hard against the wall of a coppersmith's shop. The burnished wares clanged together like a kitchen in full smoke and his new-wound turban tumbled to the ground, releasing his eunuchlike Western curls once more. I rammed my dagger through the foppish brocade under his left arm. His liquid brown eyes—I could see my beardless self in them—winced as the point of my blade stopped some-where between skin and rib.

Shopmen retreated into their back rooms. No one in Constantino-ple would lift a finger to stop a eunuch with his dagger bared. When the deed was done, they would reemerge and quietly set things in order again, merely muttering "honor" among themselves with awe rather than anger. To pry more into the matter would be decided bad taste — or decidedly dangerous.

I slipped my blade, wicking blood to the hilt, through Barbarigo's flesh, off the rib and down, until the next thing it found would be his heart. And yet I couldn't drive it home. We stood eye to eye, panting in each other's exhausted breath.

"You—" Barbarigo swallowed and tried again, almost smiling with the pleasure to find each word was not his last. "You are the *khadim* who first brought me to her."

I drew my arm back for the lunge at such a lie.

"You are," he insisted. "Didn't you come, telling me she'd borne a son and wanted a priest for him?"

I couldn't deny it. And if I acted now upon my impulse, would my part in all of this be exposed?

Barbarigo had been speaking Turkish to this point. I switched to Venetian, for he could not recognize me as I did him and would have no reason to switch on his own. The croon of our mothers' tongue took him as much by surprise as the point of my blade, warmed by his own blood. But suddenly, irrationally, I wanted him to know.

"That was not the beginning, Barbarigo. Not the beginning at all. Do you remember me now? My voice, at least, from behind a carnival mask. My voice which, against all nature, hasn't changed in the intervening years. It was I, Barbarigo, who thwarted your attempt to elope with the lady that January evening so long ago. It was I, in the Foscari's hall. I, Giorgio Veniero. And you—" I laughed in spite of myself at the mercy it would have been. "You threatened to turn me in to your father."

My adversary's face paled as if I'd hit an artery, though, by my life, I'd as yet given him no more than a scratch.

"Yes, I—I remember," he stammered. "I—I haven't forgotten— nor forgiven—in all these years."

"Nor I, Barbarigo. Nor I. Though, by my life, I wish I'd let her go with you. I pray to heaven you had taken her out of my life, to give me my life again."

Barbarigo shifted. I refocused the attention of my blade, so he would not think emotion had weakened my resolve.

But then I realized I did not truly want *him* dead. Neither his life nor his death presented any threat to me or my two ladies at all. If I'd turned and walked away from the chink in the tradesman's wall, refusing to get involved in Safiye's machinations, we would have remained safe, too. But now she had drawn me into her maelstrom once again. Who knew where it would end? And who knew what effect this could have on my lady and her tiny, precious daughter? *Evil* was the only word that came to mind.

I could not escape the thought that this was how Baffo's daughter had planned it all along. Once again I was playing her dupe. I had hoped, even prayed, that what I had suffered in that castrator's dim little house in Pera had freed me of the spell the sight of her cast on every being in the world. Now rationality glimmered in the back of my mind: The haze of jealousy I'd been laboring through for the past hour was not the way to peace in my life.

My rashness might even bring harm to Esmikhan and Gul Ruh.

I would rather, I admitted in the brute part of my brain, turn this dagger on myself. And if I no longer stood on watch for my ladies, certainly they would suffer. At the very least, *I* would suffer without sight of them, unable to watch the daily miracle of their lives.

Who benefited if I cleansed the glistening life from young Barbarigo's eyes, purified the air we panted together? Neither the empire nor Murad, my lady's brother, whose honor was most at stake here. Only she. Only the almonds-dredged-in-poison-eyed daughter of Baffo. She who orchestrated everything. The only safety—I remembered this now—was far from her sight. To kill her lover was not the way to lie low.

Barbarigo read the hesitation in my eyes and attempted a half smile to encourage it. I took the look as a challenge—the sort that drives reason away—and, in answer, drew back yet again for the final lunge.

And, as I did, I was caught by my own sable collar and thrown in my turn against the next stretch of wall. When my head cleared, I found the dagger knocked from my hand with a singing roll into a display of large brass bowls.

And my eyes were transfixed by the blue-flinted-with-green that was the eyes of Ghazanfer.

"Go! Run!" the great eunuch hissed over his shoulder at the young attaché.

Barbarigo seemed as immobilized as I was with the monstrous, crushed hands resting on my shoulders. His Venetian eyes blinked wider with fright than they had with my blade tickling his ribs.

"Go!" Ghazanfer's Turkish rumbled again.

Then I found my voice and spoke in Italian. "Stay away from her, Barbarigo." The hands came down heavier and inched towards the vulnerability of my throat. But as long as air was there, I kept on shouting. "Barbarigo, I swear to you on the graves of my family, extinguished in me. I swear Sofia Baffo will destroy you as she does every man who cannot resist the lure of that hellborn hair."

Finally, Barbarigo ran. He disappeared at the turn of a jeweler's sultry display, my words in pursuit.

Then I turned and took a breath—might it be my last?—in order to meet those hard green eyes again. By God, that *khadim* was totally without expression, without feeling, so it seemed. But when he allowed me a second breath, I used it to give a cough of shame, of threat, deep in my throat. With more courage than I felt, I let him know what I knew—and that if he didn't want me to use it, I dared him to kill me now.

The great conical turban that towered over mine shook in a slow negative.

No, you will not use this, he informed me wordlessly. Things will not go well for you—or for either of your precious ladies—if you do.

And did he really know this? This deepest, most damaging of our secrets? I did indeed read it in the laconic slits of his eyes.

You expose my lady, I read, I will expose yours. We both know full well that precious daughter of hers is no honest offspring of the Grand Vizier.

Part II

Andrea

IV

OVERTONES DRONED THROUGH the scented oleanders and roses like nocturnal bees after late summer blossom. The quartet of young ladies pursued the final chords of their madrigal and started another in the soft September Serenissima air.

Ah, Venice! Where one is duty-bound to feel romantic, no matter where his heart is.

Andrea hoped his circle of the company appeared to be the polite mingling of a bridegroom at his betrothal party and not a guilty son's attempt to keep his father on the other side of the garden.

Now, which of the young singers was Andrea supposed to claim as his? Foscari. The remembrance of the family name, the ties the match would make, called the face to mind. The girl favored her father's side—that unfortunate nose. There she was, second from the left, taking the descant part. Melissa Foscari.

Andrea took her hair to be the girl's best feature. It had been brought up in a thick coil over her brow much too grown-up for the little face below. Ropes of pearls too precious, he thought, to be given so idly to one so young, had been pressed into service to make a crown of the coil, and they contrasted with the hair in an agreeable richness.

But this only emphasized the fact: Signorina Foscari's hair was black, raven black. They'd given up even trying to give it blond highlights as any Venetian woman from the deepest brunette would do, under a wide-brimmed hat on her *altena*. They were all, in other words, trying to match Sofia Baffo's perfection. In vain, in vain, Andrea sadly dismissed their efforts.

He struggled to keep the reaction on his face towards the upper side of the scale between disinterest and disgust as he greeted a few more guests. He who had held perfection in his trembling hands, how could he have patience with anything less?

Jesu, but the canals stank this time of year of lethargic tides. Andrea had forgotten how badly, and now the labor of breathing the foul air gripped his diaphragm like an iron manacle. He rubbed exhausted eyes against the sting of yellow-green decay and the sound of splashing rats. Typhus, he recalled, stalked the poorer sections of town in this unhealthy heat.

Wisteria reached towards the palace's upper story like a lover towards his beloved's balcony. A marble nymph flirted at him through the vine's tendrils. The fortune in beeswax the Foscaris had spent to illuminate their assembly caught the statue's perfect white curves with a sheen. This idealized beauty, so unself-conscious, luxuriating in her nakedness and its power over mankind, this was like his Sofia.

Andrea, very conscious that it was his first wine in over a year, took the glass a servant in sapphire livery offered him and let the fermentation fill his head. Over the tiny pool of red, Andrea continued to consort with the stone nymph.

"Well done, lad!"

Andrea looked helplessly down at the bloom of wine on his new lace ruff. A hurried abandonment of the Turkish in his costume upon his return to Venice had led to this ostentatious and brazen style. And now it was ruined with wine caused by a slap on the back and the hearty greeting of Messer Foscari, his future father-in-law.

I am not meant to be a Venetian fop, Andrea scolded himself.

The older man, who ignored the damage he had caused, was accompanied by Andrea's father, Agostino Barbarigo, the Republic's stern-faced proveditore.

Andrea shifted nervously under his father's gaze, feeling like a child, his elopement with Sofia thwarted again in Ca' Foscari. He felt the cut under his arm itch as it sloughed its scab. He remembered the eunuch.

It hardly seemed possible that the two beings were one and the same, the eunuch in Constantinople and the masked figure in Foscari's hall. They were so disparate in time and space. And in Andrea's mind, the masked destroyer of happiness had gained in stature over the years, haunting his hopes and dreams like something supernatural.

Well, Andrea was not about to let anyone, especially a ghost from the past—a demon from hell, rather—thwart him now.

Besides, it was too late. He'd tossed the dice amongst the uprooted cobbles of the Arsenal's workyard. They must fall where they fell.

Andrea strained his attention over the rather rhythmless music of the madrigals, out into the sultry night, for one single thump that would change the evening's rhythm all together.

By God, what time was it? Surely the bells had already rung midnight and he had missed them with all this revelry. But how could that be, when any such communal sound made him jump since his return to Christendom? He missed the muezzins.

"In truth, young messere, what do you think?" Foscari laid a confidential arm about Andrea's shoulders.

What do I think about his daughter? The thought left Andrea at a loss for words.

"What do I think about what, sir?" he managed to get out before he said something more foolish.

"I mean, what do you think about Chios?" Foscari said.

"Chios?" Andrea repeated with a gulp.

"Do you think we can take it?"

Because his son failed to give an opinion, Agostino Barbarigo stepped into the breach. "This close to the end of the season, the Turk will not be expecting a new offensive."

Sofia had all but promised that if he were successful—

Foscari said, "No. And if the Genoese cannot hold such a prize, gateway to the East, the Republic surely stands to inherit."

"The chances of the success of our fleet seem fairly good, don't you think?" Andrea's father said.

Andrea tried desperately to determine where east might be, the direction of Chios, the island that was the hushed topic of conversation. East was the direction, too, of the Arsenal where, as he had seen that afternoon, the outfitting of the fleet for this enterprise was progressing apace. Because there was no telling east from west now in the dark, he feared his own plans, as opposed to the Republic's, might have miscarried.

Suppose Giustiniani—that Genoese Chian who had no desire to see Venice take what he considered to be his own—suppose he were discovered. Suppose he were already taken by the night watch. Although rash enough, Giustiniani's was not the sort of bravery that would stand up to the first hint of torture. He might be confessing his accomplice's name even as they stood there chatting among the roses and oleanders.

Andrea thought he could hear the patrol's gondola slipping down the rancid waters of the Grand Canal, over the madrigal, over the echoing night songs of the gondoliers. Any second now, any second, they'd be pounding for admittance at the Foscaris'.

"Andrea, answer our kind host," his father hissed.

"A young man." Foscari laughed. "His mind on my daughter."

"You must have something to say on the subject of Chios rather than standing there like a total fool."

Andrea swallowed the last of his wine and cleared his throat. "The Turks sets great store by Chios."

His voice started high, reminding him of the eunuch again. "Sofia Baffo's hellborn hair will destroy you." The memory made Andrea's words end in a squeak. He tried once more.

"The Turk will not be induced to give the island up so easily as we may hope."

"Indeed?" said both older men together. The rigid constriction of two pairs of brows awaited more.

"The profit from the annual mastic harvest alone is worth a fortune."

"All the more reason it should belong to the Republic," Agostino Barbarigo said, the many hairs of his chest-length beard quivering as one.

"Indeed, sir." Overcoming a Turkish hesitation to speak on such a subject, Andrea forged ahead. "But all these profits go to the support of the . . . of the imperial harem. The Turk will not easily endure such an insult to his womenfolk."

His womenfolk will not endure it, Andrea thought, smelling jasmine mixed with almond paste, remembering the last time in the Jews' shop. No, by God, say not "last time."

"Our fleet shall teach the infidel to endure it, the lecherous old lout," said the elder Barbarigo with a passion he usually reserved for redheads.

Involuntarily, Andrea said, *"Inshallah."*

"And what is that heathen word supposed to mean?" his father asked.

"Forgive me, sir. No Turk would speak of the future without uttering it. The word means, 'If Allah wills.' "

Foscari laughed, the jovial host. "The Turk would then find anathema any festivity looking to the future such as we hold tonight?"

"I think Allah shall have very little will in the matter when he comes up against San Marco on Chios." Agostino puffed out his beard like a bullfrog marking territory with his song.

Andrea could not suppress another *"Inshallah."* But fortunately, no one heard it. Santa Sofia began to ring midnight, followed closely by San Felice, the more distant campanile of the Apostles, all the many bells of Venice that had stilled him to sleep as a child. Their notes were as liquid on the sultry night air as canal water.

Over the fading peals, Andrea heard a thud. Of course, he was listening for it. He only had time to think, That must be the patrol at the door, before he knew it was not.

The *"Mashallah"* of pure astonishment with which he followed the thought was also unheard by his scrupulous audience, for the syllables were blasted from their ears by a sound that rocked the very mud flats beneath their feet. Slivers of glass exploded from the upstairs windows of the palace and shivered through the wisteria's leaves like a waterfall.

And suddenly there was no doubt which way was east, which way the Arsenal was, for the sky over that quarter of the palace's roof glowed orange and coquelicot with soot and sulphur like the approach of daylight.

V

"SHE WILL NOT come to see me."

Andrea heard the lifelessness in his own voice and knew he caught it from the great eunuch's death mask of a face. The tones echoed around the tight confines of the jeweler's back room like whispers in a tomb.

Around him were the familiar sounds of the Turkish bazaar muffled by walls. The sharp smell of gold mingled with the strong soap the Jewess used throughout the shop in a religious frenzy of cleanliness, yeasted by the little fresh-baked poppyseed buns she offered to every guest. All these things folded into the pleasant ambiance he had longed for throughout the past two months until the thought stung his eyes with tears. But these same things now all seemed bleached and faded of life.

Andrea struggled against passive acceptance of his own statement as a man struggles beneath a smothering pillow. He felt, in fact, more violently angry, more betrayed, more frightened than he'd ever been in his life.

"Sofia will not see me?" he repeated, more of his emotion wriggling free this time and gasping for air. "That lecherous prince must be in town."

"Prince Murad—may Allah favor him—remains in Magnesia," Ghazanfer stoically advised.

"Then—God forbid it—Sofia must be ill." Andrea knew his feet were pacing under him, though there was no more than two steps they could go in any direction without running into walls—or into the eunuch's great rigid green-draped knees.

"The lady is well, by the favor of Allah."

"But she will not see me? No. I refuse to accept it. She cannot turn me away, not after what I've done for her."

"She knows what you've done," Ghazanfer said. God, the creature was a statue!

Only death would have kept Andrea away. Surely it must be the same with Sofia. "She doesn't know. She can't know."

"About the Venetian Arsenal, yes, she knows. You, sir, must have been delayed by other matters, for word of the—calamity—reached us a week ago and my lady read your hand there at once."

"She can't know. She can't know how we stood on the Foscaris' *altena* and watched—"

Andrea stopped the rehearsal surging through his brain. The memory had a demonic life of its own. So many times during the intervening weeks he'd attempted the same amputation of his thoughts. By promising himself, Sofia's ears will hear it, he'd always managed what seemed a superhuman feat. I will tell her and only her. And her kiss will make it go away.

"More people would have died in an invasion, wouldn't they? Even if Venice won."

Why had he said that to this pathetic, ravaged, expressionless substitute for his beloved? To prevent more confessions, Andrea paced like a madman, his hands twenty places at once. He was aware of his actions, but couldn't help himself.

"*Inshallah.*" The eunuch committed nothing.

"She must know I did it for her."

"She does. And is grateful."

Andrea knew he'd said more than enough. The eunuch remained a godlike judge, though Andrea had always imagined God with more wrath in His eyes—like Agostino Barbarigo. Still he couldn't stop himself.

"I haven't regretted it. I haven't regretted a single action, not for a moment—none of it. Not until now. Now when you tell me—God in heaven!—she will not see me."

"Rest assured, young sir, you have my lady's gratitude."

"But nothing else. Nothing else? Not even the sight of her?"

For two months Andrea had thought of nothing but returning to this room, of renewal of the supreme pleasures he had enjoyed here. Now that it was not to be, this return to the place only evoked the memory of love, aching in its absence. And the warning of that other eunuch, that eunuch who'd said his name was Veniero, who'd said . . .

Now all he could see was that it wasn't enough.

A bit of unmeshed logic wagged its loose ends at him, more notice-able now than it had ever seemed before.

If Sofia wanted Chios to remain with the Turk, she could not possi-bly have ever planned to leave with me. Few mastic profits could be hers in Venice, even if Venice owned the island. Only if she stayed, slave to the dark lusts of that heathen prince—

Unthinkable. Something was missing, that was all. One tiny bit of the web that made his rationale a neat and tidy package—a package pre-sented by God in his favor—that was all. He simply couldn't see it right now, but he was certain it was there.

No, the only possible conclusion was that Sofia was being kept from him against her will. Someone suspected their attachment, so she was no longer as free as once she'd been.

Perhaps not as safe?

"But it was enough, more than enough," Andrea heard himself shout. "If she had seen what I saw, heard what I heard. All they ever found of Giustiniani was—the wink of the cross in his unattached ear. The wails haunt me still in my nightmares. Screams and cries I am powerless to help—in my childhood language and hers—"

Andrea managed to stop his mouth and his frantic pacing. His insides wobbled like a child's top losing its spin and equilibrium. He took a seat to keep himself from falling over.

The seat Andrea took was the edge of the cot which he and Sofia had had no trouble turning into a bower of bliss. In order to make himself sit now on this compacted mattress laid over sagging strings, it was necessary for him to brush a score of webbed associations from his mind. He had to realize that others, many others, had used this room for many purposes. The stench of such purposes seemed to creep out of the plaster and splitting boards to assault his nostrils. He joined him-self to the rest of unbenedicted humankind with this thought, and to be no better than the redundancy of the copulating, groveling, self-interested race did not do much for his own esteem.

To even settle himself down to the level of this stonelike creature be-fore him—not male, not female, nor yet quite beast—that was too much to be endured. But having endured news that he would not see the revelation of Sofia, anything else was easy enough to take.

"I suppose there is something she wants you to tell me." Andrea found the words at last.

"There is."

"Something more than that she won't see me, else she simply wouldn't send you at all."

"I am merely considering—how much of this you need to know."

"Oh, for God's sake, tell it all," Andrea spouted. "You can give me no greater sorrow than you already have."

The great eunuch shifted on his little chair with a dangerous creak and there seemed not air enough in the narrow room for the two of them. "The tale has little to do with my lady."

"Tell it, *ustadh,* and get it over with."

The green in the eunuch's eyes shifted towards the flimsy boarding of the wall over Andrea's head.

Andrea resisted the temptation to turn and follow the *khadim*'s eyes, afraid any sign of nerves would make the gelding skittish and drag the story out even longer.

"My lady bade me," the eunuch began, "relate to you something that happened to me yesterday morning."

"Nothing else?" What happened to a eunuch could be of little consequence anywhere.

"Nothing else," Ghazanfer replied. "But attend me first before you turn a deaf ear. Are you aware that I was once guardian to Mihrimah Sultan, Selim's sister?"

Andrea shook his head. He still couldn't discern any reason why he should hear the tale, drawn with such difficulty from the huge freak, as if his mind were shut by a door that had not been swung in years. But Sofia, Andrea reminded himself, trusted this creature.

So Andrea worked up more concern in order to say, "I beg you, *ustadh,* continue."

"It was almost six years ago now, when Selim, our present master, was as yet only crown prince."

Andrea noted the eunuch did not recite the customary formula praying for an eternal reign when he spoke Selim's name. Did this betray treasonous thoughts against the master who owned him, body and soul? It certainly would explain why the eunuch felt a need to confess something he dared not speak even to others of his kind, perhaps to no other breathing soul. Andrea scooted closer to the hard edge of the cot.

"There was in those days a youth among the imperial pages whose fair features and gentle manners won him a friend in everyone he met. He was all but guaranteed quick advancement among Suleiman's— Allah keep his soul—closest attendants. But then Selim came to Constantinople on an obligatory visit to his father—may Allah rain blessings on our departed sovereign—and it was not two days before Suleiman's son claimed the child as his attendant as well. And Selim demands a little more of his favorites than our departed master ever did. Alas, the poor boy's severe Christian upbringing did not allow him to accept the master's attentions with anything but utter distaste. And, you must know, Selim is not easy on his lovers, be they male or female.

"In his grief, the lad turned to me for consolation. Many's the early morning he would creep into my room before the hour of prayer. I'd wash the sex from him and—perhaps—if the master had been excitable that night—signs of rougher use—signs of favor many another slave would have been proud to wear.

"Then the lad would cry himself to sleep in my arms. Perhaps I did wrong by this. If I did—Allah is my witness—I meant no harm. Perhaps it was wrong to coddle the boy so. I should have been teaching him clearly: No love a slave enjoys can ever equal the love of his master. Unfortunately and unknown to me, my young friend began to leave Selim for my room as soon as the prince slept, without being dismissed, without learning if his master had further desire of him. One night—and perhaps Selim had been told by jealous tongues to beware—we were discovered thus—like a mother with her babe, and the master thought the worst."

How could Ghazanfer speak of such things so impassively? Yet he did, reciting these terrors as no more than credits and debits in an accounting book. The eunuch was indeed a monster, humanity cut from him along with the rest of it.

"I was taken to the Seven Towers. Surely you must know of the place on the outskirts of the palace walls, and if you have not heard of the infamous tortures that occur there, I will not disturb your nobility by a rehearsal of mine. Suffice it to say it was in the eunuch's hospital that my lady found me."

Andrea found his mind wandering to where Sofia might be now, if she could not be with him. He could not believe Ghazanfer would be sitting there, so intent on his tale, if his lady were any place but safely tucked inside the imperial harem. Although—and perhaps this was what the monster was trying to tell him—a harem might be anything but safe.

Ghazanfer continued, "Selim had determined I was to suffer eternally—eternity, at least as far as he has control over it. I was to be slowly brought to the point of death, then brought to health, then death again, as long as flesh could endure it. The master came several days to watch, and brought my friend—"

Now, with the mention of torture and in spite of his distraction over Sofia, Andrea could not help but find the taciturn eunuch's tale gut-wrenching and compelling. He shivered, as if the Towers' shadows touched him, and when Ghazanfer faltered, encouraged him to continue.

"I will tell you, my young Venetian, I'd not been under this treatment long before I was at the point of seeking my own death. It was then my lady found me and, I know not by what magic, contrived to buy me as her own. I was pleased to think Selim had forgotten his jealousy in a new love, and was easily persuaded of the fact."

Some of what the eunuch must have endured Andrea saw in his ravaged face and much-broken fingers—things that had only repulsed before. And the young man heard it in the tenderness and utter devotion with which he approached reference to Sofia Baffo.

Perhaps, Andrea jolted with the perversity of the thought and studied the eunuch more closely, Perhaps my jealousy of Prince Murad has been misplaced.

"My young friend I never saw again," the eunuch continued, "except once. That was yesterday morning. My lady contrived to have me in attendance at the minister's secret war counsel. Through our connections in the kitchen, I was set to serve drinks, and so became a hearer of their every decision.

"All would have gone smoothly. The viziers and generals were agreed that the entire army should be thrown against Yemen to beat those rebels back. The Mufti had given his blessing. But then—then the Sultan arrived."

"Sultan Selim!" Andrea could not keep from exclaiming.

"He who, in the intervening years, has inherited his father's place."

"But I thought he no longer attended either the Divan or the war counsels. That, at least, is the wisdom among the ambassadors."

"So thought we all, as well," Ghazanfer replied, "though that your intelligence should be as good may make us reconsider ours."

Was the eunuch amused or angered? Andrea couldn't tell and let him continue.

"In any case, from Sokolli Pasha down to myself, none of us could have been more surprised had we seen the Doge of Venice himself enter the chamber. But here came the Sultan with a train of followers. Foremost among them was, of course, Joseph Nassey."

"The Jew who has been Selim's companion since childhood?"

"Precisely. What people may not be so free to tell your prying Venetian ears is that Nassey is more depraved than the master. He delights in nothing so much as leading the master by the hand down the tortuous road in all the unfamiliar territory of debauch. It seems clear it was Nassey who set the idea in the Sultan's head. The Sultan himself is too muddied with wine to put two and two together to come up with any sort of plan at all if something like this irritates him. Without Nassey, whose evil stamina is ever so much greater, Selim would only rant and rave."

"Of what plan do you speak?"

"In a moment. I will get to that in a moment." It seemed more difficult for Ghazanfer to name the plan than to name his master's corruption. "First I wish to tell you that besides Joseph Nassey, the master was accompanied by—"

"Yes. Go on." Andrea spurred the balky gelding.

Ghazanfer looked down and away. "By my friend, the young page. No longer favorite, yet he was still trusted to arrange his majesty's cushions and to fetch his narghile. We were able to exchange glances across the room, glances which said, 'Thank Allah, you are still well.' Nothing more."

"And the Sultan's plan?"

"The ministers at first opposed the Sultan's plan with as much tact as they dared. 'The scheme is ill-advised,' they said. They called upon signed treaties for witness, which the Shadow of Allah may not break lest Allah Himself be called a liar.

"As they grew more adamant, so did he, then so again did they. At last Selim lost his temper. Now, our master is not a large man. Having seen him only from a distance, on his horse, in his huge feathered turban and when every head around him must bow, you may have received that impression. But it is false. He is not large, and his complexion and manner are quite pale and womanly, for he takes little interest in the male pursuits of hunting, riding, or war anymore. When he is sober, his small, dark eyes seem bland and lifeless. But fired with drink, as he was then, he is a different man. His eyes leap, his flesh burns red, and his mouth spews fire.

" 'How dare you?' he cried to his ministers. 'How dare you gainsay my heart's desire. I am the Sultan of Islam, the Shadow of Allah. And you—don't you know that you are my slaves? I could snap my fingers and see you all boiled in oil before noon prayer today. Your lives are nothing without my pleasure! Nothing!'

"None of us dared move or even breathe at that moment lest it be contrary to his will. And our fear served him as yet another draught of strong wine. Under its influence, he felt—and we did, too—that he had the strength of twenty men. He snatched the sword from the waist of the nearest janissary, then snatched my young friend by the neckband. And as he did, the look of venom with which the master fixed me announced his choice was hardly arbitrary. And I had thought myself so disfigured by my torturers that no one from before could recognize me."

Emotion swam like a fish in the blue-green of the eunuch's eyes, then froze solid.

VI

"THE LAD MADE no resistance—" The eunuch's tale continued. "—not even a whimper. Had the master asked him, he would have lain down voluntarily. But the Sultan shoved the boy down and pinned him with the sword—through the heart—to the rugs.

"The Sultan spoke. 'All of you! Grand Vizier, Kapudan Pasha, whatever fancy names you have, you are all my slaves, no better than that crawling worm there, and if it is my pleasure, I could do you all the same at this moment. No power on earth could stop me. Is it my pleasure? Perhaps. First, I must hear your pleasure in this matter we are discussing. Shall we make war on whom I decide, or shall we not?'

" 'Be it according to your word,' they all concurred as they watched—or tried not to watch—the boy's last twitch.

"Even the Mufti agreed. The Mufti, who is not the Sultan's slave, who is a free-born Turk, educated in the mosque schools, and who should have no other law than that of the Koran and the traditions of the Prophet—he who should act as a check to any madness in the Sultan.

" 'Although it is true the island has always been Christian,' the Mufti said thoughtfully, 'they did pay tribute to both the Mameluks of Egypt and Islam's first caliphs. It seems therefore justified to take it for the Faith.' "

Andrea shook his head in disbelief, watching the terrifyingly expressionless face before him. Other griefs—even Sofia—were forgotten for the moment. "Such power in one man! If ever a Doge had a will like that, the Senate has such power that the best one can ever hope for is a very weak compromise. And with other states in Europe, it is much the same. No wonder Europe is so slow in getting anywhere!"

"Except that," Ghazanfer cautioned, "the place a single man wants to go may not be so healthy for the rest of the world."

"Well, barbarians on an island like Madagascar—no matter how they may fight—it would do them good, in the long run to be joined to the Turkish Empire."

"Madagascar? Is that what you thought when I said 'island'?"

"Of course. It seems only reasonable. It is the next step towards India, which I am sure the Sultan would . . ." Andrea fumbled. "You did say Yemen, didn't you? And I reasoned . . ."

"My friend. You misunderstood me. I never said the master was following reason in his design. This is the dream of a man in his cups." A rigid sort of sorrow seemed to penetrate the eunuch's eyes before he announced, "The Sultan has his eye on the island of Cyprus."

"Cyprus?"

"Cyprus, as you know only too well, grows the best wine in the world, and the quota they have been willing to sell to Turkey in a year has never been enough to satisfy—"

"But Cyprus belongs to Venice!"

"Exactly, my friend."

The exaggerated patience in the eunuch's voice reminded Andrea he had little enough right to be championing Venice's cause. In one of the first waves of emotion he'd ever felt from the creature, he felt disdain. Disdain against himself. Disdain because he, Andrea, was moved—blinded—by carnal lust while a *khadim,* godlike, was above such constraints.

Still, Andrea couldn't help but exclaim: "But that is war—on us!"

"Now you are not as casual as you were with the lives and goods of Madagascar. And Cyprus is not so far from Constantinople as that distant land. Why must you Christians always think all barbarians are only eastward?"

"But we have a treaty of peace with the Porte. Hasn't Selim been told?"

"I have already told you, my friend, what the Mufti himself said about the bounds of honor surrounding that treaty. They are nothing compared to the honor of winning new lands for Islam—now. If you do not believe me, my friend, stop by the house of Joseph Nassey in the next few days. The master has promised to make him the island's king. Nassey has already ordered the woodcarvers to carve a plate with

Cyprus's coat of arms and 'King Joseph' on it. It will swing above his gateway for all Constantinople to see. This is what my lady wanted me to tell you."

Andrea's chest flooded with the warmth of gratitude towards Sofia. She had not forgotten him after all. But what she expected in return was still not clear, and he wanted to give her something. The desire to give was, in fact, a physical need. "Is there nothing to be done to stop that maniac?" he attempted.

"And just a moment ago you were wishing the same power for your Doge."

"But what should we do?" Andrea rocked on the edge of the cot. The rough wood cut deep into his thighs, but he ignored it. "Shall I have the ambassador request an immediate audience?"

"You have never been allowed to see the Sultan yet. What makes you think he would see you now? Besides, you are but men, and we have seen he can terrorize men and pin them to the floor like moths."

In a rising panic, Andrea reminded himself that his true love was thrall to such barbarians. Is this what she was trying to tell him? He stammered, "No power on earth . . ."

"Now, I didn't say that," the eunuch reminded him. "Those were your words. In our realm, there are one or two powers given the strength to withstand the wild whims of the Sultan."

"Pray God, what can they be?"

"Well, first, the dervishes."

"Dervishes?" Andrea repeated impatiently. "The dervishes are mad."

"They are mad, allowed to be mad with Allah, and are both powerful and incorruptible in that they never have to play by the Sultan's rules. If a dervish is corrupted to become the Sultan's lackey, the people are not fooled and he loses his power among them. And if a Sultan dares to wield his laws above a dervish—to kill or imprison the holy man as he may do any vizier or pasha—he will only make a martyr. Even dead, a martyr has power over a Sultan. The more horrible the death, the more powerful the martyr. No, by hanging a dervish, a Sultan only puts the rope around his own neck. Even the janissaries will always follow the drumbeats of a naked dervish before they'll follow the Sultan's standard."

"That is all very nice for a Muslim," Andrea said, exasperated, "but what am I to do as a Christian?"

"Yes, well, I only spoke of dervishes first so you could see how the system works. There is, of course, one other refuge from the Sultan's will."

"And that is . . .?"

"The harem, of course."

"The harem! But that's ridiculous! Those women are his slaves, as much as you are, *ustadh*. And worse than slaves. They are bound prisoners, never seeing the light of day. Why, no rat in Constantinople is more subservient to the Sultan's will than the women of his harem."

"Now you are looking at the harem with Christian eyes, my friend. As if they were your Catherine de' Medici or England's Elizabeth, to be judged by the standards not only of Christians, but Christian *men* as well. Try to see them through my eyes. My eyes, half-man, half-woman, half-Christian, half-Turk, and then you may catch a glimpse of what it would be like to be all Turk and all woman. It is their very removal from the open, brazen affairs of men that gives them such power.

"If Selim were to go about terrorizing his women and pinning them to the floor—as he could, indeed, if he wished—he would lose more than a night's paramour. He would lose his honor. Every shred of it. A thousand years of military victory could not make up for that loss, for there is nothing more important a man owns than that which is totally out of his hands—the honor of his women. He would make a martyr more powerful than a thousand ragged dervishes because it would be of his own flesh and blood, from the very center of his heart, as we say. He might as well order lepers to sleep with all his women.

"Ah, but here I am trying to explain to you something that is beyond words even as the dervish's union with Allah is unspeakable. Usually I cannot even talk to my lady about these things. 'Ghazanfer,' she sighs, 'you grow tedious and there is work to be done.' Often I fear she does not understand the very harem she lives in. She was, after all, born and raised a Christian."

Here the eunuch paused, betraying uncharacteristic introspection before continuing. "Sometimes I fear she misuses the harem's power— or, rather, rejects its power in favor of the tactics men use. If she uses that power, she must face the consequences men face, and sometimes I fear . . . Still, she saved my life. She is wise, good and brave . . ."

"And beautiful," Andrea added to complete his version of the vision that today had failed to appear.

"Yes, and the most beautiful woman in the harem besides. Few are such complete eunuchs they are not aware of this. I will not speak against her. And that she would send me to you with this message assures me she has some inkling of how the power of the harem should be used."

"What does your lady want me to do?" Andrea still found himself helpless of decision in the face of this news.

"That she did not tell me," Ghazanfer said.

"How I wish I were her slave instead of you!" Andrea burst out. "For I desire nothing more of life than to receive orders from her lips. For I myself seem . . . witless at this news."

"Would you take a suggestion from me?"

"Gladly. For you know her mind better than anyone in the world."

"I think my lady has sent you this warning so you and all of Venice now on the Bosphorus can pack up your things and flee to safety. The Porte, I believe, means to send you an ultimatum tomorrow: Give up Cyprus, or face war. That will buy you some time. You can pretend to think it over. Two days, perhaps, in which to evacuate all people and possessions safely. After that, your lives cannot be vouched or bargained for in this city, whatever the harem's power. And, perhaps, at sea, you can warn your navy of the coming storm—"

"Navy? What navy?" The words exploded from Andrea's heart-crushed lungs. "I have been instrumental in blowing the Venetian navy out of the waters!"

The thought brushed his back with a chill. Was his destruction of the Venetian navy connected not only with Chios, but with Cyprus as well? He couldn't compass the notion.

"Turn your merchant vessels into men-of-war, perhaps . . ." the eunuch ventured.

"With what? Our munitions turned the night of September thirteenth into day."

Ghazanfer shook his great white turban sadly. "These details are beyond me."

But not beyond Sofia.

Did that thought come from the eunuch or from Andrea's own mind? He squashed it. "Surely she cannot expect me to flee. Flee, like a coward, from the field?"

"The power of the harem is to preserve life. Glory such as a soldier craves is not part of it."

"But life without honor is——" Well, what was it? Could one such as himself have any honor——or life——left? None, certainly. None without the focus of all he had done——Sofia Baffo.

"You are young, my friend," the eunuch was saying mildly, as if purposely to contrast their natures. "And full of hot blood. As I told you, the honor of the harem is not the honor of men, although they do hold the honor of men in their white hands."

"You speak in cursed Turkish riddles!" The young man quite forgot his task of diplomacy. "How can a woman love a man who is a coward?"

"More, I suppose, than she can love a corpse."

Or a traitor.

Did the eunuch's eyes read that, or was it Andrea's own mind that accused himself so? He would not succumb to the thought. He had only done what was necessary. "Well, by God, I do not intend to die in this fray."

"That will be as Allah wills."

For her part, Sofia wanted him alive. That was promising; she must still love him. Then a horrifying thought occurred to Andrea and his blood seem to freeze miles from the warmth of his heart. What if she was preserving him alive not for love, but for further use? To order the explosion of more Arsenals. To torture him through years as Selim had done to the young page boy——who had fancied himself spared——only in the end to take barbaric pleasure in pinning the lad through the heart to the rugs on the floor. Was it even possible that this was why the *khadim* had told him that horrific story, a warning with two separate meanings?

Andrea looked hard at the eunuch and could see no denial of such a motive behind the creature's eyes. But he read no confirmation either.

Ghazanfer rose to leave the room. "I have done my lady's will. More than that I cannot say. Salaam, Barbarigo."

"Here, here!" Andrea shook the fears of Sofia's betrayal from him as a dog shakes off muddy water. He rose after the eunuch, pulling the locket from his neck. "Take this and give it to your lady—from me."

Ghazanfer held the fragile thing in his great, torture-flattened hand. "It may be Allah's will that she never send you another message."

"It was my mother's locket, but I do not care. No woman on earth is a better heir to it—and my love—than that woman you serve."

"Salaam." Ghazanfer bowed again. "I pray for peace, Barbarigo, both between our countries and within your troubled heart."

Tucking the locket within his breast, the eunuch turned to leave.

"Tell her—" Andrea called after, convinced now that only Sofia's well-justified fears for her own safety had kept her away. Fears she had defied for his sake. "—tell your lady I will not leave Constantinople without her."

VII

ANDREA CONSIDERED HIS options. He would go and plead peace before the Divan with such power and logic that Sofia would throw all foolish Turkish convention aside and pull back the curtain of the Eye of the Sultan. For, of course, she would be there and, no less than the viziers, be won by his speech. She would leap from there into his waiting arms . . .

After that, what should happen was not so clear. Yes, there was the problem of the room and a courtyard outside filled with janissaries. But somehow that seemed a negligible factor, once he had her in his arms.

Then there was the scenario in which he stormed the palace walls almost single-handedly, killed the mad old Sultan, and then penetrated the forbidden holy of holies. There she (he would almost write it *She*—divine) would be lying in sorrow and languor on a crimson couch, her golden hair like fire in luscious disarray. She would reach long, white arms out to him, her liberator, her deliverer, her true love. Again, he need not dream further than this point.

More elegant settings stoked the fire of his brain, but practicality had whittled it down to this: an alley beside the little neighborhood mosque-converted-from-a-church a stone's throw from the palace of the Grand Vizier. If he shifted just right, he could catch a glimpse of Sofia's sedan through the wrought-iron gates.

A sharp wind scudded straight off the Black Sea to attack his fingers and toes. It put out the moon as easily as one of his bravos had put out the light at the end of the alley just after the lamplighter had passed. Now the only illumination came through the heavy curtains drawn over the second-story lattices of the closest homes.

Andrea blew on his hands to keep them flexible. They must be able to curl firmly around the hilt of his dagger.

The call to evening prayers directly over his head brought a small congregation to the mosque. Andrea found the men who filed past his hiding place slightly unnerving, being predominantly janissaries from the exercise field. Each man carried his own rug under his arm like an open display of his soul. Andrea felt a strong urge to join them, if only for the better concealment of his own soul, one among many. But public devotion would soon make way for the privacy of tents and hearthstones.

Already the domestic miracle of fresh-baked bread served with cabbage and earthy chickpeas seeped its scent along with a warm, greasy light through the lattice stars and the curtains overhead. It overwhelmed the smell of rankled garbage at his feet. The balconies and jutting bays of the second stories sagged like matronly breasts.

This image made Andrea wonder. Though no man was likely to see the deed, what about the women? Day and men and their liveliness made it easy to forget, but he knew full well that few actions in Turkey went unobserved by the silent sentinels of harem eyes. What would women think? Wouldn't they rejoice that one of their number was about to be freed?

Earlier, from the Pasha's gardens, peacock cries had sounded. Now, with a ruffling of feathers, the birds settled. From that lesser house, jutting into the moonlight on his right, he heard an infant wail, very like the fowl, he thought. The mother hushed it. That most intimate of exchanges, surpassing, in some ways, even that between lovers, caught its talons in the pit of his stomach. How separate he felt from the joys of hearth and home!

But by these means I shall win such pleasures for myself, Andrea insisted to his seething brain. From tonight on, I shall no longer be on the outside looking in.

The only problem remained how long they'd waited. Sofia couldn't be spending the night with her friend, could she? Andrea knew harem doors were universally closed and locked at dark. But he also knew Sofia. She would have her ways around such constraints.

Another gust of northern wind, and the moon shivered out of her gauzy veil again. The faucet before the mosque would have an icicle on the end of its nose in the morning when the pious came. But he would not be there to see the prayerful, made brave by faith, crack the crust and plunge in with the muezzin's first sleepy call of the morning. The notion gave him a brief pang which was, he assured himself, only the wind, cutting more to the quick. Andrea drew the cloak tighter about himself. He let his eyes catch heat from the faint gleam of gold trim on the sedan chair seen through the palace gates.

This sight was enough to settle his resolve.

In no more time than piety allowed, the mosque emptied. Then, as if on that cue, the Pasha's palace disgorged the awaited sedan.

Rather than heading straight back for the Sultan's palace, the conveyance obliged him yet further by turning down this very passageway. It halted not four yards from where he stood, pressed against the minaret wall.

Finally, wonder of wonders, the bearers were dismissed to go warm themselves in the public house around the corner.

That left only the eunuch, leaning against the sedan door with his arms crossed over his chest, watching, waiting. And perhaps Ghazanfer wasn't to be counted as the enemy. He had dismissed the bearers, after all. Certainly he hated Sultan Selim. And loved his mistress. He would not care to be parted from her or do anything she did not approve. Once the *khadim* saw Sofia's joy at the prospect of freedom and Venice, surely it would not take much to bring him along. Particularly since a eunuch who had failed to protect his charge could not expect the respite of the Seven Towers before he'd find himself at the bottom of the Bosphorus.

Andrea hoped he could keep his minions at bay long enough to give the poor capon a chance.

Yes, the plan seemed God-ordained, just like the Arsenal plot. Or perhaps, it was merely too good to be true.

The grasping Turkish moon hazily lit the enclosing walls in solid blades and wedges. A low whistle rose from these stacked shadows. Andrea turned his concentration to the task at hand.

A second replied. This whistle was almost lost in the openness where the walls gave way to the huge space of the ruined Hippodrome. The third fellow was closest to the action. His whistle came from down this tortured intestine of an alley, near where it crumbled away altogether. The solid ground under Sokolli Pasha's palace and the entire neighborhood was here revealed to be a sham. Anciently, huge arched supports had leveled the natural sharp incline from the Hippodrome down to the sea. Horses for the Byzantine circus had stabled in these caverns. When the horses had gone, the homeless.

And now . . . Sofia Baffo.

Andrea worked up spit and pursed his lips to give the final whistle. Coming from the minaret's foot, it would seem a belated echo of the muezzin

The instant before Andrea actually sent air through his throat, the signal to fall upon their prey, the mosque doors opened to emit one final worshipper. Andrea hissed his accomplices back again, or hoped he did. The blood pounding in his ears was so loud he doubted he could have heard his own whistle if he gave it. With growing dismay he watched the soldier smoke the moonlit air with ashen breath, then claim the last pair of boots on the sacred threshold.

The footwear seemed black at first. Then it caught a gleam and was betrayed as red. This matched better with the cascade of exotic bird-of-paradise feathers that swung from the janissary's turban almost to his knees. These features pronounced the man a veteran, a battalion officer, a Chief Soup-Maker, that homey title which nonetheless terrorized Christians.

Andrea flattened himself behind the minaret's curve. Rather than coming up the alley, back towards the Hippodrome, as Andrea had been certain any soldier must, the Chief Soup-Maker turned left when he passed the mosque's fountain and courtyard.

Walking down towards the ruined stables, the janissary stopped and scowled a moment at the extinguished street lamp. Then, as if he thought, Well, so much the better for me, he went on. He sauntered right past the parked sedan and—did Andrea see aright?—nodded a greeting to Ghazanfer and pattered his fingers familiarly on the shutters. Then he disappeared down into the crumbled arches. Andrea could only hope the man he'd stationed down there had more presence of mind and skills of stealth than he'd credited him with.

One more breath and we go, Andrea told himself. But before he'd drawn that breath, the plan misfired again. Ghazanfer opened the sedan door.

Jasmine burdened the cold air like a warm blanket, lingering in layers. The veil-wrapped woman slipped out of her eunuch's hands and down the alleyway in the very footsteps of the vanished janissary.

All was silent for a very long moment. Even Andrea's dithery brain stopped sending him messages.

And then, she screamed.

VIII

ANDREA WAS DOWN the alley like a shot, barely stopping to fling the stunned Ghazanfer into the arms of the two uphill accomplices.

At the lip of the subterranean caves, Andrea skidded to a halt. Before him sprawled the body of the janissary, the bird-of-paradise plume pitched heavenward.

And struggling in the arms of the third bravo was Sofia Baffo. The bravo, having left grimy proof of several false attempts on the gauze of her veil, had finally found purchase over her mouth.

"Jesu," Andrea burst out, crossing himself involuntarily and rather foolishly for the sake of a Muslim soul. "What have you done?"

"You said somebody might get killed," the bravo answered, his wall-eye roving in spasms. "Rather him than me."

"But he has—had—nothing to do with this."

"Hadn't he?" Perhaps it was just the defect, but Andrea was certain the bravo was taunting him.

"Let her go," the scion of the house of Barbarigo ordered, trying to sound in charge. After all, Sofia was listening. More than that, she'd fixed him with the keen edge of her wonderful eyes. Recognition honed there and, was it possible? Hatred? He must cure this at once.

"What? She's not the one you want? Feels fine to me. Right fine. You don't want her, I'll take her myself."

"Let her go. Let her walk back to the sedan."

"I don't know, captain. Doesn't feel to me like she'll come without assistance." Struggles jarred his words.

"Let her go, I say."

The bravo complied, at least with the hand on the mouth. But the flailing he did with it in the air suggested his release was not so much of his own will but because his captive had bitten him.

Sofia screamed again, and the curses and scuffling coming from behind Andrea, from where Ghazanfer was being held, were not encouraging.

"Sofia, Sofia, it's me, Andrea," he said as soon as the bravo's hand had quietened the scream once more. "I've come to rescue you. To take you back to Venice. I've got a boat waiting and everything. Just come on back to the sedan and we'll carry you there."

In the same moment Andrea realized first that he was going to have to help get the captive into the sedan. Indeed, that he ought to have been lending a hand sooner. And second, that the reason he hadn't helped out was because he was hesitant to approach that belligerent bundle of silk and brocade.

Andrea approached with caution. At first touch, the jasmine fragrance filled his brain. But the fragrance was missing the undercurrent of toothsome almond; gone from her physical being was the warmth and softness of love.

Without doubt, the woman they had captured was behaving very differently from the creature of his dreams.

Then Andrea felt something more: The Sofia he held had a more prominent belly than the tight drumhead on which he was used to beat out his love tattoo.

By Jesu and Maria, she was pregnant.

Was it his child? His head was too overwhelmed to figure very clearly, but he thought it might be. No wonder she was behaving so strangely. Andrea had heard that pregnant women were subject to strange fancies and often didn't know their own minds. He would have to think for the two—the three—of them.

Between them, Andrea and the bravo wrestled Sofia a couple of paces. Young Barbarigo was trying to be as careful as he could, but he did have to use some force. The woman herself set her feet firmly into the men's shins more often than she let them touch the ground.

"Here. Let's gag her with the veil," the bravo suggested when they stopped to recoup and regain a grasp on their burden. "That'll give me another hand."

Andrea nodded dumbly.

The fight Sofia put up against the removal of her veil wounded Andrea in plenty of places, but the jab to his heart hurt worst of all. In spite of—or perhaps because of—his admiration, the bravo was ready to smack her into submission. Andrea stayed the man's hand, though having to fight on two fronts at once was wearing.

Of course she has been among the Turks so long she has taken on this extra layer of any woman's natural modesty. Andrea excused her opposition and promised himself as well as Sofia that there was no harm intended.

"Do you think I would hurt you, my love, or—or our child?" he pleaded.

Your child? You think this is your child when I could have a prince?

Andrea seemed to read these words in the glare of eyes over the bravo's hand, so he didn't think in that direction any more.

He did, however, keep up the struggle towards the sedan. His actions were, after all, in her best interest, no matter whose child it was. And he promised himself he could love any child Sofia bore.

Still he could not escape the impression that the wish to remain disguised motivated her as much or more than modesty. Like a thief in the night, like the two men having a time of it with Ghazanfer who'd both taken the precaution of muffling their faces, Sofia seemed to be masking illegality from witnesses more than beauty from lechers.

But Andrea could waste no more time considering it. Ghazanfer was gaining the upper hand at his end of the alley. A lucky kick by one of the bravos had managed to knock the monster's dagger out of reach and into the deep shadows. That was all that kept the eunuch from giving better than he took, even in that two-to-one match.

"I was beginning to wonder, captain—" The bravo on the other side of Sofia's contentious form clenched his teeth and panted his exertion. "—whether any woman could be worth this much trouble. For what you paid us, you could have found yourself several dozen obliging whores. But now I see. I've got to hand it to you. She's worth it."

Andrea didn't appreciate the fellow's sentiments, nor the roving of his defective eye, but the young lover had no choice. No way could he have kept the force he struggled with in his arms on his own.

The bravo's words, oddly enough, seemed to have a calming effect on the maelstrom Andrea held to him in a parody of the passion he'd hoped for.

Then, into the half a breath the bravo gave her while he worked the veil into a manageable gag, Sofia compressed these words. "No gag. I won't scream."

Andrea had the uneasy feeling she spoke to his accomplice as much as to him, but he pretended otherwise and signed the man to hold off. The bravo shrugged and complied, but kept the gag poised a mere heartbeat away from where he wanted it to be.

"Why did you do it? Barbarigo, why?" At least she was speaking Italian now, although he didn't like the formal name with which she distanced herself. "After the Arsenal—I thought you were my friend."

"Your friend? *Cara mia,* I love you. I do this because I love you. I do everything because I love you and can bear no one else to have you."

There was a snort of impatience in her voice. "I mean, why did you have to kill Khalil?"

"Khalil?" Andrea didn't like the caress she gave the name. Worse, the bravo heard it, too, through the language barrier, and raised a teasel brow over the mad lurch of his eye.

"Him." Sofia pointed to the ground behind them.

"The janissary?"

"Yes, the Chief Soup-Maker."

"He has nothing to do with this."

Andrea didn't like the recollection nagging at the back of his mind that until very recently, the Sultan's private army had been sworn to celibacy, living together like monks. Andrea had always found this a very unnatural—and dangerous—mode of existence for men of the sword. Such a life could not help but be dangerous for any women in the janissaries' neighborhood.

Sofia insisted, "Khalil has everything to do with this."

"An unfortunate accident. He got in the way. But not one that need detain us. Please, Sofia, don't let it keep us a moment longer."

"Excuse me, captain," the bravo said.

Andrea waved impatiently against the interruption of Turkish into a flow of Italian that, for some reason he couldn't quite fathom, was taking all his concentration to follow.

The bravo persisted. "Perhaps it will hasten things along if I mention that that red-booted fellow there made my job easy. He exposed his heart, as nice as can be, by raising his arms for an embrace."

"Infidel," Sofia hissed. "Murderer."

The bravo grinned maniacally. "Seemed the best thing to do, under the circumstances. To run him through."

Andrea felt as if his heart, too, had been punctured. But no, no, a Barbarigo could shield his heart in a gauntlet of iron.

"Get her into the sedan," he ordered, dragging the woman none too gently himself, baby or no. "Let's get out of here."

"Barbarigo, you don't understand."

"I think, madonna, I understand a little too well. What should have happened in Ca' Foscari seven years ago, I intend to see happens now. I will make you mine. You will be rescued in spite of yourself."

To Andrea's surprise, she came more complacently now. A little firmness would manage her. By the time they got to the sedan and he'd opened the door, he couldn't help but give Sofia a quizzical look.

"Well, what is there left for me here in Turkey?" she snapped at him, as if the logic was all too simple.

The child, Andrea reminded himself. Her son Muhammed.

But Sofia said nothing about any child. "The plot has failed," she said instead, "now that Khalil is dead."

"I don't notice you weeping."

"But I might. I just might." This shrill pinnacle of her voice had ugly edges. "Khalil was our only hope for Cyprus."

"Cyprus?" The consideration that there might be more at stake here than the possession of one woman's body for one man's pleasure took Andrea quite off guard. "You mean to tell me you'd corrupted that high-ranking officer?"

"Why are you so surprised?"

"But—how?"

"Andrea," she cooed. "You need to ask?"

Andrea struggled to ignore a heavy flush. "He was going to stop the invasion of Cyprus? Cause a rebellion, create a diversion, refuse to fight—and spare Cyprus?"

"Barbarigo, why would I want to stop the invasion of Cyprus?"

"Because Venetians would die, of course. Because Cyprus belongs to Venice."

"What benefit have *I* in that?" The moonlight caught a halo of her hair against the black arch of the sedan's interior. "Hellborn hair" was the description that came first to mind.

"I'm going to take you back home."

"Where I'd be one foolish, silly noblewoman among a thousand."

Andrea closed his eyes against a dizzying wave of guilt. And upon the slate of his eyelids he saw the face of one of the Republic's other noblewomen, the candlelit features of Melissa Foscari, intent on the sweetness of her madrigal. "Yes!" he shouted.

"No." Her calm was terrifying. "If Turkey takes Cyprus, my son—my princely son—will soon rule it, along with everything else. And I—I rule him."

"And—and your friend the janissary?"

"Perhaps you know—" Andrea was keenly aware that Sofia punctuated her sentence by laying her hands on his chest. He could feel their heat through both velvet and linen. "—perhaps you don't. Sokolli Pasha is doing everything in his power to stop the invasion."

"I hear he hasn't much success, not against the besotted will of the Sultan."

"Yes, Selim is a problem. What I would give the man who'd find a way to murder him." Sofia had slipped her hands up his chest now and was toying with the lace of his collar. And he had worn it for just this purpose. "However, in the meantime, Joseph Nassey is a good substitute."

"Joseph Nassey." Andrea choked on his voice's thickness.

"The Jew, Selim's most fervent corrupter. So easily corrupted himself. The Jew, you must know, is my creature."

"What would you give, Sofia? And for what?" The effects of her touch were going to his head.

"Although so far I've only been able to get Nassey to plead for invasion."

"And what did you expect Khalil to do to Sokolli Pasha?"

"Assassinate him, of course."

Andrea felt her withdraw from him with the same timing a skillful lover uses just before the enveloping climax. Andrea felt himself drawn helplessly after her, aching for that climax.

And then it came. From the bowels of the sedan behind her, Sofia had retrieved a neat silver and pearl-inlaid pistol. He had no time to consider where she got such a new-styled weapon, nor where she'd learned to use it. Not only did she travel armed, but she traveled with it primed and charged. And she didn't flinch to level it at his face. Nor to lay the cock to the wheel.

One single lazy second drawled across time. Andrea moved through it as though through water, and as if he had nothing but water to breathe.

The ball caught the walleyed bravo in the midst of his leer with no warning whatsoever.

The Pasha's peacocks set up a terrific pandemonium in reply.

Andrea ignored that difficulty for the moment, focusing on the recoil instead. With the shot's help, he flung Sofia firmly back into the sedan and fixed the outside latch, flimsy but temporarily sufficient.

The bravo's death groans had so disconcerted the other two accomplices, however, that they had loosed their grip on Ghazanfer. The monster of a eunuch, backed against a wall and holding them off with fists and boots alone, began to squeal in his obscenely feminine voice, "Murder! Help, for the love of Allah!"

People began to stir behind the neighboring lattices and the night watch couldn't be too far off. But with Andrea's inspiration, the bravos renewed their restraint and stifled the eunuch.

"Cut the capon's throat," Andrea hissed to the bravo whose dagger was most at the ready. He wasn't at all certain that three could get the sedan to their shoulders, but there was no time to beg Ghazanfer to come along.

Then blood, black but spangled silver by the moon, spurted. It was not Ghazanfer's thickly chinned and grossly unnapped throat that gave life out with a sigh, however, but the knife-wielding bravo, from beneath his flimsy mask.

A figure had suddenly dropped behind the fracas as if from the sky. When it freed itself, yet more eunuch's robes were unfurled and Andrea recognized Sokolli Pasha's head *khadim,* the one who called himself Veniero, who must have clambered over the palace walls.

The remaining bravo didn't even wait to determine this much; he vanished up the alley in the direction of the Hippodrome. A moment later, Andrea was in his wake. Not a moment too soon, for the pistol, reloaded in the sedan, fired again, spraying up dirt at his heels and, in the other direction, he narrowly avoided running head on into the night watch. But he was not so quick that he didn't overhear the following exchange between the two victorious eunuchs.

"*Mashallah, ustadh,*" spoke Ghazanfer, rubbing his thick neck as if he hardly hoped to find it still whole. His voice seemed to curl over the first smile ever to cross the impassive creature's lips. "You weren't a moment too soon on that one."

"I had been at the wall listening for quite some time. Since I heard your lady's first scream."

"And you didn't come to our aid?"

"I couldn't make up my mind that you wanted me. Or that it would be in my best interest to do so. With your lady, it's often difficult to tell."

"Yes," said the larger eunuch, more thoughtful that his usual omniscient tones. "I suppose that's true."

"But she does carry something that belongs to the realm of Islam— an heir."

"Yes."

"And after hearing about your young friend the page—"

"You heard that?"

"Yes."

"Yes. I—I hoped you would. But shouldn't someone go after that Italian?"

"My ears did hear right? He is the one they call Barbarigo?"

"The same."

"Leave him. His life, I fear, will find its own level, now that she's opened the floodgates on him."

Perhaps Andrea imagined some of this talk. He imagined all sorts of things that night, running through the hostile city, rowing through the black waters dotted with lantern light in confounding constellations as fishermen stalked the late autumn *lufer* run. This journey he'd planned to take in love's company he took alone.

IX

"HOW MANY SHIPS? How many ships?" the proveditore shouted up to his lookout.

"Hard to say, my lord," came the answer. "They're equal us. Maybe more."

"More? The devil you say."

"Perhaps, sir."

Long before dawn on the seventh of October, 1571, the Christian fleet had weighed anchor. It was a Sunday, rather late in the year and risking storms, but the night had remained clear, brilliantly star-studded. All Andrea had seen of the fleet around them was its mimicry of the constellations above on the black water below. Each lead ship dangled a lantern from her masthead moving like God before the Israelites. The others mutely, invisibly followed.

As dawn had come, the allied Christian fleet found itself straddling the ragged entrance of the Gulf of Patrai. Swollen sails and quivering pennants, Christian devices all, had crammed the straits. They hunted revenge for the brutal fall of Cyprus to the Turk.

Priests had moved from ship to ship and man to man, presenting their holy relics and heavy, thumping silver crosses, offering communion. And the men took it, perhaps with more piety than the lot of sailors had ever experienced in their lives. If die they must, they would die shriven. If captured, they'd go with the taste of God on their tongues.

But no man expected that either of these fates would befall him. His neighbor, perhaps, but not him in whose personal consciousness the world had begun and without which it would extinguish. They could feel personal immortality plastering the roofs of their mouths along with the blessed wafer.

Andrea had thought this bitterly as he'd fingered the crusty scab on his face—the gift of a year and a half of whoring—and made his own confession. There wasn't time to begin to tell it all. Others were waiting. So he didn't mention a quarter of the sins resting on his account. And he left everything he owned to his mother in a will he doubted the Republic, if all were told, would honor.

Now, several hours of sin later, the sun was brilliant, almost blinding, off the waves stilled to looking-glass polish. Against the port side, the white rocks of Corinth were likewise unrelieved by any pads of green.

A dense, low mist seemed to be hovering over the next inlet, the Gulf of Lepanto. But those in the crows' nests shouted the news down and soon enough anyone with eyes could see for himself. This was no

meteorological fluke—a fog in midday sun—but the Turkish navy itself with sails unfurled, in superior position, ready and waiting to take
on all comers.

A leaden silence fell over the Christians. Even the ships' timbers
forgot to creak and men forgot to breathe as simple wonder, unadul-
terated as yet with fear, overcame them at the sight.

Hasan Pasha was there, intelligence enlightened, the son of Barbarossa himself. Jafer Pasha, the Beglerbeg of Tripoli, and fourteen
other beys of the maritime provinces had joined him, each entitled to
hoist the banner of Prince of the Sea. Deploying his miles of ships into
one great grasping crescent, and claiming the center for himself was the
supreme Turkish commander, Muezzinzade Ali Pasha. Andrea's heart
thudded more when he heard that this commander's ship was named
The Sultana. How could he fight against that?

"And Uluj Ali," the report came.

"Damned renegade," his father cursed. "I'll take that man's balls for
myself."

Andrea knew Uluj Ali as a fearless corsair, the southern Italian turn-
coat who'd first captured Sofia Baffo and brought her to Constantinople.

And then Andrea learned there was another man known to his
love among the enemy. That was Sofia's master, her lover, Murad,
the eldest son of the Sultan, heir to the throne. Father of Sofia's
children. Andrea couldn't suppress that bitter thought. If she won't
claim me.

Murad was leading his contingent from the *sandjak* of Magnesia. Andrea almost echoed his father in claiming that man's privates for himself. But he hesitated, confused. He had given Sofia a choice, he
remembered, and she had chosen this Turk.

"Are we at them, my lord?" The men had reached the boiling point,
where their individual minds melded into one.

"Yes, by God. Yes, for Cyprus and San Marco. At them!"

Now, although the opposing forces seemed to be unified in their
ranks like two solid city walls, Andrea realized this was an illusion. Not
only were the two armadas mere flimsy wooden ships upon the sea, sus-
ceptible to everything from flaming arrows to hidden shoals, but they

were truly far from united in personnel besides. The North African beys actually got along with Constantinople and each other no better than Spain got on with Venice.

Add to this the fact that the brisk morning's breeze had now died to nothing, and both forces would have to depend on their rowers. The rowers under the Turkish decks were Christian slaves. And under the Christians, the captives continually called on Allah and His Prophet in spite of the chains about them.

Andrea looked over the backs of his father's rowers, uniform blue shirts and white caps moving like drops of water in a single swell. Their issued homogeneity disguised a crew at war with one another in their souls. The rowers would like nothing better than to propel their ship into the clutches of the enemy, who would free them from their shackles and return them home. Only full forces of whipmen and drivers kept them from actually doing so.

And the case must be the same across the stretch of green water in the Muslim hulls.

Fleets were divided into individual ships, ships into slaves and freemen, freemen into clans, father divided from son, and even Andrea's heart was not at peace with itself. He had determined to fight his damnedest, to make his father proud of him once and for all, or die in the attempt. But when, over the drums marking the rhythm of his own ship's forward motion, he heard the drums and thrilling double-reeded squeals of the janissaries' martial shawms, he faltered.

How familiar was that sound! How like home! He had heard it so often as a division of janissaries changed their station through the streets of Constantinople. How often he had stood and watched such maneuvers with an admiration he could not conceal. They were so proudly martial in their yellow and blue, their white and scarlet. Even the will of Allah in the form of a sneeze was not allowed to disturb their perfect discipline.

The sound of their mustering bands could not help but remind him of times when he'd been the happiest: days when he'd had a meeting with Ghazanfer in the afternoon, and the morning had seemed alive with hope of what news the eunuch might bring of his lady's doings. Or might bring the lady herself. Those were days he had shaken off his father's hand and felt certain of his own worth, certain it would some day bring him happiness.

As Andrea stood gripping and ungripping his sword by the rail, his father's mistress walked by him on her way to her cabin where she would await the outcome of the battle. She was a big, brazen woman with red hair. He'd never liked her and resented her presence there in the place of his adored mother, the plump, mousey little woman who had retreated for consolation into religion.

"Kill a Turk for me, Andrea," the mistress said, tweaking his ear playfully and then swinging her hips off towards the cabin.

Suddenly Andrea wanted nothing more than to see her raped by a dozen syphillic Turks. He would help them hold her down. He could no longer have any respect for any woman who dared to show herself outside either harem or nunnery.

The first shot was fired—one charged only with powder from the Turkish flagship as a warning. By God, how chivalrous! Andrea thought. Don Juan answered for the Christians—with his heaviest cannon—and it was not blank.

The sixty-three galleys under the proveditore of Venice were deployed along the left flank of the gulf's headland, which would greatly hamper their movements. What rocks and shoals were hidden under these waters were quite unknown, so Barbarigo warned his sailors to keep well clear of the coast.

Hasan Pasha Barbarossa led the Turks, whose waters these were, on this wing. Being his father's son, as the brilliant red beard beneath the white turban proved, he'd known every inlet of the Mediterranean like the back of his hand almost before he could toddle on deck.

The Turks' craft had shallower draft than the Christian vessels. And they proved themselves at once to be fearless of the rocks, knowing to the hair's breadth how close one could risk. Armed with this fearlessness—which was not foolhardiness, Andrea thought, but knowledge cold and keen as a Damascus blade—they began at once to outmaneuver the Christians, catching them up on two or three sides. Even the monstrous galleasses—planted in front of Barbarigo's force like towers on a city wall—did not daunt them.

The Turks' quick little galleys skidded past these floating fortresses as if such things could be encountered every day. As if the galleasses were not the new secret weapon Venice had gone head over heels in debt and desperation to build. As if they were only more familiar coast-lines instead of multiple decks bristling with cannon and crack-shot harquebusiers.

Through the heavy smoke the Turks sailed. With the loss of only one of their ships to the three Venetians that were now aflame, the Turks had soon engaged the entire left wing in hand-to-hand combat at which, everyone knows, janissaries are unequaled in the world.

Now, over the constant cannon fire, Andrea could hear the very or-ders being shouted by Hasan Pasha as his galley pulled close, locked oars, and prepared to board the Venetian flagship. By God, how he loved the sound of that language! Even raised in battle cry, it was music to his ears. The things one can say in Turkish that are impossi-ble to say in Italian! They were all things of glory and chivalry and love.

Andrea gripped his sword to meet his first opponent. Now he saw him, a wiry little man stripped to the waist and climbing in the Turk-ish rigging like a monkey, preparing to swing across to the Venetian rail just at Andrea's side.

Salaam. I shall greet him with peace, Andrea thought, and bid him welcome to my father's humble ship as politely as only Turkish can.

Andrea set a pleasant smile on his face, bizarre in that mêlée of blood and death. He watched as the little man tested the strength of his rope and put his dagger between his teeth to free his hands.

"Here, let me at him, boy," said old Barbarigo, who seemed all over the ship in his desperation.

Old Barbarigo shoved his stupefied son out of the way and let his pis-tols crack. He caught the Turk full in the chest. The little man lost his grip in midair and plunged, dead weight, into the water between the ships, splintering oars on both sides as he went.

Andrea looked down over the rail at the sight as if into the very maw of hell. He felt as if he had lost the only friend he had in the world in that little monkey of a man whose name he didn't even know.

"By God—" Andrea murmured aloud and crossed himself. Then he stopped. No, not by God. By Allah. "By Allah and His Prophet."

He tried it at first under his breath. Then he began to halloo it. He joined his voice to the rumble of the oarsmen beneath him, to that of the Turks who were using it as a battle cry to urge one another on.

"I surrender myself into the merciful hands of Allah," Andrea sang out. "Lead me to Allah and His Messenger."

Now the Turks had established more stable means of boarding than rope swings: planks and wooden ladders. Scimitars swinging like scythes, they reaped a great swathe on board the Venetian ship. Andrea saw that a corner of the main sail was on fire. As there was no wind, it was a slow burn, languidly uncurling its way up the canvas. It grew like weeds about a wilted scarlet lily, the flag of the Republic on top of the mast. It was, nonetheless, a burn that could not be put out.

"I surrender! I surrender!"

Men about him were joining his cry though, as they pled frantically in Venetian, it did not mean the same as his Turkish "I am a Muslim!"

The Turks didn't have time to heed every cry, and many who surrendered also died alongside their companions who fought to the end. But Andrea, perhaps because his cries were in Turkish, kept the scimitars and arrows from himself and managed to balance his way across on a makeshift ladder to the other galley. There he laid his suit at the feet of a young commander of the janissaries.

Andrea had not offered more than a few words of explanation before his captor panted out the reply, "Well, if you're to fight with us, you'd better put on this."

The janissary tossed him the length of fabric from the head of a dead comrade. With it, Andrea showed the man he already knew how to wrap a turban. This seemed proof of sincerity to the janissary, who laughed, clipped Andrea with comraderie on the shoulder, and said, "Stick with me, O Muslim!"

But already men about them were lowering their bows, swinging the nervous tension of their sword arms against air, or quickly scrambling back to their own ship, for the Venetian galley was clearly doomed. The whole rigging was in flames now, dropping volatile fragments like flower petals down upon the dead, the wounded, the unspent kegs of powder. Andrea saw his father, still shouting orders, standing on what had been the stern but what was now the highest point of the ship as it tilted dangerously.

The red-haired mistress was with him, yowling like a soaked cat. The woman tried alternately to dowse the flames about her petticoats and to get her man to calm himself. For now as he turned to profile, Andrea saw that his father had received an arrow wound near his right eye which, if it were not to prove fatal, would surely require more care than he was giving it.

That vision of his father, standing amid the flames of his ship with the mistress at his side, and half an eye running down his face, would haunt Andrea for the rest of his life. At the time he could only hope the state of his father's eye would spare him going down beneath the waves with his last vision that of his own son and heir wearing a Turkish turban.

TO THE CHRISTIAN rolls of the dead, next to that of his father the proveditore, was added the name of "My lord Andrea Barbarigo."

But Andrea was not dead at all. Venice might have discovered this for herself when her ambassador signed the new peace treaty with the Porte. If he had looked closely under the turban third on the left, just behind Uluj Ali, the new Kapudan Pasha, he would have discovered the face of his old attaché among the Turkish naval command. But the ambassador had other worries on his mind.

The allied Christian fleet had carried the day. But Lepanto, Uluj Ali promised as the treaty was signed, had but trimmed the beard of the Turkish navy. It would grow again, and thicker. Even as he signed, the ambassador knew the Golden Horn was bristling with a whole new fleet built overnight it seemed.

"If we have not enough iron, we Muslims can cast anchors of silver, and our sails shall be of silks and brocades when the canvas is gone."

It was, indeed, a finer fleet than had been sunk, and built in the space of but one winter.

"But you Venetians, by cutting off your island of Cyprus, we have cut off your right arm. You cannot grow another."

It was true and the ambassador knew it. The treaty confirmed, in very humble terms, that violent amputation.

All the Cypriot wine he wanted was now promised to the besotted old Sultan for as long as his heart could keep beating. And Venice was quickly being eclipsed by greater powers, both East and West.

Part III

Abdullah

X

THE OPERATION THAT makes a man sexless gives him an ancient timelessness as well.

"There is peace in the harem, thanks be to Allah." Ghazanfer tried to make conversation as he helped me unload my two ladies in the dim shadows before the door to the imperial harem.

I studied his face, which seemed as little altered by years as it did by moment-to-moment changes in emotion. Nor did his costume deviate, summer, winter, or spring, as the season now was. I supposed that whenever the brown sable of his trim began to grow a little thin, he scoured the furriers for just the same shade. The drapers had to produce the identical bottle green in such widths as his great figure required for the ample fall of his robes. Such lot-to-lot dye variations as the normal harem uniform suppliers produced never glanced off him.

I replied with an attempt at equal impassivity. He owed me his life, from that dark alley by my master's northern wall. But I cannot say this made me trust him any more. Ghazanfer had not heard, for example, what I had heard while his lady and young Barbarigo spoke together in Italian in that same alley, that same night. Safiye wanted my master, Sokolli Pasha, the Grand Vizier and main prop of the empire, dead. Allah only knew what that would do to my two ladies, Esmikhan Sultan and her little daughter.

Or what else Baffo's daughter might have in mind for my two charges. I glanced protectively after them, where they paused now, Esmikhan loathe to walk too far without me on the opposite side of her cane for stability. In the one spot in that dark alley where there was enough sunlight, a rosebush struggled in a raised stone bed. I remembered my lady claiming the pink blooms to liven her daughter's soft, dark hair last summer. "A rose for a Rose," she'd said, playing with the Persian meaning of the name Gul Ruh.

Now they studied the first splitting of greenery to judge how soon they might repeat the ritual. Gul Ruh, over three years old, was calling me in her most saucy, commanding tone to come and lift her up. " 'Cause you know Mama cannot."

Ghazanfer was not the sort of man to argue with, about harem peace or anything else. Nor was he one to talk with much, either. So I agreed with him. "Thanks be to Allah." But I could not resist adding, "May He not allow the peace to be on the surface only."

"You look, my friend, for a Battle of Lepanto here within chastity's walls?"

This hint of joviality was unusual encouragement from Safiye's monster. I said, "No battleships in the pleasure fountains, no. But what in its own way may equal the Battle of Lepanto on the scale used in the women's world. With no less ultimate effect."

"You refer perhaps to the—" He chose the word carefully. "—tension between Nur Banu Kadin and my lady?"

"That creature Nur Banu herself introduced into the sanctum, but who has now grown to have very definite power of her own. And the will to use that power. Safiye the Fair, once called Sofia Baffo."

Slowly, quietly Ghazanfer spoke. "The harem chooses sides." Was there threat in his voice, that I had chosen the wrong side?

"At first it was only periods of silence," I continued to challenge him, "and long icy stares between the factions as they sat together. Then it came that they sat in opposite ends of the room, whispering, and have separate hours set aside for them in the bath. Nothing overt."

"Nothing," Ghazanfer told me, "to lose sleep over."

But I could not agree with him that it wasn't dangerous. It was much more dangerous, I sensed, than a battery of cannon; and the long, slow wait for the fuse to burn down was often more nerve-wracking than had I been in the front lines on a battlefield.

And was his uncustomary verbosity a warning that my lady, too, must choose sides or be crushed in the middle? Esmikhan, I knew, would die rather than make such a choice, her dearest friend on the one hand, the stepmother who had all but raised her from infancy on the other. And though her mission on this occasion was with Safiye, my lady would scrupulously keep even hours with Nur Banu at another time.

I hurried to answer Gul Ruh's demands. I caught her up, the bundle of silk that she was, warmed by the life of her tight little body. I took the whip of her stubby little braids in my face. Then the sight of life springing from the rosebush's severely pruned and manifestly dead twigs made me cling to the preciousness of her being with such ferocity that she cried out I was hurting her and I must let her down.

"Are you certain we must visit Safiye today?" I asked my lady in a low voice and with a glance behind to Ghazanfer as I took her arm.

We made our laborious way after Gul Ruh's happy skipping to a song she made up about "Beautiful Aunt Safiye's beautiful curtain of modesty," by which I felt the child might have inherited some of her uncle Murad's penchant for poetry. Not to mention that of her natural father, with his bunches of flowers and quotes from the Persian. But I did not allow myself to think too long in that direction. For all I knew, Ghazanfer might read such thoughts in my walk and he'd already given me cause to believe he held too much of this ammunition against my lady in his arsenal.

"You know I must," Esmikhan panted. "A mother's grief is at stake." She did not say more, the labor of walking strained her breath already. And I did not argue further lest it tax her beyond endurance.

And what could I say? The two women were as close to each other as legal sisters-in-law might be in Venice. And Esmikhan always considered Safiye her best friend, though what Safiye's feelings might be were more equivocal.

And I must confess to some gratitude when Ghazanfer, having seen to the comfort of our bearers and the rest of my lady's attendants, caught up with us and offered—sincerely enough—to help. When Esmikhan smiled her thanks, he lifted her up into his giant's arms and carried her the rest of the way. And I followed, smarting in my ineffectiveness, carrying only my lady's cane.

꩜

"I RECEIVED A visit from Huma yesterday." Over an hour later, Esmikhan, sustained by sherbet, sweets, and sunset clouds of pillows on

Safiye's divan, had sufficiently recovered from her exertions and the pleasantries of formulaic greetings. My lady broached the main purpose of our journey.

Safiye was busy with her voluminous correspondence and hardly concealed her annoyance at the interruption. "Not that woman again!"

"Safiye, how can you speak in such tones of a woman whom Allah, in His impenetrable wisdom—may we all submit to Him—has chosen to use so cruelly?"

"Last week she pestered your aunt Mihrimah, the week before, Nur Banu, and in between, at every Divan, at every Friday procession to prayers, she approaches the stirrup of the Sultan himself. I have even heard your level-headed Sokolli Pasha, Esmikhan—spurred by his harem, no doubt—speak for her."

"And why not? How else is a poor, weak woman to get justice in this world of mighty men if she doesn't tear her veil and make a scene? This is what the protection of our screens and eunuchs is for."

Safiye shook her head in pity, seeing no logical connection. "Every vizier and pasha's plagued by her," she said, "until there's no room left in their heads for anything else."

"But Safiye! The poor woman—"

"She is poor. And so of little consequence."

"Safiye. On the last day, Allah will command His angels to seize and fetter those who did not urge mercy for the poor during their lives. It is my religious duty to petition the French embassy. Aunt Mihrimah has done the same. I am surprised Huma has not come here."

"She has. Ghazanfer," Safiye said with a glare in my direction, "knows enough to turn such people away."

"Even my husband the Pasha has—"

"Sokolli Pasha has refused the poor French ambassador—who's only a man trying to do his job, after all—any more concessions until this matter is resolved."

The tension showed in white patches on my lady's face. "And why shouldn't my husband refuse him? My father the Sultan—may Allah favor him—has released three French captives in good faith and hope of exchange. But nothing is forthcoming from the infidel French. Nothing."

"Esmikhan, the widow Huma's daughters were taken nearly twenty years ago."

"By the Knights of Saint John."

"So was I. So was I." Safiye could not resist a glance in my direction. We'd been taken by the Knights together, she and I. And though she might acknowledge this, the fact that our misfortunes must be laid squarely at her door was not admitted even in her eyes.

"The girls were on their way with their father and brother to Holy Mecca," Esmikhan said. "The sanctity of their pilgrimage was violated by those pirates."

"As ships going to Mecca have been known to suddenly turn pirate when it suited them and attack Christians heading towards Jerusalem."

"They haven't. They wouldn't."

"You, my dear friend, have little experience of how the world works."

"I don't want to know. Not such a world as you see, Safiye."

Safiye shrugged her perfect shoulders up into her perfect blond braids. "The fact remains that Huma's daughters have been in France twice as long as I have been in Turkey—most of their lives, in fact. They can hardly remember anything else."

"How can you say so? That any girl would ever, ever forget her mother. I haven't forgotten mine." Esmikhan's eyes misted with tears. "And she died when I was born."

At that moment, the little girls—Gul Ruh and Safiye's Aysha, just toddling—came running in from the fountain and plantings of the private courtyard. As mother of a prince, the Fair One was entitled to this perquisite of air and space in the harem world, otherwise rather sterile and cramped in accommodations. Aysha stumbled on the threshold and it was Gul Ruh who picked her up and mothered her out of her tears, although there was less than a head's difference between the two. Aysha already had Safiye's long, dancing limbs under her.

Aysha's bevy of nurses came secondarily. One changed the bands of diaper cloth covering the little girl's sex, of which she was as yet carelessly unaware. A child graduated to such swaddling when she would no longer stay put in a cradle. One nurse swept the soiled bands off to the laundry. The third stopped her mouth with a knob of marzipan knotted in a square of linen. Safiye herself did nothing but drape her graceful arms over her desk to protect the work.

I had to wonder if the marzipan had been soaked in poppy-head water as well, for very soon the toddler had suckled herself to sleep. She was allowed to nap just where she fell, a little hillock of flowered red-and-gold silk amidst the blooms of the finest Isfahan rugs laid three deep on Safiye's floors, the year as yet too early for the tile beneath to be exposed.

"Hush. You mustn't bother Aysha Sultan now," Esmikhan told her daughter. "Come here and sit by me."

Grudgingly, Gul Ruh took the second option offered her, to go and toss a ball in the yard with the now unemployed nurses for a while. Encrusted with jewels whose gold casings could cut skin if thrown too hard, the ball was in fact not much of a plaything. But it was the best to hand in this world where the most common everyday objects were too readily gaudied past all usefulness.

"Isn't Muhammed here yet?" my little lady pleaded of Safiye, leaning back as long as she could on a nurse's hand.

Esmikhan gave a little cough of warning and Gul Ruh remembered her manners. "I mean, my honored cousin Prince Muhammed—may Allah smile on his house until Judgement Day."

"You know the single-reason-for-my-being has lessons with his eunuchs and tutors during the day."

The way Safiye rattled off the euphemism to avoid using the preciousness of her son's name mimicked Gul Ruh's attempt at manners. At the very least Baffo's daughter was irritated at yet another infantile interruption. Fortunately, I think the nuances of tone were lost on the child. My little lady probably did believe Muhammed was her aunt's reason for being. She was her own mother's reason for being, Esmikhan made no secret of that. And a child of Gul Ruh's same age in Italy, I reckoned, would still be encouraged to believe in the old witch La Bafana to keep up the good behavior until Epiphany. There was no reason to confuse a childish mind by insisting on a distinction between the prince himself and the power he represented to his almond-eyed mother.

"Can't I go to him?" my little lady asked.

"Goodness, no," her mother exclaimed. "To the palace school?"

"I should like to learn at the palace school. It would be less boring than tossing a ball around."

"Perhaps, when you're older, my treasure," Esmikhan said, "We might get you your own tutor at home. A nice, pious woman."

"It would be more fun with Muhammed—may his final hour be blessed." The two phrases existed in two different childhood worlds.

"I know, my mountain spring," Esmikhan said now. "But you could still come and sit with me. I could comb out your hair for you."

"Oh, Esmikhan. You won't leave that child a hair on her head by the time she's ten with all your fussing." Safiye spoke with an impatient shuffle of papers.

Gul Ruh chose the nurses then, and thoughtfully invited the little dwarf girl Murad had recently given his lover to come and play, too. Still, in a way she couldn't quite express, my little lady fully understood that the slaves, who would treat her always like a princess, might well render her as useless for her task of living as the jeweler's enthusiasm had made the ball for play.

XI

DURING THIS INTERRUPTION by the children, Safiye had gone on with the day's correspondence. Between her and her scribe, they had gotten off half a dozen letters. Safiye's correspondents, those I saw, included viziers and *sandjak beys,* as well as the Persian ambassador: a bellicose note. Words even went to Joseph Nassey, consoling him that it wouldn't be long now before he got the Cypriot kingship Selim had promised him. Hadn't the island fallen, true to the Sultan's oath? Wasn't Safiye herself pulling in every favor she could on his behalf? But Nassey must be patient. What good would a war-ravaged countryside be for a king, anyway? It was better to wait and let the janissaries clean up the place yet a little more.

One letter Safiye even snatched out of the scribe's hand, saying with a mixture of conspiracy and impatience, "Let me deal with that one."

In no time at all, she had jotted off a note in her own hand and folded it before the ink could quite have time to dry. Safiye did not give her product the distinguishing mark of her seal, but handed it at once to waiting Ghazanfer, who knew without telling where he must go, and did so with a silent bow.

Esmikhan, for her part, could contain no other thought in her mind when children were present. Only when the rhythmic toss of the ball accompanied by a childish rhyme droned in from the courtyard with the laziness of dust motes did my lady manage to pick up the thread of her purpose where she had dropped it.

"Huma's daughters have been forcibly converted to Christianity."

"There are worse fates," Safiye said, setting aside her writing with a sigh. "Besides, why would the mother want them back now that they are so corrupted with heresy and would have to bear the punishment for apostasy if they came?"

"The law of Allah is merciful. It understands that we women are weaker than men and is not so severe on us in such cases."

"The girls'd go to prison at any rate, even if not to the gallows. I say those girls are better off where they are. Catherine has made one her treasurer. The other is a lady-in-waiting, a post of honor, not of servility as you and Huma may imagine. Besides, I understand they are married in France."

"They were forcibly married. To strangers. And too young."

"Like me, Esmikhan? Like you?"

Esmikhan shifted, and I went to help her plump the cushions up more comfortably.

"The girls must have children of their own by now," Safiye suggested. "How can the mother think it a mercy to move them from their own children? What that widow really needs is to remarry herself. I may even be able to suggest someone suitable if I set my mind to it."

"Do you think so, Safiye? And would you do that?"

"It would certainly give her something else to do so the rest of the world could get on with business."

"Perhaps the king of France would be willing to put up the brideprice so some poor but worthy gentleman could——"

"That is asking quite a bit, Esmikhan."

"A widow is in no hurry, not like a younger woman." My lady's memories of her own youthful infractions were a little too transparent in the self-condemning tone of her voice. I silently pled with her not to betray herself, for there could be no worse person to give such information to than Safiye—if the Fair One didn't already know.

Whether she did or not was difficult for me to discern, but she did snort something like a laugh.

Esmikhan forcibly set down her own memories and returned to the matter at hand. "And I think the daughters also ought to write to their mother. One little note at least, to assure her they are happy and well. If they cannot write themselves, they must go to a scribe. And I think you could write to France's Valide Sultan to order them to give their poor mother ease."

"Very well," said Safiye, letting out her breath with the force of her decision. "Luck is with you. This is my day for letters. One more cannot hurt."

I came fully alert. Safiye could be talked into doing nothing for others she hadn't already decided to do on her own. I must watch carefully.

"Oh, Safiye. You will not regret it."

To my horror, Esmikhan was trying to get up to bow her gratitude. I managed to settle her back down. No matter what Safiye's promise, I knew it could not be worth the trouble of sending for seconds to help my lady return to the divan should her constitution not prove up to the exertion.

I was greatly relieved that my lady contented herself with saying, "Allah will reward you in the next life if not in this."

Safiye waved the possibility of God away with a flash of her long, elegantly hennaed and many-ringed fingers. "This must be the most formal of letters," she then instructed her scribe. "Queen to queen."

The scribe I recognized now as Belqis, a girl of beautiful Tatar features originally bought for Murad. Safiye's greater charms, if not to say skills, had long ago supplanted her. Realizing her hopes in this direction must come to naught, Belqis had diverted her energies to the pen instead. That Safiye trusted her correspondence to this hand said something of Belqis. So did the fact that the scribe no longer bothered to conceal a premature grey creeping down the long, straight strands of her raven hair. The stains on her fingers were ink, not henna.

The conclusion of all of this was that Belqis and her art were a pleasure to watch, as fascinating as a dancer who takes equal care to hone her skills. Belqis began by taking a fresh sheet of paper out of her tooled red cowhide portfolio. The paper was thick and clearly of Eastern make, yellower than what they were making in Venice, and without watermark: Muslim paper-making firms were never so anxious to advertise their names as the profit-conscious West. The size of a large napkin, half as wide as it was long, the page's thickness and color gave the impression of parchment, which Eastern paper-makers continued to yearn for even when that medium was too dear.

Belqis draped the paper like a tablecloth over the low, portable desk she wrote at, her knees drawn up under her on the floor. Finding by close inspection that she had the rough side up, she turned it over to the smooth, so that no fibers would clog her pen. Here again was Eastern manufacture evident, for the Turks had not the mechanical hammers, a recent German invention, and relied on hand burnishing which left uneven streaks on the smoothed side.

Belqis took an agate stone that exactly fit in the palm of her hand and finished up the polish to her personal specifications. Her actions released the hard, sharp, new-paper smell of animal-hide sizing like a knife into the harem's usually cloying, heavy scent of too many women wearing too much perfume. In their sizing, too, the Muslims liked echoes of the ancient parchment.

Belqis studied her page with satisfaction, smeared now as it was with the midmorning light that dappled in from the courtyard through the lattices. The whole document, when it arrived in France, would speak of things exotic, the integrity of an ancient tradition and its opulence, even before the first word was read.

This dappling did not seem to mar the paper's perfection in her view; women are used to seeing things, half-light, half-dark, like that. Their eyes adjust from earliest infancy. "If the sun had not been female, even she would not have been allowed in the harem." An Eastern pundit had once written those words, playing on the fact that in Arabic, *sun* is feminine. Unlike the male sun in Italian, a beneficence, the Arabic is a malevolent fury, a barren woman who seeks to scorch the entire world to her own fate. Under the harem's lattices, even women condemned to childlessness like Belqis were protected from all but the most innocent of that celestial female's wrath.

Belqis laid out her pens, her inks in five colors. Deciding after the morning's labors she would have to grind more black, she did so, oak galls on a slate palette. Rose water turned the powder to liquid.

Now Belqis set a straight edge down the right-hand side of the paper, leaving a generous margin at least as wide as her own palm, and marked a crease at this point the full length of the page with the rounded tip of a stick of sandalwood. In France, they would smell that fragrance, and the distilled roses in the ink.

Then the scribe sat back on her heels and waited orders to begin.

Something did not seem quite right to me, not about Belqis but about Safiye. I could never have ease in the Fair One's presence; I told myself there was probably no more to suspect than usual. Yet I couldn't help but probe the deceptively still and murky waters a little.

"How did you become a correspondent of Catherine de' Medici?" I asked. "She is the Queen Mother and effective ruler of France."

"Quite simple." Safiye displayed no hesitation to answer directly. "Catherine sent customary gifts with her new ambassador and Ghazanfer had only to suggest to the Divan that since these were gifts from a woman, it would not be appropriate for men to accept them. They were meant to be kept behind the curtain of modesty."

"That makes perfect sense." Esmikhan's tone was warning me off. My distrust of her best friend always grieved her.

"Ghazanfer saw that they came to me," Safiye continued. "They were nothing much, nothing the outer treasury would miss: some lace, a casket of onyx engraved with nude figures."

Esmikhan said, "Such things are better suited to the harem in the first place—if not to be tossed out at once for obscenity."

"What we thought exactly. Still, any gift requires a thank-you note."

That was as far as I dared carry my questions. So I fell silent, as a eunuch ought, and determined to watch all the more carefully instead.

"The usual sort of formulaic opening." Safiye turned to instruct her scribe.

And in firm black, Belqis wrote "Allah" in what would be the largest letters on the page, leaving again an elegant, opulent margin at the top.

"Allah is the Helper" centered carefully in the field of yellow-white.

"An excellent choice of invocation on a letter that would beg the receiver's aid." Esmikhan gave her blessing, whether Heaven would or no.

I suspected the whole elegance of the parallel would be totally lost in France's court, even in a direct translation. But I couldn't dampen my lady's spirits so.

The scribe, meanwhile, dropped down a line and without dictation went on, lavishly praising the lords of the universe in descending order, all in rhymed prose couplets. Allah was "the Absolute and the Veiler," the "Originator of shapes and colors . . . exalted be He above His Creation." And that Creation was "ornamented by the perfumed sepulchre and pure soul of Lord Muhammed, the Seal of the Prophets . . . the beautiful reflection of the Garden of Paradise in the dark pool of earth . . . the crown on the head of happiness, the pearl in the shell of existence."

Over every skillful turn of phrase, Esmikhan exclaimed, sometimes so struck at the verbiage that she could manage no more than a *"Mashallah!"* of wonder.

For her part, Belqis, to whom such turns of language were second nature, most of them trite repetitions and mainstays of the imperial scribal schoolroom, had her own pleasure. For each phrase, she changed to a different color ink, until the scarlet, blue, black, crimson, and gold alternated all down the page. And the flourishes of her final letters, the great sweep of loose tails and flight of upper and lower curves gave the impression of vines and tendrils, even of birds, in a full-color garden of visual delights.

Belqis's heart was towards illumination, obviously, towards delicate and intricate replication of Allah's most beautiful handiwork on the tight, formalized confines of her page. But since Allah Himself, perhaps in jealous rage, had prohibited such blasphemy to those of His creatures who worshipped him, her art took this form instead, splitting the bounds of her casing quietly, subtly, as the rosebush did in the harem entryway.

All at once my mind jerked back from such musings as if it had been burned. I had suddenly realized that under cover of Belqis's riveting performance, Safiye had taken out a sheet of paper of her own. So may sleight-of-hand masters work their magic in the public squares. Or pickpockets.

I looked closer. Thin, white, and watermarked with a crown, I recognized Safiye's paper as coming from a Venetian firm. No one would connect it with the harem. And the Fair One had taken up a pen of her own and been writing for I knew not how long. On pretense of keeping an eye on Gul Ruh out in the yard, I slipped around so I could read some of Safiye's writing instead.

Safiye wrote in Italian, of course. Her pen was outpacing the scribe's, each painstakingly executed syllable of the Turkish equalling three or four words of the quick, hard Italian letters. And in the place of airy, meaningless flattery came much of substance.

I could not read everything over Safiye's shoulder, draped with her thick blond braids. I did not dare let on that I suspected too much, raising either her scorn or her increased caution—I'm not certain which I feared more. That she did not scrupulously hide what she wrote convinced me that, as far as this letter was concerned, she did not care too much that I knew what message she was smuggling abroad.

Then Safiye noticed my attention and smiled, thick with more diversion—flirtation. Such a look would always send a stabbing memory pain to my groin—and set me even more on guard.

Safiye addressed my watchfulness: "Any letter in Turkish would have to go through the outer clerk's office to receive a Divan-approved translation into whatever foreign language necessary. But you see, since Catherine and I are both native speakers of Italian, there is no need. I make my own translation as we go along and spare the clerk's office the trouble."

The points of almond in Safiye's glance dared me to call her on this, and I almost did.

But though Esmikhan might not see the danger in a parallel letter, she did see it in my opening mouth. "Pray Allah, you two," my lady said. "Don't start your bickering in Italian again. I can't bear it."

So, for my lady's sake, I resisted. Still my face burned under the almond sweetness of Safiye's triumphant smile. I knew she was diverting my attention, so I redoubled it, yet under such a veil that it may seem to have halved instead.

Obviously, what Safiye wrote in Italian on paper with a Venetian watermark was not going to be a faithful translation of the Turkish. I suspected she'd already written two or three lines while Belqis was still smoothing and creasing in the margin.

Just as obviously, this was not the first time the Fair One had employed this means of smuggling correspondence, not just to lovesick Venetian attachés but to foreign heads of state. France had refused to join the Christian alliance at Lepanto, I recalled. Was this due to Safiye's hand? How many other foreign states received her letters-within-letters? What else could be laid at her deceptively cloistered door? What did she offer them? And what did they grant in return? The answers to such dangerous questions were impossible to answer at the moment. But I must try to begin.

XII

As opposed to Belqis's flower garden, Safiye limited her letter's greeting to an affectionate "My dear sister queen." This gave her plenty of time to thank Catherine for the recent gift of a copy of a work that had been dedicated to the French queen's father, Niccolo Machiavelli's *The Prince*. "Perhaps no one but yourself can understand how like inspiration the words came to me as I read," Safiye's quick hand wrote. "I devoured the whole in a sitting, and have since reread it many times."

Reading this over the blond-haired shoulder made my blood run cold. I knew *The Prince,* having found a copy of it myself in a shop specializing in foreign texts near Beyazid Square. There'd been booksellers in that place since their wares had been Greek on parchment scrolls. I often browsed there, looking for things to delight my lady—such as the

Homer that had once brought us so close together—and particularly now that her health precluded many other activities. From such a title, I had supposed this man Machiavelli to have penned some innocent little romance.

I realized Machiavelli was only putting into print what plenty of people practiced anyway, instinctively, in spite of religion's best efforts, without his instruction. Safiye, for example, had been Machiavellian long before Catherine's gift arrived in her hands. My life was clear evidence of that.

Now, as I watched the dual letter to the Queen Mother of France taking shape, phrases from Machiavelli's book ran through my mind like the horrors of the little house beyond Pera where manhood had been tortured from me. "Because people are bad and will not keep faith with you, you too are not bound to observe it with them." I couldn't shake such words, though a merciful God would have allowed me to, as He ought to have allowed me to forget Pera. Both memories had the same effect, a sickness in the bowels, a dampness in the palms, a tendency to lose touch with the present when, if anything, both such words and the scarred-over event should have taught me to keep my wits—to prevent further tragedy.

"Men ought either to be well treated or crushed, because they can avenge themselves of lighter injuries, of more serious ones they cannot."

Did Safiye consider I had been crushed beyond threat? Was that why she so nonchalantly taunted me with glimpses of what she was doing? I may have felt so crushed at one point in my life, but caring for my lady had changed that. At least it had once more given me something worth avenging—if attacked.

My thoughts were interrupted as I noticed that meanwhile, Belqis had progressed to Sultan Selim. For his pious honoring of Allah and His Prophet, her flowery language honored him in return as "Khan of the seven climes at this auspicious time, the Shah en-Shah in Baghdad, in Byzantine realms the Caesar, and in Egypt the Sultan. May he live long and attain what he desires."

My lady Esmikhan sighed with wonder at the artistry the scribe displayed.

But Safiye's letter was where my vigilance must stay. She was discussing French politics with a familiarity that made it difficult for me to follow. But, as well as I could make out, her words were, "How clever of you, my dear sister queen, to have maintained the interest of England's Elizabeth in your son Alençon, albeit he is more than twenty years her junior. And in spite of the necessary unpleasantness of St. Bartholomew's Day which might well make a Protestant queen think twice. I understand your son has grown taller and managed to produce a beard, which may do much to hide his youth and imperfections. As long as Elizabeth continues to call your son her 'little froggy,' I fully expect I may soon hear that you are the mother, not only of the king of France, the king of Poland, but of England as well. You are indeed the mother-in-law of Europe, and that is not the term of shrewish powerlessness we often imagine, but praise for the greatest of Machiavellians."

Aloud, Belqis tried out her honorific formulas for Selim's son Murad. "The straight-grown cypress in the garden of kingship." Esmikhan particularly liked that description of her brother, who had begotten His Highness Muhammed, "possessor of the crown of twelve illustrious ancestors."

Safiye's letter continued in a different vein: "Further as to what you might do with these Huguenots is difficult for me to advise. I must tell you the reflex here in Turkey is to side with Protestantism, if for no other reason than that we both share Catholic countries as our nearest and most inimical neighbors. Protestants run about destroying Catholic shrines and holy pictures; Turks share the same attitude towards 'idolatry.' For this cause I find it most difficult to plead on your behalf against Protestant England here in the Divan."

A look in Safiye's almond eyes made me think she enjoyed taunting me with bits of this letter. If there was anything here I'd been able to thwart, certainly she would have put off the correspondence until later.

I read more: "Your refusal to ally against us at Lepanto was helpful. But you must know that news of the measures taken to quell your internal rebellion with the fierceness demanded to prevent a rekindling from the coals, your 'St. Bartholomew's Breakfast,' was met here with nothing short of outrage. Nonetheless, if we assume you can forge a mixed alliance with England as successfully as you did with your daughter and Protestant Navarre, things may proceed much more in our favor."

Women finally found their place in the official reality of Belqis's words. His Royal Highness Muhammed's mother, "Most favored of the veiled and modest heads, the most exalted fleshly cradle of princes" sent greetings to "the support of Christian womanhood . . . trailing skirts of glory and power, woman of Mary the mother of Jesus's way."

Safiye returned to the subject of mothers-in-law. "Mothers-in-law here in the East are given much greater power in the formation of marital alliances than I remember in the West. Mothers are, after all, the only ones in a position to know prospective brides, for such a veil of modesty hangs over womenfolk that men will never broach the subject among themselves without risking censure of the deepest kind for their rudeness. Nonetheless, it is not until I had your example that I realized just how powerful I might become in this next stage of my career."

Safiye caught my eyes and smiled slightly. How much, I wondered, of this intimacy was also flattery? Machiavelli could turn on the Machiavellian, could he not? I couldn't tell and didn't dare take my eyes from the manuscript to think of the matter longer, for the Fair One's bangles were winking even faster across the page now.

"Although the Ottoman imperial house does maintain an ancient prejudice against marrying beneath them—and since they are the greatest empire in the world, finding peers must needs be difficult—I think, with your inspiration and that of Signor Machiavelli, I shall accomplish something."

A touch of fear crackled along my spine. Now this was an area that might well affect me, my lady, and little Gul Ruh. I sent another protective glance out into the courtyard. All seemed well, but the light blinded my eyes so much that I couldn't read Safiye's writing for a moment after I returned to the dappled light within. I listened to Belqis's phrases instead, still in praise of Catherine.

"May her last moments be concluded with good. . . . Let there be made a salutation so gracious that all the rosegarden's roses are but one petal from it and a speech so sincere that the whole repertoire of the garden's nightingales is but one stanza of it, a praise which brings forth felicity in this world and the next."

I shivered again at the invocation of sincerity in a letter meant to lay a false scent and reminded myself to read more of the real one.

"I beg your understanding of the position I am in here in the East before you condemn my simpleness. I had to get to the position of favorite first. Favorite is not the comfortable once-and-for-always of a wife under the Catholic sacrament of marriage. Even having attained this position, I was still unsure of it for many years. I resisted the realization that the more children I have to bargain with, the more bargains I can strike.

"In any case, with your example, dear sister queen, what I had tried to escape when I feared my only weapon was my good looks I have now embraced. And I once thought these Turkish women so benighted in their slavery to fertility! I doubt I shall, at this point, manage to equal your own ten offspring, but I am pleased to announce that after Prince Muhammed and little Aysha—and due to Murad's visit to the capital over the winter—a third imperial heir is on the way."

This was news indeed! Esmikhan, I was certain, had not been told yet, or she would have been able to speak of nothing else, not even the plight of the poor widow Huma. Granted, before the letter got to France, the new prince or princess might well be born. At any rate, its imminent arrival would no longer be possible to keep a secret. But that Safiye would tell this distant queen she'd never met before she told my most devoted lady was a matter to be considered. I knew I couldn't break the news to Esmikhan; the hurt would kill her.

Safiye sharpened herself a new pen—one of the reeds they used in the East instead of the quills of the West—and wrote on. "What an alliance that would be, my Aysha with your youngest, Hercule. The age difference is not so sharp as that between your son and Elizabeth, and the forging of Catholic to Protestant would be nothing to it. Everything from Constantinople and Paris would be crushed to powder between that alloy. I know your priests would not approve, not to mention the muftis. Still, it is pleasant to dream.

"And there is always Muhammed to your Marguerite—should you find Navarre more trouble than you can safely keep under house arrest and in need of more drastic remedy. The muftis even encourage Muslim men to marry infidel women, hoping for conversion. And women's beliefs, of course, are of little account. I don't think I can promise you my son will not take other wives and concubines, as the religion here allows. Marguerite might be distressed—but I imagine your nature is such that you can see the advantage here, even if youthful romantic hearts cannot.

"The shrewd mother, you have taught me, must think of such things from the cradle. At any rate, the first thing in Muhammed's case, here among the Muslims, is to have the lad circumcised—he would never be considered a man and marriageable before this."

What Safiye planned on that front—converting Muslim ritual to her will—I did not read. The lavish greetings having taken up more than half of her paper, Belqis must ask confirmation for her brief mention of Huma's daughters. Then she closed: "May this reach you at an august time whose every moment is more precious than several years . . ."

But Safiye continued to write and I alone noticed the discrepancy. The light had now changed so that I was unable to see enough to make a full sentence of it. She turned the watermark crown upside down and crammed lines in the margins.

Meanwhile, Belqis was distracted by what she had left to do and my lady, who did very little correspondence of her own, by Belqis and her ritual. And, I must confess, such was the glamour of the scribe's actions that I was entranced myself and failed even the attempt to move where light on the Venetian page would be better.

An imperial scribe uses gold dust for drying the most important documents instead of sand. Belqis uncorked a vial of the precious substance and sprinkled it from the head of her letter to the foot. Then she curled the paper up into a funnel and let most of the gold slip back into its container to reuse next time. Unlike sand, however, a certain amount of the gold was expected to linger, dazzling the receiver with yet more opulence.

Safiye contented herself with sand for her letter, then quickly folded the paper in western fashion, from the top down, because Belqis was waiting. Over this smaller white packet, Belqis folded from the bottom up and finally placed the seal. Before the warm wax smell, scented with jasmine, had had time to fade and the imprinted *tughra* to harden, the scribe plucked up a little box that sat next to the vial of gold dust. She poured the contents of the box into her hand—they were gems— and chose from among them three tiny but exquisitely cut rubies and

a diamond. These she set artfully among the bars of the seal's calligra-
phy like birds in a cage. Thus Belqis, all unwittingly, crowned her masterpiece with yet one more diversion from the communication's true
import.

And this was none too soon, for just at that moment, Nur Banu
sailed unannounced into Safiye's room, her dark eyes crackling with
fury. She didn't even stop to answer little Gul Ruh's happy chirp of
greeting out in the yard.

XIII

"WHAT IS THE meaning of this?" Nur Banu's black eyes flashed like
two more jewels among the king's ransom she wore about her person.
I always found some pathos in the lavishness of her dress, as if she hoped
to prove her life was satisfying by such things.

"The meaning of what, O most favored among the veiled heads?"
Safiye's quotation of the phrase of elaborate reverence so recently used
in her own cover letter assured me she was playing innocent and had ulterior motives here as well.

"You are tempting the will of Allah and planning for Muhammed's
circumcision."

"Yes, planning."

There was much at stake between the two, for Prince Muhammed
was the son of one woman and the grandson of the other. And how a
boy takes this important step into manhood, or so the saying goes, will
determine the path of the rest of his life. Though she might conceal
them here in the East, I knew Safiye at least had just explained her motives to a European queen, or as nearly as I was ever going to learn
them.

Safiye gestured Belqis to pack away the correspondence, but she otherwise gave no gesture of welcome to the woman who, as mother of her lover, deserved respect. I remembered, as the Fair One must have done, that her eunuch Ghazanfer was away running messages, else Nur Banu, no more than the widow Huma, would not have gained entry here.

Safiye continued: "My lord, the royal prince's father, has given his permission and spoken to the necessary officials. It is all arranged."

Esmikhan offered a polite greeting to her stepmother in an attempt to ease the tension. It didn't work.

Nur Banu fumed: "I'll wager you didn't even consult the astrologers."

"The astrologers have been consulted." Safiye spoke as if to console, but nothing could be more calculated to aggravate than her words. "They have given a day a fortnight from now as the most auspicious."

"A fortnight. That's not enough time."

"It pleases me well. The weather should be settled by then."

"Not nearly enough time."

"The astrologers say there will not come a better day for over a year."

"How can we prepare for a prince's circumcision in two weeks?"

"Well, we certainly cannot if we must spend our time sitting around arguing." Safiye gestured after the departing scribe. "Personally, I have seen to many important things today and if you'll allow me—"

"The festivities that must come before, the foreign dignitaries to invite, the gifts to acquire? I don't care who you think you are, you cannot work miracles. It will seem my grandson—Allah forbid—is a merchant's brat, a peasant, a wild Turk of the steppe, no Ottoman prince to be made a man with so little care."

"Nevertheless, it is settled." Safiye shrugged the wealth of her thick blond hair off both shoulders. "My man has made a decision, since your Selim is incapable. And Murad arranged that it pleases his father as well—may he reign forever—since *I* pleased *him* so well during his recent visit to Constantinople."

Safiye smoothed her hand over the snug pearl buttons down the front of her *yelek*. She blushed with obvious pleasure—and unshakable beauty—obviously thinking of another fruit of the prince's attention which as yet only she and I knew.

Nur Banu's cheeks flushed, too, but with fury and an unbecoming clash against the redder splotches of rouge there, against her hennaed hair so orange and stiff it might have been forged of brass. "Yet you will not go where you belong, to my son's side in Magnesia."

"And why should I, when he is content to make the trip north often enough?"

"You have no shame that he may be neglecting his duties for the likes of you?"

"None. Besides, Murad knows he must have someone here in the capital to watch out for his interests."

"Surely his own mother has nothing but his best interests at heart." Nur Banu pressed the place in her chest where such concerns resided as if it pained her.

"Surely he is not convinced of that since he is content to fulfill my requests over yours. Such as speeding up this barbaric rite—if I cannot talk him out of it altogether."

"Of course it must be done, you impious girl. But not so young, not so young. What shame and ill omen it would be—Allah forbid—if a son of Othman and heir to the throne should cry out when he was cut. By old tradition, the ceremony should be put off until the boy is twelve or fourteen."

"But the vision of my sweet small son sobbing and clinging to his mother for comfort as he faces manhood appeals to me more," Safiye said.

"His tears? I have never noticed that his tears do aught but irritate you up until now. Fine mother that you are, you are probably the last person he would turn to for comfort."

"I have also heard that a few tears now are preferable to the serious threat of infection in an older boy."

"Your only true concern is to hurry Muhammed into manhood so you can wield a man's power through him ere he's cut his eyeteeth."

Safiye made no attempt to deny the accusation. "I am, after all, the only mother he has."

"Consider how my son listens to the only mother he has before you tempt Allah with such pride. Someday, my girl, if Allah so wills, you, too, will lose a son's love to an ungrateful whore."

"Any whores I find will be stoned at once."

"That's what ought to be done to you." Nur Banu threatened with a gesture.

"I see no hand lifted against me—only your empty one. And if I am fated to lose my son to another—which Allah forbid—then better to circumcise him now, before such a calamity can happen."

Through all of this, Esmikhan had offered little reconciliatory chirps which even I did not hear. But now I could not longer ignore her agitation, and moving to her side, I bent and asked if she were not ready to go home.

"I cannot yet," she murmured under the row. "I must see if the Quince has something for my pain."

I had never been able to understand why my lady persisted in trusting her health and that of her children to the palace midwife. Esmikhan could have chosen another. I wished she'd chosen another after the death of her first little son. After two more dead sons, still she had persisted. Now she could scold my scepticism, "Abdullah, the Quince gave me Gul Ruh."

At what a cost of health! I might have replied. But Esmikhan was nothing if not trusting as well as bound and determined to do things "the way they ought to be done." "Everyone has always used the palace midwife," she always said. And "you can't blame the Quince for things that are due to the hand of Allah."

So I comforted myself that if there was witchcraft, one might as well go to the witch to undo it. And the ashen pallor of Esmikhan's face urged me there wasn't time—yet once again—to hunt up someone new. Her sickly look should have reminded me earlier that we had this errand today.

The discord she was obliged to witness probably triggered this bout of pains in her lower belly in the first place, I thought as I offered her my arm. "Let me take you to the infirmary, then."

"I don't think I could make it there. Besides, you remember the last time I saw the Quince?"

I did, the haunted look that had come over the midwife's eyes, the harshness in her tone. I might almost say fear, though what the tough old Quince had to fear from my lady was impossible to guess. "Then I'll go for you."

"Would you please, Abdullah?"

"You won't mind staying here?" I looked anxiously over at the other two women, the noise between them having risen another notch. I marveled how little Aysha could be sleeping through it all and thought poppy-head water again. "I could take you to the sedan first."

"I'll stay," Esmikhan said. She made another ineffectual attempt to speak between the antagonists, then filled her mouth with a sweet laden with buffalo cream. She always ate when she was distressed and helpless to do anything about it.

In the doorway I met Ghazanfer, red in the face and puffing for breath. He had obviously heard the row corridors away and come on the run. His errand, then, had been within the palace. But I didn't care to scrutinize it more than that. I just gave him a look as to say, So this is the peace of your harem, *khadim?* I'm taking a risk leaving my lady here with you.

And then I saw Gul Ruh standing in the big man's shadow. Her little hands, working anxiously, clung to the door frame from the courtyard. Her brown, doe eyes widened and swam with tears as she tried to call, "Auntie? Grandmother? Auntie? Grandmother?" over and over again to no effect.

"My lady," I called past my shoulder to Esmikhan, "I'm taking the little one with me to the Quince."

Esmikhan replied, "Very well."

But the eunuch tried to stop me. "I'm not certain you should, brother. The little one to the Quince? It is not wise."

"Well, I'm not about to leave more than one of my ladies here in the midst of this catfight you call harem peace."

And with that, I scooped Gul Ruh up into my arms and hurried off as fast as I could go.

XIV

THE MOMENT THE sounds of squabbling died, Gul Ruh wriggled to get down and I let her gently, taking the sweet, soft petals of her hand instead. Esmikhan would always have clothes made too big for her daughter, certain, with an uncharacteristic disregard for the will of heaven, that "she'll grow." The heels of Gul Ruh's too-big slippers clattered merrily beside me, echoing off the long, marble halls as if to frighten off evil spirits.

The harem corridors wound this way and that, up stairs and down again, like the tendrils of a luxurious jasmine vine—or, as I'd once heard Safiye say—the intestines in the belly of a stone-hearted beast. There were always at least two ways to get from one place to another, depending on what one wanted to see or to avoid. Or, alternatively, there was no way at all. I took the roundabout route to the infirmary, knowing how every woman from mistress of the wardrobe to the lowest laundress would be hovering where she could hear the brawl between the two leading women, laying her bets as to the outcome and what it might mean for her own life. I'd let Gul Ruh avoid that gawking if I could.

Door after door arched, mitred, squared, tunneled down to the size of a mouse hole in the gloom at the end of perspective. Now that the women's voices had been swallowed in a gulp, off to our right we could hear a tumult of young boys' voices, full of fear-propelled enthusiasm, all reciting Koranic verses at once, at different speeds, perhaps even different verses. That was the princes' school, where the brightest of the young levy boys also studied with their future masters.

"My cousin Muhammed is in there." Gul Ruh stated rather than asked it, pulling lightly on my hand until I stopped in the corridor to listen with her.

"That's right—may Allah favor his future."

"We can't go in there." Another statement.

"No. But I could take him a message if you like."

"I'm a girl." She was very definite about this, though I could see her little mind working strenuously at something behind the intelligence of her big brown eyes.

"Would you like me to take Prince Muhammed a message?"

"But Abdullah?"

"Yes, love?"

"How can you be here with me?"

"I will always be with you, my dearest," I promised wildly.

"I mean, aren't you a man?"

My silent struggle for the right answer allowed her to rattle on elaborations.

"How can you be here with me and also go to Muhammed? And with Father and out in the market? And here with me and Mama?"

It is the nature of God she's trying to grasp, I thought with bitterness. Finally I said as simply, as unemotionally as I could, "I am a *khadim*, mountain spring."

"What does *khadim* mean?"

Khadim means what I am and all I've suffered, seemed too broad, yet too circular an explanation even for a three-year-old. "It means 'servant'," I said instead.

"But not any kind of servant." She was definite again. "A servant who wears long fur robes and has no beard. And yet no breasts like Mama."

I rubbed the straggly hair on my chin in shame and said, "Yes."

"Aunt Safiye says Muhammed must be . . . cir . . . cir . . ." She struggled for the word and then found *cut* instead. "Muhammed must be cut first before he is a man."

"That's right."

"And until he is cut, he can still come and visit us sometimes."

"That's right." My heart lightened. She was leaving the painful subject.

"Were you never cut?" No. I was wrong. "Is that why you can come and go as you please?"

I flinched. "I was cut, sweetheart. Only much, much worse

than your royal cousin will be, *inshallah*. And that's why I'm a *khadim*."

She allowed me to walk her a step or two further, then she stopped again. "Could you cut me?"

"Sweetheart!"

"Cut me like you were cut so I can come and go, too. I would like to do that."

I found my knees sunk to the floor before her like dead weights. I folded her precious little form into my sable-furred arms and held her tight, pressing the firm little globe of her head into my chest, stroking her braids, her little back possessively, releasing the already-too-feminine smell of her to fill my mind. Hunger that was all life had taken from me fed at last on her.

"I can't do that, sweetheart."

"You are a servant. I order you." She pushed me away firmly. Her feet in their too-large slippers scuffled, trying to escape me. "Or I will sell you in the market."

Only the comedy of adult insistence dwarfing her tiny body allowed me to laugh instead of crying. "Then I must go to the block which, by Allah, would kill me. Still I cannot cut you."

I remembered the possibility of rape. My lady had once equated that with what gelding was for a man—only worse, because it could happen over and over again. I needn't burden Gul Ruh with this weight of feminine life. But I did swear to myself she would never know the possibility as long as I drew breath.

My little lady read my thought, at least part of my thought. I guess my face always softened when the image of Esmikhan passed behind it. "We needn't tell Mama if you think it best," she said. "And I'd be brave. I promise I wouldn't cry. Not too much."

Tears mixed with laughter in my eyes, blinding me. "I can't. As Allah is my witness, no power on earth can do that. And I wouldn't cause you such harm even if I could."

"Why? Why?" she insisted, anger setting her on the verge of tears as well.

"Because . . . because, thank Allah, you are a girl. When I was your age, I was a boy." That was a difficult thing to say, with all the memories it conjured, and I blinked against them.

"Oh." "This girl business again," echoed behind the syllable.

Gul Ruh was silent a moment, thinking. Into the pause drifted the princes' recited words:

"In the Name of Allah, the Compassionate, the Merciful. Be mindful of your duty to Allah and reverence the wombs that bear you. Men are superior to women on account of the qualities with which Allah has gifted the one above the other. Verily, Allah is High, Great."

"Why?" she repeated, intensity dropping the word to a whisper.

"Because," I said helplessly. It was too big a question for me to answer. "Because it is Allah's will."

No sooner had I said this—an answer I had meant only to be as safe, trite, and formulaic as any other recital of such words—than the full wonder of the theology hit me. I felt myself shaking on the hard marble floor of that harem corridor at the mighty, ineffable, incomprehensible power eternity hides in such moments.

"Poor Abdullah," Gul Ruh said, reaching up a little hand to gently touch the curse of my naked face. "Did you cry when they cut you?"

"I did, little one." I choked, the memory breaking through my body with physical force. "And screamed and cursed Allah, begging him to let me die."

"Are you sorry now you didn't die?"

"No, dear heart, no. I—" And this was the first moment I realized it myself. "—I thank Allah every time I look at you."

In my mind, my thought went forward. I was even grateful I was such a man as I was, for no other being on earth save only her mother could have been present, nay, responsible both for her getting, when the sanctity of harem walls was defied, and at her birthing. And there was her teething, her every step which no man saw, no man but the Divine— and Abdullah the *khadim*.

"I thank Allah, too," she said, in the perfect faith of a child.

Still shaking slightly, I got to my feet and took her little hand in mine. Dear Allah, I was going to spoil her rotten!

"Come, my heart," I said. "Let's go get the physic to help your mama feel better."

XV

LIGHT APPEARED AT the end of the corridor, a door open to trees in their first green haze of spring. Under the trees, fresh manure on the newly turned beds and the freshly shooting perennials hummed with flies and hornets in the Quince's herb garden. We turned to the right before leaving the building, and entered the surgery.

The bellies of row upon row of Chinese porcelain, japanware, and blue Persian jars leaned in upon my little lady and me from the walls of the narrow room. The smells of their contents assailed our noses. Sweet cloves and cinnamon, sharp garlic and bitter gentian. There were the darker odors of moss, clay, and virgins' blood, as if we'd walked into the very heart of a woman's pelvis. Animal parts preserved in brine—all slaked with a wash of alcohol and a pervading sense of power.

Gul Ruh's little fingers shifted nervously in my hand and I pressed them tight to reassure her.

There was another smell, and I remembered the buzz of opium tasted under a piney disguise of mastic gum. For all her skill—or perhaps because of it—I had known the Quince to medicate herself into oblivion since before Gul Ruh was born. And, as is the way of such habits, there was very little chance the poppy had loosened its hold on the midwife during the intervening years.

Indeed, as my eyes adjusted to the gloom, I found that the room was not deserted, as I'd first suspected. The old Quince was there, slumped behind her table, snoring quietly. She appeared little more than a heap of shabby olive-green clothes, much slept in.

"Perhaps we shouldn't wake her," I suggested to my little charge.

"Yes, we must," Gul Ruh said firmly. "So she can make Mama not hurt any more."

"Madam? Madam?" With no response, I turned to Gul Ruh again. "Perhaps another midwife would do as well."

"No," she replied firmly. "Mama says the Quince is the best. She brought me into the world and saved my mama's life when there was little hope." Gul Ruh tried her shrill little lungs: "Madam?"

At this point another woman bustled herself into the room. I recognized her as the Quince's new apprentice, a black African everyone was calling the Fig, "to make a regular fruit basket of the infirmary." She was as blue-black as a fresh fig—and who knew what seeds her heart contained? A large gap between her front teeth exposed only shadows within, as if even enamel couldn't quite close over the African in her.

The Quince and her apprentice were rumored to be more than co-workers. I didn't think it was my business to probe further into such affairs, certainly not among women the Sultan and princes were not likely to claim. Slaves must find comfort where they can.

Other rumors were more disconcerting. I'd heard the Fig had been powerful in her homeland—a priestess. No, more. The incarnation of a deity called Yavrube. Yavrube would come to the call of a drum and possess her. And the aura had been exported with her.

The Fig certainly dressed like a queen. Contrasting richly with her skin were more pearls and golden sequins than all but the most favored odalisque was likely to earn. The Fig's countrymen, I'd heard, would deposit with her any treasure they might earn—or steal—from their masters against the possible purchase of their freedom. Sick or ill-treated slaves might find refuge, and all this she protected under the brilliantly flowered skirt of her power.

Whatever the truth of all these rumors, I sensed them—and more—in the cypress-shadow chill the woman brought into the room with her. The Quince had chosen her replacement well—or perhaps it was the Fig who had chosen. That thought, too, entered my mind as the African came to stand protectively between me and her still-snoring mentor. Finding comfort in slavehood was one thing, fomenting rebellion—and certainly demonic polytheism in the heart of Islam could be nothing else—was another thing all together.

Still, since I had no proof—more than the distinct feeling, a knot of fear in my stomach, that it was actually Yavrube I addressed—I kept my thoughts to myself and merely stated my errand. Wordlessly, she went about fulfilling the order. I read *birch* and *willow* on the jars into which the black hand dipped.

"No opium. We want no opium," I said, casting a glance at the Quince, exposed in her helplessness again.

The Fig honed her ebony eyes——shooting her demon out to scrutinize me?—but said nothing.

Then, as if *opium* were the word that conjured, the Quince began slowly, slowly to rouse.

"Madam Quince?" I greeted her politely around the flash of her assistant, whose gold- and pearl-polished movements were gaining velocity. "Peace to you, madam."

"Hello?" There seemed to be gravel in the older woman's chest.

"Hello, madam. I've come——"

"Who . . . who are you?"

"Abdullah, madam. From Esmikhan Sultan. I've come——"

"Esmikhan?" The Quince bolted upright as if I'd blasphemed. Her old, lined, fuzzy face paled, then grew greener than the scarf around her head. "Esmikhan Sultan," she breathed. A curse.

I didn't know what to say. Gul Ruh chirped instead, "My mama has a pain in her belly and wants you——"

"Who?" growled over the gravel. The Quince lifted one knobby finger that tremored out of control. "What child is that?"

The Fig shimmered defensively, catching her mistress and spilling the handkerchief of simples she'd gathered in the process. I stepped, too, trying to get between the threat of that finger and my little lady.

"This is Esmikhan's daughter, Gul Ruh." I spoke soothingly. "You remember, madam. You birthed her."

"Dead!"

A violent jerk flung the old woman out of the Fig's arms and across her work table. Stacks of books and mortars and pestles in three sizes went flying into a filigree stand that held a small glass bowl over a lamp's flame. Glass shattered. The flame went out and threw up a pall of acrid smoke.

"That child should be dead. With the rest of them. The rest of them. Dead. Babies. Dead."

I was beside my little lady in a moment, sweeping her up into my arms and inching backward. The Quince, possessed, staggered in our direction. The Fig pressed a kerchief in my hand and me towards the door. I needed no more encouragement. Gul Ruh stared, wide-eyed but too surprised to whimper.

Before I managed to get us out of sight down the corridor, the haunted woman had lurched into her garden, pursued by the Fig. Here the Quince stood, saying the same things over and over to the barren earth, the denuded trees: "Babies. Dead. Their insides bleeding out."

And then I had the task, which I finally gave up as hopeless, of trying to explain this mystery to my little one, apologizing for the will of Heaven that made drugs that eased pain but also wildly deranged.

"What pain does the midwife have?" she asked.

I couldn't answer.

Gul Ruh took it bravely and soon was distracted with other things that loomed larger in her childish life. But, unlike the previous explanation of the sexes, I could tell she wasn't satisfied. How could she be, when I brought no comfort even to myself? I could not understand why the Quince should have turned suddenly so violent. And worse, why that violence should have been turned so personally, so specifically against my little angel.

Unless—unless it had something to do with Yavrube.

XVI

A WEEK BEFORE the day the astronomers had picked as auspicious for the beginning of the festivities, preparations for the young prince's circumcision were well under way. One thousand poor boys had been chosen to join Muhammed in this rite at the cost of the palace. Their presence would give the young prince the honor of mass charity and the unfailing devotion of these boys and their families for the rest of his life.

Each boy had already been sent a new suit of clothes—nothing to compete with the cloth-of-gold in twenty changes that were being readied for Muhammed, but rich enough, with a striped silk turban each that would be worn with feathers. Tent stakes were driven into the lawn both within the palace walls and outside in the Hippodrome to take the overflow of entertainments from the kiosks.

And heat from the kitchens filled the whole palace.

My lady had abandoned her own harem for the palace's "to help," as she said, "with the preparations." What a woman who could hardly walk might do to help was never asked. She would sit and bask in the excitement, of course, and her daughter would learn something about what made boys different from girls as she watched this ceremony in her cousin's honor. That was enough.

As soon as we arrived, I went to the kitchen. I had to supervise the deposit of ten trays of tiny tartlets filled with ground dates, nuts, or apricots, heavy with honey, all arranged in elegant pyramids which my lady had had her women prepare at home as a gift. Although not more appreciated, they were more practical than the jewels and fine fabrics that were to be her main gifts to the boy, his mother, and grandmother later on.

In spite of the extensive remodeling and rebuilding the palace has undergone between that morning in April and the present, the form of the kitchens has proven so functional as to always be renewed along the same lines. And even those who have never been within the Sublime Porte will have some idea of their layout. The row of ten stone chimneys rising like the necks of wine flasks from their individual domes is the most distinctive palace structure the average citizen can possibly view from a boat on the Marmara.

The average citizen, too, will have a good notion of the activities of that complex of kitchens. Turning live sheep and goats, sacks of hard, raw grain, and whole fruits and vegetables into the numerous hot and cold dishes upon which people feed happens in his own home: merely multiply it a hundredfold.

The average citizen will certainly have a clearer notion of these activities than many a child born and bred in the harem does. Sometimes such royal children know no better than that Allah Himself must have created meat just so in bite-sized pieces tangy with herbs and spices.

They never imagine that there should be separate plants for fennel, basil, and coriander, that pepper must come from so far away or that salt is really a mineral mined from the earth, and that only the skill of the cook blends them with success.

The harem had its specialists in sherbets, preserves, and candied delights, of course. But for the majority in the heart of the harem, much of cookery was likewise a mystery. The women liked to regale one another with tales of how far and at what expense snow was brought from distant mountains packed in straw, as they told tales of flying carpet rides. But one for whom "far" may be to the end of the garden and back, she may suppose that the white cold falls on those mountains in perfect little rounds of sherbet flavored with raspberry, lemon, or rosewater.

Whereas in most kitchens the women do the cooking, in the palace, it is a profession for men with years of training; women never set foot inside. The kitchens must, after all, feed the outer, men's palace as well, sometimes several thousand mouths on a Divan day.

Young eunuchs and young odalisques both begin their duties by picking up the steaming trays in the outer harem corridor and delivering them to the rooms where the women wait in happy, chattering clusters. Male servants called halberdiers actually cross the open court from kitchen to harem. The halberdiers leave the trays on special heating stones in the corridor, careful to glance only circumspectly through the long fake tresses dangling from their hats, careful to vanish before the head eunuch rings a bell announcing dinner.

Each of the ten chimneys seen from the Marmara surmounts not only its individual hearth, but an entire kitchen. Each kitchen has a separate entrance off the main corridor, each has its own allotment of produce.

The first kitchen, with the sober food taster and his five underlings watching every move of the small army of cooks, is that of the Sultan alone. Then comes that of the Valide Sultan—Nur Banu had it now—then that of that of the Sultan's current favorite. Under Selim, she (or he) changed so frequently that that room was always in a state of confusion. It tried desperately to meet each new taste, sometimes two within the same afternoon. The favorite's kitchen was a synonym for chaos.

"How was the market today, *habibi?*" one might ask. "I understand the new shipments from China are causing quite a stir."

And the reply one might receive: "Yes, by Allah. A regular favorite's kitchen!"

The fourth kitchen was for Safiye to share with the women of royal blood; the fifth for the chief white eunuch; the sixth for the viziers and other members of the Divan when they dined in; the seventh for the rest of the eunuchs, pages, and other lesser officials; the eighth for the rest of the female slaves; the ninth for the attendants of the Divan; and the tenth served the three hundred men who manned these kitchens as cooks, confectioners, accountants, butchers, grocers, chandlers, dairy-men, icemen, water carriers, scullery hands, herbalists, tinkers, and apprentices. You notice I didn't mention bakers—the palace bakery, every bit as large as the kitchens, was in another place, in the outer or first court of the palace.

A mosque stands at either end of the complex, serving five kitchens each. The hours of prayer are devotedly kept here because it often happens that this is the only time a cook can sit down. Otherwise, even their meals are taken on the run; a bite here of whatever is boiling, the scrapings of a bowl. On a normal day, as I have said, they have about a thousand souls to feed, more on Divan days. But for the circumcision, there would be over six times that number for the week-long duration, when family and friends not only of the Prince but of the charity boys would have to be served as well.

In spite of her separation from the heat and noise, and in spite of the kitchen's massive, all-male hierarchy, it was still possible for a woman of the harem to make an impression on the food preparation, however. No favored woman would give up a single route to influence the men of the *selamlik,* certainly not one available to her sisters even in the poorest households.

And, however little Safiye knew about the inner workings of her young son's mind, she did know that dates were his favorite food. A boy given to frequent sulks, Muhammed could always be coaxed out of them with a handful of the sticky brown nuggets. So Safiye had contrived to have six dates smuggled out of an oasis in Arabia which was the only place in the world where this particular variety grew. They were known to most, if not all, of Constantinople by name alone because the natives were so jealous of their prize that they posted guards day and night in all seasons about their trees. And, though they might honor a pilgrim with a taste, they required that every pit be returned again to a careful account.

Each date was as big as Muhammed's eight-year-old fist, as sweet and creamy as honey whipped with butter and so rare outside Arabia that their weight in gold could not purchase them. With these treasures, Safiye planned to beguile her son during his suffering.

However Safiye's messengers managed to get the dates out of Arabia, it was no more difficult a task than getting them into the harem. Or so it seemed. They got as far as the kitchen storerooms, brought in like any other foodstuff. But when Ghazanfer came to pick them up to bring them to his lady's room for safe keeping, he found Nur Banu's eunuchs already there, making similar claims of possession.

This, at least, was one version of the conflict. There were several other versions in circulation including its mirror image told by those in Nur Banu's camp. If Nur Banu couldn't have her way over the age of her grandson at circumcision, she would certainly provide herself with the best of gifts to celebrate the occasion.

So while I was having the porters set their tartlet trays down in the storeroom, the overseer came and stood behind us, watching with an eagle eye that we didn't come too close to the encrusted gold casket that held the dates. It was in his neutral custody until someone higher up should come and tell him whether Safiye's eunuch should claim it or Nur Banu's.

"Present bias does seem to favor Nur Banu," the overseer confided to me with a philosophical air. "She does have the greater authority. My personal inclination is, however, that the actual facts favor Safiye. It would be too bad if authority overruled the facts in this case."

My immediate thought on meeting this man was, What a time his mother must have had birthing him! For his head, though narrow, was incredibly long. His turban sat ill upon it, looking more like some Venetian dandy's hat than the usual neat, tight knot because of the stretch. Although he was a slim man, a double chin or, rather, no chin at all beneath a beard neither present nor yet quite shaven added to the length. In the very middle of that head's length rested a mouth of disconcerting smallness, held constantly in a rather simple pout as with some persons born feeble-minded.

Upon acquaintance, however, it was clear that if not particularly profound, he was neither witless nor inattentive to duty. When he was certain he could trust me, he let me have a look at the dates, more valuable than the casket in which they nestled like half a dozen eggs in a nest. As I could never taste them, there was little point in taking more than a peek to verify that such wonders did indeed exist. Then I turned to leave.

I let the porters go at the door with a suitable tip then, hoped to make my way back to the harem through the kitchen corridor, on to the white eunuch's quarters by the Gate of Felicity. But before I could, the pantry overseer stopped me.

"A friendly warning, *khadim*," he said. "I wouldn't go down past the kitchens if I were you, not if I valued my life."

"How so, friend?" I turned to him and laughed. "I am not afraid of a little heat if it will cut my walking time in half."

"Yes, well, there's the heat. But something else besides."

"What's that?"

"Oh, it's all on account of these—ahem." He gestured towards the casket he hardly ever let out of his sight, even when the room was empty.

"Yes?"

"Well." His long face grew longer still. "It's those two kitchens. Nur Banu's and Safiye's. They both crave the supreme honor of making the dishes to complement these dates and both claim the other unequal to it. Even the head chefs are not above flinging insults at each other in the hall."

"I think I can dodge flying insults." I smiled.

"Ah, but the underlings. They do not stop at words. Kitchen slops, fire brands, skillets—even knives have been flying. And all on account of these dates—and those two women. I don't envy you, having to go back to the harem. It must be very frightening there, so close to the heart of the flame when this is what we find at the edges."

I bowed to him, thanking him for his concern. I was going to go against his counsel nonetheless, but I think stopping to hear it was one of the most provident things I'd ever done. Just as I turned to continue, heedless, on my way, what sounded like a thunderclap came from the very spot I would have been at that moment if I had not stopped.

I do not know what the sound was. And no one who was close enough to see what it was lived to tell the tale.

XVII

THERE ARE THOSE who think it was only a fire such as any kitchen with piles of wood and pans of grease is subject to. Maybe it was only the words the overseer had just finished giving me, but I'm afraid I must refute that notion. That sound and the awful speed with which smoke, then flame was soon pouring down the corridor in both directions make me suspicious.

Suspicious of what, I can hardly say. And I did not take time to think about then, for the overseer and I were shoving each other out the door and into the courtyard to shout the news to anyone who had ears, "Fire! Fire! Quick!"

Not a moment later we were followed by all those who managed to escape the kitchens if they did not jump out the windows in the other direction. One man had his eyebrows singed. Others, overcome by smoke, were carried by companions. One brought fire with him, clinging to his clothes like a playful little monkey. Screaming wildly, he flung himself to the dust and rolled while some came to his aid.

They answered our call quickly: janissaries, pages, officials of all descriptions carrying water in vessels just as varied. Soon several hand-to-hand chains were set up to carry water from the Fountain of Execution in the first court. The fountain's steps, brown with dried

blood, grew red as the water splashed on them—here the head executioner and his assistants always washed themselves after carrying out
their function. Now it was called on to save lives instead. But soon the
fighters were halted at the kitchen door in their efforts, and then one
or two were seriously injured as the roof of the portico collapsed in
front of the door.

A strong breeze like the breath of Judgment came off the Marmara,
pushing my robes against the fountain and making them wetter and
heavier still.

"We shall have a time of it if that wind keeps up," the man closest to
me shouted, and I agreed.

The wind working like a great bellows trained right on the hot spot
and fanned it towards the main part of the palace and the harem. Where
a corps might have set themselves to strategic advantage, none did because that would mean violating the Sultan's women.

As soon as I saw this, I left my place in the brigade—there were
plenty with pinched faces beneath the sweat to replace me, and firefighting was not my first responsibility. I walked as fast as a eunuch's dignity would let me through the Gate of Felicity.

I found my lady gossiping with friends. In their *oda,* no sound of the
fury out in the second court had entered. I waited as long as I dared,
but then felt obliged to interrupt.

"What is it, Abdullah?" Esmikhan turned to me still weak and smiling from her last fit of giggles.

"Lady," I said, "there is a fire in the kitchen."

Her face puckered and then burst into laughter again. "I am glad
to hear that," she said. "They will need something to roast our shish-
kabab on."

The others joined in her laughter.

"You misunderstand, lady," I said. "There is a fire gone out of control.
Several men have been killed already and the whole second court is in
alarm."

"Oh!" some of the ladies exclaimed and wondered if, from the lattices in the female slaves' dormitory on the second floor, they could get
a view of what was going on. They went to find out.

For my lady and even for some others not so handicapped as she, the diversion was not worth the trouble of climbing stairs, so they picked up the conversation where they'd left off.

"But lady," I persisted, "I think perhaps I should call the sedan porters to have them on alert, at least, in case we are forced to flee."

My lady sighed at this second interruption. "Abdullah, don't bother them to no purpose. No, I'm sure they'll have it put out long before we have to worry in here."

"Allah willing, it will be as you say."

I bowed to her words and made my way back to the eunuchs' quarters by the gate where I joined a crowd of my colleagues, watching anxiously from the windows. We heard a shout and a groan from the firefighters, but what caught their attention escaped us, the angle of the wall blocking our view.

We didn't have long to wonder. The head eunuch soon came running in. "To our charges, *khuddam.* They tried to hold the flames back at the gate, but it's breached now. Come, to the ladies."

In some respects, it was good the head eunuch's quarters were on the outer side of the gate; he had already lost his possessions to the flames and was now able to think clearly about other things. When his seconds stopped by their cubicles to gather what they valued most, he was able to knock silk robes, fine ceramics, and books from their hands, saying, "Put that down, my friend. You will need your arms for the children."

"But where shall we take our charges?" someone asked.

"The garden," the head eunuch said. He answered on the spur of the moment. Nonetheless, given all the time in the world, anyone would have come to the same conclusion; the garden was the only sanctuary.

"But we can't take them into the garden. It's not ladies' day in the garden. The Sultan is there, entertaining friends."

"I'm sure the men will be circumspect enough to look away if they realize the only alternative is the flames. And if they are not—well, then, you will have to work harder, won't you?"

We were met at the harem vestibule by several ladies who had been drawn by the smoke and came to wonder.

"Into the garden. Into the garden, ladies," the head eunuch said, and set one of his seconds to accompany them. They stood at the door to the outside, blinking and hesitating, as skittish as horses when the stables are on fire. Inside was safety. Outside was something worse than pain or death—a loss of honor.

"Come on, come on," the eunuchs encouraged.

"We'll have a time of this," I warned the head. "I know many women have gone up to the second floor to watch from the windows. You'll have to get them down."

"Yes, thanks for the word," he said, and went up the first staircase we came to with half of his staff following.

When I opened the door of the room where I'd left my lady, the smell of smoke followed me quite strongly and gave force to my words. "Come, lady. It's too late to leave by the front in the sedan. That way is already in flames. We must go out the back on foot, into the garden. Come, I'll help you."

I'd given all my seconds the day off because I'd assumed, in the Serai, I wouldn't need them. I cursed that assumption and the lack of another pair of strong arms. But three of her maids and I managed to half carry, half support Esmikhan out of doors. Our task was made even more difficult by the fact that, as soon as she saw we were in earnest, as soon as she saw the smoke, and caught the panic of the fleeing women passing us, my lady remembered her daughter.

"Gul Ruh!"

"I'll go for her when we've got you safe, lady," I promised.

She called out her daughter's name again and began to struggle, making our task more difficult.

Gul Ruh no less than her mother was my responsibility to see safe. I knew that, but I couldn't be two places at once. To calm her, I spoke to Esmikhan as if I were already working on that problem.

"Where is she, lady? Do you know?"

"With Muhammed, her cousin. I haven't seen them since this morning. They went off to play together. Allah knows where that might be."

Allah knew indeed.

XVIII

ANYWHERE IN THE palace was possible, for the girl was only three, and if the Prince's school was not in session, under few restrictions of honor. It was proverbial how those two had been found, hand in hand, gaping at the sick in the infirmary, watching the boats from the wall, dropping pebbles on the turbans of petitioners as they passed beneath the Sublime Porte, stealing (Allah forbid they were there now) dates from the kitchen stores. This spunk was mostly the girl's doing, for it was known that by himself or even with other playmates, the Prince tended to be quiet and pouty.

Once they had even wandered into the Sultan's baths when he was sporting with his favorites. Neither of the children had ever seen a naked man before, and one erect had been a sensation. Investigations on their own persons were found wanting and their questions continued to be the scandal of the harem. My earlier attempt at an explanation of the will of Allah paled by comparison.

"That is what will happen to me when I am circumcised," I overheard the little Prince tell his cousin.

"You will grow big like that?"

Muhammed nodded soberly. "That is what it means to be a man."

And Gul Ruh was duly impressed.

But though their nurses and tutors slapped them and the less conscientious merely hid their faces and tittered, no one thought of prohibiting the children's rambles. The Sultan merely doubled his guard when he wanted to indulge.

"I'll stay here," Esmikhan said firmly now. "Now you go find Gul Ruh."

"Lady, you're too close yet. The roof of this kiosk could easily fall down on you if it should catch."

"Then here. I'll go no further without my baby."

"Lady, I still fear if this wing goes, you may get scorched."

"I can make it on my own from here. Please, please, my baby."

"Here. We've given you that expanse of lawn as a break. Allah willing, the flames will not leap to these trees across that. Unless, of course this wind keeps up. Here, then. I'll leave you with these ladies here."

"Abdullah." She caught my hand. "I'll go with you. I'll help you look."

"By Allah, there isn't time!"

I had never shouted at Esmikhan before and instantly regretted it, for she fell to helpless weeping. Had she been any other mistress on any other day, I might have gotten a beating for it. But I didn't even take time to apologize, only to tell the girls beside her that if they were not Allah's greatest fools, they would do all in their power to see that she did not try and follow me.

Tears were infectious. Either that, or things had reached the boiling point and there was overflow. Everywhere were women weeping and their discomfort was added to by the fact that many men were also in the garden, either having no place else to escape to or trying to fight the fire from this angle with water from the fish ponds.

It was a difficult task to keep veils on demurely and yet watch the fire, or watch for children and friends, at the same time. For most, the choice finally fell with keeping honor, perhaps because all who were going to get out safely must surely have done so by now.

One face I did see, and that was Safiye's fair one. She didn't even care to keep her hair covered, so any firefighter might feast on what was Prince Murad's property alone. Perhaps it made them fight harder, but their success seemed no greater.

"Lady," I heard Safiye's Ghazanfer pleading, "we cannot go back into the kitchens. The kitchen is the heart of the fire. Are we like Indian mystics that we can walk on flame?"

"But I must know if they are safe," she insisted, wringing her hands.

By Allah, I thought. The two children had gone to rifle the kitchen storerooms.

I bowed and asked for confirmation of a thought that was too terrible, almost, to think, let alone speak.

"No," Safiye replied curtly.

She had been asking after the precious dates. She had no idea where Muhammed was. She had assumed his nurse—but even as she spoke, that woman came sailing across the lawn towards us, almost unveiled so the grey grief was very plain. I think she was so distraught that she had no idea there were men present.

"Lady, lady, I've looked everywhere." Her sobs stumbled her and brought her to her knees at Safiye's feet. "I cannot find the young Prince. Oh, Allah, Allah, I shall die. Oh, Merciful One, I pray take me instead!"

Safiye did not bother to remind the woman that it was *her* baby, as she had always taken care to do before lest this nurse become as attached to him as the ill-fated first one had. Now Safiye realized that her dates would be of precious little use if there was no Prince to give them to. And her status—well, she couldn't stand idly thinking about that. Against protests, she insisted on joining Ghazanfer, myself, and the others in the search.

It was too hot now to get very close to the harem at any door. As I circled around the building, looking for a way in, the sea breeze blew that heat upon me in gusts. I saw the copper dome over the great harem throne room glowing orange as if newly forged. I wondered what the ravenous fire could find to consume in that room that was mostly mirror and tile, but I smelled burning wool and silk—an awful stench—and remembered the thick rugs, cushions, and hangings. Then the very air inside seemed to catch in little explosions. Squares of copper crumbled down like no more than bone left buried in a trash heap for many years.

The flames shot up as in a giant potter's kiln, higher than the three stories of the palace at any point. They ran along the rooftops like flood waters; the afternoon was warm for that time of year and against that natural heat, the flames appeared clear and shimmering as if they were water indeed. Above the conflagration, seven or eight minarets and lookout towers still stood, reaching heavenward like hands imploring aid.

Among the other smells of things that should not be burned billowed that of human flesh. I hurried on.

So effective was the division between *selamlik* and *haremlik* that even the fire could not breach it. The firefighters had managed to cut off the flame at the Divan and kept it there throughout the day. This men's part of the palace, then, I searched thoroughly from the Eye of the Sultan to the grooms' quarters until I was satisfied that the children were not there.

After that, I looked throughout the outer palace, trying to see everything with a child's eye so as to catch a clue as to what might have attracted them. The crowd of firefighting men around the Fountain of Execution remained the most noticeable thing: They were weary now, black with smoke, washed with sweat, and short of patience. No child could pester them long without being swatted on his way, even if he were a prince.

Above the fountain and behind were the blocks on which malefactors' heads were displayed as example. Two were there now, their faces melted by the heat and by a day or two's decay into grins that seemed to mock those who'd thought it was punishment to mete out death.

The Church of St. Irene across the great yard had been turned into an armory when the Turks had conquered. All those empty weapons and uniforms made me think myself a witness to a battlefield when all the living had gone home. Perhaps the church had looked just so on the morning after the Turks' conquest when the thousands who had crowded there hoping either heaven or the enemy would see in it some sort of asylum had been disappointed. And the Turks had left it just as they found it at the end of the battle for these hundred years.

"Gul Ruh Sultan!" I called. "Prince Muhammed!"

But my voice echoed without reply off the polished brass of a wall of shields.

I thought I would save time in the infirmary, because the sick could reply if they had seen a little girl and boy that day. But they would hardly answer, grabbing my clothes and demanding news of the fire. All their doctors and attendants, as well as any who could walk, were out carrying pots of water, and those left behind had suffered the greatest anxiety, smelling the smoke for hours.

Had the children gone beyond the Imperial Gate, then, out of the palace altogether? To Aya Sophia, perhaps, whose great domes were even now casting long shadows over the wall? They were not allowed there, but it was better to think they had the whole wide world to wander in rather than that they were still somewhere in the harem.

I had gone so far, close to running all the time. It had been several hours, through one call to prayer at least. And my heart, which fear sent racing even faster than my pace would actually have caused, begged for rest. Who knows? I rationalized. Someone else may have already found them. I should at least check with my lady to see how she fares.

I took the long way round through the Gate of the Dead ("Allah shield us," I said for protection against the restless souls, louder than usual). The shorter routes were blocked by flames. I met Ghazanfer on my way and he told me, in no more than eight words, that they'd found nothing, that his mistress had gone one more to look in the Eye of the Sultan and sent him to look in the garden again. His face, which was as tight and as hard as a mustard seed, told me he was blaming himself, as he always did when things did not go well for Safiye.

Some enterprising soul had set up the division of *haremlik* and *selamlik* there in the garden—a row of cypress and a rose hedge were the demarcation—so at least there was the relief of modesty. How they had moved my lady to this place I do not know, for she was too prostrate now even to take the water her ladies were offering her, and she had to take it on her wrists and temples with a cloth instead. One glance at her was enough to tell that she had had no news, either.

Esmikhan met my eyes with her huge brown ones and I shrank from them. I remembered the night of the lovers' nightingale in Konya, how those eyes had fixed me in that same way and demanded a miracle. And I had given it to her, given her a man's love in the only way I knew how, given her the blessed wonder of that child.

Even the cuckoo has fled this garden this afternoon. There will be no nightingale in the smoke tonight. I can work no more miracles.

I tried to pass that message to those eyes, but they would not hear it. If I offered no comfort, they would not let me near. So I left with just that glance. I must appear to still be full of hope in the search. I must.

XIX

I STUMBLED ACROSS the men's section, unseeing, unconscious of where my feet were. Someone, I became aware, was giving the call to prayer. At this point no one thought carrying one more pot of water could be more important than an appeal to the One Without Equal. All around me, men instantly dropped what they were doing and, rugless, turned to face across the ashes of the kitchen, across the Sea of Marmara. They faced that City which for most would always remain only a dream, but which, at that moment, was more real than anything else in between.

My mind was in such confusion that I remained standing, and might have stayed so, a scandal and, to some, a curse to all the proceedings. But fortunately a tug at my hem brought me to my knees in time for the first prostration.

The slow, rhythmic movements of the ritual brought a calmness to my heart I had almost forgotten. We progressed through the form— but progress is not the right word unless going around in a circle and ending up where one started is progress. But as we followed our cycle, I began to see that it was grass into which I buried my face. There were tulips blooming beside me with the dull black scent of their anthers. And overhead were trees. Trees! Plane trees with their new yellow-green foliage! And I had begun to feel as if all life had ceased. The end of the sunlight filtered through those leaves and came down upon us like a shower of gold coins. A shower of gold coins, the ancients said, brought the god to a maiden and gave her new life. These coins, too, would buy nothing in the market. Only in one's soul did they purchase the love and peace of God.

At the final prostration my ransomed soul at last looked out for others. I noticed the man beside me, the one who had tugged me down, and then I saw I knew him. It was the long-headed overseer of the kitchen supplies.

Why is he not still by the fountain in the fire line? I asked myself, but immediately received the answer: Both of his hands were swathed in rags. He must have burned them quite badly. How careful he was, even laying them on his knees as he prayed. With those hands he had tugged me down, saving me blasphemy, bringing me peace. What pain had it caused him? I was grateful.

We smiled at one another in the peace at the end of the prayer, and when that was past, I asked him politely how he'd got his hurt.

He made a brave attempt to smile, though the memory tinged it with grimace as he replied, "Those damned Arabian dates."

My heart leapt to panic pace again as I heard those words and recalled what my hopeless, before-prayer task had been. It was only with the greatest effort that I beat my heart to a calm and made myself stand and hear the end of his tale.

"After I fled the building and was already lending a hand with the water," the fellow said, "I remembered them. The storeroom was thick with smoke when I got there. The smells—I cannot tell you. It was as if a Bedouin were cooking—no art, they cannot keep from burning everything. Scorched rice, blackened joints. The jugs of very fine oil in the corner leapt to a blaze that water would only spread.

"But I found the casket and brought it out. The closest exit, towards the kitchens, was now totally engulfed in flames. Like a straw sucking up a lemon-orange colored sherbet, they came so fast I could hardly turn before the smoke was affecting me terribly. Just at the door, I tumbled to the ground. A janissary—may Allah forever favor him— saw me and pulled me feet first from the flames. But not until the casket I clutched in my hands like life itself became so hot that it took my baked-on skin with it."

I winced and murmured some blessing upon him.

He braved another grimace-smile, and continued, "But, praises to Him, it has pleased Allah to send a favorable outcome to this little history. The physicians have great hope for my hands, and the dates, though somewhat melted as if they'd been baked inside a pastry, are sound— or at least they were when I left them. Still, knowing with whom I left them—"

I interrupted here, as calmly as possible, to tell him why his story did not have a happy ending. "The young Prince will never enjoy those dates at the hand of his mother," I said, "and your brave sacrifice was in vain."

To my surprise, the man laughed. "Well, from his mother, yes . . ." Then he stopped himself because here in the open with the harem just a rose hedge away, one couldn't gossip as freely as in the closed store-room of the kitchen. "Let me tell you what I did then."

I saw he had not understood the import of my message. The heir to the Ottoman throne was dead, and with him my pretty little mistress, the joy of all our lives. But before I could say so in so many words, he continued.

"As soon as I regained some sense after my ordeal, I sat with the casket between my knees and I grew angry. All I went through—and for what? That woman—whichever one it would be in the end, the mother or the grandmother—she would give me a *ghrush* or two for my pains and take the prize to the boy to win the glory for herself. As if she had dived into the flames to get them!

" 'Fool! Fool!' I cursed myself. 'You may be a cripple for life, set out on the street with no pension to beg, and no one will ever hear of you again.'

"Then I thought, By Allah, there is so much confusion here. Surely everyone will consider it a miracle that these dates were saved and got to the Prince's hand at all. They will never stop to care by whose offices. But if I give them to the Prince myself, he will remember me as the others would not. He will remember me when, Allah willing, he is Sultan. He would never let me go begging then.

"And just then, as luck would have it, whom should I spy but the young Prince Muhammed and his lady cousin."

"You've seen them since the fire!" I cried. "Alive?"

"Oh, very much alive, Allah bless them. They'd heard the fuss and come running to see. They were really a nuisance to the firefighters as well as a danger to themselves. Here is something I can do, I thought, to help the struggle, even though my hands are now useless.

"So I went at once and salaamed before the young Prince and offered him my gift. Then, as I led them out of harm's way, I told the two of them something of how I'd saved the casket." (Knowing him, he probably drew it out with great detail.) "The little lady—oh, such a tender soul! She wept so delicately at the tale, and, though the Prince, being so superior, was at first loathe to say anything to me, she insisted that I honor them with my company."

"You have been with them?"

"The honor was mine, I assure you. If nursemaiding is always this pleasant, I wonder that it is not the most sought-after job in the Empire."

"Where were you?"

"Down at the bottom of the garden."

"At the end of the garden!" Why hadn't we thought to look there? Perhaps because it was the safest place.

"In such a pretty little bower . . ."

"How long?"

"Oh, hours and hours. I only left them when the sun began to sink and I knew I must pray soon."

"Are they at the end of the garden now?"

"Well, I don't know." The man seemed surprised at my eagerness. "I told them they should try and find their mothers. They might be worrying now that it was coming dark."

"Oh, if you only knew!"

"You know, his highness, the young Prince, let me have a bite of one of those dates. The young lady held it for me, and fed me like a little bird so I wouldn't injure my hands. I tell you, I shall not taste anything so divine 'til I, with Allah's favor, enter Paradise. And when I got up to leave, the young Prince rose on his feet, to his full height—oh, and he looked the very embodiment of his great-grandfather, Suleiman, may Allah have mercy on him.

" 'By Allah,' he said, 'and you, Gul Ruh, are my witness. I swear this day that when I, by divine favor, wear the sword of my father Othman, I shall not forget this man and the bravery he has shown this day. I swear I shall . . .' "

But by now I was laughing so hard with relief that tears were streaming down the sweat dried on my face. Convulsed with sobs and chuckles, I could do nothing but hug the fellow, then leave him standing there, muttering, that he never could understand the sexless ones.

I found my lady in the same state, laughing and crying by turns as she washed the remains of the priceless dates off her little daughter's face with the edge of her veil. She tried to scold, but she was too relieved to make much of it.

I remember Muhammed standing by, too, his sulky self again now that he was in public. He was crying, and that exaggerated the scar on his cheek, a reminder of a time when his mother in her ambition had had other things on her mind. Someone had told the Prince, in haste more than unkindness, that that was the end of it. He would have no circumcision now, for the fire had thrown everything into disarray and besides, it was an awful omen. They had forgotten to add that the ceremony would surely only be postponed a year or two. He was quite convinced this meant he should never be a man.

If he could not be a man, then he would have his nurse. At this they told him hush, no, he couldn't have his nurse but they would run and get his mother instead, who would be greatly relieved to see him alive and well. Muhammed knew, as only a child can, that he would get no comfort from his mother. But what he didn't know, and what they couldn't find words to tell him, was that his nurse would never comfort him again either. Mad with worry, she had thrown herself back into the flames to try and find her charge. Some had gone after her and dragged her back by force, but the agony of her burns would not let her live the night.

It had been a common curse under the boy's tyrant of a great-great-grandfather to say, "May you be Selim's vizier." Those officials lost favor so quickly and were so short-lived, it was said, that they never left the house without their last testaments on their persons. Some in the harem took to saying the same sort of thing with reference to Muhammed— "May you be chosen as the young Prince's next nursemaid"—for he had lost two under very bitter circumstances in the eight short years of his life.

I could hardly help but pity the boy. Nor could I blame him when the next person he threw his much-agitated affections towards was neither nurse nor tutor. The one with whom he hoped to share his own immortality of childhood was my own little mistress Gul Ruh. I instantly wished to turn his affections otherwise.

XX

WITH THE FIRE contained but by no means cold, and with what had been their home only ash and black, heat-cracked marble, the immediate problem became where to house the nearly eight hundred women of Selim's harem. The janissaries and male attendants could sleep on the ground in the garden. Indeed, they were trained for nothing if not such hardship. But to have his women sleep exposed to a naked sky was a dishonor even—or especially—a sultan could never live down.

We took over a hundred women into our home that first night. Such a perturbation! Sokolli Pasha removed himself and went to sleep in the Divan so we had use of the *selamlik* as well.

By the end of the week, however, we had no more than one of my lady's stepmothers and Safiye with their two suites. This came to less than fifty extra women, which we thought we could manage for a while. The others had moved to other places outside Constantinople, some as far away as the summer palace at Edirne.

During the summer, when there were all the gardens for this trebling of our household to disperse into, we managed quite well. The young prince and Gul Ruh, one might have thought, had indeed died in the fire and gone to Paradise, so blissful was their small existence together. We only had to watch they didn't try bathing or sleeping together, as they would have loved to do.

And Safiye was pleased to have daily access to the grille overlooking Sokolli's main guest room.

With these three happy, we were all pulled along to contentment, too.

As the cold weather descended, however, tensions which had been covered or at least tempered by sunshine and flowers erupted quite unbearably. My master grew wise and took to holding his most sensitive councils in the Divan. Denied access to the Eye of the Sultan altogether, Safiye was always irritable. I suppose we should have been glad that Nur Banu, the only one Safiye could justly accuse of malice against her—was in her private garden palace near the Edirne Gate—even further from the powers of government than she was.

Safiye herself was obliged to admit that she was at times unreasonable, like a caged animal who may strike at the hand that feeds it. Sometimes she even apologized. But that might just have been the child everyone at last knew to be growing within her. It is common wisdom that a woman is not herself when she's pregnant.

And that was how Safiye's third child, a second prince, came to be born in our harem. Cowardly, I sent one of my assistants to fetch the midwife. But the Quince, who had refused on some excuse or other to be watchful under our roof all summer, did not appear even for this. The Fig came instead, and so late there was little at all for her to do. Safiye did always get her woman's business done in a hurry—although this time Allah willed not successfully.

The little prince died without a name.

"It was the fire," some said. "It came at a very delicate time in the pregnancy—before she'd even told anyone. It did great harm to the unborn child."

But Safiye had the gracelessness to accuse my lady's rooms of cursing births. Esmikhan did not shake off this accusation very well. The memory of her own three dead little princes did not rise off our hearts for weeks. Even Gul Ruh proved a poor antidote for a while.

And I was more disturbed than I could even tell my lady by the word the Fig left me with as I helped bundle her back into her sedan. "Revenge," is what I thought she said, looking straight at me. Her thick African accent made me hope I'd heard wrong. But even more unnerving was the impression she gave me that I should be glad of this information.

Safiye recovered from the tragedy faster than anyone. A stint at the grille overlooking Sokolli Pasha's *selamlik* was tonic enough for her. She did have Muhammed and Aysha in compensation, growing quickly as children will.

Still, I think we were relieved—all but poor Muhammed and Gul

Ruh, who wept as if their little lives would end—when Safiye finally conceeded to Murad's entreaties to join him in Magnesia. At any rate, they were gone before the worst of winter set in.

WITH ESMIKHAN AND her stepmother there were no personality problems whatsoever. In fact, after all the excitement of having Safiye with us, I would at times find myself suddenly and excruciatingly bored. If one of my lady's stepmother's handmaids had not been among Selim's current favorites, I think I might have gotten into some mischief of my own, just to keep in shape.

This girl was not foremost of the favorites: Those had been given a room close at hand in what was left of the main palace. And Selim's desires were not what they once were: The burning palace had put some fear of Hell in him and he had taken to calling for the Mufti for long religious discussions almost as often as he called for debauch.

But every once in a while he would send a messenger to us for the girl. She had no attributes to speak of save this alone: She was the best of the booty Cyprus had to offer after the fourteen months of starvation and disease that were the siege. He sent for her on days when he wanted to drink the wine so much blood had been spilled for, and to glory in the one great success of his reign—the conquest of her island.

For my own diversion, whenever the girl was called for, I would see to it that I was free to accompany her. Some may see no great excitement in a long evening reading poetry or playing chess with a colleague while I waited for Selim to grow sated. It is true I would have whiled away the time in much the same way at home. But at least here the rooms were not quite so familiar. There were new faces in the company who might have new tales to tell, and I could stop by and observe how the rebuilding of the palace was coming along. Progress here was but very slow, for Selim's heart wasn't in the task. Nonetheless, this provided other news to bring home to my mistress. The new foundations ran along the same outlines as the buildings that had burned, so she imagined it easily.

I did keep thinking I might some day pick up some news there so close to the Sultan that would prove of more importance. But Selim had long ago forgotten there was a world outside that would shake if he but spoke. My own master Sokolli Pasha was in full control of the vast empire in all but name. Selim had retreated more and more into his own pleasure—or, as relief from that, into his own morbid guilt, equally indulgent because it was likewise of no practical application.

I was disappointed in everything I learned—until one late afternoon just shortly before Muslims were due to begin the month of fasting in their nine hundred and eighty-second year. Christians were in the midst of Advent in the last months of 1574.

I remember I was alone in the eunuchs' sitting room, reading a collection of pious tales. Lack of activity more than anything else had sent me to seek such reading. I was on the story of how Moses asked Allah where in the universe He was. And the ancient prophet received the reply, "Know that when you seek for Me you have already found Me."

I had looked up for a moment from the manuscript to contemplate that divine answer, but was denied inspiration of my own by the appearance of the Cypriot girl. Every retelling of that old tale brings the events that followed so vividly to mind that I sometimes fear I shall never be able to seek Allah properly because of this stumbling block.

It was evident at once that the girl had not finished her stay. She was not dressed to go, but had only a bath towel to hide her nakedness in; because of her agitation, it wasn't serving very well.

He's been more perverse to her than usual, was my first thought. But things will only go worse for her if she seeks to escape him. There is no escape for a slave of the Sultan. Allah help me. How shall I convince her?

But then I noticed a high glow in her cheeks, rather more of excitement than of fear or disgust. It made her actually radiant, and if I had thought before that being a Cypriot was her only claim to favor, I now decided there was some other beauty present.

"Abdullah, please come." She did not squeak it in a passion or shout it in fear, but whispered it, as conspiracy.

I was confused. "Into the presence of the Sultan?"

"Please, just come."

So I marked my book with a scrap of silk and followed the naked kneading of her buttocks.

They had been in the bath. It was Selim's fancy to lay the girl out in the pool like an island reposing in the Mediterranean, and to move upon her like the Turkish flotilla out of Latakia. She would be obliged to feed him—peeled grapes and draughts of her people's wine like their blood—as the island had fed the invaders, with nothing reserved for itself. He would move over her curves as the Turkish cannon had rumbled over the terraced hillsides until he besieged the prize—Famagusta on its harbor—where victory was won with the utmost violence and revenge . . .

I went in prepared to make my deepest salaam, and to keep my eyes averted as was proper in the Sultan's presence. But the room seemed to be deserted.

The Cypriot led me down three tiled steps to the cooling room in the center of whose octagonal piers an octagonal fountain bubbled. At the bottom of the steps of the far pier lay a body.

It was hard to believe that the Sultan of all Islam could be found in such indignity. A slave, perhaps, or a beggar at the end. He was spread-eagle, stark naked, and where it was not pale and flabby as a fatted, plucked hen, too much liquor blotched his flesh the color of dried liver.

"Is he dead?" the girl whispered.

I forced myself to overcome not awe but revulsion and to bend and find out. When I put my hand at the back of his head, it felt mushy and came back bloody. But the movement made him open his eyes and catch the girl's face. She drew back, startled and afraid.

A tongue thick with wine moved in the Sultan's mouth and I bent to hear what it said, "Cyprus . . . shall . . ."

"Cyprus shall what, majesty?" I asked, but never heard. A pulse continued, very faintly, but there was no consciousness to accompany it.

"He slipped," the girl explained. She had given up the towel as a cover altogether now and was wringing it anxiously in both hands.

I stood up and looked at her. Yes, that seemed reasonable. Stumbling drunk, he'd been pursuing her around the fountain. The floor was wet. He slipped, fell, and cracked his skull.

There was, of course, another possibility. Even as I stood there, I thought I heard a voice echoing from the dark recesses of the bath where, the superstitious say, are the haunts of jinn. It seemed to be the voice of the Sultan saying, "Come, my splendid Cyprus. Give me a hand."

And she gave him a hand: to his tipsy feet a firm, well-placed shove.

I looked in her eyes and saw that vision was a very definite possibility. Those sad brown eyes had seen her whole family and all her friends starved or butchered, the indignity of the slave block, the continued embraces of the rotting man whose fault her entire sorrow was. Unlike other favorites, she never thought the getting of a son might improve her lot. A hardness in her features hid other ambitions. That was why she could never be very pretty and why, perhaps, Selim still called for her when he wanted to tempt his vulnerability.

"You may pray," I told her quietly, "he doesn't live to speak again."

Then I looked away from that hardness, for even I could not stand in its presence.

I found a towel to cover the man's nakedness so that the next to find him should not be exposed to the same shock I'd suffered to learn just what frailty we'd all been subject to for eight years. Then I told her she had better learn to weep for her master quickly before I returned with help to carry him to a bed.

What was done was done, I thought. Even boiling the girl in oil for treachery would not improve matters, only give ideas to others who might not have considered it on their own. To this day she and I alone know that what was everywhere pronounced an accident, "Allah's will," was really the revenge of Cyprus from a cask of its best wine and the hand of a hard-faced slave girl.

XXI

IT TOOK THREE full days for the ghost to pass from him, but even before we got the dying Sultan to his bed, the messenger was on his mad dash to Magnesia with the word for Murad: "If you would inherit your father's throne, come at once before the news gets out and other claimants have a chance to mass."

Again I had to wonder at the cool way in which my master, the Grand Vizier, carried off the change of power. Of course, had he done otherwise, he might well have been out of a job—nay, out of his life. But cucumber flesh could not have been slower to color and betray itself. Me he trusted, the girl he ignored, and only the two I'd called to help me when the Sultan fell had their tongues removed as a precaution. Otherwise, even Esmikhan was not told, Nur Banu did not guess, and the other viziers and officers of the Divan did not have an inkling until Murad himself arrived at Moudania.

Sokolli had the imperial galley on alert, ready to ferry the new emperor across when he should come. But Murad was not expected for another day, and had not been told of these arrangements, so he hired his own passage on a little fishing boat. Thus he arrived on the deserted shore of the Topkapi peninsula.

Now, Murad had been camping out on the fourth day of a hunt when he was alerted. He did not bother to change clothes before riding and sailing like a madman for ten days. For speed he had limited his suite to no more than four trusted companions. Ghazanfer was among them—Safiye's eyes and ears, her fist of power—and there was also Uweis, an illiterate and rather wild Turkoman of original stock whom Murad favored because he knew the mountains and steppes and could hunt them like a fox. It would take more than just a change of robe to give that man a dignified appearance.

So this road-worn party had come to knock on the empty seaside gate to the palace wall after midnight. My master had warned the gatekeepers to be on their guard and, on their lives, to admit no one without his express orders. These men took one look and then did not need to look or think more before following those orders—and shutting the little peep window again and firmly.

A winter storm was blowing in off the Black Sea. The winds were high and the waves left precious little shore—and that very exposed—for five men to stand on before the rise of the great walls. Perhaps Murad had seen through the peep window, past wind-whipped cypresses, to the blackened carcass of a palace he was to inherit; he had heard of the fire, of course, but not yet weighed the reality of it. Tired, hungry, cold, shut out from his own palace—a ruin—and now it was beginning to rain. The new Sultan must have been very discouraged indeed. Even stray cats had deserted that exposed spot that night.

Murad sent one of his men running at once to warn my master of the situation. But it took more than an hour for the man to make it around the point, over the great rocks slick with rain with the waves crashing on them, to the city gates where he could gain access.

Eventually my master Sokolli Pasha, with a few men (I was among them) and torches, opened the gate and let the wayfarers in. Yet we did not at once fall upon our faces and welcome our new sovereign. No, Sokolli Pasha had warned us as we hurried to the gate. One of Selim's five younger sons might have somehow gotten word and was now set on usurpation. It had been at least two years since any of us had seen the heir. Murad's next youngest brother, in spite of their different mothers, was very like him in features, and the journey had made this man both thinner and darker. We raised our torches against the wind and peered intently.

"Only if you would stake your life that he is Murad," we were warned. None of us could go so far.

Sokolli Pasha coughed apologetically (for the man might very well be our next master) and said one more test would have to be passed. Although he had just traveled ten days almost without pause, fresh horses were brought and we rode to the palace on the outskirts of town which had been Nur Banu's residence since the fire.

Many have called my master "Sultan Maker" as if there were some sort of blame to that. But let it be known that never was the harem more powerful than on that night. Nur Banu came from her chamber, still in crumpled clothes and bleary-eyed from sleep. She stood, stared, then threw open her arms with joy. "My lion," she cried, the term of endearment all mothers of princes give their firstborn sons. With those words and those words alone, she made an emperor.

I suppose had I had a plot up my sleeve, I could have wielded my own power that night. As neither my master nor any of the other officials went into the room where Nur Banu was, nor would have known her from any other woman if they had, it all rested on the testimony of my two colleagues—Nur Banu's Kislar Agha and Ghazanfer—and myself.

But the thought never occurred to me to counter the will of Allah in this matter. I gave the sign to my master as we reentered and we instantly all fell flat on the floor, declaring Murad to be our new master, the power of our lives and the Shadow of Allah.

A weary but happy smile crept over the face that wore the paprika beard. "By Allah, I'm famished," he declared. "Have them bring us some food."

As we got to our feet to fulfill this order, even the least suspicious among us could not help but exchange guarded glances. That his first words as Sultan should be these! That was an ill omen in anybody's eyes.

XXII

MY LADY TOOK these events—the death of her father and the succession of her half-brother—quite well. Considering that Murad's success meant the death of all five of his brothers including Esmikhan's own full-blood brother, Jehanghir, she took it amazingly well. She never held it against Murad; it was ancient Turkish law.

Murad had, in fact, wished to show mercy. But the Mufti soon convinced him that individual mercy was never so great as mercy shown to the people at large. The new Sultan's vast subject populace would ever praise him that he had spared them any opportunity for civil war. So five little turbaned sarcophagi joined their father's great one in the high-ceilinged and heavily tiled mausoleum on the grounds of Aya Sophia. There they rest as unashamedly as if the plague had merely touched them with the hand of Allah.

My lady's stepmother's sorrow was not so tempered by faith, and this grieved Esmikhan more than the actual murder. But her stepmother was soon moved along with the little Cypriot and any other woman or boy who had ever known the late Sultan to permanent retirement at Edirne.

Esmikhan wept at the separation as if at her stepmother's death—she knew she would never be able to make such a long journey as that to visit—but in a few weeks distance made all those griefs bearable.

Selim's death caused Safiye griefs, too. Though they were less permanent, they were no less hard to bear—at least for the fiery daughter of Baffo.

She, along with her son, daughter, and the rest of her suite, arrived in Constantinople after a more leisurely journey from Magnesia—though one not without discomfort as it was midwinter. Safiye then discovered that she, no less than Murad, should have made the trip in ten days if she wanted to be certain her position was consolidated. The way it was, Nur Banu had had two or three full weeks in which to immure herself in her son's affections, and when Safiye did arrive, Nur Banu was well prepared.

Nur Banu had arranged an elaborate ceremony whereby every member of the harem—from treasurer to wardrobe mistress, from keeper of the jewels to Mother of the Heir Apparent—would pass in review before her and, by placing her hand under the Queen Mother's foot, swear her unquestioning obedience to her will. It was along the lines of the more public ceremony a new sultan always held whereby the head of the janissaries (primed by a lavish gift), the head of the enclosed school of pages, of the corps of eunuchs, the poison tasters—all vowed to fulfill the master's least desire as they loved their lives and Allah.

This ceremony with her enemy's crimson satin slipper was almost more than Safiye could endure, but she had little choice in the matter. Murad approved his mother's move and was seated, nodding with agreement, at her side throughout. Safiye dared not even balk. But she comforted herself that oaths by Allah did not mean quite so much to her as they did to people who had been born to that Faith.

And Safiye found herself desperate to please the Sultan at every turn. Now that he was Sultan, she wanted to be at Murad's side every moment, for every decision and firman. But Constantinople and the Empire at his fingertips gave Murad other diversions he had not had in the provincial *sandjak*.

The rapid rebuilding of the palace to his own extravagant specifications was, for example, a high priority. Murad had gained a taste for building with his mosque in Magnesia. Now he even ordered the construction of an observatory in the grounds under the direction of the great Egyptian astronomer Takeiddin.

This scholar's observations had led him to theories not unlike those of Copernicus, that Pole who has caused such a flurry in Christendom by saying that the sun, not the earth, is the center of the universe. The same Arabic scholars laid the foundation for both of their work. Takeiddin found no more favor for his notions among the Muslim clergy than Copernicus among the Christian.

Perhaps this is just as well. Not that I do not believe these men; their arguments are convincing as far as my knowledge of physics and mathematics will carry me. I just do not think, for the sake of the common man—that man walking behind his oxen on a clear, still day with no time for science—that God should be allowed to be any further above us than a voice will carry.

Be that as it may, in the end, at the Mufti's insistence, the edifice was turned from an observatory into just another kiosk in the gardens. Instead of allowing the stars to become our guideposts to higher Being and His knowledge, they now serve as they have always done: to mark the leagues of love in nights full of more earthly pursuits.

Now as Sultan, Murad was able to indulge in his fondness for poets, musicians, and dancers as well. He brought artists from as far away as India, no expense barred. A pair of Italian painters were popular for a while, their naturalistic lines finding favor more because they were exotic and magical—like a conjuror who can pull a real orange from midair—than that anyone thought to emulate them. True art, as anyone knows, does not need to copy life exactly, but rather give a light and airy, delicate representation of it so we may see through familiar forms to higher things.

One day, instead of waiting to be called for, an impatient Safiye sent to interrupt her lover's business with herself. I was present when the reply came.

"My master begs to decline," Ghazanfer said, his green eyes downcast. "He has just received inspiration for a new poem he would write to share with his friends at their next banquet. He said you would understand."

A look of absolute panic crossed Safiye's face before she could check it. She realized she was no longer so young. She had born three children, one dead, one of them a girl. She was twenty-five, an age at which slave girls were customarily retired from waiting on the Sultan, it being assumed that after that age, there was no hope of them catching his eye. They were given to faithful *spahis* or janissaries to honest wifehood, or they became seamstresses and laundresses to those women who still had hope.

Safiye had taken good care of herself. She had neither borne too many children nor sat too long on cushions to lose her figure. Her hair still had the wonderful luster that had first drawn the Prince to her, but anyone who saw the great baskets of lemons that followed her to the bath each day knew it was no longer so easily come by.

Her influence might last only months, weeks. Maybe one could count it in the stanzas of Murad's latest poem. Every moment the Sultan spent at some other pursuit was time lost for her. Safiye knew it. And she was scared. Scared as neither pirates nor storms at sea nor roaring flames in the harem had been able to frighten her before.

And so Baffo's daughter determined to do something neither books nor paintings nor even the stars could compete with her in. By the summer of that year, after two or three dearly bought private interviews with the master, she had accomplished her design.

It was at a party given by Nur Banu in the gardens of the summer palace for the purpose of admiring the lilies in bloom. Aunt Mihrimah was the one who spoke first as Safiye came forward to greet her with a kiss.

"Safiye, my dear, are you——?"

Safiye, who had been wearing heavier garments than the heat would allow and unbuttoning her waist higher than she really needed to yet, was elated that it had been recognized at last. "Yes, madam, it's true. Gul Ruh will soon have another little cousin to play with."

The party was immediately alive with exclamations, congratulations and questions: when was she due? what did she hope it would be? (another son of course), and how did she feel? Those who were barren came to her to crave a talisman that Allah might likewise favor them.

While all of this was going on, I stole a look at Nur Banu to see how she was taking this disruption of the order of her party and the usurpation of her status as hostess and center of attention. To my surprise, I saw neither anger nor frustration in her eyes. Her demeanor seemed as sweet as the heavy scent of the lilies that hung like a liqueur over the garden. Her look seemed, like some of the gaudier hybrids, to have a cultivated, almost artificial air.

I could not suppress the thought, nor yet would I find explanation for it: It is as if she knew all along. Almost as if she planned it this way. Nur Banu, I thought, might well have learned of Safiye's condition from spies or bathhouse attendants, but that it could in any way serve her purposes I could not imagine. Yet, I thought, it almost seems as if she sees that Safiye has fallen into her trap.

Nur Banu bided her time. She sat on a rug with her hands quietly folded in her lap until the furor raised by her rival's announcement had settled like dust in a stifle. Nur Banu was content to wait until, of her own accord, every woman fell silent, took a seat, and looked up at her hostess expectantly. When even Safiye could not resist the raising of the bow of her brow in wonder, Nur Banu at last began.

"Oh!" exclaimed the Valide Sultan as if suddenly coming to herself under this general scrutiny. "What sort of hostess must you think me? That you have all been here so long and I have yet to offer you refreshment."

She clapped her hands sharply and immediately a slave girl stepped through the doorway of the kiosk, bearing a ewer of rose water, an empty bowl, and a napkin. With downcast eyes and perfect manners, the girl moved among the guests from the most honored down to the least to allow each to wash her hands and face of the dust of the road. There was utter silence as she did so, but not because of her actions. It was a courtesy expected even in poor homes where only a pitcher of well water might substitute for that of roses and a younger daughter, perhaps, for the slave.

But "Not since she first presented Safiye," one who had been in attendance on both occasions recalled afterwards, "Never since Safiye has Nur Banu—or anyone else for that matter—produced a girl of such exquisite beauty."

She was like some tiny white porcelain vase in which one sets a single violet upon a shelf and it beautifies the entire room. Beneath the lucid skin, her bones seemed like a bird's, supple and breathtakingly fragile. Although it hurt one's stomach—the fear that even breath might break her—yet one could not hold back the desire to immediately scoop her up in one's arms, protect her, fondle her, prove to every sense that she was not just air.

Her blackbird eyes showed intelligence beneath the thick and perfect curve of lashes, so there was more than just a shell. Her hair, which Nur Banu had dressed for her under a small purple cap and gossamer veil, fell to the knee, thick, black, and curly, of such mass that it seemed greater than the rest of her body put against it. And her breasts, which on any other frame would have seemed of average size and beauty, on hers were voluptuous, two soft mounds of honey-almond paste.

No two women could be more unalike than Safiye and this girl, the former tall and fair, the latter tiny and dark. But each was the perfection of her type. Probably only once in so many years does the Almighty allow such beauty upon the earth, or we should all destroy ourselves for its sake, like offerings upon a heathen altar.

At last the party could contain itself no longer and began to ask all at once: "Where did she come from? How did you find her? She must have cost a fortune. What do you plan for her?"

Nur Banu smiled and replied, "She's Hungarian. I can't tell you how we scoured the markets for her . . ." until the questions and answers were all a jumble and could not be matched. Then it was better to let Nur Banu have the floor and say what she would say.

"I can only hope," she said quietly with a heady, lily-scented smile, "that my son is as full of questions as you, my friends, when he sees her. He is prone to addictions, and the only way, it seems, to rid him of one is to give him another. And for that next one, yet another . . ."

"You mother of the jinn!" Safiye hissed under her breath. "You wouldn't."

Others bade her be still and not insult their hostess so. Had they not all vowed before Allah and under a satin slipper to obey her? But Nur Banu continued in calm confidence and raised her hand as a sign of peace. I have known the ambassadors of such peace to wear daggers up their sleeves in the Divan.

"Forgive me, mother of my grandson, if I offend." The Queen Mother smiled gently. "You are with child and cannot wish to entertain Murad now. Truly, I thought only to give you a rest after these thirteen years. Even Suleiman was never so constant to Khurrem Sultan, and her power never seemed to lack because of it."

Safiye was on her feet now, calling her ladies and eunuchs to her. She would leave at once and endure such treatment no longer.

When she had gone there was an awkward pause in which the little slave girl stood dumb and helpless in the center of the room, very near to tears. She thought she had failed in this, her first test.

"Nay, come here, child," Nur Banu called to her when she saw her dilemma.

The girl went at once, like a mouse scurrying to the safety of its hole, and sat submissive at her mistress's knee.

Nur Banu reached out, lifted up the heavy hair, and laid the back of her hand against the girl's white marble cheek. "Supplant one addiction with another," Nur Banu murmured.

The girl looked up with bewilderment and tears in her black eyes. "Excuse me, lady?" she asked, and I knew she could hardly put two words of Turkish together as yet.

Nur Banu smiled into those eyes. "You'll do perfectly, my dear. Just perfectly." And she planted a tender kiss on that alabaster brow.

Even so, I don't think the girl quite knew what all the business meant. All she did understand was that the hands that fed and clothed her, that had come now to be like those of her lost mother, they were pleased with her. That was enough. She leaned up against her mistress's knees and purred in gratitude.

XXIII

ESMIKHAN AND I saw no reason—indeed, it would have been rude of us—to leave Nur Banu's party with Safiye. Then, as the afternoon progressed and the lilies lost their scent with too much smelling, we noticed several curious activities. First, one of Sofia's eunuchs (not Ghazanfer, a new *khadim*) came and murmured something to one of Nur Banu's, who passed the word on to his lady.

Nur Banu smiled, stroked her pet girl's hair, then called the Fig to her. The Quince was not present—I could never escape the thought that this was because my lady had come. But the Fig pursed her lips as if at something sour and then turned a little of her mentor's green. Nur Banu gave the apprentice a whiplash look. The Fig bowed and left with Safiye's eunuch.

They seemed totally disconnected events at the time, and nothing for us to worry about. But when, at our own leisure, we finally did return home, we found Safiye there—and in labor, in imminent danger of miscarriage.

"You've brought this on yourself, haven't you?" The Fig, laying out her simples on a low table, hardly offered sympathy.

And Safiye was hardly subdued. "I? It's that demon's dam of a mistress you've got. She's the cause."

"No. I know. A little powdered fern, a little iris root—it's the oldest trick in the book. Girls have been ridding themselves of the fruit of illegal love with that since time began. By Allah, I wouldn't be surprised if Mother Eve herself brought those plants with her from Eden, they're so useful, so divine."

"You think I want to lose my baby?"

"Of course. How else will you ever compete with Nur Banu's little Hungarian?"

"By Allah, two live princes are worth much more than one not even lusted for yet."

"Very well. Let me have a look at you and see what we can do."

"Don't you dare touch me."

"Do you want to save this baby or not?"

"Not by your hands."

"What's this?"

Safiye shot the Fig a withering glance. The midwife got the message, whatever it was, and looked sidelong at Esmikhan, fearing she might have understood, too. She was more cautious with her next words.

"You've always trusted me before."

"You're in her employ." I wasn't sure who that "her" was. "She'd like nothing better than that I lose it—and maybe other things while we're at it."

"Didn't the Quince give you a fine, strong son? Without even a stretch mark, by Allah."

"That was then. Now—"

"Why did you send for me, then? The lilies were so nice—"

"I didn't send for you. It's that new eunuch. He got in a panic and didn't do as I told him. I'll see he's punished. Ghazanfer wouldn't have made such a mistake."

"So where is Ghazanfer?"

"Away. On other business," Safiye answered laconically. "Ghazanfer wouldn't—"

She interrupted herself to press her eyes together and pant heavily for a moment or two—the first such interruption we'd seen since we'd entered the room. I found myself disbelieving that distress. Even at six months, Safiye was as tight as with her first. Quince or no, I said to myself, she's not going to lose it.

Esmikhan was much more trusting. "Please, Safiye, dear," she said, sitting at her friend's side and taking her hand. "Let the midwife look at you at least."

"Esmikhan, if you're a decent hostess, you will take that pagan woman out of this room this instant."

"Safiye, please—" Esmikhan knew what it was like to lose a child.

"Esmikhan—" Safiye was vicious.

"Perhaps, madam," Esmikhan said quietly to the midwife, "if you'd be so good. Just for a moment. While I talk to her and try to make her see—"

"And you don't need to be polite to her, either," Safiye snapped. "What has she ever done for you?"

"Safiye, how can you say such a thing? After all—"

"You can't even walk any more, thanks to the Quince."

"Safiye, I was almost dead. At least I am still alive. And I have my precious Gul Ruh, thanks to Allah and the Quince."

"Yes? Well, what about the others?"

"Please, Safiye. Don't speak of what is Allah's will."

"Allah's will? Was it Allah's will?"

"Yes, of course." Esmikhan was truly shocked—and the most horrible thought Safiye's words could conjure hadn't even crossed her mind. It was merely the suggestion that something could happen in this world that was not Allah's will which appalled her.

"Hhm." Safiye sniffed skeptically, but then turned her concentration to her distress once more.

"It's all right, Esmikhan Sultan," the Fig said with a sniff of her own and began repacking her supplies. "You don't need to ask. I'm ready and willing to go."

Still Esmikhan was so distressed that such unpleasantness had happened under her roof that she made the supreme effort and personally saw the midwife out of the room with only one of my assistants to take her arm.

I watched them go, then I turned back to Safiye. My mind was unsettled by things that had been said and I wanted to know—

Safiye was on her feet. I grabbed her eyes with mine as one grabs a naughty child to give it a firm scolding—not for standing, but for putting on what was obviously an act. It could be to no good purpose.

She was prepared for my glare, however. She met it not with firmness, but with an all-consuming softness like some animal gone limp and playing dead as the hunter approaches. I dropped my eyes at once in self-defense, but it was too late.

Sweet Jesus, but she is beautiful! I thought. The reversion to Venetian language and faith were but emblems of the surge of youthful passion I felt. I managed to offer this prayer before rationality left me altogether: Lord, don't let her ask me anything. I won't be able to refuse her if she asks me . . .

I saw her eyes roll into a fog of unconsciousness like almonds rolling into a vat of honey. Whatever there was of a man left in me rose, then stumbled, awkward on unused feet. My arms took her weight in them as she fell. The satin of her robe was slick with body heat and with straining to meet across her growing belly. I could feel the coursing of her blood beneath it.

I let that golden head sink back into the pillows on the divan and my hand reached for a taste of that pomegranate cheek.

"Ghazanfer," Safiye murmured.

My hand fell back, confused and hurt that it was not my name her lips formed.

"Where's Ghazanfer?"

"I'll see if I can find him, lady," I said coldly, finding I was indeed able to rise to my feet.

With surprising speed and strength for any woman, but especially for one about to miscarry, she sat upright and caught my hand. "Veniero," she hissed at me. "There is a doctor in the *selamlik*. A Venetian. A guest of Sokolli Pasha. Bring him to me."

The lapse into Italian and her laconic style made me believe she was on the very edge of delirium. But her brown eyes caught mine totally washed of their honey sweetness, sharp as arrow points.

I appeased her with a baby word my nurse used to use, full of endearment, yet promising nothing.

I left the room and stood a moment or two in the next, trying to shake her influence from me as a dog shakes water. In the end I still could not sort out what she wanted me to do from what I really ought to do and so I sent my fastest assistant to find Ghazanfer. I saw Esmikhan, her ladies, and the rest of my seconds in to sit with Safiye and—maybe—to keep her from rashness or dishonor in the meantime. Then I myself went down to the *selamlik* to see about this doctor.

Many of Murad's scholars and poets had, like Safiye, taken to sulking on Sokolli Pasha's hospitality when they were out of favor. Six men were in the midst of a lively discussion when I entered the room. Their language was Persian, for the physician, though he had traveled widely in lands further east, learning the lore of his profession, had but passed through Turkey before, an omission he was swearing to remedy.

My master, among his six or seven other languages, had a smattering of Venetian on which he would sometimes fall back for politeness, but which he was too unsure of to use readily. He found it more useful to pretend ignorance and overhear.

Three of the other men—the Egyptian astronomer and two of the best-loved poets alive—knew not a word. It can be unnerving to learn that the tongue you grew up thinking all the world spoke has not been worth the while of such great minds to learn. Only the sixth man present, the sea captain and dragoman, once Andrea Barbarigo, now called simply Muslim, would have been more comfortable in Italian. But this meeting was not to honor him, so he could be content to sit quietly to one side and try to pick up a phrase here and there of the Persian.

Barbarigo looked at me as he always did, with eyes one could not help but pity. He had tried, I knew, many times to reestablish contact with Safiye now that, as a renegade, he had made a name for himself in the Turkish navy. But now that he was all Turk, she no longer had any use for him. He was all Turk, he had to have the morals of one. I could not take any more time to feel sorry for him then.

My personal interest in poetry and the mystics had increased my knowledge of Persian so I had no difficulty in catching the drift of the conversation—the medical works of Galen as they are translated and commented upon by the Arabs—nor in finding a pause when I could present my problem to my master.

"Abdullah," he said, falling into Turkish and touching my arm as if he feared I had the fever. "Abdullah, whatever can you be thinking? A woman of the Sultan? To expose her to the scrutiny of a man, and a stranger at that?"

Barbarigo overheard and raised an eyebrow as he must any time the word *woman* was pronounced in his hearing, however rarely that must be. I shifted so my back was more fully to him and tried to speak lower. I pleaded that she was a Venetian and more used to male doctors than a Turkish lady would be.

But my master replied, "She will not have the usual midwife? Then send for another and wait for her to come." He continued then with something I had not considered. "If we set this precedent, all of our women with skill in medicine will soon be overshadowed by the men who have more interest in high fees than in health. The women will have no place to practice and never receive the honor due to them. My guest has just been telling me how in Venice many women of the higher families have men, men not even of their kin, attend them in labor. It has become the fashion. What, may I ask, have men to do with the things of birth? Muslims cannot dishonor their women so."

I made one final, desperate attempt. I pleaded that the Sultan would blame his Grand Vizier more if, because of his negligence, either Safiye or the child were lost than he would if he allowed the best and most immediate medical treatment, even if it happened to be male.

Now my master touched my arm again to calm me and said, "Very well. Until the midwife comes." He added that he would be interested to see this man's art in practice. "But you must arrange it so that when this veiled one is treated, not even her face may be seen."

We moved quickly and there was really not so much to be done. Gul Ruh had female tutors for all of her subjects from recitation of the Koran—at which she did very well, having now almost a third of the scripture committed to memory—to needlework. But for Persian, Sokolli Pasha was unsatisfied with anyone but this great poet with whom he even now conversed. Gul Ruh was as yet a child but it was still a delicate situation as many of the texts they were to study would of necessity be love poems. By devising a large screen to stand between student and teacher and having a eunuch present at all times we managed to keep the tongues from wagging.

We set this screen up for Safiye and the doctor in the *mabein,* the room a neutral zone between the *haremlik* and *selamlik.* Our *mabein* had more the air of a schoolroom, smelling of ink and book bindings, for the master hardly visited my lady any more, even in duty.

The little window through which Gul Ruh could pass her written exercises for examination now served to pass Safiye's wrist. I do not know how much the man could learn from that pulse alone. It was hardly the natural pulse it might have been had a woman taken it. Safiye's breath must have come with more difficulty through the veils in which we'd robed her in lest the screen fail. Then, too, the touch of a man's hand was not something to leave her unaffected. My master's anxieties were plain now: How could a mixed doctor-patient relationship ever produce the objective diagnosis necessary for proper treatment?

Whatever the man found in that wrist, it was both interesting and informative. The two remained huddled on either side of that screen for a very long time.

"What did they say?" I asked the assistant I'd put to oversee the meeting.

"I don't know," he replied. "It was in no language I can understand."

I cursed myself soundly. Of course! They would speak in Italian, and I was the only one who could understand that. Why had I thought my first responsibility was to Esmikhan, who was taking the whole business very hard? Because, I realized, Safiye had suggested it with a weak roll of those wonderful eyes.

I spent a long time afterwards going over the physician's features in my mind. He was an old, withered man interested in little beyond his art. Even his next meal was of little concern when there was scientific study or doctoring to be done. He had a small, pointed white beard and the grey eyes of a grandfather. Although Safiye could not have seen these things except from a distance through the harem grille, surely his hands would show her that in the rest of the man there could be of little interest for a lover. These were hands thin and bulging with veins and knuckles until they seemed more mechanical than flesh and blood, hands that had handled drugs and diseased limbs from Spain to Cathay.

Others might have been reassured by such thoughts, thinking romance was the worst confidence those two could have exchanged. But something Esmikhan said made me guess otherwise and gave me more ill ease.

"Is the doctor still seeing her?" Esmikhan demanded of me when I came to comfort her. "Is he seeing her?"

"Yes, lady," I replied, giving her my hand. "Allah willing, she may be made well now."

"Allah willing, it may be so. But I would not trust my body and my unborn child to that Christian."

"Do not fear, lady. Medicine, the knowledge of Allah, may cure whether the practitioner be Muslim or not."

"Still, I cannot think what Safiye can be imagining. She must be delirious, poor child."

"The doctor may help delirium," I said, though "poor child" had never been an epithet I'd give to Safiye, even when she was much younger.

"But after the things we overheard him say to my husband and the other gentlemen yesterday . . ."

"What did he say?"

"Why, he said—actually bragged—that many of the great authorities had known much of the ways of the child in the womb, but that he had learned more than any of them. In some distant land he had learned to give abortions without danger to the mother. He can make it look like a miscarriage. And he can bring on a case of child-bed fever look-ing as natural as the real thing. He also knows, he said, more of poisons than anyone who has ever lived, both antidote and administration. Surely that is black magic and ought to be avoided, don't you think?"

I left Esmikhan as soon as I could after this without causing her alarm and ran to the *mabein*. But by then another midwife had arrived and my assistants were diligently ushering the doctor out as they had been or-dered.

XXIV

WHEN SAFIYE THREW off her veil to let the old woman examine her—the old woman clucking against any witchcraft the unbeliever might have applied—I had never seen Baffo's daughter look healthier.

And Ghazanfer had arrived. Where he'd been all this while was a mystery, even to Safiye it seemed. I remembered how fearfully she'd asked after him in the midst of the crisis. Now, as I entered, the great eunuch's back was to me as he paced at the foot of his lady's makeshift bed on the divan with unaccustomed agitation. Perhaps our recent en-forced closeness had also helped to make him more transparent. In any case, this was the first time I realized that the *khadim*, usually so cautious of what his face revealed, could sometimes be gauged in his unguarded back.

There I now read, Why have you done this to yourself, lady? To yourself and your unborn child? It is my job to protect you and I do so—with my life. But how can I protect you if it's your own hand you turn against yourself?

I also saw a slouch in the wide space between his shoulders, a slouch that spoke of a case of the sulks approaching childishness.

What I heard aloud, in the eunuch's rising *voce di testa,* was this:

"Against Selim, yes. I hated Selim. You know I had cause and he was the ruination of the land. But Murad—Allah keep him—is not his father and I can't continue to serve you against him and against innocents, to bring chaos to the lands of Islam!"

Safiye saw me in the doorway. Her eyes shifted and Ghazanfer caught the message. He managed to suppress the storm inside to his usual glassy calm exterior. With the intake of a single breath, even his back fell silent.

"How fares the cradle of princes?" I covered the intermittent awkwardness with my most formal language.

"She and the child are out of danger," the midwife declared with self-satisfaction.

"Allah be praised."

Safiye smiled an addictive smile at me, which I resisted. Then she allowed her attention to be consumed with midwifery.

Ghazanfer took another breath and took the burden of my presence from his lady. "I am conscious, *khadim*," he said, "of the disruption all of this causes the peace of your harem."

"Do not mention what is Allah's will," I replied with equal stiffness.

A glimmer moved through Ghazanfer's eyes, as if to say, It's never Allah's will in reference to her.

Before I could raise my own brows in surprise, he spoke aloud in a different vein. "I fear we must impose upon your hospitality yet further."

"The guest is a gift from Allah."

"His Highness the Sultan, hearing of the danger that has threatened his peace and majesty in this room, is very desirous to see the well-guarded one with his own eyes."

"His Highness's wish is my command."

"But as it is not thought wise to move the object of his concern in her present state—"

"We will not hear of it."

"His majesty will come here."

"We will be honored."

"Now. This very afternoon."

What could I say? "We will be honored."

"I know it's a great inconvenience." Ghazanfer dropped his formal tone in an approximation of apology. "But what else can we do?"

For one moment I thought, Nur Banu must be beside herself with fury. Surely her new girl was condemned to failure from the start, if Safiye the Fair One remained so vital in Murad's heart. For the only other being a sultan had ever gone to see—and did not send for to await his own pleasure—was Allah Himself in His mosque at Friday prayers.

What else could we do? the great eunuch had asked. I couldn't spare thought for alternatives the rest of the day. I wasn't the only one who noted parallels: Some of the same ceremonial could be applied here as at Friday prayers. But though this parallel lent the self-propulsion of centuries-old tradition, I could not trust to that. I personally had to see to every detail.

I ended up claiming part of the Hippodrome's summer dust as I tried to find places for all the attendants that had to come along on this lovers' tryst—and the mounts of those who claimed the honor of riding the short distance. The viziers made a field of green, the muftis in white, the chamberlains scarlet, the sheikhs a block of blue. All these had to be made comfortable with refreshments and small guest gifts according to rank.

My master himself had to unpack his most formal robes of heavy green silk from among scented aloes, his conical turban ringed with gold. He saw to the highest dignitaries in the *selamlik*. The harem, of course, was mostly left in peace: Even a sultan could claim no access to any household's inner sanctum. But my lady had to rise to the occasion and little Gul Ruh, too, had to wear her best to greet her royal uncle.

I take it all as heaven's mercy that I had no time the rest of that day to consider the ramifications of this visit, either for Nur Banu or for anyone else in the empire. But I do recall thinking, on one hasty passage through the *mabein,* that this man from whom I so scrupulously averted my eyes as the Shadow of Allah had once tried to best me in a hand-to-hand fight. It had been when I'd first come to the harem and I'd stood my own against him until Safiye's declaration that I was a eunuch had finally removed me from the young prince's threat. I wondered if Murad remembered.

On that same quick passage on silent, watchful eunuch's feet, I saw little out of the ordinary in the familiar faces: Gul Ruh's straining to whiteness in her attempt to be a grown-up lady, Esmikhan's blooming to renewed health in her brother's presence, Safiye's calmly triumphant—this much was expected. That Ghazanfer's flattened cheeks wore a brush of high color—of pleasure? or shame?—was more surprising. But I took no time to consider the curiosity then.

So it came as something quite unforeseen when at last I closed the harem doors and thought we had done with the world for a while that my master should call me back out to him in the *selamlik*.

Sokolli Pasha's private rooms had less of the feminine about them than a soldier's barracks, than a monk's cell. A spartan divan of rumpled cushions, a worn rug rutched at the corners, stacks of dispatches, pens and ink, maps on a low writing desk. That was all the furnishings save the overwhelming smell of masculinity barely tempered by the requisite aloe shaken out of his ceremonial robes. I could count on one hand the times even so feminine a creature as myself had entered these rooms. They were, from my perspective, a more closed sanctuary than the harem.

The Grand Vizier looked at me keenly over his falcon's beak of a nose. "It went well, Abdullah."

"Thank Allah."

"And thanks to you as well, Allah's servant."

"And your servant, my master." I bowed, arms across my chest, straight from the waist.

Sokolli Pasha shrugged out of his ceremonial robe. I moved to lend a hand, a gesture I could tell he was unaccustomed to, still in many ways the raw Bosnian recruit. I found myself averting my eyes from the sight of his shoulder blades. Though still covered by underrobes of lighter silk, they seemed old and tight—achingly tired. Any other man would have called for a massage. I felt tempted to undertake the task myself, but did not dare, unbidden.

The Grand Vizier was now closer to seventy than to sixty, the small vanity of henna becoming an ever deeper red on his beard as he sought to cover the encroaching grey. And his eyes—tonight—seemed rheumy with exhaustion. No one but Allah would ever know—or truly appreciate—the weight of the world that rested on the lids of those eyes.

"Tell me, *khadim*."

"Master?"

I was not prepared for what he wanted to ask, "Tell me what you know of Ghazanfer Agha." I was even less prepared for the title he attached to the end of my counterpart's name. It took me a moment to imagine whom he might mean. *Agha, lord,* though euphemistically applied to all eunuchs, was a rank above *ustadh* in honor.

"Ghazanfer . . . Ghazanfer is a *khadim.*" Well, that much was self-evident. I had to say more. "Ghazanfer is a *khadim* who knows his duty and does it." Surely no one could argue with that statement, no matter whose side he was prompted to take.

My master nodded. He had guessed as much. No, more. But I had given him the impression that this was a man after his own heart, someone he could trust. I hadn't meant to do that.

"Why, sir, do you ask?"

"It seems he is to be *kapu aghasi.*"

"*Kapu aghasi?*"

"Senior officer of the palace, yes. Not 'is to be.' Already is. Our master the Sultan declared him to that high post this afternoon. On his visit to our—to his harem."

"But *kapu aghasi* is a post—a post almost equal to that of Grand Vizier—to your own, master."

"Indeed. And it was greatly enhanced when our sadly mourned master Suleiman—may Allah give him the paradise he deserves—transfered the *awkaf* of the holy cities Mecca and Medina as well as that of over seventy of the largest mosques to his superintendence."

"Safiye!" I couldn't help but hiss between my teeth.

"Yes." My master took off the heavy gold-banded turban and rubbed the infant nakedness of his carefully shaven scalp. "I know my master the Sultan's harem is none of my business. But I had to suspect that a woman who could call the Shadow of Allah—heaven grant his reign last 'til judgement day—to her bedside could also get him to appoint whomever she wants to a vacant post. I know his mother the Valide Sultan was putting forth candidates of her own. I even got a note or two shuffled through the sacred curtains. But—it seems the old woman has lost this round."

Sokolli Pasha remembered himself and went to kindle more lamps in the growing darkness. Where are the servants to do this? I wondered. I bent myself to straighten the rug. At least I could do that for him, even if I couldn't find a way to tell him of the scene I had witnessed between Safiye and her eunuch—now the whole empire's eunuch—that afternoon.

In truth, I didn't know what to make of the exchange myself, not in light of this latest appointment. I would have liked some help in the task. But, though I admired my master's wisdom—the entire empire must be grateful to it for getting us through the years of Selim's negligent rule—I was quite certain he was not the man to help me unravel the faces of women and the most taciturn of eunuchs. In the ordinary way, Sokolli Pasha behaved as if such creatures did not exist.

The Grand Vizier chuckled rather harshly—at himself, it seemed. "I guess after eight years of Selim—Allah favor him—I've grown too used to making appointments as I see fit. This is the Creator's compassionate way of reminding me I am not Sultan. I am just the Sultan's slave, after all."

"And I, master, am your slave." Could he take any comfort in that? Probably not, but it was the best I could offer.

The lamplight made his smile seem thin and crooked. "Yes, well, let us hope the Sultan himself be not a slave."

"To the harem?" I asked, astonished at the idea.

"Yes. To his favored women. But Allah knows best."

My master turned a lamp to the papers on his desk and I understood that, as I could or would say no more, I was dismissed.

XXV

I HAD TO confess the name Ghazanfer Agha had a certain melody to it, slipping off the tongue as if grown together in one piece. And I certainly heard it plenty of times off plenty of tongues in the months that followed. Everyone in the world, or so it seemed, had business with

Ghazanfer Agha. And, as rooms for a *kapu aghasi* had yet to be rebuilt in the Sultan's palace, they had to be found in ours, etched out of the Grand Vizier's space in the *selamlik* because more often than not, the matters of Safiye's head eunuch were with men. The most powerful men in the world.

Safiye watched the office grow with more satisfaction than she watched her own belly.

And my master threw up his hands and took his work elsewhere, a stranger in his own palace.

The most pressing order of the new *kapu aghasi*'s business was to get the pilgrims off to Mecca. The seventh month of Rajab was fast upon us, the time when the faithful would have to set off from Constantinople if they hoped to make the arduous journey in time for Dhu'l-Hijja. Of course, all the imperial city, especially the Sultan, would have a hand in their send-off, deputizing their proxies, displaying the largesse they would commission to go in their place. Some of the treasure would be given as safe-passage insurance to the wild Bedouin who beset the pilgrims' path, some to be traded with pilgrims from other lands, the remainder to enrich the dual shrines themselves.

The gifted mosque lamps—many, I was quietly gratified to see, of Venetian glass—stacked up in our hallways and closets. Gorgeous rugs of the finest knotting, the gold-embroidered green case which contained the Sultan's bejeweled compliment to the Sherif of Mecca . . . Then of course there were the black lengths of finest silk embroidered with Koranic sayings in pure gold that would go to replace the covering of the Holy Ka'ba. The first half of a thousand needlewomen's work had gone up in the palace fire, so this lot had to be scrambled for.

Finally came the day when those obliged to stay behind gave the departing pilgrims a rousing procession. Albanians and Bosnians, leaping with new converts' enthusiasm; wild, anciently pious men from the Asian steppes; naked and flagellant dervishes from Anatolia—these swelled the ranks of the locals. This year as every year, the journey began with a joyous circuit outside the city walls while man and beast were still fresh and exuberant enough not to require that every step mean progress.

The display was always so stirring that many dropped their pedantic responsibilities then and there and joined up. The rest promised themselves and their god, "Next year, next year, *inshallah.*"

The Sultan's proxies formed the high point of the entire parade, the head of the column, great as a small army. These in turn were lead by two sacred camels of ancient and reverend pedigree, never used for profane burdens. The first camel, draped in rich clothes of scarlet and gold that hid it almost completely, carried the *minhal,* the high pinnacled litter of gold that caught the sun and winked its holiness in all directions. The second camel bore only a small curved saddle of green velvet with silver trappings. This represented the saddle of the Seal of the Prophets himself.

"Allah, Allah," a hundred thousand throats moaned as the shadows of this simplest, yet holiest of sights touched them. Some of the more credulous dropped to the ground and rubbed their foreheads in the dirt as this camel passed by, as if indeed the Prophet Muhammed had not died nearly a millennium before but rode there in our very midst.

After these two first camels came many, many more, just in the Sultan's party alone, for every night on the way a great red and gold tent would be erected to house the Sherif's letter and the green saddle. This tent had to be carried, along with twenty camel-loads of treasure for the maintenance of the holy places, and all this needed grooms, drivers, slaves to load and unload, water carriers, and cooks; and many of these contrived to bring their families along.

This was only the beginning. Thereafter followed thousands of the Faithful, equal, we are told, in the eyes of Allah, but hardly so to human eyes. There were great men, easing a guilty conscience with the journey but still unable to travel without a great following. Their women came behind in closed sedan boxes—sometimes it was hard to tell harem from baggage and eunuchs from porters. There were poorer folks who had saved all their lives for a donkey which, Allah knew, would never make it through Syria let alone the waterless Hijaz. Or a mangy camel which they could as yet drive only with difficulty; the balkings, runaways, and sudden sit-downs were a constant disruption to the proceedings.

A large division of the army marched by like rods of iron in the height of discipline, reminding one and all that more than nature might be the enemy on the journey. Then, in a generous sprinkling like salt over the whole melange, there were the very, very poor—dervishes, beggars, and paupers—who meant to walk the whole way. Some had not even made provision for carrying water and could hardly be told from the empty-handed audience except, in some cases, that they seemed even less prepared for an arduous journey. They would have to look to the mercy of Allah and a propensity for charity among their fellow travelers—greater on the road than at home—to carry them every step of the route.

※

NO SOONER WERE the pilgrims safely on their way than, in her eighth month of pregnancy, Safiye's rooms were ready for her under Sultan Murad's roof at Topkapi. The Fair One would let nothing hinder her from returning there, to the thick of the fray, although her new midwife thought it very ill-advised in what had already proven to be an eventful pregnancy.

Organizing the exodus without much help from the over-burdened Ghazanfer Agha caused me a great deal of stress. Before the last casket of gems was quite out our harem door, I had come down with that bane of all my race, a urinary infection so excruciating I could not leave my bed. I'd begun by passing blood through the silver catheter my lady had given me as a poor substitute to flesh. In the flurry, I'd ignored it until fever and nausea allowed me to ignore it no longer.

I dosed myself with the usual flax tea and quantities of pomegranate juice. But on that particular day at the height of my illness, I'd long since drained the juice pitcher. The tea water had gone cold and unappetizing on an indifferent stomach, and I was too sick to go for more. Well, it was my own fault, wasn't it, for being so efficient when I was well that no one else in the palace ever learned to take any responsibility on his own?

I was feeling so miserable, lonely, and uncared for—this being a disease of such indignity, the very embodiment of our mutilated, less-than-human state—that I had begun to actually hope it might kill me. I would not be the first of my kind to die this way. Nor—and this added to my grey outlook—would I be the last.

Earlier I had hoped for a visit from my lady. Wouldn't she be anxious that I was not at her side? Then I did not wish it, knowing only too well that getting her down the stairs and through the corridors to my room would be more trouble than it was worth. And though such a pilgrimage may not begin that way, in the end it would be *my* trouble she caused rather than the relief she hoped for, so basically lazy and helpless were my seconds. I wished Esmikhan happy—and quiet—where she was.

Perhaps, then, my young lady would come, having the run of the place as she did. For a while I hoped for that cheer, and regretted that her mother must have warned her "not to bother poor, sick Uncle Abdullah today." Then I did not want to spend the energy it would take to meet Gul Ruh's liveliness. I didn't want to see the cloud of concern that would drift across the vivid whites of her eyes. And since nobody else in the world mattered, I wanted death before I'd let others see me in my shame, even one bringing me more juice or giving the embers in the brazier a stir on that cold, wet fall afternoon.

Presently, however, before a forgetting sleep could come, someone else did enter the room. It was the last person I wanted—or expected. It was Ghazanfer Agha.

I made a clumsy struggle to get to my feet; any man who drags *Agha* around after him should at least have his hem kissed.

"Pray, do not stir yourself, *ustadh*," my guest insisted hastily. Don't I know the agony of such things? Is that what his tone implied? It was impossible to tell.

Ghazanfer made his great bulk comfortable on my rug—the only place left in my small cell to sit, what with me taking up all the divan. I hoped this did not denote an extended stay.

Once settled, my inexpedient guest launched into a long and formalized speech. He thanked me and mine profusely and wished us "the eternal blessings of Paradise" for the "saintlike hospitality" we'd shown to him and his.

What does this man want? throbbed through my aching head. It occurred to me—I was not so fevered as all that—that high officials are removed from the normal rounds of sociability. They never make personal visits—unless they want something.

I tried to think of some belonging he or his women might have left behind. I tried to remember some unintentioned slight, some word I might be required to pass on to my master—in my condition! I worked my fever-papered tongue in dry desperation.

Ghazanfer suddenly stopped in midflattery and scowled like a demon at the low table set between us. Whatever I've failed to do, I thought, I will pay for it now. At least with those monster hands about my throat, it will not be the lingering death of the infection for which I'd been preparing.

The Agha could move quickly for one so large, and such movement was invariably frightening to us lesser mortals. In a moment, he snatched the pitcher up off the table. I flinched and covered my tender groin, expecting to be showered with broken crockery in an instant. Instead, Ghazanfer stormed out into the hall. I heard him collar the first maidservant he came to, shame her for neglecting "the *khadim,* your most careful protector" and ordered "more juice and more hot water, quickly, as you fear Allah."

I heard the scurry of terrified slippers. What fear of Allah when Ghazanfer Agha was in the room? Then the awesome man returned and sat down quietly again as if half ashamed of his size—or his calling— and what it did to others.

He worked on the brazier a little but said nothing until I made an attempt: "How . . . how is the peace of your harem?"

The great, torture-hardened face cracked into something like a smile. I must be delirious. A *kapu aghasi* could hardly be burdened with a harem. Unless you called that greatest of all sanctuaries, Mecca and Medina, his preserve. But this man, at this time, did not set his sights quite so high.

"My lady Safiye," he began chattily, almost amiably, "had just received news of a 'weakness in the enemy lines,' hence her haste to return to the palace of our imperial master."

"Weaknesses? In enemy lines?" I was too sick for riddles.

"The little Hungarian—Nur Banu's Hungarian—who wasted no time in captivating Murad's heart, has also wasted no time in becoming pregnant." Did I detect a little native pride in this fellow Hungarian? Against his own lady?

I decided I was seeing things and said, "So Safiye and her shortly-to-arrive little one have some competition then?"

Ghazanfer presented me with another quiet almost-smile. "But my lady has two new weapons in her own arsenal."

"Weapons?" The fever worked on the image and made me shiver.

"And, like a soldier more foolhardy than courageous, she can hardly wait to try them out against the enemy."

"More than the awaited child I read you to mean."

"Yes. The first is the doctor."

"Doctor?"

"You know, the Venetian you fetched for her when her life and that of the awaited child were despaired of."

"She's gotten people to believe that he was responsible for her sudden, miraculous recovery?"

"Even Murad—Allah extend his reign for eternity—even the Sultan was impressed cnough that he has given his own personal permission to allow the man of medicine access to her anytime she felt the midwife was not doing a good enough job."

"Poor Safiye," Esmikhan would say when she heard of this, echoing the opinion of many other women. "My brother no longer loves her as he used to. To be so careless about whom she sees! Where has the old jealousy gone?"

But I remembered the fellow's purported skills in the ways of women. At the time, I'd thought Safiye wanted them for herself. I should have known she was subtler than that. Now I saw, without words, that there were other wombs in Murad's harem. The doctor would not have to enter the harem, just pass his knowledge and potions on to Safiye. Could Safiye blind a man who, by report, had endured untold other privations for the sake of his science? The man was old, the juices drying— Still I did not doubt it. In the shadow of her strength, he, too, could believe that all acts done in her name still had a virtuous objectivity, would still lead to knowledge that would still lead to truth that would still and ever be good.

God knows she'd blinded me. I suffered for it continuously.

While my thoughts waded through fever, Ghazanfer's quick mind scampered on ahead. " 'Spare no trouble, no expense.' " He was reciting for me Safiye's instructions to him concerning the acquisition of her second new weapon. He had not.

"Her name," he said, "is Mitra."

XXVI

"MITRA, THE NEW slave girl, is a Persian and of a noble family," Ghazanfer said. "Her father was posted to a border stronghold from which she was captured during a recent offensive when—*mashallah*— Allah punished the heretics."

"This Mitra is beautiful, I suppose?"

My guest hardly required my encouragement for his tale. "Not stunning, not like the Hungarian, not like my lady. She is of light complexion, something which isn't at all unheard of among Persians although it is the darker folk we see more often. Her hair is the color of amber in some lights, a fine setting for either emeralds or rubies, the bigger the better. But by itself, unremarkable."

"You are a connoisseur of slave flesh, my friend?"

"I suppose I've learned the jargon during these last months of search."

"So all your business was not for the pilgrimage?"

"No, it was not. Anyway, this Mitra was taken some four years ago as no more than a child. Few could have been able to see through her fear, awkwardness, and only slightly above average looks to find the pearl hidden there. But a woman of the nobility invested the hundred *ghrush* and the thousands of hours needed to complete all she lacked in Turkish taste—which you know, of course, favors the Persian where it can. Mitra sings like a lark and poetry—most of it in her native language—she recites in a fashion that others, even with years of training, might only aspire to. They can never achieve an inbred grace."

"I perceive she has touched your heart, agha."

"Indeed. I love the poets." And it was not without some bitterness that he continued, "She was reading poetry when Murad first met her: An enterprising poet had rented her to present his latest creation before the throne."

"I suppose it won a royal prize for him."

"Beyond all imagining. But the man flattered himself. And even Murad the Sultan—may Allah favor him—even he did not realize for the glory of the reciter that the poem itself was really quite mediocre."

I found lucidity enough to wonder, "Where is Nur Banu in all of this?"

"It was actually the crown of the veiled heads who first heard of the event, heard the poem on someone else's less-inspired lips, and realized that it must have been the reciter that inflamed her son's heart instead. A new route to her son's ear, she realized, had just opened up. She sent to the noble woman and immediately offered equal what she had once paid for Safiye for the girl."

"Then?"

"Then I got wind of the purchase. I brought word to Safiye. 'Offer her half again so much,' my lady said.

"The dealer was dumbfounded and came apologetically. 'I must be honest with you, agha,' she said, 'or I may loose your favor and the honor of your future custom. The girl is not a virgin. The men who captured her—well, the heat of battle and all. And maybe they, being only rough soldiers, never guessed what a little careful training could do. Perhaps it would be better to let the Queen Mother have this one, less than whole as she is.'

"Safiye consulted with her doctor. Then she heard that Nur Banu was ready to offer five hundred, so she stuck to her original price and gave six.

"Nur Banu stepped down. 'She's not a virgin, after all,' the Valide Sultan said. 'I'll save my money for others, better ones.' "

I asked, "Do I sense you did not mention the Venetian doctor in vain?"

"You sense correctly." His words made me shiver again. "Now the doctor had only heard of the procedure for restoring virginity in some far land, never seen it or even its product for himself. But, in the interest of science, he relished the chance to experiment. And now—" The eunuch spread his great, flattened hands in a gesture indicating self-explanation.

I suppose the fever was still slowing me. I asked, "Now?"

"Now the Venetian has reason to congratulate himself."

"And Safiye has won her six-hundred-*ghrush* gamble."

"She has."

I let my end of the dialogue drop for a moment while I forced my mind to consider the implications of what I'd just learned: Safiye buying slave flesh, creating Murad's addictions on her own. As I paused thus, the maidservant scurried in with cold juice, warm water.

"This is well," Ghazanfer said to her. "But see you do not neglect him in future."

The girl bowed deeply the instant her hands were empty. "Agha, I am your slave." She hurried from the room.

With hands that might have crushed porcelain had they been careless, Ghazanfer poured me the cooling juice. He was up on his knees; I fully suspect he would have tried to help me to drink like an infant if I had not refused him.

While I drank—finding myself almost faint with the relief the shock of cold brought my parched throat—Ghazanfer turned to the hot water. The rising steam spun silver comfort up through the damp grey air, lightening the weight of those monstrous hands.

"The flax is here," I said between swallows, gesturing towards the plump little jar.

But my guest—or was he now my host?—reached into his own bosom where I could not help but see how femininely the mutilation laid the fat on him. Ghazanfer pulled a kerchief out and opened it flat on the table. I saw and smelled a grey dried jumble of herbs.

"What is that?" I asked.

"A mixture. I have it of the Quince."

He must have seen me stiffen at the name, even spill a little pomegranate juice on my coverlet.

"Yes, I know there is ill ease between your household and the old midwife."

"I don't know why," I admitted. "I mean, besides the opium. It must be something besides just opium, to be so violent."

"Do not mind it now," Ghazanfer calmed me. "Her drug sends her no ill dreams against me, and this is what she makes for me—when I am afflicted like you. She does not even know I am here, and need never know. And it works wonders."

"What is the concoction?" I asked, still uneasy.

"Certainly I will tell you, so you may make your own next time, and I will leave you the lot in the meanwhile. Dog's grass mostly, six parts of that."

Now that he gave it a name, I could smell the clean, meadowy smell. "But dog's grass?"

" 'Note where the dogs go when they are sick.' That's what the Quince told me."

"That tough-rooted bane of farmers?" Perhaps it was a hopeful sign that I was considerate of somebody else's bane besides my own. But I did not think it so, being still desirous of death myself.

" 'Personally, I'd rather have an acre of dog's grass than of carrots for my herbary,' the Quince once said to me."

"Yes, that does sound like the tough, skilled woman I remember from—from before."

"Three parts of ground root of butterbur, three of onion, two of rhubarb, two of horsetail." Ghazanfer concluded the recipe. "I thought you might not be in a condition to remember it all, so I've written the directions here." A slip of paper joined the kerchief on the table after a pinch of the mixture had gone into the water to steep.

"Thank you," I said, dumbfounded beyond that.

I drank the tea, made palatable with honey.

Then, to divert the great *khadim*'s attention and already feeling somewhat revived, I said, "Thank Allah, the departure of the pilgrims went well for you."

The green in his squinty eyes brightened. "Yes, thank Allah."

I couldn't stifle my surprise at the true joy in his voice and tried to imagine what might cause it. "Took in a lot of baksheesh, did you?"

"Baksheesh? You speak that way? It is an honor to serve as custodian of the sanctuaries. Do you take baksheesh from those who wish access to your harem?"

The idea shocked me. "No. No, of course not."

"Then why should I accept it from those hoping for access to the greatest harem in the world? Our divine Master decides who may enter that sanctuary, whether we consider them worthy or not. True, some people did confuse the mundane with the spiritual and press a gift upon me. Such is the way of the world. But in each case, for the fear of Allah, I gave that gift away at once, as alms."

"Of course." But I wondered when the empire had known such a *kapu aghasi* before.

"It has been . . ." I saw him struggle to find words to express what, up until then, he had kept carefully locked in the harem of his heart. "It has been a great blessing to serve. As Allah wills, I hope I may always be found worthy of such service. I have particularly enjoyed my correspondence with the head agha over the shrine in Medina."

"The head guardian is a eunuch?" I guess I had known that, but, especially in my present fevered state, it was difficult to fathom.

"Of course. Brotherhoods of our kind serve at all the greatest shrines—at al-Aksa in Jerusalem, the tomb of Ibrahim in Hebron, in Cairo, at the tomb of Ali, fallen for the moment into the hands of the Persian heretics. In Mecca. But the greatest of all—for us—is in Medina, al-Medinat an-Nebi, the very City of the Prophet."

"I guess I see why it should be. Female pilgrims journey to all those sites in numbers equal to the male. There must be guardians who can deal with both sexes in honor."

"But it is more than that," Ghazanfer insisted. "In Medina particularly. You see, when the Angel of Death, in fear and trembling, came to ask the Messenger of Allah—blessings on him—if he might take his soul, Muhammed, with a perfect knowledge of the will of Allah, agreed. He died in the room of his favorite wife, Aysha."

"I wonder if Safiye was aware of all this history when she named her little daughter."

"Safiye was at a loss for feminine names," Ghazanfer replied, forgiving my diversion. "I suggested Aysha myself, having always had particular reverence in my heart for the well-guarded one Muhammed likewise chose to honor."

That a eunuch should name a princess of the blood seemed amazing to me. I even wondered, although everyone knew it was the great Suleiman who had given the heir apparent the ancient name, whether a suggestion hadn't come, somehow, from Ghazanfer in the case of Prince Muhammed as well. Both Safiye's children had been given names heavy with piety, lacking the flowery inspiration of more popular appellations. Simpler, more straightforward names were, of course, more appropriate for men, particularly men who would rule the realm of

Islam. But such possibilities occupied my mind for a while so I let my guest speak uninterrupted.

"The Prophet, blessed be he, was buried right where he died, under the floor in Aysha's room. And when his successors, the right-minded caliphs Abu Bakr and Omar, died, they likewise claimed the honor of burial next to the Messenger in whose great footsteps they had tried to lead Allah's congregation. Aysha stayed until her dying day in the room next to her buried lord, and when she died, she likewise joined these great men in the ground—and in Paradise.

"The great mosque in Medina grew up on this spot, incorporating the form of the Prophet's house: the rooms of all his wives and the rooms of the *selamlik* around a common yard. This is the form it maintains to this day."

"So these are the rooms of women," I proposed. "They need eunuch guardians. Even in death."

"Yes. But it is more than even that. As you can imagine, the grave of the Prophet contains great divine power, great *baraka*."

"Why else do people visit it?"

"Such power can be of benefit. But, poorly honored, it can also be dangerous. For example, while Aysha of blessed memory yet lived, a woman of Medina came to her, begging that she might pay her respects to the holy tomb. Aysha gave in and let the woman have a glimpse. So brilliant was the light within that the woman was turned to ash for her presumption and was buried where she fell, a warning to others.

"Still, being made only of the clay of this earth, the shrine needs mundane care. Earthquakes come by the will of Allah, and sandstorms. The stone and mortar crack, threatening destruction of the world by exposure to the divine power within. The black drapes with which the tombs are hung—like the Ka'ba in Mecca—these tear with time and must be replaced. But who may dare to step across the gulf between the worldly and the divine to undertake such duties?"

"Only the *khuddam* you mean to tell me?"

"It is so. And our power was discovered in the following manner. One day a great stench began to arise out of the tombs in place of the usual sweet smell. The stink grew so that even the most faithful of pilgrims could not bear to perform their devotions. Several men went to try to see what the matter might be, but none returned alive. Then a child was let in. He came out, but had been stricken deaf, dumb, and blind and could not say what he had seen. Still, the fact that he had lived pointed the right track. The task requires the innocence, the sexlessness of a child—but a man's wisdom. So a *khadim* volunteered himself. For three days, he fasted, kept vigil day and night, and prayed. Then he went in—and returned carrying the carcass of one of the sanctuary's pigeons that had died and rotted within.

"Ever since that day, it is eunuchs who have kept the hallowed place. Forty of them live, eat, and sleep within the precinct at this present time. All are men of greatest piety, known for their learning, their charity, their austerities."

I rubbed my hairless chin thoughtfully. "But if I drive you back to your original analogy—"

"Yes?"

"That eunuchs must keep guard at the boundary between the mundane and the divine as they keep guard between male and female—"

"Just so."

"Does that mean this miserable state of ours is half of this earth, half of paradise, as it is neither male nor female?"

"All is Allah's will."

"You will not commit yourself to such blasphemy?"

Ghazanfer smiled his tight, half smile. "All is Allah's will."

"Would you go so far as to say that our failures to keep the boundaries between men and women may be visited by destruction similar to what you have described in Medina?"

"That, my friend, is my firm belief. In either case, the two worlds combine but poorly."

"Like oil and vinegar."

"Rather like fire and powder—one kiss and all consumed."

"Except in our own persons."

"Except in us, yes."

I shifted on my cushions in my discomfort. "Which is, nonetheless, an uneasy state."

Another half smile. "As Allah wills."

"And if we fail in our duties?"

Ghazanfer looked at me hard—and yet not without kindness. Once again I got the firm impression that he was not at all ignorant of the breach I had allowed in my sanctuary wall, the breach that had allowed my heartbroken lady, once in her life, to know the blinding force of a true lover. That conjunction was responsible for Gul Ruh, the little girl child that was such a light to our lives. Did the *kapu aghasi* begrudge her—us—this? Did he condemn our mortal failings? Worse, would he try to take the pleasure of that breach from us?

"The righteous pilgrim must not be denied entry to the sanctuary," he said instead of what I had imagined from him. "Nor as many of its blessings as he can contain. It is up to a *khadim*'s pious wisdom to know what to let in, what to keep out."

"Awesome responsibility." I wasn't certain I believed his tales of lightening bolts from the blue but still I found my voice a whisper. "It cannot devolve upon mere mortals such as myself."

"Yet it can and does. This is the will of Allah working in us. The knowledge of when to keep the boundaries He Himself has set—and when to let the curtain down, if but for an instant. Such is the work of the truest servants of Allah."

XXVII

GHAZANFER GREW QUIET, pensive. "I cannot say I have always used my power in the wisest way. But I must say I am grateful for the calling I've recently received. To better help me understand what the will of Allah must be, how to serve Him. I think it is easier for you, Abdullah." And he said my name as more than just a name.

I would have held this thought and driven it further, but suddenly the tea had done its work and there was something more urgent I could hold no longer. With a groan I said, "Excuse me a moment. I must—"

Ghazanfer half smiled. "It works quickly, doesn't it?"

I could only nod as I struggled to get to my feet, biting back the pain with clenched teeth.

"Here, let me help," Ghazanfer said. And I welcomed the bone-cracking strength of his arms.

"Oh, God!" I gnashed my teeth over what wanted to be a scream when we finally reached the privy. "I've forgotten the catheter."

"I'll go," Ghazanfer said, helping me to sit on a bench for the agonized wait. "In your turban?"

"Where else does a eunuch carry his parts? It's on the table."

He will find another maidservant to send for it, I thought. I begged God—whatever God there might be, for certainly Ghazanfer's merciful, half-smiling deity was not in the swirl of my pain—to let me die quickly of the shame. And of the pain.

But Ghazanfer Agha did not delegate this, no matter what a *kapu aghasi*'s natural reflex must be. He returned, and the heaving of his breast told me he'd forced his huge bulk much more quickly than his usual dignified gait.

The *kapu aghasi* helped me up and held me while I began my straining business. The catheter shook in my hands.

"I cannot," I moaned. "The way is clogged."

But it was only the silver tube choked with hot pus. Ghazanfer rinsed it out and then let me try again.

Relief left me shaking with weakness as great as a child's. The huge *khadim* all but carried me back to my room, helped me to plumped-up pillows, plied me with yet more juice. I never wanted to have to pass anything else in my life again, but I drank at his insistence and my lips wavered in thanks; speech was beyond me.

Then my guest settled back on his rugs and took up all the burden of talk for himself. His tones were those with which he might lullaby an invalid child. But rather than a child's fables, these were a eunuch's. Too full of wonders to be believed, and yet, in my fevered head—

Ghazanfer told how Medina's guardians sat all day on a raised platform between the sacred tomb—veiled with black silk and latticed with scent-releasing aloewood—and the gateway to the mosque. Here, in happy brotherhood, they sat, read and prayed. The scene entered my fever-forged brain, grew vivid by the vivid force of Ghazanfer's words.

From this platform, the *khuddam* had a perfect view of every pilgrim who ventured in. They could instruct the ignorant, male and female, in the proper worship to make. They could mediate with the greater Mediator on the pilgrim's behalf, calling into the shrine, "O Prophet, a faithful one comes" as we everyday eunuchs warn the women that a man is about. Should a *khadim*'s keen eye detect impiety, he could be down off the platform in a moment, brandishing the cane he carried (no other weapons being allowed in the precinct) to soundly teach the careless a proper fear of Allah.

Scholars even kept the biographies of the tomb's most famous guardians, so their names and great deeds might not be forgotten. The present head agha had sent his Constantinople counterpart a leather-bound collection of such histories. Ghazanfer had many of them memorized, the heavy swing of their Arabic.

One of the *khadim* of olden time, one awesome Kafur Agha, so the story ran, had possessed a wondrous voice. "Such a wondrous voice—" Ghazanfer's own high tones made this seem rather ludicrous. And yet— "That when he raised it to chide misbelievers, the very ground would shake and glass could shatter. One day the muezzin, concealing secret sin within his heart, heard that voice from high up on his minaret and plunged—for fear—unto his death."

Medina's eunuchs, so I learned, tended the Garden of Fatima, two dozen date palms clinging miraculously to the desert sand in the open space between gateway and shrine. Ghazanfer described how the dates could not propagate without the eunuch's hands. The long spurs of the male tree must be cut off in the proper season and hung amidst the female blooms. In due time, the eunuchs gathered the fruit and sent it as gifts to those in the world they felt most deserving of such divine favor.

"Such favor is not bought," my guest assured me, then added laconically, "It is for the humble, the weak, the truly pious as only Medina's *khuddam* know humility and meekness, as only they can teach it. For the greatest of men, from the world of men, must come and kiss their hands and hems, these sexless creatures they have scorned elsewhere. You would not, for example, see an imperial kitchen explode into flames over Fatima's dates.

"When it comes time to replace the sanctuary's black silk curtains, six of the most pious *khuddam* alone are chosen. They fast, they pray. Then they blindfold themselves and thus bring the ladders. They climb and replace the worn drapes with new, all blindfolded to spare their eyes the fearsome *baraka* of that within." There was, Ghazanfer reminded me, such a veil in Jerusalem's temple of old.

"And then, every evening as dusk begins to fall, the eunuchs rise up off their platform. Solemnly, they drive every worshipper burdened by sex out and lock the great silver-studded doors after them. Then they take up lamps, our brothers do, in the gathering dusk, and solemnly circumambulate the darkening shrine. With their own hands and the purest oil, they kindle the wicks hung from silver and golden chains that will illuminate the holy place in the still desert air until dawn.

"It may be—yes, the head agha told me it is so—that some whole man or other sometimes makes pious supplication to the guardians. He is desirous to watch this final, private rite. The agha then may scrutinize him, obtain references, train him for months. And if, at length, the supplicant is deemed worthy, he is permitted within yet a while after the gates have closed. And he may—just may—even be allowed to carry oil and fire, to light the lamps, to pray. But if it is to be so, he must give up the trappings of a man for that one night. He must wear the long, spotless white robes with full, long sleeves that are the eunuch's dress. He must wear a eunuch's turban; he must gird his virile loins with a eunuch's sash. He must become, in other words, one with us, before he may safely enter that most holy of spaces.

"Then, at length, this final duty done, the faithful *khuddam* retire to their platform once again where they sleep in turns, some always watchful, always on guard. There—twixt heaven and earth."

The tale ended with sleep, as many a child's tale does, happily ever after. And I murmured from a deep drowse of my own the traditional tale's beginning: "Once there was a man—and once, there was not."

Perhaps I slept a healing sleep, perhaps not quite yet. I was aware of some commotion as one of my seconds came to the room, bowed deeply before the *kapu aghasi* and informed him that he was wanted "by many great lords in the *selamlik*."

I heard Ghazanfer sigh as he heaved himself up to his feet. "Duty calls, my friend," he said. "I told no one where I was going, but the world has found me out anyway. Allah grant you——" He seemed to want to wish me much more but in the end limited his prayer to "—— Allah grant you health."

And he was gone. Sleep came almost instantly to me now. There was room, however, for two more thoughts. And most curious ones they were, too.

The first was a feeling I couldn't shake. Everyone who knew the details of the *kapu aghasi*'s appointment, including my master, assumed the great eunuch had taken the post at Safiye's behest, to work her will as a counterpoise to that of the Grand Vizier. But then, with the eunuch's presence still lingering in the room, it seemed quite otherwise. Perhaps even Safiye assumed she had nothing but the firmest of allies. And yet Ghazanfer himself gave off another purpose—if you looked hard and close enough. Was it possible that the *khadim* had taken sanctuary in the office so heavily charged with religion, with *baraka?* Was this his way to escape in some measure from the demands of his mistress instead, Safiye's spell being, as I knew only too well myself, difficult—dangerous—to break?

My second thought was to wonder about the tale I'd overheard Ghazanfer Agha tell Andrea Barbarigo concerning the death of the page boy at Selim's hand. Throughout the three and more years since, I'd thought it hardly a thing one told to an unbelieving stranger. Ghazanfer would speak so? Ghazanfer, usually so taciturn even to those who knew him?

I remembered, in the moment before sleep, the flit of green eyes towards the chink in the Jews' wall where, I'd thought, I was so cleverly hidden. And it occurred to me: Maybe he meant the tale not for Barbarigo, who had been, after all, a lovesick fool, dragged helplessly towards his fate by the codpiece.

Perhaps, like all that afternoon's effusion, Ghazanfer Agha had meant the tale for me.

XXVIII

I HAVE OFTEN been disquieted by the thought, then as I am now: Isn't a manufactured virgin very like a eunuch, likewise manufactured? It is clear that Safiye's new Persian girl Mitra always suffered pain in being a woman. This—coupled, perhaps, with the pains of her earlier life, more than any sort of training—made her the remarkable reciter she was.

It could be seen in her eyes. Plain eyes as God made them, they became heavenly blue through experience and seemed always filled to the brim with a sort of petulant vulnerability. They not only made her more attractive—one wanted to swim in those eyes like in shivering cool pools on a hot summer's day—but they lent to her poetry a beautiful, wounded longing that I have never heard matched before, even by those who claim more art.

Now Safiye, with her two new weapons, gave a party to celebrate her return to the palace and, as she said, "To repay Nur Banu's kind hospitality," sorry only that it had taken her several months to do so.

It was the excitement. The heat. The shock the sight of Mitra gave her. The pressure Nur Banu poured out upon her afterwards. Nur Banu's sudden increase in the magical regime she had the girl on to insure a male child. All of these were put forward as causes for the very serious trauma the little Hungarian went through that night in which she almost lost her child.

I have my own suspicions about the matter.

I know for a fact that Safiye had gotten a vial from the Venetian doctor that very morning. She said it was part of her own treatment, but I also happened to see her wave one particular dish to the little Hungarian that evening and saw, when she turned from the slave, that she had hidden something about the size of a vial in her bosom.

I said nothing of my suspicions at first because I could not believe in anything so horrendous. Then, too, I had no proof and no one else to share in my conjecture—unless it were Ghazanfer and he was busy with his new office.

The Quince, however, must have suspected something immediately. She roused herself from her haze and managed to halt the untimely contractions, bringing the pregnancy back to normal. But she was very jittery—and sober—after that. Or so I heard. She wouldn't let Safiye near the Hungarian girl when she came to offer her condolences and congratulations on her recovery. And the midwife, aided by the Fig, did her best by calumny and gossip to try and undermine the power of that man, the doctor, in "their" harem.

On the whole this made for an ironic Ramadhan, that month when Islamic unity asserts itself stronger than at any other time save perhaps during the pilgrimage. We managed to maintain something of the usual air under Sokolli's roof by inviting the imperial ladies by turn, Safiye one night, Nur Banu the next. Even so, ambiance was delicate and my lady, who hadn't a malicious bone in her body, felt like a constant conspirator. She had to bite her tongue more than once having started a comment with, "But only yesterday Safiye told me . . ." or "Somebody was saying it wasn't like that at all. Who was that, Abdullah?"

And I would give her a look that said "Nur Banu" and she would blush and say "Oh, yes," apologize, and fall into a confused silence for the next half hour.

It was Nur Banu's night and some such careless phrasing sent the Hungarian, who had seemed volatile ever since we'd known her, flying from the room in tears. Esmikhan was in great distress and blamed herself although I couldn't remember anything threatening that might have been said.

"It's pregnancy, you know," Nur Banu assured us. "She cries all the time—for no reason. But, thanks to Allah, she gets over it just as quickly."

After a time, when the girl did not return, I thought perhaps I should go look for her. The cool of a balcony beckoned me outside and for a moment I forgot my search, entranced by the vision of the Aya Sophia Mosque just across the way. It was illuminated for the holy month against the black night sky, each of its four minarets twinkling with a thousand little oil lamps. Rising like heat from every home and cottage, bazaar, and dervish lodge were the sounds and warmth of the feast and celebration. They rose and filled my heart and I smiled at the inward peace I felt in my—could I say it?—adopted religion.

Then suddenly, for no reason I can tell, the celebrating seemed to die for a moment and—from clear across the water in Pera it must have been, with no more strength than an echo—there came two or three clangings of a Christian bell. Suddenly I remembered that Ramadhan happened to coincide that year with the Christians' commemoration of the birth of Jesus. It was the very night. The event had just been an-nounced, however faintly, to the world.

Those few distant bells suddenly recalled to my mind so clearly the Christmases of my childhood. I remembered the eery skirl that seemed to rise like mist as the peasant folk came down from the mountains in procession with candles and led by their pipers. I remembered the chill, the thrill of nighttime, candlelit boat rides towards the old church on the island of San Giorgio. How, as a child, I had thought the holy sea-son somehow special for me alone because San Giorgio was *my* saint.

My mouth was filled with a warm sweetness, for although Ramad-han cakes are sweeter than those old cook used to bake for our Christ-mas, those cakes of my childhood had a flavor all their own. That flavor must have been mixed with the warm taste of firelight and the care of loving arms about me. My back prickled and my eyes grew moist.

It was one of those sacred moments. All religions can create them. I've often been aware of the same feeling as Islam creates it: upon see-ing the minarets illuminated and several times among the brethren of the dervish order. Such moments are windows through which we catch a glimpse of the Eternal, of what true religion is. In me, however, I re-alized that Christianity had and will always have the advantage in pry-ing open those windows. Those arms that first hold us, Mother's arms—or, in my case, those of my old nurse—are closer to God than anything we learn later in life. An irrational prejudice, I'll admit, one never destined to help in the search for Truth. But a very real feeling, nonetheless.

Just as quickly the feeling was gone. A door from the *selamlik* opened below me and one of the master's guests slipped into the garden, mak-ing it no further than the nearest rose bush before he had to empty his bladder. Then the sounds of Islam in celebration closed over creation once more, losing the divine moment for me. But something lingered to keep me above the most grimy of mundane thoughts presented by the view of the man in the gardens: that we are mere animals, no more.

A throttled sob called my attention to the next balcony. There in the dark I could just make out the very pregnant figure of the little Hungarian. I was going to call out to her cheerily to forget her sorrow and to come into the party again, but something about her stance stifled me with the realization that more than a few tears were at stake here. She was teetering dangerously, intentionally on the edge.

I'll never know what it was that saved the little Hungarian's life that night. Surely it wasn't my presence—I don't think she ever realized I was there. I cannot help but think she must have heard the distant ring of bells and remembered . . . I do not know what sort of Christmas Hungarians remember. I only have this impression: deep, all-silencing snow, and in the heart of that bitter cold and dark, warmth and light by a fire.

The little Hungarian collapsed with a fearful sob—on the safe side of the railing. And it was there, just moments later, that Nur Banu found her and caught her in her heavily bangled arms.

"There, there, don't cry, my little mountain stream," Nur Banu crooned as if the girl had been an infant. And when, after a time, the sobbing failed somewhat, the crooning turned into a sort of singsong, the words of which were these:

"Have I ever told you, angel? No, I suppose I have not. Of when I was a girl. I don't tell many. There isn't much to tell. I left, of course, when I was only four. Paros is the name of the island where I was born. Paros. And when the Turks conquered—" She limited this train of thought to: "Well, my life has never been the same.

"But still I do remember. We had a festival, too, during the winter. A festival called Purim. I don't remember now what that means or what it was about, Purim. All I remember is that there was a very wicked man—Haman. Oh, how that name still sends shivers up my spine! They would say his name. I didn't dare say his name with them. The very posts of the house would shake with fear. Grandfather pounding the floor with his cane. Grandmother shaking dried beans in her cooking pot. Brother battering the woodbox with the flat of his little ax. I was so afraid. I thought I should die.

"But there were my mother's arms. 'Esther, Esther,' she crooned. Esther, that was my name. She placed on my head a crown made of woven palm. 'Esther. Esther. Queen.' And the darkness of Haman vanished. There was calm. And smiling. And sweet food. And finally, wonderfully, sleep, safe sleep to the sounds of ancient, ancient songs with words I do not know. Only the melodies linger. I always thought . . . I always thought, since that night . . ."

Here the singsong stammered to a self-conscious halt.

"Lady, what did you think?" the Hungarian had recovered enough to ask.

Nur Banu's tone was more prosaic now and matter-of-fact. "In my saddest days, when I was sold and hungry, cold and alone, I would always remember that night, that crown. 'Esther the Queen,' I remembered, and I knew I was born for higher things. And you see, here I am. I can pin this diadem into your lovely black hair and it is not simple palm but real, emeralds and pearls. No, keep it on, my child. It's for you. A gift. To remember this evening by as I remember that one so long ago. A queen. My sweet little cloud from a foreign land, rise and be a queen."

And they did and went back into the festivities.

I have often wondered if the fact that that crown was real made the feeling it could convey to the heart less real in the more important realm of the mystical.

IT WAS ANOTHER night not too much later in the same month that I happened to be out in the streets breaking my fast on some sherbet bought of a street vendor. Since sundown he had been turning such a thriving business that he hadn't had to clink his glasses together once for advertisement. Who should happen to be just behind me in line but Ghazanfer?

We exchanged polite salaams and then I asked, formally rather than from real interest, whether there was anything serious that caused him to be out instead of feasting at home.

"I was at the Fatih Mosque," he explained.

"Come, come, my friend! This is Ramadhan," I said. "We sit famished in the mosque all day, drowsing to the recitations, trying to find the strength to be interested in the relics which are on display these days and no others. But once the sun sets . . ."

"I had a vow to fulfill."

I saw at once that the holiday had made me more jovial than I had meant it to, or than Ghazanfer was able to imbibe at the moment. He bade me good holy days and then went on his way. It was only afterwards that I realized what events lay behind the brief lines he had given me. I remembered then that he had made a vow to donate enough money to feed all the children of the orphanage associated with the Fatih Mosque for a year should his mistress be safely delivered.

Safiye had had her baby, then. And since I hadn't heard the cannon boom from the fortress except to greet sunset, I knew it was a girl, and the fusiliers would put off announcement of the humiliating fact with three blasts until the morrow.

Safiye had paid the doctor a lesser price—but Ghazanfer had paid Allah all. The child's name was set in the harem book as Fatima. Another simple, pious name. I guessed who'd had a hand in that naming.

Safiye's face was not as black with shame as one might have expected. I noticed this at once the next time I saw her. It was the final feast of the holy month, and we'd been invited to spend it at the palace.

But why should she be downcast? Her Mitra was also carrying the Sultan's child, and with the Venetian doctor to oversee the pregnancy from the beginning, it was sure to be male. Mitra was in such favor that, despite her condition, Murad insisted that she spend every night of the holy month with him. She had so enlivened his interest in the arts that when she was not in the presence, it was his old poets and musicians he called for, no other girl.

Even on the twenty-seventh night, the Night of Power, Mitra had been at his side, reciting in her sweet Persian singsong. Most men refrain from visiting their harems on this most holy night of the year. This is the night when Allah took all creation in His Hand, gave them their fates, and then demanded, "Who is your Lord?" To which we are all said to have replied, "Thou art, O Lord." A visit to the harem might, I suppose, make some men give divinity a different answer.

To the Sultan, however, this sober prohibition does not extend. Should he sire a child on this night, it is seen as one destined to be very powerful indeed.

"So even though we knew already that Allah had filled her womb, we were very thrilled and flattered by Murad's choice," Safiye explained. Mitra had been returned to the harem now and Safiye sat holding the girl's hand and speaking as if for both.

Safiye, dressed in lush ruby reds set with golds, riveted the eye with her beauty. She had already regained her former willowy figure: No one would ever guess she was the mother of three—and the little dead prince besides.

Mitra herself did not look so well, although in the glare of her mistress few would notice. Pregnancy excuses one from the rigors of the fast, still I could see that the month of sleepless nights had not been easy on her. And Mitra wept outright when the traditional roast lamb was brought in. Her memories of previous lambs included the encirclement of her mother's arms.

And I could not help but think that, even though her new Fatima was only a girl, Safiye was missing out on a great claim to power by allowing a nurse's arms to hold the babe at that time instead of her own.

XXIX

I WAS NOT present, being safe in Sokolli Pasha's palace with my ladies at the time. But the events were discussed so often over the next weeks that I might have been and can reconstruct the story well.

The Quince had fallen asleep over her water pipe. Most remembered the old midwife as one who understood and controlled the workings of things too well to have to resort to hysterics. Fussiness or a sharp bite of sarcasm were her old methods of dealing with life's difficulties. So when she woke up screaming, it curdled the blood. Such a sound could only be imagined coming from unearthly realms of ghosts and jinn. Or from the flaming pits of the damned.

"Babies!" was the first coherent word the Fig, who came running with rose water and valerian, could make out.

Then, "Their insides all bled out." As she had done on that day in the presence of my little lady and me.

When the Quince had recovered herself somewhat, the Fig adjured her to tell what horrors she had dreamed. But the old midwife pursed her lips tighter than ever, turned green, and would not. She would not tell even when the nightmare came again. Again, and then when she dared not go to sleep days on end because it came every time she closed her eyes.

Thinking the drug was the cause, Nur Banu and the Fig tried to keep the pipe from the old woman. But they could not keep her from her pharmacopoeia because her skills were needed, now more than ever as the Hungarian came near to her time. If anything, the prohibition served to intensify the Quince's intoxication.

And the Hungarian came to her time, but without the Quince. At first the old woman said to her assistant, "Well, see how she does for a while and call me if you need me."

At the end of the first day the Quince sent potions to help, but no one was ever quite sure they were administered correctly. At the end of the third day, Nur Banu had her eunuchs drag the midwife to the birthing room by force.

The Quince, it was clear from her staggering and stammering, had fortified herself—not the laboring woman—heavily with drugs. But to no avail. As soon as the midwife stepped over the line of gunpowder into the smell and warmth of the birthing room, the dream came to her awake. Her screams evidenced more torture than those of the Hungarian.

In sore straits now Nur Banu sent for Safiye's midwife. The closest assistance turned out to be the Venetian doctor. She let him come, but it was too late. Or it was too early, and he was the final cause. What happened depended on whom one asked. The Hungarian died and her child as well, that is all we know for sure. The girl, like her country, could no longer bear the battles of empires being fought over her small body and what it contained.

Some shook their heads and said, "Four days of labor and then death. But think if she had lived, she and her son. What ravage then . . . ? Allah favored her with mercy."

Nur Banu lost her Hungarian, but Safiye lost her doctor; he was not trusted in the harem again on anybody's word.

As for the Quince, her mind slowly stewed to the viscous consistency one gets if one cooks the seeds of that fruit with a bit of pulp for a long time. I don't think she spoke another coherent word, although her babble was perpetual. I never saw her again, for as I had already noted, she had developed a particular aversion to my mistress. The mere report that Esmikhan was visiting sent the older woman in a frenzy to the highest parapet or darkest cellar of the harem. Sometimes we would hear her, the sharp, inhuman barks of a tortured soul, and they sent shivers down our backs.

The Quince lived on in this state for years. Indeed, I don't remember her death at all. She simply faded away, mind first, into the world that tormented her so, the voice lingering on last of all, finally coming only at haunting times. One came to think of it as no more than the sound of rain on the harem's copper roof.

NUR BANU BOUGHT two or three promising new girls in an attempt to replace the Hungarian and to break the spell cast on her son by Safiye and Mitra. In a market inflated by demand of her own making, they must have cost her a small fortune. I know even a scullery maid I went to buy for my mistress cost over three hundred *ghrush* at the time. But so far, Nur Banu's money had only been wasted, and with more girls than she could reasonably keep busy, their idleness got them into mischief. They were not maintaining a good name for themselves as is absolutely necessary if one would see the Sultan.

One day I happened to be passing through the newly reconstructed Black Eunuchs' Quarters where I heard a most dreadful sound. It was someone crying out in pain, yet one gone so far beyond humanity that it took effort for me to consider it human and to go and see if I could be of some assistance. I shouldn't have gone. Two burly blacks had a girl laid out cruciform while a third turned her bare white back into deep red furrows with a rod.

"By Allah, they will kill her," I exclaimed to the first unoccupied *khadim* I met. The screams were all-permeating and our conversation was marked by severe distraction on both sides.

"By Allah's will, not," the man replied. "At least, not yet. Their orders are to give off as soon as she is unconscious. Then they must wait 'til she rouses, then try again."

Though all *khuddam* are called upon to administer discipline from time to time, it is rarely more than a few heavy blows to the soles of the feet. If the girl suffers the embarrassment of an ungraceful walk afterwards, that soon passes. But blows to the back mean her career is ruined. The Sultan will never put his arms about scars, no matter how pretty the face.

"What can be wrong," I asked, "that calls for Nur Banu's destruction of her own property?"

"It's not Nur Banu's slave," I was told, "but Safiye's."

"Ah. But would she destroy every girl Safiye buys so that none may come to the Sultan again? What a waste!"

"The charge is more serious than mere jealousy."

"What's that?"

"Witchcraft."

The girl stopped screaming at that moment and my overtaut nerves leapt into the silence and onto that word like biting onto a cherry pit when one expects a smooth, well-cooked sauce.

Witchcraft. No more heinous crime can infest the soul of a harem than that.

"Murder and treason are less insidious." I found my voice shawled in a whisper.

"Yes," the man replied, "for in those cases the culprit is swiftly dispatched and that is the end of the business."

"With this darkest of crimes, however, the witch herself may be unaware of what she has done."

"What other explanation can there be for the Quince's sad end?"

"Indeed." I hadn't considered that.

"If a woman of such intelligence can be turned mad, almost rabid—"

"This is true."

And I couldn't help but think of the assistant Fig, her reputed familiarity with the world of spirits. But what reason would the Fig have to harm her mentor?

"Confessions drawn under torture," I suggested, "may only ever uncover a fraction of plots devised in the company of demons and jinn."

"And who could say what are lies? All has to be taken as real."

"But, my friend," I suggested, "even death is no answer, no safeguard against the power to lurk from beyond the grave."

"Indeed. And insubstantial spirit may haunt in silent talismans, in any dark corner, and under every flagstone."

I felt suspicions rise from the very paving stones as I left the *khadim* to go about my business. There was the Fig, of course, but I seemed to be the only one who considered her.

Mitra's blue eyes had made her suspect from the first day of her arrival. Safiye herself had taken to pinning a little mirror to her bodice so that the evil inherent in such eyes, even if inadvertent, might be reflected back again. It must be unnerving even—or especially—if a woman has no malice, to find her face reflected back off every soul she meets. But because she was still carrying royal blood, Mitra was immune from all but the most irrefutable of implications, and this Nur Banu never was able to extract, though she tried.

Safiye, as mother of Murad's only children to date, shared this immunity. And in the end, it was only a few poor serving girls—some from Safiye's suite, three who had waited on the Hungarian or the Quince, two Persians, and a Genoese, who, because of their origins, were suspected of setting their sympathies where they ought not to— only they ever felt the rod.

The Genoese and one of Safiye's own girls were all who paid the supreme penalty: Tied in weighted sacks, they were rowed out into the Golden Horn one night and then pushed overboard. One could not pity them too greatly. By then the black eunuchs' rod had wrecked such havoc on their limbs that they could never hope for more than a life of meanest drudgery.

After that, Murad, who had never seen full pregnancy before except as a child too young to remember, grew uneasy around Mitra and the swelling fruit of his own loins. He sometimes had her recite from behind a screen but without the magic of her eyes, the spell was somehow broken. He began to chose others for his bed, others his mother held out to him. By the time Mitra was delivered of a fine, healthy boy she called Mustafa—for some dear brother, perhaps, or her father, long dead—the Sultan had a new infatuation.

And witchcraft was allowed to sink for the time being into the dark and bottomless pit from which it had arisen.

I lose track of Murad's infatuations now. One seemed much the same as the next, and as Safiye and Nur Banu were pretty well matched in determination and skill at choosing, the crown went first to one camp, then to the other. The only effect was to make the Sultan all the more defenseless before the onslaught.

What experience I have had with love—or, rather, I should keep to the word infatuation, for to use that other here is blasphemy—convinces me that there is indeed something of the dark powers in it. And time and again throughout the coming years the word *witchcraft* was heard, first from one side of the harem, then the other.

Some strange signs scratched on the post in the hall to the baths. A pile of decomposing bones and skin found in a corner. No more, and no real indication that accident rather than malice might have caused these things. No matter. The great black eunuch would bring out his rod again, like a shadow from the dead himself.

I never liked that *khadim*. The cutters would have done better had they left him a man and sent him to the front lines somewhere to defend the faith and put down heresy. He enjoyed his job too much.

Even if you profess no superstition yourself, an awful shiver must come to you when you hear the word *witchcraft,* once you've seen what it can do.

❧

It was that same year that another kind of witchcraft made its presence felt in Constantinople. This was the effect, or so it was said, of Murad's first words as Sultan: "I'm hungry." There was famine in the land. The first year of his reign the harvests throughout Anatolia had been bad, and this year they failed altogether, with the drought spreading to both the northern coast of the Black Sea and into Europe.

Bread reached twenty aspers a loaf in the markets, and not everyone could pay. No one in Sokolli's house went hungry, of course. I actually gained a little paunch as I fed more on rice and bread to thicken up the thin meat and vegetable stews. My master increased his gifts of charity to the mosques so they could feed more of the poor in their soup kitchens. As for the imperial palace, I suspect some there have forgotten there ever was a famine. Their bread remained as white as ever and the goats' production of milk, whenever it dropped off, was augmented by greater flocks that fed on the Serai's irrigated lawns.

It was one morning during this time that the Sultan was speaking to an Italian goldsmith about a new sweetmeat service he wished to commission. The tray would be a silver pond, the bowls lilies, and lapis lazuli, pearl and ruby dragonflies would perch on each spoon . . .

And how do I know of this meeting? I learned of it later, from the third man who was there, the interpreter, one Muslim, formerly Andrea Barbarigo, now dragoman to the imperial navy.

"Yes, your most sovereign majesty." Andrea translated for the smith, keeping his eyes trained on the fastidious craftsman and averted from the sovereign. "The design will be the most beautiful thing I have ever been privileged to make in my career. Your majesty certainly has an artistic eye. It is my wish, however, that only the best materials be used—anything less and the toil and design will be wasted."

"Yes, only the best," Murad agreed. "What is the use of melting down a little on the side to line one's own pocket if it isn't the finest to begin with?" He signaled quickly to Muslim not to translate that part but said instead, with an unfeigned smile, "Of course. You shall have the best. The best in the world, and I am the Shadow of Allah."

"That is my only concern." The smith grew red with embarrassment as he suggested, "Perhaps it would be best to wait. I know there are many demands on your coffers at the moment, what with the famine and all."

"We have a saying in Turkish," Murad assured the man. " 'If prices were all equal, there would no longer remain such a thing as the best people.' You shall have the materials you desire, and by the end of the week."

When Muslim had translated that into Italian, the Sultan added, "What day is today? Sunday? Well, then the Divan should be sitting. Would you, my honored guest, like to see a little of the workings of the Islamic government?"

When the smith replied he would enjoy that very much, Murad said, "Come with me, then. And when we have seen this, you will not be concerned about your materials any more."

Murad conducted his guests through the twists and turns of the palace until he came to the foot of the stairs that led to the Eye of the Sultan. This was the grilled and curtained space that looked out over the Divan. From this hidden closet the Sultan could watch the court's proceedings without its knowledge. Or he could not watch, as he chose. And everyone from minister to lowest waiter must behave as if he were there, just in case.

At the door to the Eye, a young, gangling eunuch, obviously a new fellow, was taken by surprise. The Sultan and his guests had already passed him by before the *khadim* recalled how to salaam a Padishah. And after he'd finally negotiated that, he tried desperately to make some sign of warning.

"Later, *khadim,* later," the Sultan said, and led his guests up the stairs two at a time like a boy half his age. He flung open the second door at the top, then stopped short.

Muslim suddenly found himself doing something more than translating words. He had to interpret customs, and that was much more difficult.

"Good signore, I think perhaps we should leave his majesty and complete the arrangements for the casting of this project at another time." Then in Turkish: "You'll excuse us, majesty?"

The Sultan gave them a wave over his shoulder but no glance and Muslim hastily steered the goldsmith back down the stairs and into the courtyard by the shortest route. The yard was crowded for a day in the Divan. They would have to be content to watch the workings of government from this perspective. Muslim was glad the eunuch was a novice and more concerned with his own failings than in apprehending others'. He was also glad he had been the one just on the heels of the Sultan and that what was behind that door was his secret alone.

He had seen her. He'd known at once it was she. It could be no other. In pink and green, the colors of a peach tree in bloom. Her golden hair spun out across her shoulders and breast like a halo. With the cushions and rugs about her like the flower and bunting decorations of a holy day, she reminded him of the Madonna in the little chapel in his mother's convent. He thought he might swoon from devotion before they reached fresh air.

XXX

AND THIS NEXT scene I owe to the green eyes of Ghazanfer Agha, who had been sitting in the Eye of the Sultan watching the Divan with his lady.

"Peace to you, master." Safiye hardly wasted a moment on surprise before getting to her feet and making her obeisance.

"And to you, Safiye," Murad returned.

"Forgive me. I was only watching the Divan today for a little diversion. I shall leave at once."

"No, no. Stay. Sit down."

Sit down quickly, please, the *kapu aghasi* read the Sultan's thought. From the level of the floor where he continued to bow his huge bulk with difficulty, Ghazanfer saw Safiye was as tall as their common master was. The young prince may have found the woman's height enticing once. No doubt it unnerved him now.

"My companions seem to have gone, Safiye," the Sultan said aloud. "We shall watch the Divan together for a while."

Murad seemed to curse himself silently. Why did he grow so red? He ran his fingers around the stifle of the sable collar that lay like a wet noose about his neck. After all this time, that she should have such an effect on him, Ghazanfer thought with renewed admiration for his lady.

Murad had had a string of girls young enough to be his daughters, and still none of them could move him like this.

Murad scratched his beard distractedly, perhaps painfully aware that grey had begun to invade it like mealworms in the paprika. Could it be that her appearance had a stronger effect on him than it had had that first evening? Ghazanfer had not been present, of course, that Id al-Adha, festival of the sacrifice, when Nur Banu's gift to her son had been this prize, served up to him like pastries on a tray. But he could guess.

And, he guessed, there were other emotions mixed with the desire now, indeed, quite overcoming it. The Sultan knew that Safiye knew of his amours. She knew how weak he was, while all the time she sat there—so he thought—in perfect constancy. If the mere glance of her eyes were not enough to tell him she was faithful still, then there was Ghazanfer, Ghazanfer Agha settled like a bell jar over her on which was engraved the word *virtue*.

Ghazanfer rose inobtrusively and watched how humble his mistress became before Murad, devoted to him still. Her actions proved it. It gave her awful power over him. The lord of three continents could not meet her in the eye. He was ashamed.

"Safiye, I . . ." he stammered to bring forth some sort of apology.

"Say nothing, my lord, if you do not wish to."

The Sultan took the mantle of sovereignty she handed him with those words and flung it hastily over himself for protection. But still he realized, and realized that she realized: If he was Sultan, she was Sultan Maker.

"Please, please, be seated, my master." Safiye gestured with a sweep of her graceful arm. "Your counselors are just coming to the important decisions now."

Murad let her reverence and the formality of the situation give him the royal will he needed to sit as if it had been his own idea. Then Safiye curled up at his feet like some faithful dog. He tried to protest and invited her to sit beside him on the divan. But she would not. And there was such power in her humility, he could not resist! He didn't stop to think that the seat on the rugs gave the best view and hearing of the affairs in the room below, and that a modicum of comfort was the only advantage he had on the divan.

The Agha of the Janissaries was in the midst of complaining before the viziers: "I swear by Allah that if something is not done, the entire corps will have turned over its supper kettles by the end of the week."

"And the cavalry will join the rebellion," added Ferhad, the handsome Master of the Horse.

"There's ground stone in the flour."

"Rotten vegetables."

"No meat at all last week."

"You cannot feed your army on that and expect them to be faithful."

"I agree," came the sober voice of Sokolli Pasha, sitting just beneath the Eye where they could see little more than the bubble of his gold-banded turban. "Something must be done and immediately. With the general populace also hungry and restive, discontent in the army is like a firebrand in the powder stores. You've had a chance to take our offer to your men. What is their answer?"

" 'A tax for wear and tear on our teeth and stomachs.' That's what they're calling it." The young Master of the Horse enjoyed a smile. There was no doubt of his charm.

The Grand Vizier gave the man a hard look which he had difficulty meeting. "They joke at it, then? They will not accept our best offer, one that will break the empire in any case?"

"My colleague did not say that," the Agha of the Janissaries spoke for Ferhad, who at the moment could say nothing. Ghazanfer wondered briefly what there was between the young cavalryman and the Grand Vizier. "They are willing to bargain over such a 'tax.' They will take a hundred *akçe* a man per year."

"We only offered fifty." Sokolli Pasha was grim.

"A hundred is what they want."

"Very well. See if they'll settle for seventy-five. And we in here—" He looked around at the other viziers seated with him on the Divan. "—we will see if it is possible to meet them there."

The two commanders bowed their way out of the room.

"By Allah!" Sokolli Pasha exploded the minute the men had gone. "It is blackmail. They will destroy the empire. They will destroy Islam. Don't they care?"

"I doubt they do," said Lala Mustafa, the second vizier. He spoke quietly. "It is not their empire, after all."

"Of course it is their empire."

"They were taken from their homes as boys. Remember?"

"So was I, by Allah. So were you. I knew if we let them marry they would begin to get personal profit on the brain. Ah, but I forget. You are in favor of this scheme." The Grand Vizier's voice sharpened, like a knife, as he added, "You and whoever pays you."

"I see no other way out, my lord Grand Vizier. Do you?"

Sokolli Pasha was desperate, but he had to admit he saw none. " 'The encroachments of the rich are more dangerous to the State than those of the poor,' " he quoted instead.

"I beg your pardon?"

"Nothing, Pasha. Just something Aristotle once said."

"Heathen blasphemer." Lala Mustafa brushed the quote aside.

"Be that as it may," said Sokolli Pasha, "let us be united, gentlemen, now, and try to figure out where we are to get that extra twenty-five *akçe* a man. There are no taxes coming in; the *sandjaks* have nothing to tax, nothing but stubble in the fields. Jihad is at a stalemate on all fronts, so there is no booty."

"There are still the bankers and moneylenders standing by." Lala Mustafa again.

"Vultures waiting for the carcass. No, by my life. That I still refuse."

"All the Christian governments do it."

"Yes, by Allah, and they are condemned to hellfire."

"Still, if we want to compete with them in the economy of the world . . ."

"By Allah, we do not have to compete. We are the realm of the Faithful."

"There are some who would call that opinion short-sighted and parochial."

"Would you call it that, Pasha? Would you?"

Lala Mustafa did not dare.

"As the realm of the Faithful, what Allah has strictly forbidden we may not do. We may not take money at interest."

" 'Allah's legislation has no other purpose than to ease the way of His servants through the exigencies of the times.' " Lala Mustafa quoted from a famous Muslim jurist.

"It is blasphemy to suggest such a thing in this context," said Sokolli

Pasha. "In any case, I could never agree to something that is neither more nor less than the bartering of the lives of future generations of Muslims into slavery. And the Mufti will agree with me."

The reverend representative of the Faith was not present, but Lala Mustafa sadly shook his head. He knew it was true. "Then we have no choice but to get the money where we got the first fifty *akçe*."

"How can we?"

"Debase the currency. Instead of fifty percent copper to a silver coin, make it seventy-five. So the army will really be getting only the twenty-five *akçe* we can afford. But they will think it is more. And the grocers they buy from will think it is more. And the merchants. And the whoremongers. And the jewelers."

"You really think they will do this?" Sokolli Pasha was grim. But then, he often was.

"They'll be obliged to. It will have the Sultan's name on it. Otherwise they would be committing treason."

"By the Merciful One, how I hate money!"

"There speaks a man with all the fine things money can buy and a full stomach. You would not say that if you were poor."

"It smacks of usury no matter how one wants to deal with it. We are still borrowing on the lives of our children. When a state has been dependent upon growth and growth and more growth and it finally reaches the limits of Allah—Why can't even I accept that limit? Why can't I see within and see what must be done and have the courage?"

"No one will call you a coward if you take this bold step."

"No, because they're all such damnable cowards themselves."

"It is only a temporary measure."

"Yes, and as Allah is my witness, I shall see that it remains so. I will not live to see temporary measures like these become tradition."

"Amen," said Lala Mustafa.

"As if one could say one day there was a famine, the next it was over," Safiye could not help exclaiming up in the Sultan's Eye. "Oh, he is a tedious old man, that Sokolli Pasha. I only wonder, my love, how you endure him."

"Endure him? I must. He made me what I am. And my father before me."

"There is always the executioner's block for Grand Viziers who've outworn their stay."

"Now, my dear. One way or another, I always manage to have my way. Sokolli Pasha or no."

Murad himself seemed startled at how easily he had fallen into conversation with this woman when politics were the topic. Even the endearments came easily.

They are like some dottering old couple, Ghazanfer thought, beyond the needs of sex, who only use the bed as an excuse for a good chat.

"You are in favor of debasing the coinage then, too, my love?" Safiye asked her master.

"Yes."

"But I remember in one of their earlier discussions of the problem, Sokolli said, 'What man would want his name stamped on a lie?' The coin says on it that it weighs so much in gold or silver and can be traded for so much, but any man with a scale can see that it does not. And there is your name affixed to it forever."

"Yes, that is a consideration."

"Which you considered, my love?"

"Yes."

"And?"

"And—other things seemed more important."

"Your new sweetmeat service for example?"

Murad seemed embarrassed that she knew of that. "Yes." But he continued firmly. "The future might forgive me a lie on the coins. It will not forgive me if I let the janissaries take over and lose the empire."

"Or if you show yourself as a weak ruler by bartering your jewels. My love, did you take a bribe for this?"

The way he returned her glance betrayed himself.

"Ah, I thought so. Who promised?"

"I'll let you guess, my sweet little politician."

"I guess it was Lala Mustafa."

"You are very wise."

Safiye blushed a controlled, enticing degree. "And he was bribed by lesser officials who were bribed by lesser ones who were bribed by the bankers and moneylenders. It must be a substantial pile by now."

"It is. And you know its genealogy better than I."

Ah, she was sitting at his feet now just in the attitude she must have had when as a young prince he'd first taken those golden curls into both his hands . . .

"Are you terribly disappointed in me?" he asked hoarsely.

"Disappointed? Oh, no, my love. I shall affix a string of those debased coins and wear them on my caplet proudly." She shook her pink and green caplet set with sequins now most coyly. "Did I sound disappointed?"

"A little."

"Well, I'm not in the least. In fact, I am very pleased. Some of that bribery money—well, you may as well know. It's mine."

"I see." Murad smiled in wonder and some little relief.

"Surely you don't expect me to live like Sokolli Pasha wants us to."

"Away with your fine clothes?" Murad teased, plucking at the diamonds that buttoned her *yelek*. "And my slave girls?"

"You could not do without your girls, my love," Safiye agreed.

"I just wanted to know. That's all." He said it into the pillow of her neck.

And Safiye pulled herself up on the Sultan's knees and kissed him tenderly on one cheek. Murad repaid the kiss, then their lips met lightly.

Ghazanfer did not move a muscle. He willed even his eyes not to blink.

"Tell me, how is your Mitra these days?" Murad murmured into the golden hair. His nuzzle released the smell of heliotrope and lemon.

"Just fine. Lonely, though. She misses you."

"And I miss her. She has such a way with the poets."

"Yes, she does. Oh, but you've been so busy with that new girl of your mother's."

"Yes. Well, she's a silly little thing."

"Aren't they always?"

Murad grunted into a smile that committed nothing. He took another deep breath of that hair, then sighed. "Send her to me tonight, will you?"

"Mitra?"

"Yes."

"Of course. Your wish is my command, my master." She kissed him again and was gone. The big Hungarian eunuch slipped after her dance in silence.

XXXI

"KING JOSEPH" THE sign read beneath the shield of red lines and silver crosses. "Barry ten azure and argent," the description of Christian heralders might have read, "lion rampant gules." Yet the words were not as foreign to Constantinople as one might imagine. *Azure* comes from the Arabic for dark blue and *gul* is the red rose in Persian, as in the name of my young lady.

The lions had faded pink, the stripes to a pastel blue. Five years of wet cold and blistering heat had passed since Joseph Nassey's dream of a kingdom of Cyprus had reached fruition in the Sultan's heart. Yet the Jew had never enjoyed the fruits of his labors. At first there had been famine on the conquered island. Selim had fumed, not so much because his new subjects were going hungry but because part of their hunger was that nearly every vine on the island had been cut down during the war. It would be years before there would be another decent vintage and Allah only knew if the cuttings imported from the mainland could ever make wine so sweet.

His friend and inspiration Nassey, the Sultan had declared, would only be given the island when it was worthy of him. Until time had healed the ravages of war it would be best to put the place in the hands of one used to desolation, a soldier, Muzzaffer Pasha.

Muzzaffer Pasha had done a remarkable job. The Cypriots were now hailing the Muslims as deliverers. I can understand this, from my present perspective. We Venetians had insisted that every priest on the island be in communion with Rome. Muzzaffer allowed the beards and cossacks of eastern orthodoxy back. If the man in charge of the island's secular law was a mufti, the people cared little as long as Greek could be the tongue that sent them to heaven and incense and icons greeted them in their churches every Sunday.

Muzzaffer Pasha also allowed the people, who had lived on their lands as serfs according to Byzantine custom, to buy those lands for a nominal sum and to work them as free men. That was Turkish custom. It seemed to produce better results.

Within three years a pressing from new Cypriot grapes arrived in Constantinople as per the tax schedule. But no one was able to tell whether the vintage was as good as that in former times. Selim was dead and could not say whether the price he had paid in Turkish lives, subject suffering, and drain on the treasury was worth it.

Selim was dead and with him, one thought, Nassey's claim to Cyprus's throne. Nassey had no friend in the new Sultan. No one was surprised, when the time came to reward Muzzaffer Pasha with a fourth horsetail to his banner and a transfer to a *sandjak* closer to home, that the Divan totally overlooked promises made by a predecessor. Nassey would fade, we all suspected, like the sign in front of his house.

So I was somewhat startled to see, as I happened to pass it one day, a eunuch from Nur Banu's suite entering under the shadow of Cyprus's wooden coat of arms. But Nassey, when he was in favor, was favored by Safiye. I could find no explanation for the *khadim*'s presence there, and I had business of my own to attend to, so I soon forgot the event.

I remembered it again in a hurry as things progressed.

At the time, that afternoon was more memorable to me for another reason. I was the last soul to leave the street in front of our house. The heat had closed all shops and driven all other errand-runners indoors some time before. I was grateful for the cool that greeted me in the cavern of cypress trees and jasmine of the master's garden. It was cooler still within the house and there I was welcomed by Gul Ruh's joyful shouts. Their echoes were to my ears like sherbet to a dry tongue. I decided to put off entering the *haremlik* for a moment to follow the sounds and refresh my eyes on her as well.

A fountain splashed in the middle of a courtyard in the *selamlik* where, when he chose to pray at home, the master could perform his ablutions. About this, like sparkling water herself, the young mistress was scampering, skipping, playing tag. Whenever I saw her like this, I was always glad for the sin that caused her to be, even when the master looked at me and commented that she seemed to have nothing of him in her at all.

She was a beautiful child—young lady now, almost nine years old. She had her father's (her real father's) height as well as his fine features translated into feminine terms so she could have been older. Her coloring was burnished and healthy—Esmikhan's, only brought to life by exercise and sunlight. Whenever she lost that color occasionally during a childhood illness, it always came back quickly with more vigor than ever. Each scrape, however, drained Esmikhan with worry and her bloom did not return. Sometimes it seemed that the transfer of health and strength between mother and child had not ended when the midwife cut the cord. Or even at weaning.

When the girl was healthy, which was most of the time, Esmikhan needed something to fret about and she found it in her daughter's hair. True, it was not curly, thick, and luxurious, "strong" hair, as fashion preferred. "You'll have to eke it out with skeins of black wool when you are older," Esmikhan told her daughter with a sigh nearly every day. But it grew long instead and the two braids which bounced behind her that afternoon seemed to have life of their own that heavier hair could never possess, and life of a more ethereal sort. No thicker than heddle ends, still when they flew, they could set the sleepiest old cat in the weaver's shop to playing.

Gul Ruh was playing with Muhammed the Prince who was, I think, at our house more often than his own, at least as often as he could escape his tutors. That afternoon their play was even livelier than usual, for they were joined by Arab Pasha.

Arab Pasha was the son of the old black slave woman who had served Sokolli Pasha before I even came. Although deaf and nearly blind, she seemed to shed twenty years to have him home again. I'm not good at picking out features when they're set in dusk, but I've never doubted that old Ali was his father. Still, some gossiped that Sokolli himself had sired the man in a time when a purchased African was all the progeny he hoped to ever deserve.

It is true that Sokolli Pasha had given Arab Pasha all the advantages a father could: a splendid education among the palace pages and then the influence to secure him the best posts. Yet, had the young man not had so much intrinsic ability, I'm sure Sokolli wouldn't have seen him past a scullery job. Now that he had earned three horsetails to his standard practically on his own, Arab Pasha was the name the Grand Vizier had put forward as the new governor of Cyprus to replace Muzzaffer.

My master admired and loved (in as far as he was capable of such emotion) the young pasha; while neither beauty nor weakness moved him, ability always did. My young mistress in her own, much more open way, adored him, as sister never loved brother before, and it was her name for him, "Brabi," given before she could talk straight, that composed half her shrieks around the fountain that afternoon.

From the breast of his shirt, Gul Ruh had stolen Arab Pasha's pouch of Turkish tobacco. They were playing keep-away all around the fountain with it, and the girl, who had Muhammed on her side, managed to keep ahead of the pasha's great long legs for quite some time on her dancing thin ones.

Prince Muhammed thought by his devotion to win back some of his adored cousin's attention, which always suffered when the black man came home. The prince served her long and well in the fray and then could not understand why, when the pasha cheated and won—leaping right over the fountain with his long black legs and pouncing on the girl like a panther—why she curled and giggled in his arms as if *they* had been conspirators from the first.

Initially, Gul Ruh struggled, leaping like a little puppy after a table scrap for the pouch the young Pasha held high over his head. She had force enough to tumble him, with her on top, to a seat upon the fountain's edge. Here tickling and toying slaps fell exhausted at last to a cozy embrace, with her head on his shoulder and her hand still in the breast of his caftan. I noticed the contrast of skins: hairless white against the thick, curled black.

Muhammed sat to one side of the pair like a discarded cloak by the bedside; I couldn't escape the image. He scuffed his crimson slipper against the flags and whined from time to time, "Gul Ruh. Gul Ruh. Let's play . . ."

Then the master arrived. He entered by the same archway I had. A few steps behind me, he said, "Ah, Arab, I was just——"

A few steps beyond me he stopped stock still for a moment. Then another moment passed. He had taken the scene in and knew what he must do. His only struggle now was with his own awkwardness. He could command armies, but this put a blinding glare in others' eyes and in his own at how helpless he was in the shadows of the harem. Times like this made him wish that between this awkwardness and the last he'd taken some time out from the Divan and the training field to practice these black arts.

"Daughter, come here," he said.

The two faces, the white and the black, looked up from themselves, startled not only by the sound but by the recollection that there were other people in the world. Once over her shock, Gul Ruh smiled and luxuriated her head back against the young pasha's shoulder.

"Hello, Papa," she cooed.

The uncomfortable softness her voice gave him put an edge on his. "I said, come here."

Her eyes grew big with wonder, almost—should it be?—fear. She got to her feet and came to stand before him. A single toss of his head said, "To the harem."

She went, her braids as stiff as rods. The only backwards look she dared was for her father.

The Grand Vizier now motioned me to him. That was easier. I was at least half a man. He took my elbow as if for support, but was very firm when he said, so quietly neither of the others could hear, "It is time. She is your charge now."

I understood and bowed. Later I heard the voice of Prince Muhammed wailing, "I want to see Gul Ruh. I have to see Gul Ruh again," echoing into the heart of our harem like the disembodied voice of the jinn in the cypress on a windy night. It was the same wail he'd given as they'd driven his nurse away when he was a baby, only now there were words to it.

Only then did I finally feel the full impact of the day and realized that, for the two cousins, this was a very real sort of death. From now on, even when she went to call on the boy's mother, Gul Ruh would have to veil closely if ever the young Prince came in the room. And I would have to speak for her while she quickly withdrew.

Muhammed was beyond the prohibited degrees of relationship: father, brother, and uncle. Sex was conceivable beyond that pale, hence, face-to-face contact was inconceivable. From this I understood that Arab Pasha was not the master's son. If he had been, then their contact would not have startled Sokolli Pasha into seeing how close his daughter was to puberty, for brothers and sisters are always allowed to be intimate.

Gul Ruh had no brother. Until she married, her male companionship, beyond her father, was at an end. Her grief, unlike her cousin's, was soundless.

And some weeks later Sokolli Pasha freed, then married one of our slave girls to Arab Pasha. It was the master's rather awkward (awkward because so extravagant, especially on top of the appointment to Cyprus) way of showing his protégé his affection.

When we took the bride for her day in the bath, Gul Ruh had to run back to her rooms in tears. She barely survived the Henna Night, and the wedding night she couldn't endure at all.

I'm not certain what particulars of the marriage bed Gul Ruh knew. Unlike in the West, women safe in their harems never curb their tongues in the presence of children when discussing such matters. Esmikhan was somewhat more inclined to modesty than most, probably because any mention of intimacy must call to her mind but a single event, and that stolen event was one she must not, under any circumstances, divulge.

Gul Ruh knew at least that marriage entailed great intimacy. She knew that this freed slave of a bride was allowed to go with honor and ritual to the presence of her adored Arab Pasha, whereas she, a princess of the blood, could only ever catch a glimpse of him through the lattice again. The hurt, grief, and jealousy was almost more than Gul Ruh could bear.

Something else about this marriage should be mentioned, not because I found it important then but because of what happened afterwards. The guests were eating wedding soup spun with threads of egg and plenty of lambs' fat making rainbows on the surface, such a pottage said to give the couple the strength they need for their exertions. There were also great pyramids of party pancakes, dipped in orange blossom syrup, heaped with buffalo cream, and sprinkled with pistachios. My lady was an expert when it came to filling the house with the smell of warm butter and sugar.

In the midst of these festivities, Nur Banu put in an appearance, by which we were much surprised and professed great honor. The Queen Mother at the wedding of a slave! Esmikhan offered her stepmother a seat of honor next to the bride, and Nur Banu took it as if she would have demanded it had it not been immediately forthcoming.

Here she spent a great deal of time speaking to the bride in an undertone. That is, of course, a matronly guest's prerogative and it is thus that a girl learns what she might expect from the married state. Many women take this opportunity to exercise their souls of griefs and disappointments in their own lives. So I suspected nothing. Even the words I did happen to overhear as I offered the Valide Sultan a narghile, though I found them odd, did not make me suspicious.

"Too bad he is black," Nur Banu said. "The seed of a black man can curdle your inside. It is work, I tell you, to get healthy children by them."

Here she stopped to screw the mouthpiece she had brought with her—it was the old, mellowed jade one—to the smoking apparatus. Then she continued, "It is the same with the governing posts they are sent to. They begin by serving as well or better than any white man. But soon, Allah alone knows why, their affairs turn muddy, black . . ."

It is unfortunate the girl was so young and fresh from the hills of Caucasia, too, where people are very isolated and superstitious. She believed, her eyes wide and frightened, what the Queen Mother told her.

XXXII

CHRISTIANS IN CONSTANTINOPLE will remember this time. Their solemn feast celebrating Our Lady's Ascension was tragically interrupted that year. The janissaries were restive because Murad had declared no war at all that season—something that had never happened in the history of the Ottomans before—in consideration of the famine.

Having nothing better to do, a band of soldiers were spending their seventy-five *akçe* "tax" on wine. The wine sellers were wise to the debasement and only offered drink three-quarters water to match the three-quarters copper in the coin. Still the men had managed to imbibe enough to get rowdy and they began to take as their entertainment a mockery of the Christian solemnities. Some young acolytes, seeing what a small and disorganized band the soldiers were, decided to defend themselves. The brawl that ensued ended only with the death of a priest, the rape of several pious Christian matrons, and the church itself a pile of smoldering ashes.

Muslims will remember these days as well. Not for the brawl: that had little effect in their quarters but a few bumps and bruises, all imported. Nonetheless, it was the day after the brawl that my master entered the Divan smoldering like the apse of the ruined church.

"By Allah," he said, "these Christians are our wards. They are People of the Book, people who pay tribute into our coffers—practically all we have coming in now—so that we will protect them. We must let them live their religion—inferior as it is—in peace. We are honorbound before Allah to shield them. How shall it be when word of this comes to our borders? There are people—Christians and Jews—recently surrendered to our sway because we gave them our word they would receive protection and rights far and above what they had under the rapacious, petty Christian kings before. 'Well,' they will say, 'even in the capital, Muslims do not keep their word.'"

Sokolli Pasha was also unnerved by the unquiet mood he sensed in the troops. If such a mood were indulged at this moment, when there was nothing left with which to buy them off, rebellion was just around the corner. Sokolli Pasha conferred with the Agha of the Janissaries and got clear support from the Mufti, whom he never failed to impress with piety. The measure passed easily and in a matter of moments went from the Divan to the courtyard where it was read: "Any Muslim found drunk on wine against all command of Allah and His Prophet will suffer the pain of death."

Heavy sobriety met the announcement and reigned, only slightly appeased by the return of the Sultan from a late summer hunt in the mountains near Edirne. Murad was not like his father, an incurable sot, to seek to overturn the law himself. He did indulge from time to time, but the way he did it—always eyeing the red crystal closely like a miniature painting, sniffing and sipping at it with an artist's care— made drinking, to go along with the liturgy of his poems, something more like a sacrament. If left to himself, Murad might have let the whole thing pass, like the twenty other times such a law was on the books, as a useful piece of present discipline to be slowly relaxed, conveniently forgotten over time.

As his companion in the hunt, however, Murad had taken Uweis the Turk, and that man returned to the smoldering city with him.

Surely I have mentioned this man Uweis before. He was one of the faithful four who stood in the wind and the rain that night when Selim was dead, Murad not yet Sultan. When he'd stood there, he'd been a short, quiet man somewhat afraid of his first trip to the city. Like some exotic woodland beast, we all thought when we first learned of him. But years in Constantinople among the favorites had changed him.

Uweis had put on a lot of weight, which did not set well on his short legs, relatively long waist, and stubby neck. It gave him the proportions of a dwarf. A huge mustache he vainly curled and tended and the yards of gaudy-striped turbans he affected made this frame seem top-heavy and unstable. From one ear he dangled a foppish parade of jewels, and his trousers were shimmering satin, shot with gold, and so voluminous they would be useless for horseback. Someone must have told him that tying the layers of a sash around his midriff accentuated the fat. He'd taken to wearing it bound tightly around his hips instead (or maybe it simply wouldn't stay up on the globe of his stomach), tourniqueting his legs. Such a sash forced the belly out into an even greater bulge, which sagged despondently over the bands like a merchant's pouch. It was ironic that the costume designed by the original Turks who rode lean and fast off the steppes with scimitars flashing should suit this Uweis, the only man of pure Turkish descent I knew, so ill.

One who had never met the man before would have sensed something incongruous about him at first glance. Then one had only to wait 'til he opened his mouth for the mystery to be made plain. His Turkish was rarified—the language of peasants and thieves. In the palace, even the simplest page keeping the back door peppers his speech with gracious allusions to the Persian poets or the Arabic religion. And Uweis had tried to pick up these affectations, too. But they came to his throat in hiccups of bad grammar and botcheries. If he'd had any sense, he'd have kept his mouth shut. But of course, such restraint was foreign to Uweis.

We often wondered what it was that made Murad keep the man about. Murad was, after all, one who strove for high culture. It seemed the Sultan might have done better to leave the Turk, like a favorite horse, at his hunting lodge where he could be kept and groomed and exercised to be in good shape when the master wanted him. That was always the excuse given for his perpetual presence—Uweis could track anything over any terrain for any distance. Those of us who'd never been hunting with the royal party wondered how that could be so, at least any more, when those dwarfish legs must send him crashing through the brush like a wounded bear, that awkward weight might well make even a workhorse stumble.

I suppose, like the poet who wrote of the fresh mountain breeze blowing through the heavy, scented garden, Murad liked the aesthetics of sharp contrast. Uweis was allowed to stay like a jester to give life at court perspective. Still, I cannot understand why Murad sought sense from mere shadows, no matter how dark and full of contrast they were.

After the fact, I learned of a particularly graceless remark Uweis made in the Divan which, because of that Turk's favor, Sokolli Pasha had to let pass unchallenged.

"By Allah," the little man had said between his teeth in language that made the hearers cringe, "what is a born Christian doing, dictating virtue to those of us who were born to the muezzin's call, whose fathers have taught us Islam since his father was still a barbarian? Watch him, my lords. I wouldn't be surprised if beneath that holier-than-thou mien there lurked a heart plotting mischief."

That four or five others present were also originally drafted from the subject peoples and the quotation of the old proverb, "There is no faith like new faith," left him still unsubdued.

Coincidentally, it was that same day my mistress mentioned she had been visited by Nur Banu while I was out.

"What did the Valide Sultan want?"

"The same old pleasantries. No new gossip. She did seem disappointed that Sokolli Pasha had not yet returned from the Divan." Esmikhan took a stab or two at her needlework and then said, almost to herself, "Strange."

"What is strange, my lady?"

"Do you remember that wonderfully heavy golden girdle the Queen Mother used to have?"

I didn't, but I pretended to because Esmikhan grew impatient with me whenever I indicated that fashion was not among my major interests.

"She didn't wear it today?"

"Oh, she did," Esmikhan replied, "But it used to have such a wonderful pearl on the end of it. As big as a bantam's egg."

"And?"

"And it didn't today. You can't imagine that she could have lost something like that, can you? The whole palace would have been turned inside out until it was found. And if it were stolen, surely we would have heard about it."

"Yes. Well, she must have given it away."

"Yes. But to whom? Whom does Nur Banu favor so?"

I had no answer.

My master did curious things under stress. That Sunday—for some reason the Divan did not sit that day, though its pressures pursued him—Sokolli Pasha insisted that the entire household join him for a sail on the Bosphorus.

Most of the girls, of course, were ecstatic with the prospect of such diversion. My job keeping them from becoming too diverted and my hope of pleasure practically canceled each other out. My lady had to be bodily carried onto the boat, but once made comfortable with cushions and sherbets I think even she enjoyed herself.

On the strait, in the sunlight, a stiff breeze sent wavelets flying like a swirl of so many autumn leaves. The air was good and strong and the heave of the rowers and the smell of fish and salt and tar brought days of my youth to mind. Gul Ruh and a few of the other girls pressed me and so I regaled them with memories. Sometimes in the midst of a recollection, I would catch Esmikhan's eyes and we would smile at one another, remembering. It was a healthy day, indeed, for I managed to tell my tales without expressing or even feeling bitterness.

Any man passed thirty-five has learned that his life will not be all they promised when he was a boy. Perhaps my youth as I told it was a little more lively than the reality, but I could leave it behind now with less regret.

Gul Ruh grew bright-cheeked and laughed, and she and the girls went to the side of the boat and pretended to catch fishes like we sailors used to do. I scolded and told my seconds to keep an eye on them. The girls pretended to repent, but when I went out on the prow to enjoy the full, fresh spray on my face, I continued to see a flash of white arm creep out between the red and gold curtains from time to time. They pretended to repent and I pretended not to see their later transgressions. Those flashes of white, I thought, could not be seen by any but the closest passing ship. And even to them, those arms must remain anonymous.

I looked back at my master's boat. Yes, he had come with his family, but in a separate, smaller boat and never so close as to make it appear to any that there was any relationship. The Grand Vizier sat cross-legged under a fringed awning, yet without the close curtains a harem bark was obliged to carry. The only companions he had brought along were not for pleasure, but for work: A pair of secretaries and a pasha visiting from an eastern *sandjak* kept him thoroughly occupied. Did Sokolli Pasha realize we were on the water at all?

We had crossed the strait now and were halfway through the excursion. The far shore of the Golden Horn, beyond the enclosure of Galatea, spilled unrestrained by walls or fortifications down to the very water—unpainted wooden houses with rickety balconies on stilts dipped in like hasty bathers. This was Pera, the main colony of Venetians and other Christian foreigners.

"Careful some housewife doesn't come out and throw her slops down on us," I cautioned the captain as we sailed very close under the railings.

He saluted and we laughed together. He would try. Although that was a distinct possibility—as the rubbish we floated through testified—it was much more likely that we would be spied on by some foreign diplomat. These houses on the shore, though old and shabby, were great favorites for such men because they could sit on the balcony, gaze over the water at the domes of the Serai and imagine for their reports home all sorts of things one could never actually see.

So let them look! I said to myself.

I gave one brief thought to Andrea Barbarigo, now Muslim, the navy's dragoman, to wonder if he missed that diplomatic life. One good whiff of sea air assured me he didn't. I sat back to enjoy the journey.

XXXIII

PRESENTLY I HEARD sounds that reminded me of another thing for which these seaside houses were popular. Christians, to whom wine is allowed, keep public houses there to attract sailors—and anyone else desirous of a quaff. In the realm of Islam, Sunday had ceased to be the very different color from any other day of the week a pious nurse had given it in my childhood. But had I stopped to think that it *was* Sunday, it might not have taken me quite so long to notice. The explosions of laughter carried on by riotous talk and snatches of song that reached our ears from a festooned balcony up ahead had curiously unchristian tones

in them. We had rowed close to the inn's back door before what I saw
made me unable to trust my eyes. I referred to equally bewildered
ears.

The balcony was crowded with janissaries like a harvest basket with
fruit, their blue trousers pressing through the railings like plump, ripe
plums through wicker. Their songs were Turkish and familiar—my
master would recognize them as those that came from the camp of the
Faithful after Allah had granted them victory. Now these songs were
being blasphemed.

That was my first reaction: to wish to throw up a curtain before my
master as if he were part of the harem, to keep these renegades from
seeing his nakedness and dishonoring him. Or is it the harem we would
protect from profanation with the world? At any rate, God alone knows
where I might have found a curtain so big as to keep Good from Evil in
the world. By the time I'd freed my gaze from the powerful latch impiety has, I saw that Sokolli Pasha, too, had already seen, and his reaction
was now beyond my power. All I could do was to command our rowers to do their best to bring the women, at least, away from there.

I saw my master giving orders to his sailors to find a landing on the
beach and then to one of his servants to run quickly and find the first
sober squadron he could to come and arrest these miscreants. The servant, I could tell, didn't much like the idea. He'd rather they were on
the Hungarian front and he'd been asked to run espionage behind
enemy lines. Surely the chances of death were no greater; it was the
grade of honor attached to the death that worried him. Nonetheless,
when the beach was hit, he got off the boat and disappeared up among
Pera's firetrap jumble of raw wooden houses.

I've always had the impression that our outing was known and that
the entire episode was staged. What happened next tends to confirm
this.

Drink had made the lookout in the inn (if indeed the caution to post
such a man had been taken) very lax. Now at last we were sighted from
the shore. The vision of my master in white and gold beneath his
canopy—and only the Sultan himself is allowed more rowers, more
pomp, and more horsetails on the prow for a pleasure outing—could
not help but silence even the most indigent lush, and the words passed
back from the railing in a hush: "Sokolli! Sokolli Pasha is come!"

Up from their midst there arose——if a man of just over five feet can be said to rise in the midst of the finest figures of manhood the western provinces can produce, all topped by the tall turbans typical of the elect troops——the round, bloated figure of none other than Uweis the Turk. He heaved his great belly onto the railing for support and the two antagonists stared at one another across it for some time.

A jewel even more remarkable than usual hung in the little man's ear: It was a pearl the shape and size of a bantam's egg.

Then the little Turk, the bantam-egg pearl adangle from his ear, raised his right hand in a salute. In that hand was a goblet full of the forbidden drink. With great but mock solemnity, he toasted: "Sokolli Pasha, your health."

Behind him, all the troops stood as to attention, likewise raised their flasks and repeated, "Your health, Sokolli Pasha!"

Then they all drank deeply and in unison. But the riot of laughter into which this formation disintegrated was like no other loss of discipline the Ottoman army had ever seen before.

A shower of rotten fruit and vegetables pocked the water like cannon charges. There was also a skin or two of wine thrown as the revelers invited the Grand Vizier to join them in a practice that was "as lifting to the heart as if we'd all died and gone to Paradise already. To hell with martyrdom on the battlefield!"

But wine was too precious to spend in a jest so. The men soon toppled one of their number over the rail and into the water to flounder drunkenly about in an attempt to retrieve those skins. Throwing one man over offered such amusement that two or three soon joined him, along with the innkeeper's wife . . .

Our rowers were laying to as hard as they could, and after this, distance added to the general chaos so I could no longer tell details. I could no longer bear to, either.

For the women behind their curtains, the episode passed without effect, almost without comment. Even if they did understand in a vague sort of way what it meant, certainly none of them took it to be a personal threat to themselves. The rest of the excursion was so pleasant, in fact, that my lady played at seasickness in an attempt to make it last longer.

The segregation of sexes, we are always told, is to keep the weakness of women from interfering in men's more important business. Once again I wondered if it isn't also to keep women in honor above the ugly mire that men's business wallows in.

My master returned much, much later, having spent hours arguing his case with Murad. To no avail, of course. The Sultan would not hear of injuring the honor of one with whom he'd just enjoyed the pleasant camaraderie of the hunt, much less injuring his neck on the chopping block. Even the honor of a Grand Vizier, the honor of the State, were trivial matters in comparison.

Like other similar laws before it, that law has never been rescinded. It remains on the books for future rulers to ignore or to apply as the whim suits them.

Sokolli Pasha alone seemed to feel the weight of what this might do to the discipline of the troops and to public morale throughout the courtyards and back lanes of the empire. It was there the tale had flown as fast as pigeons gone home to roost. Of course it was upon Sokolli's shoulders that the scandal and dishonor fell most squarely—and for no reason, it seemed, but a mad whim of Allah. My master wore the face of a man in the prime of life who awakens one morning to find his whole left side paralyzed.

That night I stood at my post to see if he would send to the harem for a girl for comfort—simply to beat her, perhaps, as others do. But my master was never like that. I stood longer to see if he would like to talk, but he was never like that, either. My master never trusted but a very few with even a half of his thoughts. This hard time might have been eased if he had been a different man.

But had he been a different man, such a time would never have come to him.

My master went alone that night into his room and shut the door behind him. I could consider myself dismissed, but I sat up much later, seeing the light under the door and knowing Sokolli could not sleep either.

That night Sokolli Pasha wrote a very long letter in his own hand. It went to the one person he trusted most of all—Arab, now governor of Cyprus. Arab Pasha, who'd come as close to flesh and blood as my master ever knew.

XXXIV

"ABDULLAH, COME HERE."

It was Gul Ruh's voice stifled into a whisper that drew my attention up into the big plane tree by the wall.

That girl! A year since she'd first been sent to the harem and still she was fighting it. I'd put one of my assistants on her full time. A jolly, fat eunuch, I'd chosen him because he could tell tales and jokes and sing songs that kept her satisfied at his knees for hours on end. But he did like his narghile with a few grains of opium in it, and when he'd start that bubbling, you could bet Gul Ruh would not sit quietly beside him doing needlework. Then I had to go off and find her myself.

"No, come right up here," she insisted, pointing to the limb beside her. Simply standing at the trunk to break her fall was not enough.

A plane tree by a garden wall on a cool day in early spring. It reminded me of another day and another place when another girl—just slightly older than this one as the sun tells time, but much, much older in reality—had piped me to my fate with a bawdy song.

Turkish women's *shalvar*, I noticed, made climbing tress much easier than full Venetian skirts and farthingales. Once up there, they were basically more modest, too. Still, they could be pulled suggestively tight. The gauzy bodice (and Gul Ruh's vest was perpetually missing a little pearl button or two) revealed more than a hard bone corset just how close to being a woman she was. Her satin slippers were scuffed from the climb and hung from her feet by only the toes. The bare ankles, white but firm, crossed and uncrossed with excitement at just my nose's level.

Had I been the man who'd climbed the convent's garden wall, I would have refused to join her. Pride and a little petulance would have hidden the flush in my face, the racing of my heart and the tightness in my codpiece. The victory of forcing my will over hers, of getting her down from the tree when she wanted me up—by physical means if necessary—would be practice for the more intimate forcing I would have had next in mind.

But I loved my little mistress in a way that was foreign tongue to the passion of my youth and yet, I believe, having known them both, was more true and enduring. I tried the branch carefully to see if it would hold us both, then joined her there. It had been a lifetime, I realized sadly, since I'd climbed a ship's rigging like a little monkey. The long, heavy robes of my office did not help matters, either. Gul Ruh had to cover her giggles with her hand as she watched my struggle up.

"The Jew, Joseph Nassey," I replied, panting from the struggle, to her first question, "Who is that?"

But to her second, "What is he doing there in front of our gate?" I could not answer at all.

"I'll go ask," I offered, but she did not send me and I didn't go at once. We both just sat and watched with wonder the spectacle that appeared between the naked branches of the plane tree.

Had we not been the only ones about, I would have dragged the girl down from the tree in an instant. In spite of the meager and unknown audience we made, Joseph Nassey walked to and fro in front of the master's gate with a mincing stiffness in his hips that said he expected more eyes. His head was thrown back, singing or shouting, I couldn't tell which in the distance. And, hung around his neck by its heavy iron chain, he wore the wooden coat of arms that had swung so long and so vainly in front of his own house.

We watched this spectacle together for some time. Gul Ruh reached through the branches of the tree to hold my hand for protection against the strangeness of it. But finally a question without an answer bored her and she scrambled down of her own accord and went back into the house to provoke her personal guardian into entertainment.

As I had more means to unscramble the puzzle at my disposal, I pursued it much longer and was finally able to discover the man's purpose. He had taken heart by the recent and public displays of Sokolli Pasha's weakness and thought the time ripe to bid for his long-denied kingship once more. Since Selim's death, free access to the Divan had been refused to the Jew and so he determined on this plot to call attention to himself.

Years of heavy disappointment weighed on him: Few who saw his protest did not consider it at least halfway mad. But the intelligence I received from the palace led me to believe Nassey would, indeed, have earned his Cyprus by this ploy if for no other reason than that it would give a slap to Sokolli and to his favorite Arab Pasha.

Fortunately, the hand of God moved in. Whether it was a damp, cold night in the street he couldn't stand at his age, whether his madness, or whether foul play was involved (there were no sure signs of it, so my master escaped suspicion), the man was found dead in the gutter in the morning. His coat of arms hung rudely awry about his iron-cold neck, as if it had choked him.

It fell my master's lot to see that the deceased's property returned to the royal coffers. The house and furniture were sold, the gold, silver, jewels, and slaves were confiscated and brought in bulk to the rooms beyond the sacred protection of the Prophet's Cloak in the palace. This was the usual practice when a Jew or a Christian whose wealth was so largely due to the favors of the Sultan died; they cannot secure their goods' separate perpetuation by the founding of charities attached to the mosques.

※

ONE WEEK AFTER Joseph Nassey's death, my master had me collect some women's clothes "of substantial size," and a full apricot-colored veil. He instructed me to bring them to a house near the Small Khan, then pick them up again—on the person of the new addition to our harem.

"Bring her to me!" Esmikhan cried when she heard. "I will scratch her eyes out!"

The thought of such a confrontation I did not relish. Although I had only seen the new girl in her veils, even then I could tell she was no mean figure. At least one advantage she had over my lady: She was mobile on her feet, if somewhat heavy. And that heaviness might be due to her awkwardness with a veil if she were new to the land of the Faithful.

Still, somehow I doubted her novitiate. Though I'd been unable to provoke a word from her, not even the statement of her name, she

seemed to understand quickly enough when directions were given. She
climbed into the sedan chair and turned right or left down the hallway
with none of the usual hand signals and gentle shoves a eunuch had to
use with new slaves.

Irrational as it was, one could hardly blame my lady's reaction. Never
had she had cause to be jealous before, never had the master given her
one. She was one Sultan's daughter and the sister of another. No woman
bought on the block could ever supplant her in that harem, should she
bear a thousand sons. And it was perfectly legitimate that Sokolli Pasha
should find someone younger, stronger, more beautiful to be his companion in idle hours. Indeed, gossips only wondered why he had not
done so years ago. Still, it was not a comfortable position for my mistress to find herself in so suddenly and so without precedent.

Her discomfort tended to out-and-out panic, mostly because the
new addition remained a complete unknown. There was no chance to
observe her strengths, plot to combat them, or to wheedle out weaknesses and find them great enough for eternal damnation. The new
slave remained in the *mabein*—that room of connubial bliss which had
been unused for years—and was allowed no visitor but the master and
myself. This was not Sokolli's mere suggestion; it was a holy commandment to which he made me swear my life.

Normally, Sokolli Pasha made few requests concerning the harem.
Like weather and seasons, we came and went and carried out our business as if by the will of Allah alone. He gave little thought to the
processes which were my whole occupation. Therefore, when he did
choose to take a stand against the elements, I would certainly do my
best to see that he was obeyed, almost as if he were a wonder-working
saint.

And so my lady alternately tried on new jewels and gowns to improve her attractions, swore violence, and conferred with a whole string
of midwives and holy women about spells, amulets, and potions. The
house reeked of wild rue and Job's tears, the prime ingredients of such
concoctions. I nearly lost my heart out of my throat one time when I
came upon the dried skin of a snake and viper's fangs set carefully in a
niche—witchcraft. But desperate measures were called for, anything
that might serve to improve Esmikhan's position, with the help of Allah.
Her own powers, it was clear, must fail miserably.

I alone visited the *mabein* twice a day with food on a tray. From curiosity as much as politeness I would offer the newcomer a bath or try to draw her into conversation, or even only try to get her to take off her veil so she might have more air. Although every scrap of any quantity of food had vanished when I returned, I always locked the door to the *mabein* behind me unsatisfied.

"I do not know," I had to reply to my lady's distraught enquiries after anything and everything.

"But my husband," she said, biting her lip, "still spends time with her?"

"Several hours at least every night."

"Night only?"

"As far as I know."

"Oh, Allah, night is night! What do they do?"

"That, my lady, is their business and Allah's alone. But I have heard talking. Low talk at least. That's more than she's ever given me."

Here my lady would burst into tears and exclaim wildly, "She must bathe soon or the neighbors will complain of the smell. She must have her menses some time this month and he will not approach her then. Unless, oh, Allah forbid, she is with child already and then . . ." Things of that nature babbled over her lips until the stress overcame her with silence.

One day I met Gul Ruh dawdling about the *mabein* door when I brought the new girl the evening meal. My young lady was there when I came out again so I knew it was not just by chance.

"Abdullah, let me in to see her, please. I won't scratch her eyes out like Mother would."

"Off with you, silly girl," I said, giving her backside a playful swat.

Gul Ruh's eyes watched me narrowly as I replaced the *mabein* key carefully into my belt for safekeeping.

"Abdullah," she stopped me to ask a day later. "Do ladies in your country relieve themselves standing up?"

"We are not like the wild Arabs of the desert," I told her decidedly. "Our women squat the same as you. Why do you ask such a question, little monkey?"

"No reason. Just wondered."

As she turned to run off, I noticed a smear of dirty red brick color on one sleeve and across the neighboring hip. I called her attention to it, warning how angry the laundress would be when she saw that on new yellow silk.

"Oh, she'll get over it," Gul Ruh said carelessly, dusting vigorously as she disappeared down the hallway.

Thinking, she's always running somewhere, I turned myself in the opposite direction and proceeded about my own business. As I did, I felt an unusual draft and then saw that the latch on one of the lattices on the windows of that hallway was open. When I went to close it, I paused a moment before the vision of sky, iron-grey with a relapse into winter. Then I saw a clean patch on the red tile just below the window. It was the very same dirty brick red as Gul Ruh had worn on her jacket sleeve.

And then I saw something that made my heart stop. Not far from the smear of red was a missing tile. My young mistress had come within a hand's breadth of falling to the courtyard, two stories below. By Allah, and she hadn't even been out of breath!

Looking to either side to see I was not watched (even as she must have done), I climbed onto the ledge myself and then onto the tiles, my legs shaking as they felt for other loose spots. I looked down and grew dizzy, not fearing for myself, for I usually have no such fear, but fearing for her. On the pebbles of the courtyard below I saw a glint of gold— a woman's broken bangle in a place it could never have gotten except from the air, for that yard was in the public *selamlik*.

Very well, it was quite clear Gul Ruh had been out on that roof and saved from a horrible accident only by the Merciful One. But what had she been doing there? To the left, the housetops of the city lay in a fascinating jumble: the back alleyways and open markets, the parks, mosques, and caravanserais. To the right, over the rather ill-defined mass of the palace, ships on the Bosphorus with the hills of Asia, gauzed that day like women's breasts, lay in the distance. There was much for a child to see there, indeed, a child grown oh-so weary of being cooped up like a rabbit in a hutch.

The view towards Asia was blocked somewhat by the cupola that domed over the *mabein*. I could just press between it and the wall of the harem—it would be easier for a ten-year-old—and when I had done that, I saw what she must have seen. There, on the other side of the cupola, was a tiny courtyard with a dried-up fountain, weedy beds, and trees sadly in need of the pruner's hook. It was a courtyard that could only be reached from the *mabein,* where the architect had imagined the lord and his favorite could spend many delightful hours together. Although in demand throughout the Believing world, Sinan the architect had woefully misread the needs of this particular client— until now. Now I saw how commodious the yard was. There was even a tiny outhouse in one corner, open with large windows to let in fresh air—and the spying glance of a girl on the harem roof.

So I discovered that Gul Ruh must have seen—well, something. I climbed back inside, latched the window tightly and immediately called in workmen. They fixed the tile and then hammered a well-placed nail in the lattice to hold it to the frame. While they were at work, I cordoned off that part of the harem for them and made sure one of my seconds watched their every movement. I also dropped a word to the veiled figure in the *mabein:* She should keep indoors during daylight hours if she didn't want to be seen.

Then I went down into the courtyard of the *selamlik* and retrieved the broken bangle. When I'd had it repaired, I found an opportunity to speak with Gul Ruh alone. I caught her by the wrist from which the ornament had broken and replaced it, saying simply as I did, "I hope you don't make me do this again."

I think she understood my message, for I left her fingering the mended hoop in a subdued manner.

XXXV

WHAT GUL RUH suspected after that I didn't know. But I had begun to have suspicions of my own.

It was incredible. Such things happened only in the Thousand and One Nights. Gul Ruh, for whose child's idealism life still had the qualities of a fairy tale, might leap to such conclusions easier than I. That I should begin to reach them, too, was one more point towards substantiation.

The matter was clinched, in my mind, at least, by the events of the very next morning.

"Abdullah, come here."

From my master's tone I caught the fact that we were on display now. From his eye I caught more than that: an almost desperate look that I must not fail him now.

"Master?" I replied, and made obeisance to the ground, a formality we never had recourse to when we were alone.

"Abdullah, these men would like a word with you."

He turned, and turned me with him, to the room. The visitors—if they could be called that, for they had penetrated far into the house, to the very door of the *mabein*—were brazenly making a search of every alcove, pulling back curtains, opening blanket chests, and peering into large jugs. Their uniforms and swords told me at once who they were: from the palace, the Sultan's personal bodyguard.

And my master and I were on the opposing side.

"You the head of the Grand Vizier's harem?" One of them confronted me.

"By Allah's most merciful favor," I replied, bowing again.

"Tell me, *khadim,* how's the honor of your harem?"

"By Allah, it's my life if my master's honor is not beyond reproach."

"But might it not also be your life if you do not aid your master in concealing something behind the walls of your precious harem?"

"Sir, my honor and my master's cannot allow you to continue in this vein. You will please retract such insinuation."

The captain of the troop now came face-to-face with the *mabein* door. He looked at it hard as if he wished to see through it, his hand reached out to try the door, but in the end the sanctity of the place kept even him from trying it. He turned his piercing stare on me then and I met it with what I hoped was discretion as solid as the wood of the door.

"Very well," the captain said. "I'll take your word, *khadim.* But you should know that this is a very serious matter."

"Wealth belonging to the Imperial coffers—to the Caliph of all the Faithful—has been lost," my master explained quietly, with a quiet hand on my shoulder. "Lost in the business of the death of Joseph Nassey."

" 'Stolen' is more like it," the captain said. "And if you are found to have had connection with this business, it will not go easy with you."

My master replied: "Good man, I assure you and his graciousness the Sultan, once again I assure you that no crime has been committed at all. My agents sold the Jew's goods exactly as I commanded them and every *akçe* was brought to the treasury. The accounts were carefully kept. I have shown them to his majesty many times. There is no failure there. If he expected the Jew's property to amount to more, that I cannot help. I cannot help that what the records say Sultan Selim—may he find mercy in Paradise—paid out to the man is more than three times the figure we got. Please remember, gentlemen, the present state of the currency and its effect on the marketplace. Besides, Joseph Nassey was obviously a spendthrift. We cannot be held responsible for that, just because of the dark suspicions that peasant Turk Uweis may harbor."

"Better that my lord Uweis harbor suspicions in defense of our master's goods than that you harbor the man wanted for questioning in connection with the pilfering—that man, Feridun Bey, your secretary. He has very curiously disappeared from the city."

"Would it were our master's goods that concerned Uweis. Unfortunately, the Sultan promised that small Turk all the dead Jew's goods as his own. It's greed that fuels his suspicions."

"Be careful what accusations you speak against Uweis Bey unless you can explain the whereabouts of your secretary."

"Feridun Bey is an honest man," Sokolli said. "Were every soul in the Divan as honest, they would recall that he was Keeper of the Imperial Seal for a time, and had proven his worth there long before I was fortunate enough to gain his talents for myself."

The captain moved in close to Sokolli Pasha, threatening. "Tell me where you have hidden this man of many talents, then."

"I do not know where the man is," my master repeated firmly.

And I came to my master's defense with these words: "What man would jeopardize the safety—not to mention the honor—of his harem by inducing something of that nature into it?"

But by the time the soldiers had turned on their heels to leave, I was convinced that when I next took a meal into the *mabein,* the features and gestures I might discern beneath the light apricot veil would be those of the secretary, Feridun Bey.

IT SEEMS UWEIS was not totally convinced by the blank wall of the harem, either, for that afternoon, in company with Nur Banu, the little Turk's wife came to pay a call on my lady. They had hardly been on speaking terms before.

We received them with customary and polite formality, with rosewater, tea, and little saucers of preserves. I didn't even bother to try to caution my lady against it. I knew as soon as the formalized phrases— "We are all well, Allah be praised"—had run out, nothing on earth could keep Esmikhan from bemoaning the fact that her position was being usurped by a newcomer. Had she suspected there was anything to hide, she could not help behaving in a suspicious manner, trying to cover up something that consumed her every waking thought. Better to give her free rein on this subject, common in all harems.

"Bring the girl out and let us judge the depth of the threat for ourselves," Nur Banu said.

Uweis's wife, a simple, silly woman, had been reduced to tears of sympathy in the first few minutes. But the Queen Mother was much shrewder. Indeed, Nur Banu probably endured her companion only because she could carry messages quickly to her husband, the Turkish hunter who had the Sultan's ear.

"She will not come out," my lady moaned.

Uweis's wife wanted to stay and talk. She knew only too well what it was like to have a younger, more beautiful woman catch her husband's fancy. But Nur Banu had learned now what she'd come for: that there was a newcomer in the harem whom nobody had seen. She did not draw the visit out.

"Thank heaven they're gone!" Gul Ruh exclaimed when I returned from seeing the ladies into their sedan chairs. My young mistress threw her arms about my waist and, in an unaccustomed display of affection, stroked my chest.

I looked down on that pretty young head—noticing it was not so far down any longer, for she had inherited her father's height—and caressed it in return.

"Why do you say that, little garden flower?" I asked.

"Because—" she said, catching my eye with an intense stare. "Well, Abdullah, aren't you glad as well?"

I had to admit I shared the exuberance. But our momentary relief did nothing about the live charge fusing in our *mabein*.

XXXVI

BEFORE SUNSET THAT evening, the soldiers had come again, but this time they would not be put off by the *mabein* door.

"We must hear her voice," the captain said. "To make certain it is indeed a female."

"She may not speak," the master stammered. "She is very shy."

"Then you must make her speak or all Constantinople will suspect it is a man you hide in your harem. I leave you to wager how long you may remain Grand Vizier with that shame on your head."

My master took a breath and went to the *mabein* door. He knocked very gently and had to clear his throat to get the words out.

"Fatima! Fatima!" he called. As if he'd called her Maria in Venice! That name was so common it probably arose suspicion in and of itself. My master was so transparently naive about women!

"Fatima, there are men here." Best he warn his secretary at least, if he could do nothing else. "There are men from the palace and they would hear you speak. To make certain you are . . . what I say you are. It is a matter of honor. And of life and death. Fatima, can you come to the door and say something?"

There was no reply.

"She is modest," my master protested, but the soldiers were not satisfied.

"Let me go in and encourage her with the gravity of the situation," I offered.

"No," the captain grabbed my arm. "You may be in on this hoax, *khadim*. It would be only too easy for you to open the harem door and let some slave girl in to speak for 'her.' No, either that person you say is in there speaks up by the count of ten or I shall be obliged to break down the door in the name of the Sultan."

"Sir," said my master. "I ask you to recall that this is not the mountains of Yugoslavia where a soldier may lose discipline with impunity. Violence against virtuous women of the Faith can be death."

"And shielding a man wanted by the Sultan is also death. I think the odds are even. At least I am not afraid of the wager. Are you, Pasha? I am a great man of the gamble, by Allah. Men, prepare to force the door on the count of ten!"

And the captain began to count.

"Fatima, please. Won't you come and speak? Spare both of us the shame of this violence."

My master was pleading, and it was not an edifying sight in the person of the Grand Vizier. What he was pleading for I supposed to be the quick escape of Feridun Bey out through the *mabein* courtyard. But then where? Nothing else, short of a miracle, could be hoped for.

Perhaps it was the same blind hope for heaven's intervention that kept me rooted to the spot. To bolt at that moment, to run around through the other doors and make an escape for the fugitive through the harem, though there might be time before the door was broken down, would be a clear expression of guilt. And somehow I continued to believe that right might still win heaven's protection.

The door tore off its hinges and the soldiers burst in with drawn swords. My heart sank. The figure in the apricot veil had not even bothered to flee, but stood cowering in a corner. This took the soldiers aback for a moment, too. They had fully expected a man with a drawn sword to meet them. Still, they were convinced of their purpose. The captain, backed by his men, strode across the room and caught the apricot figure by one swathed arm.

As he pulled the veil tight, one could see the light swelling of young breasts beneath. Then a voice no one could doubt as a woman's cried out, "Please, sir. For my sake and yours. Let me go."

Had I still been the Christian I was born, I would never have believed it, even seeing it with my own eyes. Five armed men turned and fled for their lives from that cowering female figure as if from an army of thousands. My master made a sign. I was to have his bodyguard cut them off at the gateway. As I ran to carry out this scenario from a battlefield—excitement I thought Fate had deprived me of forever— I laughed aloud.

And I also saw, out of the corner of my eye, the master move clumsily to embrace that apricot-swathed figure. For both of us had recognized the voice at once when it spoke. It was Gul Ruh.

The violators were apprehended and the master assured of vengeance. The captain would be hanged to deprive Uweis of one of his most devoted cohorts and the others would be beaten soundly to teach them some proper Muslim manners.

I fully expected a beating myself—for being so careless of a princess of the blood—but the master and his secretary were exulting too much over this narrow escape to bother with me. I passed them, laughing and clipping one another on the shoulder in the *mabein* courtyard where Feridun Bey, still absurd in women's jacket and trousers, had hidden himself. I passed on into the harem, realizing that the punishment I expected from others I would mentally give myself over and over in the weeks and months to come.

For I had felt in my belt and found the key to the *mabein* missing. Gul Ruh must have stolen it to satisfy her curiosity during our embrace. For having been so careless, for having succumbed to women's wiles—in my condition!—I would have loved the bite of a studded lash.

"All right, young lady," I said, turning some of my anger against her. "I'd like you to give an accounting of yourself."

"Me, Abdullah?" She played innocent. "Whatever have I done? I've been quietly playing chess with my *khadim* Carnation all this while. Isn't that right, Carnation?"

And Carnation, my assistant who was just coming to see normally again since his last pipeful, assured me she spoke the truth.

That liar I motioned from the room, telling him I'd deal with him later.

Then I turned to her and began to lecture, "Young ladies should never—"

She interrupted me. " 'Young ladies should never!' But how are we supposed to learn to behave ourselves when men are allowed into our sanctuary?"

"He wasn't in the harem. He was only in the *mabein,*" I protested, but I knew she had a point.

"That's still the harem."

"The door was safely locked, and well you know it."

"I suppose you'll be wanting the key back," she said, and, pulling it from her bodice, dangled it enticingly in front of me. When I reached for it, she pulled back and said, "But first you must tell me who he is."

I shook my head.

"I saved his life. Surely I have a right to know who he is."

My heart was working up a sweat. I thought I saw the glimmer of romance in her eyes and the scene I imagined to have happened in that room before the soldiers burst in grew more and more torrid in my mind.

"You have no business. You have no right," I declared in panic.

But as we bantered back and forth, I soon came to discover I was the only one who saw romance there. She had had time to stare a second or two at the equally startled Bey—no more.

"I didn't dare to use the key until you'd gone into the *selamlik,* Abdullah," she said, "and suddenly, there was the pounding of the soldiers on the door.

"How funny he looked"—not handsome—"a man in women's clothes. He didn't look at all comfortable and was only too glad to see me, especially when he could toss that veil to me and run out into the yard in an instant."

Gul Ruh had boosted herself into a window sill to stand her ground against my scolding. Here she could swing her legs back and forth defiantly. Now a blush came to her cheeks and a tear to her eye and I feared once more that there might be some awful confession. "You know, Abdullah, that's the only time my father has touched me since he sent me in here." That was what would remain as the most important aspect of that evening to her.

I decided to conclude my lecture, picking up on her sentiment for her father. "Now you must promise me you will never go opening doors you shouldn't or climbing on rooftops again. It is your father's honor we have at stake here. If you do not come pure to the husband he may someday, Allah willing, choose for you in his great love and concern, you will break his heart."

She nodded her head, the tears too thick now for speech. She kicked her heels against the wall instead, and the repentant, sweet yet impish picture so touched me that I embraced her. We each took in that embrace more than reality could ever give; she, the love of a cold and clumsy father and I, the love of the child my loins would never bear.

❧

SOKOLLI PASHA REALIZED now he could not hope to keep his faithful Feridun Bey in the harem until the Sultan's rage over the trumped-up charge should pass. And so, before the next Friday, I had escorted the secretary, still in sedan chair and apricot veil, as far as the master's farm outside the city, where he gratefully changed into male attire at last, took a horse, and rode into exile.

Feridun Bey carried letters with him to Mustafa Pasha, the master's nephew who was beglerbeg, governor, over the difficult border territory around Buda. If Mustafa could not find a place for the secretary in some out-of-the-way Hungarian village, then he would certainly be able to help him across the border into Christian territory until such time as Allah should change Murad's heart.

I cannot tell you what a relief the apricot veil's disappearance brought to my lady. "I knew it. Such a silly thing. I knew he'd soon grow tired of her." And because Esmikhan was relieved, the harem in general was relieved.

And Sokolli Pasha went to his room and wrote another very long letter to Arab Pasha in Cyprus.

Part IV

Ferhad

XXXVII

THE MASTER OF the Imperial Horse strode across the hoof-churned dust of the Hippodrome to where the group of horsemen were practicing. Their efforts focused on an exhibition exercise to be performed at night in which rags dipped in saltpeter were lashed on shield, sword, and helmet, then set afire. It always made a grand spectacle, but as for practical application, little was accomplished more than training the horses not to balk at flame.

Ferhad Pasha had just come from the other side of the field where practice with the more useful but not so showy skills of lance and target was an utter shambles. The incompetence bothered him much worse than usual, he knew, because they were in the Hippodrome, the very shadows of the Grand Vizier's palace just shortening off man and beast. Anything to do with Sokolli Pasha must always have that effect on him.

What chance that the Grand Vizier had nothing better to do than to look out his palace gate and decide which units were hopelessly incompetent, by implication which commanders? Ferhad Pasha had no real need to drive the men so hard as he always did in this milieu. Shouting, swearing at them, calling on Allah to witness his grief, driving them through the same moves like a fury, over and over again until he could see their limbs quake with exhaustion and their eyes blaze with murder. When the time came, Ferhad hoped, that blaze could be turned against the enemy rather than against himself.

Of course, what Ferhad Pasha felt like spurs to his flanks was not the eyes of Sokolli Pasha alone. There was also Sokolli Pasha's harem, his wife, his daughter. Ferhad felt his neck and shoulders warm at the mere thought. He knew one man had no business thinking of another's harem, especially not in such particular terms. But Ferhad couldn't help himself. The wife was *his* wife, the daughter his as well.

Sometimes while at drill in the Hippodrome, he would catch a glimpse of the closed sedan as it left the rear harem door. It would never do to stare: How could he expect discipline from his men if he himself were as undisciplined as that? Yet he did not need to train his eyes. He could feel the progress of the sedan skirting the training ground. It moved like a branding iron across his back, turned his head like a spiked bit.

And as the unseen sight burned his back, the men before him would shift at their commander's unusual distraction. He'd watch himself lose control within the tight confines of his mind and there was nothing he could do about it. All the wonderful night in the holy city of Konya would come flooding back to him. Only when he extracted himself from the fit could his fierce attention to duty return. Indeed, then he would triple its intensity.

The irony of the whole affair was that Ferhad Pasha had never, never sought to do anything that wasn't duty. It was while he had been about the most secret of trusted duties that he had first found himself a guest in Sokolli Pasha's home. A guest of enforced inactivity with nothing to do but wander in the Grand Vizier's garden until, all inadvertently, he had found himself standing before a pavilion draped with autumn roses. Within had sat his host's wife, playing the oud and singing songs of ancient and mythic love. She was those myths made corporal. A vision, he'd always thought, of paradise.

And no more than Allah's offer of paradise—or martyrdom on the battlefield—could he escape the conclusion of that scene. All was, in the end, Allah's will. Seeking refuge in duty only set him ever more firmly in Allah's hands.

It had seemed a duty, a compulsion, to pick the flowers by whose secret code lovers communicate and leave them where the harem grille could read the meaning. Ferhad had read poets who had felt the same obligation to write or perish at the wrathful hands of their muse.

Through duty again he had found his unit back in Konya—at the very time the Grand Vizier's lady had been there, begging in the most pious way for Allah to take her in His hand as well. When winter in the mountains had called his unit back to Konya, how could Ferhad, with a guest's duty, have refused the governor there his duty of hospitality? Yes, even in the full knowledge that Sokolli Pasha's woman was likewise a guest under the same roof.

And the eunuch Abdullah had come to Ferhad Pasha that night, uncustomarily distracted, speaking disjointedly of the lady's attempts to do violence to herself in her hopeless grief. How could he, Ferhad Pasha, a slave of the Sultan's house, have resisted the duty to answer such a call to aid?

Images of that night came back to him at the most inopportune times. Blissful images. Esmikhan's pink-tipped breasts splitting free of their confining silk with the same fragrance as roses. Her black curls had been like jasmine tendrils, the sticky taste of her like honey.

He'd known she was no virgin. She'd borne the Grand Vizier three sons, none of whom had lived through two prayer times. But he'd seen by the wide, surprised delight in her eyes, by their pupils' dizzy blackness and the fresh bloom on her cheeks, that he'd been able to give her something she'd never known before. And that had fueled his own delight.

The memory of her shuddering beneath him could make him shiver on the warmest days. A seagull's cry would sometimes sound so like her own that it took his breath away, even as her desperately panting mouth had stolen it from him on that night.

As for his own needs, well, he'd paid high-priced whores since then, coming with great recommendations from his comrades. And all their skill had come nowhere near granting him a similar satisfaction.

There was the child now, the daughter of that night. Gul Ruh. His daughter. She'd be ten years old by now. More. Only such calculations placed the night its proper distance from the present. Otherwise, it seemed no more removed than the last dawn.

The daughter he'd never seen. He liked to imagine she favored her mother: a rose, soft and pink. That was her name, Gul Ruh, the rose in the enclosed garden which the nightingale was forbidden to love.

There was, of course, no reason why she shouldn't favor him. He realized that, particularly every time he felt Sokolli Pasha's sharp scrutiny. Sometimes Ferhad Pasha felt the old man did more than guess. He knew.

Yes, the daughter would be ten, a young lady, well guarded and in veils. Ferhad Pasha doubted he could tell mother from daughter or from any other woman if he saw them now so swaddled. And, of course, there was no opportunity to test that ability. Abdullah the eunuch had closed the harem doors behind him as dawn had leaked into the sky, putting an end to the night. And ever since then, Abdullah, who had once opened the doors of paradise, now stood a guardian as stern and unflinching as ever flaming-sworded archangel stood before Eden.

Time ought to have faded the memories somewhat, brought new loves, new diversions. In other men, perhaps. Not in Ferhad Pasha. And other men might have hated Sokolli Pasha for lording that paradise which clearly belonged to Ferhad, none other. But the young Master of the Horse had no such feelings. Obedience continued to force his thoughts. His superior had rights to these blessings because no man in the empire, nay, in the world, was as submissive to duty as Sokolli Pasha was. The Grand Vizier deserved his post and everything that went along with it—including the family—because he had paid his due to the Sultan and to Allah.

Paradise, Ferhad knew, could not be besieged and taken. It must be earned, by the will of heaven. And by strict adherence to duty. That was, after all, how he had gained his one glimpse of the place.

And so Ferhad continued to strive to match his service to the old man's own, hoping in the end to inherit that man's reward. It might well be. If he were faithful enough. The Grand Vizier—no matter how many times one said "May he live 'til Judgement Day" after his name— could not, after all, live forever. And already Ferhad Pasha was one of the handful of men standing to inherit. He was, in fact, the only possible heir as yet unrewarded with a royal bride. And he had not married lower, finding, in his memories, no need to. Knowing that those who married lower never advanced.

There was only one royal bride in which he had any interest. And the constraint of monogamy seemed no hardship.

The Grand Vizier could not live forever. But still, as Ferhad walked to the fire riders, he thought, Death should come no sooner than Allah wills—to anyone. And, considering the message he bore, he would have dragged his feet to the fire more slowly, more slowly. Except, of course, he would rather be seen, by the Grand Vizier as well as by any shadow peeking at him through sedan lattices, to be overseeing the more flawless unit rather than the clumsy lance throwers.

Ferhad Pasha's nose twitched horselike at the smell of sulphur just barely fumigating the training ground of its usual dust and manure. Burning swords passed just fingers' breadth from the horses' tails, which were tied up against sparks. The precision the team displayed as he approached was quite remarkable even by daylight and Ferhad wondered idly why this exercise always attracted the best men and their mounts.

Ferhad motioned the head of the fire unit to him. The ranks closed in over the place the man vacated like magic. The man rode his horse at a canter past the water trough, where he doused his flaming equipment with a flourish. Then he pranced his horse up to where Ferhad stood, showing his animal off to best advantage.

By Allah, where did he get that mare? Ferhad asked himself. She was the pinkish white color of some roses and seemed to be a mix of the best qualities of both Arabian and Turkish breeds with some of the power of the Europeans thrown in as well.

How is it that these subordinates always manage to get the best animals? Ferhad wondered again. Far better than mine. Better, even, than any in the Sultan's private stables.

But Ferhad knew that if he asked, the rider would merely shrug and say, "Oh, her? Ah, I picked her up for a song—skin and bones, nothing promising there—from an old trader. No pedigree at all." But, "No," he would continue, "I cannot part with her. She isn't much, but we're friends, best friends. No, not for any price."

Perhaps it had been the man's mother who'd first called him Iskandar the Horseman. Maybe he had always been that way, little, lithe, dark, hairy, with a black mustache like a curry brush. Or maybe it was just a streak of opportunism he had, like the best riders always seeking out the showiest exercise: In any profession, by hook or by crook, he would rise to the top. Was this why Lala Mustafa Pasha had specifically asked for this man?

But now the man had dismounted and stood at attention. Why am I so intimidated by this fellow? Ferhad wondered. He felt if he spoke he would betray something to give that man an edge, so he merely handed

Iskandar the written orders. Reading, at least, was his weak point: Let
him struggle with it for a while.

"We're to ride to Hungary, then?" Iskandar asked as soon as he'd
made out the gist of the writing.

"Yes."

"When, sir?"

"As soon as you can get your men together. My men have already
been notified. Meet at the Edirne Gate."

"We'll be there before noon prayers."

"Good. I needn't reiterate how important secrecy is in this mission."

"It goes without saying." The little man grinned. Then he whispered
so no one else could possibly hear over the pounding of horses' hooves
in the background, "We go to knock off the Grand Vizier's nephew
and you need to remind me it's a secret?"

Ferhad felt himself grow red—and a little sick. "No one said anything about 'knocking off'. Our orders are merely to speak with the
man. 'Obtain satisfaction concerning the disappearance of Feridun Bay,
secretary to the Grand Vizier.' "

"But we both know what 'obtain satisfaction' means." Iskandar had
not been able to read the orders word for word, yet he had read more
between the lines than Ferhad had.

"Let us hope it will not come to that," Ferhad said.

Iskandar grinned in response, then asked, "Was there something
else, sir?"

"No. Well, yes. I was wondering what you did with that letter I ordered you to deliver from Sokolli Pasha."

"I took it to the captain of the ship bound for Cyprus, as you ordered."

"And no one read it in between?"

"Whatever do you mean, sir?" Iskandar grinned.

Ferhad realized now what was so disconcerting about the grin. It was
broken by missing teeth, like a lacunae in a manuscript.

"Nothing," Ferhad said. "Forget I mentioned it. The Edirne Gate before noon?"

"Yes, sir."

Now for the life of him, Ferhad couldn't imagine what it was that had
ever made him trust the fellow. It must have been something, and some-

thing that affected others, too, for Iskandar had risen so rapidly through the ranks. But the last advancement had been Ferhad's own responsibility and now here he was, catching the attention of viziers, leading the fire exercise, knocking at the door to the post of the Master of the Horse itself.

Why did it feel like Iskandar was head of this expedition to Hungary and not he himself? Iskandar got the best horse, the flashiest drill team. Did he gain trust in the same way, and for the same ulterior motives?

XXXVIII

"THE BEGLERBEG SAYS he knows nothing, and that is that. What more can we do?" Ferhad asked Iskandar two weeks later in Buda.

"He says so," Iskandar repeated skeptically, almost sarcastically. "But what sort of 'satisfaction' is that? It is merely his word. The word of a man entrenched so firmly in Sokolli Pasha's own camp you'd have to drain out all his blood to change him."

"In any case, it's clear Feridun Bey is already over the border."

"Yes, alas."

"There is nothing more we can do."

"Nothing? I am not satisfied. I doubt Lala Mustafa Pasha will be."

"Sokolli Pasha is the Grand Vizier. Why go on tormenting his favorites without cause?"

"Because his days in this world are numbered. Best to latch onto those whose star is rising, not those about to set, whatever title they may presently hold."

"Your talk, *spahi*, sounds of treason."

"Treason is talk against the Sultan which, Allah is my witness, I never say. Where is the treason in a few words against the Grand Vizier who, after all, is a mere slave, no better than you or I? Besides, I said nothing but what is obvious to anyone. Sokolli Pasha is not only a slave, he is an old slave. He's over seventy. Allah may call him to his reward at anytime. Anytime."

"Allah forbid," Ferhad murmured automatically, a wish Iskandar did not bother to amen. Perhaps because it was a vain wish indeed.

Later, a dismal rain seemed about to wash all of Buda down the muddy streets. Ramshackle houses of the refugees and sturdier buildings alike seemed on the brink of flushing into the Danube, off towards the sea, and finally, Constantinople. Night was hardly distinguishable from day under that sky. Ferhad had to notice that the streets were empty now in order to tell the time. They were empty save for mud, rain, and himself. Anyone with honest business had taken the first excuse to leave them and go home.

Why am I so devoted to that man Sokolli? Ferhad asked himself. Even if—Allah willing—he dies a natural death, it cannot be far off. Since that night, he felt obliged to his superior with a debt no amount of servitude could repay. Sometimes it seemed to be the only night in his life, compared to which this drizzle was but an uncomfortable dream.

It is almost as if he has graciously allowed me to share her with him, Ferhad thought. Like he gives charity to any beggar who comes to his door.

Ferhad didn't like to think of himself in beggar's guise, so he swaggered a little in the empty street until he lost his balance on the mud.

French masons and Italian artists had once made Buda a gem of a city, but nearly half a century as a border outpost had not been easy on such fragile beauty. "Once the Austrians back off a little more, we may rebuild it to Turkish taste," the promise always was. But to date, a bath or two at the mineral springs were the only niceties that beglerbegs could not do without. It was a wild, rough aesthetic to Ferhad's Constantinople-trained eyes, made wilder and rougher still by the years of misunderstanding between conqueror and conquered.

The rain had soaked into the city everywhere and enlivened foreign smells: Tokay wine, paprika, sour cream, cabbage. Pork sausage. The sounds, too, were guaranteed to cause homesickness: The language seemed shackled with consonants and somewhere a gypsy fiddler played with little care for melody or feeling, only breakneck speed.

"Gul Ruh", Ferhad said aloud. He had never framed the words in public before and wouldn't until he died. "My daughter." He looked up for the moon, as he always did when his mind rode on such things, but of course there wasn't one that night. "Gul Ruh. The old tale of the nightingale's love for the rose. It means something that can never be."

Ferhad knew very well what he was doing. He would have rather been warm and dry by the fire in their lodgings, and away from such thoughts. Who would not on a night like this? But this walk was like Christ's sop to Judas Iscariot, telling Iskandar "That thou doest, do quickly." Ferhad knew full well that when he returned, the first words of greeting would be: "The beglerbeg! He's dead! Assassinated!"

Not that the beglerbeg himself deserved much sympathy. He was a weak, corrupted excuse for a nephew and Sokolli Pasha had seen him to this position prompted only by duty. But still in Ferhad's mind there was Sokolli. There was still that abominable, inexplicable devotion to the Grand Vizier. As if because of that night he was related to the man closer than any nephew.

"Gul Ruh," he murmured again. And was glad, that dripping night, of the name's impossibility.

Ferhad stopped to examine the facade of one of the buildings he passed and to wonder at the barbarous style—what was left of it, for passing armies had found it a good place to pick up souvenirs. Ferhad saw that another one of the bricks was loose: a small bit of plaster in the shape of a rosette the rain had turned a rather pleasant, glossy gray. He pried it off, feeling no remorse for defacing a building already marked for the wreckers—when peace should come—and held it in his hand. It would fit just nicely in a woman's.

"Iskandar should be done now," Ferhad said to himself, put the rosette in his sash, and turned back wearily to his lodgings.

"THEY'VE MADE ISKANDAR Master of the Horse, Abdullah *ustadh*," Ferhad told the eunuch as he handed him the rosette made by a jeweler into a pleasant little necklace for Gul Ruh to wear.

"Yes," Abdullah said. "And I hear you've been promoted to Agha of all the Janissaries."

"Yes," Ferhad shrugged as if it were nothing.

"Congratulations."

Ferhad shrugged again. "I can run no more messages for Sokolli Pasha."

"Well, he has other means."

"Yes."

"This. For your lady."

Ferhad handed the eunuch a bunch of fresh blue rue. A similar flower seemed to branch and bloom in his heart as he recalled all the messages that had passed thus between him and Sokolli's harem. Secret messages in flowers and fruits, innocent messages—to all but the love-trained eye. And to such eyes they expressed a world lush with passion. A plane leaf for the lover's hand. A clove to represent how slender, how sweet he found her figure. A lock of her soft, curly hair, in his bosom yet, that said he was the crown of her head.

And now the rue. It meant the same thing in the East as it did in the West: "Remember me."

Abdullah accepted the bouquet with a nod and turned to go.

"Oh, *ustadh?*"

"Yes?"

"Tell your master I am sorry about the death of the beglerbeg in Hungary. I know—I know they were close."

"Allah's will," the *khadim* said with disinterest. He had not known the man.

"And—"

"And?"

Ferhad struggled to conceal any meaning in his eye. His red leather boots of office scuffled on the flagstones and he looked at them as he said, "And please warn your master to be on his guard."

"Against what?" The eunuch was suddenly all ears. "Against a similar plot?"

"I cannot say. He must only beware. And I—I would not see—see orphans and widows made."

Ferhad turned and hurried away.

Part V

Abdullah

XXXIX

"YES, MY FRIEND Abdullah. I swear by Allah, you are wise to keep your eyes on that one when he gets anywhere near your women."

The voice, like muddy water flowing over gravel, and the monstrous hand of Ghazanfer on my shoulder startled me out of what had been the gaze of an idle daydream, not watchful care as he imagined. And "my women" for whom he so feared, were nowhere in sight. They were in Safiye's rooms comparing costumes and jewels for the upcoming holiday, the Prophet's Birthday. The pilgrim caravan had only just returned from Mecca and Medina, well-ladened from contacts made with the Faithful from India, China, and beyond. By such trade many a man had funded that holy journey of a lifetime. There was plenty to keep the ladies busy.

What had attracted my attention—and thereby Ghazanfer's—was the woman walking with the eunuch. Of course there was nothing odd in this—it is our duty to walk with them, either behind, hearing their orders, their complaints, their gossip, or ahead to throw up curtains, close doors, and otherwise clear the way of men. In fact, I had found nothing really strange in what I saw. It was like a panel of painted tiles one passes everyday until in a moment of idleness one notices it for the first time and it sends one's mind soaring.

The woman was Mitra, Safiye's Persian, whose poetry had won her such a place in the Sultan's heart that she was pregnant again. The eunuch was likewise Persian, the startlingly handsome one new to Nur Banu's suite. Between them was neither a veil in preparation for going out nor a list of errands she wanted to send him on. It was a folio of poetry and—though for all my study of both the romantic and the mystical poets, I still could understand but a word here and there when natives spoke Persian—I knew their subject was not the compassion of Allah.

Very well, now that I thought of it, it was a remarkable sight. Things had become so polarized in the harem that for one of Safiye's camp to be seen with one of Nur Banu's was immediate cause for suspicion of spying, poison, or witchcraft.

Ghazanfer left me and crossed the atrium to the couple. A few stern words on his part sent the girl fleeing to her room and the eunuch, with nothing left to do in that place, dawdled off with the folio under his arm.

"Well!" I was over my start enough to joke a little when the huge man returned to my side. When I did speak to Ghazanfer, it was usually half-serious. Such a man one doesn't care to become earnest with.

"What was it?" I asked. "Was he spying or poisoning?"

"Allah shield us from both," Ghazanfer replied. Then, "I shall never trust that man."

I made a sign and a sound to pacify him—he was so huge even a little anger in him was frightening—but he continued as if in explanation, "I knew his castrator."

"So?" I said as lightly as one can who has felt the knife himself. "A butcher is a butcher."

"Mu'awiya the Red always called himself an artist, not a butcher. But butchers a man can usually trust, except when there's a meat shortage. Artists, never."

I still dared not take him seriously, but his words made me able to name something else that had been curious about that couple. Between them had seemed to be the attraction of lodestones. I had not seen such attraction since the heavily chaperoned but harmless dances of my youth. The Turks generally worked on a system that either defied this natural law or gave it full rein. That uneasy hanging in abeyance is foreign to them.

I made some careless comment in the direction of this new observation, asking Ghazanfer how there was any room for jealousy between eunuchs. "Our fate is everywhere and eternally the same."

Ghazanfer fixed me with a look which might have been the smile co-conspirators exchange across a crowded room. On that great, tortured face, however, it was difficult to see more than a grimace. He gestured then for me to join him.

To one side of the atrium a slave had set up cushions and a low table covered with documents. As *kapu aghasi,* Ghazanfer Agha had offices elsewhere. But when he was not busy out in the world, it was his custom to sit here. This was the heart of the harem, a sort of *mabein* between the rooms occupied by Safiye and those of Nur Banu.

Nothing that went on between the two women could miss his scrutiny. I'd never known anyone to join him on his cushions—who sits companionably with the tax collector when he sets up shop in the village square? It never occurred to me that he might not like things this way, and I accepted his offer not knowing whether to be flattered or afraid.

Ghazanfer clapped his hands for service and offered me my choice of any of the palace dainties, just as if that corner were his home. To be polite, I took only a lemon sherbet, poured through a ball of snow fixed to the mouth of a brass ewer into a small glass. I intended to make the drink last as long as need be. Ghazanfer had his narghile lit and it bubbled comfortably.

We spoke trivialities—as if indeed I were a guest lately come to his villa instead of just withdrawn to his corner of the harem. But then, suddenly, and without preface he said, "All *khuddam* are not created equal." Before I could reply, he continued, "Some are more resigned to the will of Allah than others. Some actually prefer this life to any other."

"No." I waved him off. "None of us asked to have the better part of our life cut away like that."

"I did," Ghazanfer said.

I could tell he was not jesting, but still I could not believe it. So I said nothing.

"When I was a boy. In Hungary," he said. The narghile bubbled like a pot come to the boil, but whether it should be a wholesome soup or a spell of black magic that had reached its time I could not yet tell.

"I do not remember my father," he said. The spell was cast. He was going to tell me. And I could not have pulled away from the fascination if I'd wanted to.

"When I was less than two months old," the great eunuch said, "my father was killed defending Valpo against the march of Suleiman—on whom may Allah smile—towards Pest. Valpo is a small town. I doubt you will have heard of it. But I heard of nothing else as a child. My mother would smile and brag that my first word had been 'Valpo' followed shortly by the word 'revenge.'

"I had no father, but I had four uncles and a grandfather like a grey, grizzly wolf. We had lands and herds, but they were neglected. An excuse for a living was made by raiding Turkish outposts, and when the snows came and drove the Turks down from our hills, the men of my family would still never lift a finger to help the women, my mother and my aunts, who really put the turnips and beetroot in our pot. One uncle carried a janissary musket ball in his shoulder proudly, for all that it made him less of a warrior than the rest. For compensation, on those long winter nights, he'd taken to composing epic poetry in which our family played the parts of heroes.

> 'On the great, grey walls of Valpo
> The brave, the chosen few stood,
> Grim on the face of Valpo,
> Swords like pines in the wood.'

"I remember one day in particular after such a recitation. I'd been keeping a fierce time to the meter with my ax—hearing the rhythm, not the words—just outside the door. They wouldn't touch the wood pile, not them. The fire would go out and they'd freeze to death before they'd set iron to anything but human flesh. Rather than see my mother weary herself with it, I'd taken up chopping the moment I could swing the ax without letting it scrape the ground. I was tall for my age and strong.

"But chopping wood was woman's work, so my uncles would say when they'd call me away from the wood pile for target practice or wrestling. A new powder horn and musket. A sword stolen from a fallen Turk. These were my toys. And what boy of any age could resist that play? But I did.

"My mother came out when the poem was over to carry in another load of wood and she said, just as acknowledgement of my presence, 'Someday, Bela, you'll revenge Valpo. I know you will.'

"I stopped the ax and looked at her, bent under her load. 'No Mother', I said. 'I'd rather stay here and chop your wood.'

"It would have been bad enough had only she heard that, for she was an emotional woman and prone to believe anything set to the intoxicating rhythm of epic. But my grandfather heard it, too— he'd gone out to relieve himself hidden by the shed. He came up behind me as I chopped and set his hands on my shoulders. The weight broke my swing and the ax sank among the chips of wood on the dirt floor.

"Grandfather felt my shoulders, testing their strength as he had taught me to weigh a new bow. Then he began to exert pressure, increasing it slowly, as if I were a branch he would break with his bare hands.

" 'So you want to stay with your mother, do you, boy?' he said between teeth gritted with the effort of causing me pain.

"I could only gasp in reply. But then the pain made me angry and the anger made me strong. Strong enough to free myself from my assailant and to throw the ax at him with the energy I'd learned to throw at overaged cherry wood. Fortunately, much as I truly wanted to kill him, I had aimed in anger rather than with care. As soon as I could see straight, I saw my grandfather's favorite fur hat pinned to the wall of the house behind him, but he himself was unharmed.

"When he'd caught his breath, the old man laughed aloud. He took the ax and his hat down from the wall and laughed again until the tears came as he poked his short, powerful fingers through the rent in the fur. He dragged me into the house by the arm, showed the hat, and told the tale. Soon my uncle had added a new verse to his poem about the 'bold generation that is to be,' how I would not submit under pressure, and everyone roared with new laughter.

"But I grew sick to my stomach as the full impact of what I had done came to me. Such a black and violent thing! It had turned me against my own flesh and blood. This thing, to which my family was addicted— how could they tell, when under its influence, whether what they did was right or not? I had spoken of my concerns to the village priest and he affirmed my feelings. 'They who live by the sword die by the sword,' he quoted to me.

"Yet, I realize now that when it serves them, priests are just as able to quote words about how the enemies of God should utterly perish and 'he who is not for me is against me.' At that time, however, our priest had Protestant leanings and preferred being subject to the Turks than to Austrian Latin heretics, and so peace is what he spoke. I believed him and set my heart on the priesthood as a vocation."

XL

WITH HIS WEB of words, Ghazanfer Agha returned me to the world of his childhood, his dream of a monastic life. "Of course, even a whisper of this notion spoken at home brought down the wrath of heaven," he said. " 'And have I fed that fine, strong body of yours and clothed it these ten years that it should rot in a cloister? What about your father? What about Valpo?'

"My uncles and grandfather turned all their energies now—when they weren't beating Turks—to beating me. To make me tough, they said. If they only knew how many times I crawled with their welts on my backside to the little icon I had hidden in my bed in the loft! It was a picture of Jesus whom the artist had rendered beardless and effeminate to suggest his meekness and gentleness. That became my ideal in all my suffering.

"When finally he did catch me at my devotions, my grandfather tossed the image out the window, which shows you what sort of Christianity he was fighting Turks to keep. Me he dragged down by the scruff of the neck to be whipped once again in the presence of all the family.

"The old wolf was livid, growling in his throat as if he'd missed his kill. When he made me drop my pants and saw that the wounds from his last beating were still raw, it made him furious that so much pain should have so little effect. Before he could pick up his riding whip once more, his madness drove him to leap at me with his knife drawn, like a wolf to his prey.

"My male member contracted as it felt the cold blade against it. 'By God, I shall unman you!' he cried. 'You are not fit to be numbered among us.'

"I was shaking with fear, but somehow I managed to whisper, 'Go ahead.'

" 'What did you say, boy?'

"My voice came much louder this time; it was high and thin as a woman's. 'Go ahead and cut,' I said. 'If to be a man means to be like you, I don't want to be one.'

"The wolf's eyes narrowed to slits and fire spat from beneath his mustache. He turned from me as from an obscenity. And it was obscene, was it not? For him, castrating the son of his son was like castrating himself—unthinkable. The wolf strode to the corner of the hut while all my kinsfolk watched in horrified silence. Then he began to bay as if at a full moon, to growl as wolves do the minute before they leap. But in my grandfather's case, the sound was laughter. As soon as they saw it was laughter, the rest of the household laughed, too, from relief and because their master was no longer angry.

" 'You'll be a man,' he turned to me and said. 'You'll be a man, never fear. Which of my other sons ever had the courage to say that with a knife at his crotch?'

"Then they laughed louder and stronger and my grandfather tousled my hair and told me to pull up my pants. I did so and they laughed even more.

"My face was on fire and, rather than give them the pleasure of seeing the tears that must douse that heat, I fled out into the snow. My family's laughter pursued me like the howling of a pack of wolves on the trail.

"Two feet of snow lay in drifts where the night wind had blown it, but the air was now still and grey as iron. I hardly dared to breathe, lest the air stick to my lungs and rip them raw on the exhale. I immediately wished I had put on more clothes—another pair of mittens and a shirt or two more under the sheepskin—but I was not going back in that house, I swore, until I was dead and they carried me in.

I picked up my ax: Exercise, I thought, might serve in place of those clothes or a fire, for I was young and had no real desire to die. So armed, I set off through the drifts towards the woods.

"I decorated tree trunks with blobs of snow—heavy eyebrows and a white mustache—the old wolf; a tree with a crooked limb—my uncle with the bullet in his shoulder. Then I charged with fierce, tear-strangled yells until I hacked the trees to bits in a mad slaughter that lasted over an hour. The bits that were left were too little and green to be much use in the fire. I left them where they lay. Besides, I meant not to give those back at the house any more service.

" 'God have mercy on any enemy of yours, young man.'

"I turned to the voice with a start. I had been standing, the ax limp at the end of my exhausted arm, the cold slowly creeping in where the heat and the anger left. A wild sort of laughter (had I been listening, I would have found it all too like the wolf's) escaped from my lungs, pushed with white steam by my excruciating panting. I had heard no one approach and when I saw the man, I was reduced to only panting—and that I kept as restrained as life could bear.

"The man was a stranger. I had seen few strangers before. Everyone in our village was known to me since childhood and I had only ever been taken on one trip to the town of Szekszard in my life. There was some strangeness in the man's dress and in his voice as well, but as far as I knew, the whole world beyond Szekszard dressed and spoke like that. I was curious, but not very anxious.

" 'So tell me,' the stranger said, moving closer, leaving his horse tethered to a tree behind him. 'Who was this dangerous enemy you so bravely slew just now?'

"I didn't dare answer truthfully, 'My grandfather,' so I gave the pat answer: 'The heathen Turk.'

" 'I see,' the stranger said, and his dark eyes twinkled merrily. 'And have you ever seen a Turk before?'

" 'No,' I replied, 'but my father . . .' And I gave him a brief recital of my heritage, complete with snatches of my uncle's poetry.

" 'Bravo,' the stranger said. Then: 'Does your doctrine include rendering aid to strangers?'

"I didn't remember it doing so, but my religious bent assured me it ought to, so I said, 'Yes.'

"The man told me he had lost his way and would be obliged if I could point him on the road to Szekszard.

" 'Are you from Szekszard?' I asked.

" 'From a little village just south of the town,' he said with a smile and added, as an afterthought, 'If you can just tell me the way to Szekszard, I can manage the rest by myself.'

"I told him the way, proud of my knowledge, but 'It will take you until sunset or more to get there.' He confessed his obligation to me nonetheless. Then we stood there looking at one another in silence. I do not know what was crossing his mind, but mine was forming the question, 'Tell me, in your village south of Szekszard, would you have any use for a boy? Strong, willing—just watch me with an ax . . .'

"But before I had courage to express my thoughts, his made him laugh and slap his knee with pleasure. 'Look here, boy. Just to show you how grateful I am, what do you say we build ourselves a fire with your wood and sit down together and have some lunch? I just shot a deer. You see, I spent all night lost in the woods without any supper, so early this morning I decided even if I was lost I didn't have to starve. Now that I am found, there's no need to let the meat go to waste.'

"I accepted his invitation gratefully. In other circumstances, I might have invited him to our house, but I was in no mood to return there, to show a new friend my disgraceful origins.

"The stranger knew all sorts of tricks. He got the green wood to burn as if by magic. We set our wet clothes out to dry, and never have I tasted venison so good. He knew how to make a boy talk, too. I had soon spilled all my troubles to him, every detail I could think of about my relatives' fights with the Turks, their personal quirks and habits. Where they stored their ammunition. Even the priest had never shown so much concern over what a boy had to say. Finally, I even confessed to him what particular and humiliating family episode had driven me into the woods.

"The stranger laughed, but not like they had laughed. His chuckle was gentle and, it seemed, inspired by compassion.

" 'Next time your grandfather tries that trick on you,' he said, 'you just tell him how the emperors of Byzantium used to have their own sons castrated because they knew there was no better way for second- and third-born boys to come to power than to remain forever just behind the throne. If your grandfather knew any better, he would not laugh at the sexless ones as he has done.'

"And then he told me that, though he had been born in the little village somewhat south of Szekszard, he had seen much of the world, including Constantinople of the Turks. He was full of tales to make a boy's heart glow. He gave me hope that the world need not begin and end with one's kinsmen and the mud of the village road. In particular, he spoke of the *khuddam* not as freaks and subhuman, but as honorable opponents in a complicated game for very high stakes. What the game was eluded me in my youth and naiveté.

"He said, 'I do like to come to Hungary, if only because the women do not have *khuddam* on their side and here my side wins, as easily as taking sweetmeats from a sleeping infant. But then I always like to return to the land of the Turks again. I find the game insipid without the mystery and the challenge! Like a war without an enemy.' And he laughed out loud again and slapped his knee.

"It grew late and we both knew our time together was at an end. We kicked snow over the last of the coals and I walked with him to retrieve his horse. Then, because I felt myself too dangerously close to tears, I said good-bye and turned at once.

"I had not gone four steps before I heard my name shouted. But it did not come from my stranger. It was in front of me: My grandfather had come into the woods to find me before dark. I had no sooner seen this than a cloud of smoke shrouded the old grey wolf and the crack of a pistol shattered the air like a wall of icicles crashing from the roof in an early thaw."

XLI

Ghazanfer continued, " 'Grandfather! Grandfather!' I shouted. 'Don't shoot. He is my friend.'

"But it was already too late to speak. My friend had been knocked to the ground by the shot and his horse behind him reared and screamed in fear.

" 'Your friend? You little fool!' Grandfather shouted back at me. 'The man's a Turk. A Turkish spy.'

" 'No, no. He's Hungarian. He was born—'

" 'It doesn't matter where he was born. That horse, those trappings, that turban, that scimitar. He's a God-cursed janissary. And a dead one, thank God.'

"No, the stranger was not dead. He moved, struggled to rise from the snow stained with his own blood. My grandfather saw the movement, too, and began to reload his gun.

" 'Get out of the way, boy, and let me finish him off.'

"I didn't move except to shift my weight from foot to foot and finger the ax handle nervously. Grandfather raised the pistol to sight, found me still in the way, and scowled. But then he thought of something that made him smile as he lowered the gun again.

" 'All right, boy,' he said. 'This is your time to prove yourself a man. You finish him off. Yes, you. With that famous ax of yours. Go on. One quick blow between the brows and you'll be a man. Easiest thing in the world.'

"I turned from him and faced the stranger. I brought the ax automatically to my shoulder. It would look good from behind. But under this cover I bade my friend, 'Run!' with voiceless lips.

"When I actually caught the horse's reins to steady it while my friend mounted, his wounded arm useless to help him, the pretense was over.

" 'Get out of the way, you damned little coward!' my grandfather cried.

"But, 'Ride, ride!' I shouted to my friend and did not move from between them until the trees folded in on him and he was out of range.

"The abuse I received was first verbal but then very, very physical. It was so severe that I more than once wished my grandfather had not been so cautious of my life earlier, but put me quickly out of my misery with a bullet through the head. Nevertheless, when at last I was allowed to crawl off to my loft without supper, I did not mind as much as before. There was the stranger's good venison in my belly and I was no longer alone with only a wooden picture for a friend. Besides that, I felt for the first time in my life I had won a victory from the old wolf. And I had won it not by being meaner and stronger than he, but by mercy and friendship. It was just as the very effeminate Jesus had said."

"Was the stranger a janissary?" I interrupted Ghazanfer's tale for the first time since he'd begun.

"Of course," he replied. "I know of no other man who could ride four hours through the snow with a wound like that in his arm and come alive to his garrison."

"So he survived?"

"Yes."

"But you'd told him all about your family's anti-Turkish activities?"

"I had indeed."

"And he returned your favor to him by not telling his superiors what he had learned?"

"No, he told them. Two weeks later our village was raided and all my uncles and grandfather were killed."

"That must have been a hard lesson for a boy to learn: that people are generally ungrateful, even to those who save their lives."

"No, I cannot say he did not return the favor. For when the sword, drunk with killing and carried on by its own momentum, was just above my head, he called out and stayed it.

" 'Stop, sir. That's the boy. Spare him.' Of course I couldn't understand Turkish at the time, but I'm sure they were words something like that.

"My friend spoke to his superiors and then to me, describing how I should be taken to Constantinople and trained in the Enclosed School to become a janissary—just like he had been. I felt as if St. George himself had delivered me from my awful family. I did not say no.

"But then, that night, after other likely boys were rounded up and the prettiest girls spared their virginity for a better price on the slave block, the soldiers celebrated their victory with general violation."

"It is the way of war," I said. "Every army does it."

"Yes," Ghazanfer Agha agreed. "But I had never imagined that men and women come together in that way before, and it was a rude, violent, ugly awakening.

"My mother was among them. I heard her screams over the crusted snow. They were as pitiful as if she had been a helpless child, not one whose hot hand and sharp scorn I had felt so, so many times. I had to plug my fingers in my ears and still could not escape it.

"They stopped short after a while and I thought 'Peace at last.'

"But I was wrong.

"My friend came and quietly told me that she was dead. She had plunged a sword into her own belly rather than have to accept another man that night, bury all her men in the morning, and then live with herself afterwards. My friend came to tell me I might say a few words of devotion over her if I wanted to. I had no words to say to the bloodied, mangled corpse. But I did speak to the man, my friend, who stood, clumsy with sudden sobriety, over her.

"He still bore his arm in a sling from my grandfather's bullet, but the only blood on him was hers and that of my kindred slain. My stomach rose at the sight and I was ill on the spot.

" 'Why?' I choked over the vomit and the tears.

" 'Why?' He shrugged rather shamedly. 'We are men.'

" 'And this is what men do?'

"My friend shrugged again. 'When we see women . . .' But he could not explain it more.

"As soon as I was no longer ill, I spoke some very violent and angry words about how I would rather 'my friend' kill me than turn me into a butcher like himself—no better than the grandfather he had slain. I no longer had any idealism, not even for the flashy blue and yellow of a janissary. The man, I will say this to his honor, was duly humbled, horrified at war gone out of bounds. But even as a child, I could tell that war always does that, and therefore it should have been no surprise to him.

"When I shouted that I would rather become a eunuch than join ranks with him, he nodded as if he envied me. One quick cut under careful and skillful hands did have its advantages over the haphazard aim of war. When I did not change my mind, he said he would be sad to lose a companion such as me, but he supported me every step of the way and got the best cutter in Belgrade to do the job. He fired two after the preliminaries, unwilling to trust me to just any man with a knife. I went under Mu'awiya the Red. That is how I know of his artistry.

"My friend was there, holding my hand throughout, just as if I were his companion wounded on the field. As I healed, he came to visit me every day and brought me sweets and talked. He chose my name for me—Ghazanfer, bold lion—a name for the battlefield and not the harem where I was bound.

"And when at length we parted, we stood and looked at each other, aware and aching with fear and sorrow at the vast gulf that now separated our stations, a gulf that mortality could never bring together again. If ever Fate did put us in sight of one another, it would be as opponents, not friends, his male world bent on invading mine, and I must see that it did not. But we parted appreciating that without this conflict we would live very shallow and meaningless lives indeed."

There was silence when Ghazanfer finished. We were devotees who had just shared a mystery of our religion and to speak would be to profane the moment with the mundane.

After a suitable period of reverence, silent even in the thoughts, my mind began to work again. I realized the monument of what this man had just shared with me, this man I'd hardly ever known before. Indeed, I'd often taken him to be neither more nor less than an enemy and a formidable one at that, in spite of his visit during my illness and the dog's grass potion. I began to rack my brain for some part of myself I could share in return. I found nothing, and felt poor indeed. But rather than leave him empty-handed, I decided to divulge the one bit of information I had on him that was unauthorized.

I said, and hardly as flippantly as it may seem on paper, "Tell me.

Since Andrea Barbarigo has become a Muslim, whom do you visit for your mistress on the outside?"

I didn't really expect an answer. I didn't want one. I only wanted to let him know that I knew.

He looked at me closely. "The shopkeeper next door to Kira's?"

"Yes," I replied.

"I thought you were there." Ghazanfer nodded in appreciation. He took a puff or two on his narghile and then spoke a name, "Michael Cantacuzenos."

I had been so far from expecting a candid answer that I had to ask before I realized that he had just honored me with one more timely piece of information: the name of his current contact.

Michael Cantacuzenos was a Greek, "flotsam and jetsam of the Byzantine Empire" my master liked to say, but he said it good-naturedly. Cantacuzenos was a friend of his and, since Feridun Bey had been forced to flee, my master's closest confident in the capital, what with Arab Pasha in Cyprus. That was nice for the Christian community, but a sad commentary on the state of affairs in the Divan when the only man the Grand Vizier could trust was someone totally out of the political arena.

The moment Ghazanfer Agha made his meaning clear to me, I instantly saw Safiye's hand in any number of decisions Sokolli Pasha had made in the past months. My master was incorruptible and my mistress totally uninterested in wielding her influence over him. So Baffo's daughter had turned to the next closest thing to counteract the weight Nur Banu carried in the Divan with Uweis and Lala Mustafa in the palm of her hand. Cantacuzenos was nothing if not a talker. Sokolli Pasha only ever half listened to him, but that carelessness could make the thoughts seem to arrive in one's mind on their own.

I nodded congratulations to Ghazanfer on the success I perceived. I also let him know I would not betray this secret—not unless absolutely necessary—and he in turn knew I would not.

Not after what had passed between us that afternoon.

XLII

THE PLAGUE CAME late that year, but when it came, it hit hard, and in places that had hitherto been spared, at least in common memory. Pestilence hung over the late summer city like a shroud, tied in knots around the harbor and the barracks, where it always lurks, but also pulled in tight, choking bands even around the homes of the wealthy.

The Italians left Pera in droves and as many natives as could sought refuge on the Princes' Islands out in the Sea of Marmara. Two boats, both sorely overcrowded, collided in rough seas and untold scores were drowned. And when the islands were reached, even there was not guaranteed safety. Some brought the disease with them and it spread in the unnatural conditions of the islands faster, even, than in the fetid streets of slums.

On the islands, too, there is no natural water. The water caught in cisterns and barrels during the winter rains was stagnant by summer, and that caused disease and death of a different and no more pleasant sort.

No. Once again events proved that the best thing to do against the plague was nothing. Best to stay where one was and wait it out, trusting to Allah. Even if a body—the Merciful One forbid it—did take sick and die, there was this consolation. Those that die of the plague, like those who fall on the battlefield in the cause of the Faith or women who die in childbirth for the life of a new infant Muslim, all are counted martyrs and taken at once to sweet-scented gardens in Paradise.

The Mufti, Sheikh al-Islam, was among this year's victims. An old man, we all knew it would be only a matter of time before the fever killed him; he had no strength to fight it off as youth sometimes has, if Allah wills. But the news seemed to us a great justice, if not an actual joy. His position and somber learning, though evidence of great piety and favor of the Almighty, had always seemed to lack the full assurance of martyrdom since he'd allowed himself to be swayed by Selim into taking Cyprus. Now that the crown of death seemed inevitable and well deserved, our whole household removed to his home. The contagion of such holiness was something no one wanted to miss.

My master sat up in the room where the man lay dying, amidst the smell of sickness and fumes of garlic and sage burnt to ease the way to Paradise if the not pestilence. Here disciples droned a night-and-day recitation of the Koran. The local imam tried out phrases for the eulogy while the old ears were still alive to hear and praise it. And the Mufti's sons and a host of friends came and went as time permitted them, taking turns sitting at his side, holding his hand, renewing the wet cloth on his forehead, and exchanging conversation on topics hardly different from the somber, reverent ones the man's dignity had always required.

My master had great respect for the man. Although their opinions in the Divan had not always coincided, Sokolli Pasha appreciated the fact that it was only on a single occasion—when the page boy lay writhing with death, pinned through the heart to the floor—that the Mufti had been influenced by anything but the most pious and learned considerations. That was more than could be said of any of the others.

The Mufti and my master were the only ones left in the high chambers of government who had served under the magnificent Suleiman and remembered what it was like before the word *bribery* was even considered. The choice of a new Mufti lay with the religious institution and not with the palace. Nonetheless, my master could not help but think that the face of the *medrese* had changed since his dying friend Hamid had been elevated. The heavily bearded scholars in attendance at the death told beads not of glass or simple quartz but of lapis lazuli and gold. And Sokolli Pasha recognized among those present some who were little better than the purchased slaves of the Sultan, Uweis, and even Nur Banu.

Sokolli spoke aloud to his dying friend of his most secret concerns. "What shall happen when you are gone, dear friend?" I suppose he realized this was the last time he would be allowed such luxury.

"What will happen will be Allah's will," the Mufti said, no less pious in death than he had been in life.

The lesser scholars continued to drop their beads in unison with the rich sound of a woman's jewelry case. They said nothing, but, as my master told me later, it was clear they would not forget this scene in days to come, when the choosing of the successor took place.

We of the harem were, of course, forbidden direct access to the man in the process of attaining martyrdom. We waited out the time with his wife and daughters. Here things were not quite so somber, and not quite so charged with intrigue.

Umm Kulthum, a woman with the appearance of a fat-tailed sheep, was a faithful wife, but two more different temperaments can hardly be imagined. To his stability, she was flighty, to his reason, emotion. She could not even stumble her way through the simple Arabic of the *Fatiha* without coaching, whereas he was famous for having had the entire Koran memorized by age ten. It is certain that without the harem curtains to divide their worlds, they never would have lasted so many long years together.

Now in the final analysis the only ill effect of this union of opposites might have been to confirm the Mufti in his opinion—easily gained from much of his reading—that all women were silly and hardly to be trusted with the serious demands of religion. What color, if any, this may have painted on his judgments throughout his life no longer seemed of importance, however. The next Mufti might just as well have a harem full of understanding and true religion—no less easy to endure without the division between them, but every bit as likely to influence his opinions.

It was clear that Umm Kulthum's mourning would be wild and intemperate. But it was also clear grief would not begin until her eunuchs brought the word of the actual death. Until then, sorrow, like her religion, was based mainly on outward forms—which must be just so, of course, like the proper, most fashionable sort of veil. But once those forms were seen to, there was no reason to trouble her mind with deep reflection. The consequence of the next few hours, not only on her life, but on the Empire as a whole? What worry was this of hers?

If questioned, you would hear her be as dependent on Allah's will as her husband's study had taught him to be. But for her, pious phrases were born not of having stared the wonderful power of the Divine in the face and understood the utter vanity of all human endeavor. In her mind first you met all the forms, then it was Allah's will, with the sneaking suspicion that if you'd done everything just right, His will could not help but conform to your own.

And so the professional mourners, already called in, were allowed to pass a mirror from one face to the other. They chattered among themselves as they applied heavy coats of kohl to their eyes that would run most impressively when the time came to practice their trade. Trays of preserves and fruit in just such somber proportions as tradition called for appeared from time to time. A Koran reciter read, although no word was understood. Then, to give the professional woman a rest, Gul Ruh was coaxed into showing her skill, for my little charge had major portions of the holy book down as well.

"A remarkable child." Umm Kulthum smiled, and then kept up her duty as hostess by real entertainment—gossip. In her mind at least, it was gossip geared to the somber situation at hand, but it was gossip nonetheless.

"When it comes your turn to become a widow, Esmikhan Sultan— Allah will that the day is years away—how I shall envy you."

Everyone carefully avoided laughing at this absurdity and my lady asked politely, "What do you mean, lady?"

"I mean, of course, that your man is being prudent. He is putting away money now to take care of you when you are alone."

"But my husband is a slave of the Sultan," Esmikhan said. "When he dies, all his wealth returns to the treasury. He cannot bequeath any of it. My daughter and I—Allah have mercy on us—shall be left with only our allowance from the palace. It is the great fear of my life."

"Ah, yes." Umm Kulthum winked slyly. "But everyone knows Sokolli Pasha is keeping some by, off the Sultan's records. Under your bed, isn't it? That's what somebody told me. Well, I'm sure you'll know well enough when the time comes. Allah will it may be a hundred years from now, of course."

Esmikhan said nothing, but I could see the thought pinch in her plump face: Everyone knows? Then how is it that I do not know?

A little while later I was called upon to help move a screen into the sick room, for the Mufti had sent word that he felt the Angel near and would speak somewhat to his harem before he answered the call. I took this opportunity, while my mistress was out of earshot, to ask the almost-widow, "Lady, forgive my asking, but where did you hear about my master's hoarding of loot?"

"Hhm? Well, oh dear me. Simply everywhere. It's common knowledge."

If it's common knowledge then does even the Sultan know—or think, rather—that he is being cheated? I thought this, but did not speak it aloud. Instead, I asked, "Well, tell me where you heard it most recently, then."

"Let me think. Yes, of course. At the palace. I was calling on the Valide Sultan. She was the one who mentioned it."

"Nur Banu. I see."

"She said it was common knowledge. It must be common knowledge, else I wouldn't have brought it up, now, would I?"

"I suppose not, lady." Unless someone had only wished you to think it was common knowledge.

I heard the dying man say to my master, "You'll excuse me, Pasha, my friend," as we approached.

"Of course," Sokolli replied, bowing out of the way to let the curtain encircle the bed.

But the Mufti held on to my master's hand for a moment longer as he said in a hoarse whisper, "Look to your harem, my friend. That is my one regret in this life, that I did not spend more time with those behind me. Don't you answer the Angel making the same mistake I have."

My master nodded. These were the words of an almost-saint, after all. I thought, How pleasant that the Mufti did spend so little time with them, that he is still able to say that. If he'd spent any more, his regrets might have been as great, but they would have been for another, more bitter reason.

When at length she returned to her own domain, the Mufti's wife looked the farthest thing from a woman who had just said her final good-bye to the man she'd been married to for forty years. She was aglow with news and excitement and could not even be induced to take a seat before beginning.

"I suppose they want me to keep quiet about it for a while. You know men. No feelings at all. But I cannot keep still. Listen. Such news! Esmikhan Sultan, you and I are to be relatives! My husband has suggested and yours has agreed that your daughter should marry my youngest son."

Esmikhan gave a gasp of disbelief which Umm Kulthum was quick to reassure.

"Of course, my son's father didn't know anything about Gul Ruh until I dropped a word or two—how she recited today and all, and what a good, pious child she is. It is his death wish. Sokolli Pasha dare not grow perverse later and change his mind. Oh, my husband spoke on and on about the unifying force of the harem and all sorts of other things too deep for the likes of me. But my Abd ar-Rahman, he did blush so nicely all the while. He always was my favorite—well, the youngest always is. I'd say the wedding sheets are all but spread. And it does make my heart sing. Allah bless you with many sons and me with many grandsons," she said now, turning to Gul Ruh. "We shall be so happy together, mother- and daughter-in-law."

After reciting, Gul Ruh had taken to keeping the vigil by playing on the floor with the Mufti's grandchildren. Although condoning adults had smiled and said she was giving their mothers relief by minding them for a while, I had seen clearly that she set the pace for their wild frolic.

Now she suddenly froze and seemed to shrink. Suddenly she was grown up. Suddenly she could no longer laugh and shout or even speak out of turn to her elders. I could see she so wanted to call her hostess's announcement into question—or to refuse it outright. But she was grown-up now and when Umm Kulthum came to pat her on the head and kiss her cheek, she grew white as if growing up had given her the plague.

"I am surprised," Esmikhan finally found breath to confess. "Indeed, I had thought a match between Safiye's Muhammed and my Gul Ruh would be made. Nothing has been said, of course. I just assumed . . ."

Gul Ruh got up off the floor, shaking herself of the children as she did of dust and went to stand beside her mother for support—whether hers or her mother's it was not clear.

Yes, yes. It's true. My cousin, Muhammed. It is he I should marry. We have been promised since we were children. But it was only Gul Ruh's eyes that spoke. She said nothing at all aloud.

"Oh, but you know as well as I—Allah willing—Muhammed is to be Sultan. Sultans do not marry. Who is their equal in the world? Marriages should be made between equals. And Sultans cannot afford to let their matches become victims of all the politics and bickering that normally go on. It will not go on between us, my dear, of course. But just the presence of some foreign father-in-law is enough to suggest against it."

"But we thought it was time the dynasty freed itself from the machinations of slave girls and their particular interests. If Muhammed marries his cousin—and I think they are fond of each other—" Gul Ruh could not keep her head from affirming this with a quick nod. "—then the dynasty will be firm, Ottomans on both sides."

"That is only Safiye's wishful thinking," Umm Kulthum said. "She doesn't want her son ever to be lured from her influence as has happened to Murad and which is even now breaking poor Nur Banu's heart. Actually, Esmikhan Sultan, if I may be frank, I should think you'd be glad to keep your daughter out of that brawl which is sure to break out—Allah forbid—when Muhammed comes of age."

Such observations were too clear and too insightful for them to have originated with the Mufti's wife herself. I think even my lady realized they, too, must have been gathered at this last visit to Nur Banu's part of the Serai. Esmikhan had this advantage over her hostess: She had been raised in the palace where tact had more value than an orthodox adherence to truth. She reminded herself severely of the more sober purpose that brought them there and she smiled politely.

"I mean no insult, lady," she said. "If I appear hesitant, it is only through disbelief. I am unable to believe that Allah should bless such a house as ours, tinged with politics and war and slavery as it is, with the blessed peace and wisdom of a great house such as yours."

Umm Kulthum, without Nur Banu's coaching, could never suspect duplicity. She sat on her cushions and smiled broadly and simply at my lady's comment and comforted her forthcoming widowhood with thoughts of a wedding soon to follow.

Fortunately, there was no time for further discussion on the subject, for at that moment one of Umm Kulthum's eunuchs brought a message from the men's quarters. We had to leave at once. With all our concern for the old Mufti, we had ignored the earlier notice we had received that the Vizier of the Cupola, Piale Pasha, had failed to attend the previous day's Divan for some indisposition. The indisposition, we now learned, was the plague and, as if it had the help of his younger, stronger body instead of its hindrance, it had done its work much faster than on the frail old Mufti. The Vizier lay now at death's very door and it was only with the utmost haste that we could hope to arrive before the last *Fatiha* was said for him.

Selim had given Piale Pasha his second daughter, Esmikhan's half-sister Gewherkhan Sultan, to wife. The union had not been blessed with children, but it was a union of hearts uncommon even when the marriage is for love. The passion, even after so many years, was so intense that many, including the Sultan, said it interfered with the Vizier's duties and Esmikhan would be the first to admit that her relationship with her sister had not been the same since those sheets were first bloodied.

But if ever Gewherkhan needed her sister, it would be now. Some even chose to take a lesson from this: Let not your marriages grow too close, for Death and Allah are the portion of all. It was clear that Gewherkhan Sultan would not enjoy the easy, gossipy drift into widowhood Umm Kulthum did.

Sokolli Pasha was not without his emotion at this passing, either. Indeed, he left us to find the way to the Vizier's house on our own and hurried on ahead, as if a brain for deployment of troops and political intrigue could do anything against the plague doctors had not already tried. Piale Pasha, although close friends with Uweis and his circle, was not below opposing them when his conscience told him so. He had the passion of a virtuous woman behind him and there were some things Gewherkhan Sultan would not let him stoop to. My master would find the Divan a very lonely place indeed with both the Vizier and the Mufti gone hand in hand over the hair-thin bridge to Paradise.

Ineffable are the ways of Allah. By nightfall, both men were dead. The professional mourners from the Mufti's had offered the names and addresses of their sisters and cousins to fill the quota at the Vizier's. Between the two houses, the women had earned enough to keep them 'til the next plague before two parallel columns inched their way to the cemetery come morning. My master took the privilege of carrying the bier in both.

And when he returned home, he sent for Michael Cantacuzenos. Until the Greek came, Sokolli Pasha took comfort in composing another long letter to Cyprus.

XLIII

SOON THE FIRST rains of autumn came, flushed out the disease, and cleared the air. Everyone breathed easier and freer; merely filling the lungs brought a smile to the faces one saw in the street.

But there was one major hindrance to free breathing in our harem, and Umm Kulthum's visit certainly did not help it go away. She came and kissed Gul Ruh moistly on the cheek and asked pointedly how work on her trousseau was coming, for she would soon have need of it. Gul Ruh, who never pierced needle with thread with any confidence, balked at the idea and said nothing.

"We must get to know each other better," Umm Kulthum pursued. "Please, feel free to stop by my house anytime. Yes, I fully intend to make your marriage bed within the year . . ."

As soon as manners allowed her escape, Gul Ruh left the divan and, lest they seek her in the garden or the bath or any of the other usual places, she came bursting into my room for asylum.

"I cannot! I will not!" she shouted, then succumbed to tears.

I took her gently in my arms and let her cry it out. Emotion came over me in surges as I felt the woman in her body that was quickly overtaking the child. Had I still been a man, it was emotion that would have been dangerous for us both. As matters stood, I felt only a terrible craving to protect her from anything and everything evil, destructive, or even sad in the world. In either case, I knew I would gladly die for her sake.

When the tears had given her some measure of peace so that speech was at least possible, I said, "Now tell me what is so frightful about this Abd ar-Rahman ibn Hamid to cause all these tears. For I have never even seen him myself and all I have heard comes from his own mother. I know enough not to trust those glowing reports, so tell me what it is that you have heard."

Gul Ruh was silent, so I guessed. "You know nothing about him either, do you? So I thought." I spoke gently. "How can you judge a man so unseen?"

"I don't want to see him! I don't want to know anything more about him!"

"But I do," I said. Before she could do more than fling a glance at me such as is usually reserved for the most vile of traitors, I continued, "How shall I know how to most effectively fight against this marriage for you if I don't find out about the man?"

"Oh, you dear Abdullah!" The hug and kiss she gave me then were more than recompense for all my years of service.

"The trouble is, how to learn more about him? If I suddenly appear at the *medrese* where, as his mother says, Abd ar-Rahman spends all his time in study, I will be immediately suspected, an ignorant oaf like me among all those scholars. No, I'm afraid, my little heart's oasis, there is no other way. You must feign some interest yourself to give me a chance to accompany you. Not too much interest, of course, or your mother-in-law will find you forward and undesirable."

"What a good idea! I shall be so interested, I shall scare him right away for the shame of a forward wife!"

"Easy now. If you make yourself a name for being forward, no one but a gypsy would have you, even if you are an Ottoman. No, let us try this tack first and then, if that doesn't work, we may consider more drastic means."

Umm Kulthum's house was right against the city's western wall. Its roof proved an excellent place for my young mistress to watch the annual pilgrims' departure for Mecca. Of this great festival she otherwise must have been content to only hear reports.

It pleased Umm Kulthum to no end that the only member of Sokolli Pasha's household who accepted her invitation should be the girl she intended for her youngest son. And she was very helpful in providing opportunities for Gul Ruh (and myself) to view something more important than the pilgrim's procession, and that was a glimpse of the man she was to marry.

The men of the household—those who were not elsewhere in town, officiating at the attendant ceremonies—did not have such a good view as the women from their second-story window. To see over the walls, they had to climb onto the roof of the kiosk that served as the family's prayer hall, mosque, and library. This was mostly slaves and young boys, a rather undignified bunch with no supervision. One passing might have thought them the household of a tanner or a goldsmith rather than that of one of the greatest family of legists in the world.

A single young man alone did not join their antics. He sat below, reading a book. He was in sight and earshot of the festivities, giving the impression of joining in and enjoying the diversions. It was, after all, a religious holiday. But his delight in the book gave him such powers of concentration that he might have been sitting in the hush of a deserted mosque the whole while. The catcalls and laughter of his peers might have been no more than the rustling of sleepy pigeons in the rafters.

"There he is," Umm Kulthum announced proudly. "That's my heart's delight."

Under his father's influence, Abd ar-Rahman ibn Hamid al-Mufti had been named *muderisler,* or professor in the *medrese,* when he was circumcised at the age of twelve. Although, like his father, he could recite the Koran from memory by that age, he was by no means capable of giving lectures on religious law to men of forty. That required grey hairs, or so the saying went. A man more qualified was chosen to represent the boy in these duties for a small salary and, in most cases, that would have been fine.

This boy, however, could not escape a horrible sense of responsibility which by now, after six or seven years of the pretense, was heavily commingled with guilt. There was his father's name to live up to, as well as a whole chain of older brothers who had attained positions of importance. Abd ar-Rahman was determined to succeed, but full-heartedly and idealistically trusted in study to do it. His brothers had known enough to develop personality and social relations as well as their study. At eighteen, such a life seemed burned from the young man by the white heat of books.

His flesh was as grey as an ash pit, and though it could not be denied he knew much, it was hardly to be called wisdom. When asked what he knew, learning came from him in endless yet disjointed streams that could never be discerned to have anything to do with the subject at hand. There wasn't the solid base of experience to give flesh and rationality to his comments. When his opinion was not called for—which came to happen more and more frequently as he matured, instead of less—he would sit to one side wearing on his face a pallid yet firm look of superiority: They were all fools basing decisions on no authority, and if they'd only ask, he could set them all straight.

The final outcome was that Abd ar-Rahman was painfully, sometimes viciously, a loner, and proud of the fact. He seemed frail, old, and senile, but had never enjoyed full use of his faculties between this state and the folly of youth.

When the head of the procession could be seen approaching, the other lads called down from the roof of the kiosk to say he had better come up now or he would miss it altogether. To us up behind the second-story grille, this was our first view of the young man on his feet. His mother gave no apology for the sight. Still even she, a strong and robust person herself, could not help but be touched, perhaps even frightened by the thinness of his body as it appeared beneath his festive robes. His body was not the product of a restrained diet forged into strong wiry bands by exercise. It was pasty and unsound, the back and limbs already curled and permanently creased into unnatural shapes by too much sitting and cramped reading. His mother couldn't apologize. She only let what had been a steady stream of prideful commentary fall into uneasy stillness.

We all held our breath as Abd ar-Rahman made his attempts—at first pitifully abortive—to use the window ledges and railings to climb to the roof. He very nearly gave up the project and used this as an excuse to return to his book. But the others wouldn't hear of it. Some of thcm climbed down, and pushing and pulling, they managed to get him up in time for the passing of the two holy camels. We felt at once that the lads would have done better to leave him on the ground. As every other head bowed in wonder before the spectacle, Abd ar-Rahman turned his head in superior disgust. Such ignorant people, bowing before no more than an empty saddle and a garish mound of black and gold! One could almost hear him reciting chapter and verse where the Faithful are enjoined not to add gods to God.

Before our arrival that morning, one portion of my mind had nurtured the hope that a glimpse of the young man would change Gul Ruh's youthful heart, making any machinations on my part unnecessary. I could see now that that hope must be abandoned. My little monkey who still climbed all over roofs and trees the moment my back was turned—I was to stand by and watch as she was married to that man? He was old before his time, a pale, limp rag such as others use to mark their places in their books when they go off to more important business. I looked down at her protectively then and vowed that it should not be so.

Certainly her mind was filled with thoughts of similar purpose. But as I looked down I noticed something about her determination that disquieted me. It included the thoughtful fingering of the golden hoops she had put in her ears that day.

At last we bade good-bye to the Mufti's widow, having waded through many more wishes for the joyful union of our households. When we were finally out of earshot, packing up the sedan chair to return home, my young mistress sighed wearily and said, "By Allah, Abdullah, I do hope you come up with something to prevent this."

"I shall try everything in my power," I assured her, and she kept her face outside the curtain for a moment to fix me with a look of gratitude. I touched that face, coaxing a brief smile from it. Then I gently, purposely fingered her earring as she had done. "But," I said, "I cannot even dream of getting you the man who gave you these."

She looked away at once and closed the curtain with her own hand, which told me I'd guessed aright. Those earrings had come from Cyprus, a gift from Arab Pasha. It was not so much that she was opposed to Abd ar-Rahman ibn Hamid as that she still dreamed of gaining substantiation for her youthful infatuation for the big, strong black man who was like a brother to her. Even her suggested preference for the Prince Muhammed was only a blind. After two years of life, can an infatuation still be brushed aside so? Such a match was out of the question, too, of course. Poor child, I murmured as I secured the latch over my treasure and pulled the curtain to. Poor child!

XLIV

WE WALKED HOME through the early evening streets. The pilgrims were across the Sea in Asia now. It seemed they had taken the soul of the city with them. The muezzin's call was lifeless. ("Hurry," I told the porters. I had not realized it was so late.) What virtue could be claimed by turning the face and heart towards Mecca for the few brief minutes it takes to pray? Those of true virtue had given their prayers action and set their feet already on the pilgrims' trail. We were left behind with but the form, the hollow shell of religion. Such was the dark feeling of premonition that came over me.

Oh, Allah, I prayed, be merciful to us now.

A dark figure pressed by me hurriedly in the narrow street. I noticed curiously the clink of chain mail and the knobbed helmet of a *chiaus,* an imperial bodyguard.

How odd, I thought. What cause has a *chiaus* to run? His will—his master's will—is the supreme law of the land. He should have no cause to cover his tell-tale red trousers and chain mail with a dark cloak nor to run furtively like a thief.

We turned the corner then into our lane and the porters stopped with a jerk, uttering spells against evil. "Keep going! Keep going!" I told them, but had to shove one man quite roughly to make him obey.

Gul Ruh drew the curtain back inquisitively. "What is it, Abdullah?"

"Are you a whore that you must go showing yourself to every

passerby?" I spoke to her more sharply than I ever had before. But I was not so afraid she would be seen as that she might see.

I hurried the sedan in through our gates, warning the porters they must not upset the harem by reporting what they had seen. I told the gatekeeper to fetch the master in a hurry, and one peek out of the gate was enough to give him wings.

Still, it seemed I stood a very long time alone in the dark street in the shadow of a dead man. At first I had thought my duty was to protect him from dogs or the desecration of human stares and jeers. But as the only live thing I saw—a lean, grey cat—skirted the lane as if were bewitched, I shivered and came to crave protection myself.

The holiest ones, I suddenly remembered, had all left us for Mecca that day. We were at the mercy of the influences of the Pit. The body swung from its hook as if, even though the life was gone, his spirit still stirred with an angry craving for justice and revenge.

At length the gate opened. I jumped at the sound as if it were the chains of a ghost. The master came out accompanied by three *chiauses* from the Porte he had lately been given as a bodyguard. The sight of their round-knobbed helmets made me remember the figure that had so quickly rushed by me and it touched my back with cold. I also remembered that when Sokolli Pasha had been given the guard he had been surprised and asked the Sultan: "Master, why do I need a bodyguard? I have always walked the streets with but a few unarmed attendants and feared nothing."

Murad's reply was evasive, but seemed to suggest that he knew things he was not telling.

The master was dressed in the plain, simple robe and small, loose turban he always retired to on the rare evenings he had to himself. I realized then that he must have been at his prayers. I could imagine him, kneeling on his rug, when the doorkeeper burst in out of breath, gasping the news: "Master, the Greek is dead. Hung from a lamp hook just outside our gate."

For one brief moment, Sokolli Pasha would have lost his place in the recitation. Michael Cantacuzenos was the only man he would receive in that state of easy undress, the only man he trusted not to be influenced by the cloth of gold of his robes or a large gold band around his turban.

Cantacuzenos had been expected to arrive before the prayers so their talk could begin immediately after and go on long into the night. When the man had not come, Sokolli had rolled out his rug, anyway. Now when he heard the reason for the tardiness, it did cause him one brief stumble in form. But he soon found the words again: "Praise be to Allah, the Lord of the worlds, the Merciful, the Compassionate, the Ruler of the Day of Judgement . . ." And he did not even raise his hands from their prescribed place at chest level to indicate to the gatekeeper he must wait. He let the intensity of his prayer give that message, and the intensity also gave him fortitude, for he was able to step out of the gate minutes later and look on the street as calmly as he might have greeted his friend on the doorstep alive.

Christian priests were sent for to give the man the rites he had clung to in life. I heard one of them mutter: "That's what comes of dealing with Turks and renegades. Even those who put on a show of protecting us, underneath, they are still not to be trusted."

I was glad the master was not nearby then to hear that. It would have hurt him more than the death itself.

Before the priests arrived, however, the master's *chiauses* climbed up and cut the body down. Seeing them there undoing what I had reason to believe comrades of theirs had only shortly before done made me draw the master to one side and tell him what I had seen and what I suspected.

"The Greek did not hang himself," I said. "Where is the stool he kicked away? He couldn't have done it otherwise."

Finally I showed the master the slip of paper I had retrieved from the dead man's chest before any other had seen and read it. It said, "Defiler of Muslim women. Condemned to Hell."

Later Ghanzanfer Agha offered this information to me without prompting: "By Allah, I knew the last time I met the Greek with a message from Safiye that we were seen, but I never imagined it would end like this." And even though the man was not a believer, Ghazanfer prayed, "Allah have mercy on his soul."

"Men from the palace must have been here—somewhere near— watching our gate," I whispered to my master that night. "Waiting for him to arrive. They have done this, master, though for the love of Allah I know not why."

But Sokolli Pasha only nodded at my passion and my words. Perhaps it was only the calmness of the prayer, but I had the feeling he had expected this all along.

Once more, after the death of the Greek, my master spilled his grief into another very long letter to Arab Pasha.

The only reply the messenger brought back from the island was a plain dark blue woolen cloak. The cloak was hard and black in spots and rent near each spot with a ragged slash. The governor of Cyprus had been wearing it when, the report said, he was set upon by brigands ("The island crawls with them since the war's desolation") and killed.

"His bodyguard?" My master managed to ask this in a tone as if the news were only the reports of the wheat harvest in Bulgaria.

"That's good news, my lord Pasha." The messenger forced a smile. "They all escaped by the favor of Allah."

"All?" My master's eyes wandered for one brief moment to his own bodyguard, the *chiauses* from the Porte, standing at attention on either side of him. He shook his head firmly against a thought. No, impossible. That would be too obvious.

"Without a scratch," the messenger replied, losing his smile. "My lord, what's the matter? I thought that bit of news would cheer you at least."

"It should cheer me that one as dear to me as a son should be killed and his bodyguard of one hundred men should not raise a finger in his defense?"

"It . . . it does seem odd, doesn't it?" the messenger admitted.

"Yes, indeed. 'Odd.' " The master's thoughts were elsewhere, so it was a moment before he concluded, "Thank you. That is all."

BUSINESS IN THE harem kept my mind facing another direction. The latest-made widow returned, seven months gone with Arab Pasha's child. She had to be eased from wife of governor back down to one slave among many again. That was a noisy, weepy affair, and when the child was born, there was more wailing. Not only did the mother weep over the fact that she'd borne no son to carry on the governor's name, but the little girl was sickly and demanding, yet stubbornly refused to die. And everyone else moaned, too, as the stress told on us all.

On the other hand, there was Gul Ruh's grief. It was quiet and terrible. She wouldn't eat for nearly a week until we forced her. But the curtains of the harem closed over this grief, too, like skin over a wound. No scar remained to show the world where it had pierced so deeply. Only after that, Gul Ruh was never the same girl—or rather, young woman—again.

Just how changed she was I couldn't imagine until some weeks later when Sokolli Pasha asked that I bring his daughter to him in the *mabein*. He had not seen her, I realized, since Feridun Bey's disappearance, for he never gave himself cause to deal with women anymore. I could tell he was nervous, but so was she, with wide eyes and a heart one could almost see, fluttering in the color on her cheeks.

I gave no more thought to this dilemma, but laid my hand on her shoulder as we slowly walked to the *mabein* and I promised her once again I would see to it she never married anyone she didn't want to.

"Hello, child," Sokolli greeted her.

"Hello, Father." Her head was down, her chin right on her chest. One could hardly hear her.

"Well, come here, child. I won't bite." He laughed at this nervously as if even he didn't expect to be believed.

She went to him, but at a certain point, covered her face with her hands before him as if he were a total stranger, which, indeed, it might be said he was. Finally, he coaxed her on his knee. He was remembering the child: The young woman looked very awkward there, and rigid with nerves. But in that position he was able to work the hands away from her face, lift her chin, and look at her. I could see her face gave him quite a start.

If he had flattered himself when she was a child that there were shadows of his features in her face, in the immobility that had come to young adulthood, he could no longer do so. Was it so plain that even he could see exactly whose features those were, or was he merely struck by their dark, young beauty—the soft, full mouth, the large, black eyes, cheeks thin, but full of bloom? Did he think, perhaps, there was something attractive in the mother he must have overlooked all these years?

Sokolli Pasha had to look away for a moment to lay those thoughts aside. When his eyes returned, he came to the business at hand: "Do you understand, Daughter, that I mean only the best for your future happiness and care?"

"Yes, Father," she murmured.

"Good, for I have decided not to put off giving you to a good man any longer. At first I thought to do so, in deference to your youth. But if you are still young, I grow older every day. I do not know how much longer Allah may allow me to remain as your father."

"May He will you a hundred years, Father," the girl prayed formulaically.

Sokolli Pasha nodded his thanks at the wish but continued, "Still, I feel I must no longer put off arrangements for your future care. You may not have heard, but on his deathbed, the Mufti Hamid, Allah favor him, spoke of marrying you to his youngest son. It was his dying wish. I should try to fulfill it. They came to me today, the Mufti's older sons, and said they craved the pleasure of calling on me tomorrow night. I know they mean to set the bride-price and once it is set, we cannot in honor back out. You understand?"

She gave a quick nod.

"I only wanted to make certain the match was agreeable to you. I do want you to be happy. I can, you know, drive the price up so high they will be insulted and turn their backs on us forever. But they are a good family, a strong family, and unless the Sultan is a fool, many more Muftis may come from them. Even young Abd ar-Rahman I understand is already famous for his learning. Allah may will that he become the Sheikh al-Islam. But remember, I want you to be happy. You may speak your mind to me, Daughter, now."

I could not believe my ears. She spoke lowly but no less plainly. "I will marry Abd ar-Rahman, Father, if that is your will."

The child is intimidated, I thought angrily. I must speak for her. But it was neither the time nor the place. I had only one day before the brothers came. I must think of a plan quickly.

XLV

SOKOLLI PASHA GAVE me no time to think just then. He finished the interview with signs of pleasure but signs of relief as well, and dismissed Gul Ruh quickly. She ran off, no less relieved. But when I tried to follow, to reassure her of my support and that this marriage still might not be, the master held me back.

Perhaps now is my chance, I thought hopefully, but he did not ask my opinion. That much, he assumed, was settled. I had heard her agree to the match with my own ears, had I not?

Instead, Sokolli Pasha told me, "The Mufti said on his deathbed that I should spend more time with my harem. It would give me peace, he said. I see now it is true. You must help me in this, Abdullah. Tomorrow, there is the Divan and in the evening, the visit from the boy's brothers. But then . . ."

He did not finish the sentence, yet it seemed to finish our conversation. So I said I would certainly help him in every way I could.

It occurred to me that simply coming to know his daughter better would put an end to the marriage plans.

But though Sokolli had turned away, I could tell I was not yet dismissed. When he turned again, I was startled beyond words to see tears in his eyes. The Grand Vizier? Whoever would have imagined him capable of tears?

"I know . . ." he said, struggling to swallow the grief. "I have known from the first she was not mine."

My heart seemed to die. Did he also know my part in the matter? Was I now, after all these years, to finally be brought to justice?

"By Allah, there were times when I wished the inspiration of the Prophet had not spoken out against the disposal of unwanted girls. How easy, like the ancient Greeks, simply to take one's shame, the proof of how little a man one is, out onto the hillside and expose it there.

"But I said then and I say it now, from the Sura of the Bee: 'His judgements are faulty who allows dark shadows to settle on his face when a girl child is born.' Even a girl child that is not one's own. I have seen that it is so. For your part in her creation, Abdullah, I not only forgive but thank you."

His generosity shamed, confused and made me grateful all at once.

"There is an old peasant song," he continued without a pause for me to express my emotions in, which I don't think I could have done anyway. "Sometimes the wisdom of the peasants comes close to competing with that of the Koran. The song says:

> My own daughter
> My face was shadowed when you were born.
> I did not want your shame.
> But years and Allah have taught me
> The error and pride of my ways.
> O daughter
> Pretty, joyous child in the light of our family hearth.
> Now I would rather die myself than ever lose you.
> The bridegroom is my foe.
> He cannot pay me enough."

Again Sokolli Pasha fell silent, but again I understood we were not finished. This time the silence seemed endless. It was possible for me to take in the full import of what he had just confessed. I let the confession produce tears in my eyes as well. I let it bring to my mind all of the scenes I'd witnessed and abetted between Ferhad and my mistress.

Then there was still time, after those emotions, to go on to consider other related topics. I was in the midst of wondering just how, after such a confession, I could possibly break the man's heart with news that his daughter—and she was his daughter, after all—could not really ever be happy obeying his plans for her. In the midst of this wondering, Sokolli Pasha, whose mind must also have wandered far and wide in that time, got up from his seat and began to pace. His steps soon brought him to my side, and then he laid a gentle hand on my shoulder.

"Do you remember, Abdullah," he asked, "the day you first came here and stood in the courtyard for my approval?"

"Yes, master." It was curious, but my mind had leaped to that same time in the past just before he spoke. No doubt it was the hand on my shoulder, for he had given me that very same touch then, and at no other time in between.

"And to think I left you on your own with my harem all those years—what was it? Four or more?" He laughed, then sobered. "Well, it's easy to see my confidence could not have been better placed. All these years, you have served me well. I hope I may count on you to look out for my interests in years to come."

He had dropped his hand, but now, as I gave some clumsy words of promise to do my best, it returned. His hand seemed to have become some tender creature, a dove or petallike butterfly. It landed on my shoulder and, though I grew stiff with its presence, I did not dare to shrug it off for fear I might do it harm.

"When I was a boy," Sokolli Pasha said, "growing up in the Enclosed School, I learned to find release in the love of men rather than the love of women. It took less time than climbing harem walls, caused less trouble, and although I may be biased in this, was less nerve-wracking while being more satisfying.

"I was steeling myself to change all that and marry Selim's daughter—she was my first and is still my only woman—when I saw you. I saw you there in the courtyard. And suddenly, I was excited about being married. Many a time I came to the harem—to her, yes, but mostly to see you. I didn't notice there was a lack of eunuchs in my household because you seemed more than enough for my needs . . ."

As he spoke, I became aware of a very strange sensation. In my parts I'd thought dead and gone for so many years, I felt a strange stirring. I had strolled through the bathhouses full of naked women and felt nothing. But no one had suggested the possibility of my enjoying the throes of love before—before this.

That was just my first reaction. It was the reverse of the old proverb: the flesh, indeed, was willing, but the spirit was weak. Twenty years among the Turks where such things were natural could not overcome my earlier years where the thought had turned my stomach rotten. Stammering, I tried to explain the dilemma to him.

"I know," he stopped my self-torment with a word. "I have known you could not feel as I do ever since I learned about—about my wife and the other man. You took her part against mine, even in such a case. I have known since then you could not love me. And perhaps that hurt more than being a cuckold. Still, I will not force you—I will not even ask you, if you cannot. My dreams are happier this way."

The force of his passion brought me, helpless, to my knees before him. I bowed before the greatness of his soul, all it bore, and the vastness of the lonely abyss through which he carried it. Even at this hour, when every friend in the world had been taken from him, he was a gentleman still, and perfect in honor. I bent over his hands and kissed them for their honor.

I performed this obeisance against my will, and as soon as rationality caught up with me, I panicked: Now he thinks I have capitulated and will submit to his caresses. Even as this thought formed, one of his hands stirred to touch me ever-so-slightly on the cheek.

I raised my head with a jerk as much to escape that touch as to look with fear into his face. There I saw tears, fresher and more copious than he had shed when his daughter left him. But I also saw, through them, that he was resigned to my departure, too. I was free to go.

I managed one final, deep salaam to his greatness at the door, then I fled, like a woman, to the safety of the harem.

XLVI

My earlier plans to go at once to Gul Ruh and promise her I'd thwart her marriage moved me only in fits and starts. I did look in her room and found it dark. I took a tour of all the usual places, although my mind was so occupied I sometimes forgot why I was there.

I even tried the shutters on the windows over the roof. One where the nail had worked loose I opened, not so much with anger at the shoddy workmanship but with gratitude. It gave me a chance to look out over the tiles, slick with an icing of night rain, to clear my head with the cool, dark air. Had there been signs of Gul Ruh going out there, I certainly wasn't so distracted I wouldn't have panicked for her safety. She was no longer the little monkey she had been even one year before. Her limbs were now long and, though graceful while walking and dancing, she would be ungainly on all fours. And on those slippery tiles!

But there were no signs, and the panic that overcame me then was for myself instead. My future in this house stretched out below in a treacherous, endless abyss as deep and friendless as my master's loneliness. How long I sat on the dark stairs down from the roof and brooded over this I could not say. At last, some noise below (like someone approaching, but it was not) brought my thoughts into cohesion and myself to my feet and to the matter at hand.

My path to the next place I'd thought to look for Gul Ruh took me past her room again. It was still dark as before, but some sense of presence drew me in this time. As my eyes were more used to the dark by now, I was soon able to make out figures on the floor, then the slow and gentle breathing of women in easy sleep. There she was with her maids, just where she should have been at that hour. And from the depth and solidity of their sleep, I guessed they must have been there when I'd passed before. I had only credited to my young mistress the sleeplessness that haunted me.

It is customary to give a bride a week or so of festivities and rituals to get her used to the idea of being a wife before the night of the actual consummation, I thought. But was the nervous bride I spoke of Gul Ruh—or myself?

I returned to my room alone to brood over these matters most of the night. But at one point I was drawn to leave that haven and creep back down into the *selamlik*. The master, I discovered, could not sleep either. More than that, the Grand Vizier of all the Faithful had been unable to bear this night alone. The sputtering of lamps had not been enough company for his troubled soul. He had called for his personal secretary—and though the man grumbled and nodded with craving for his own bed, he was obliged to watch the night with his employer.

The secretary was not like Sokolli's previous one, Feridun Bey, whom we'd hidden all those days in the *mabein*. He was a man of the Porte, a slave of the Sultan. Of course Feridun Bey had been, too, but never in quite the sense of this man. We all knew this new secretary to be neither more nor less than a spy of Uweis's faction. How my heart wrenched with pity to see this great man, my master, reduced to such a one for company!

Of course there could be no intimate conversation with such a man. Sokolli Pasha was having him read instead from the history of Murad's predecessors on the throne of Othman. Nothing, being reported back to unfriendly parties, could be discovered to be more loyal and pious and at the same time harmless and innocuous. Had he only wanted to be loyal and pious, Sokolli could have read the book for himself, I suppose. But he needed it read aloud. Such was my master's craving for even so much as the lifeless drone of a fellow human voice on that dark night.

As I stood outside the door, they came to the part in the tale where Murad the First, after all his great victories, is mortally wounded by the Serbian rebels. Here my master waved his hand for the reading to stop.

The secretary who had seemed to be reading with glazed eyes now took on some life. I suspect the coincidence of names—Murad the First with our present Murad the Third—made him hope vent might be given to seditious comments. But it was not so. My master was as true to the present son of Othman as he had been to Selim and Suleiman before him. He simply used the pause to recite the first Sura of the Koran for the dead Emperor's soul.

That image of my master is branded forever on my eyelids. An unearthly light filled him as he recited, though his body remained so very grey. He huddled with age against contact with the divan beneath him, the dusty old cushions behind him and anything else physical around him. I had never thought him old until that moment. I could not help exclaiming in my heart: Here is one truly good man according to anyone's upbringing. By Allah, I love . . .

I did not finish the confession that at any other time would have been disgusting to me. My thoughts were interrupted by spoken words. "Would that the All Powerful might give me," Sokolli Pasha said with a quiet fervor, "just such a death in His service."

And I slipped off before I was seen.

Sometime near dawn I must have slept for I totally missed the call to prayers and the master's early departure in full procession to attend the Divan. But the moment I awoke, all my tumultuous concerns for our future life together, once these confessions had been made, came crashing down upon me again. I began to wish Gul Ruh would soon get married. Then I could ask to go with her to her new home.

But what sort of betrayal was this? I had promised to help her stay unwed, not hurry her enslavement to that shy, dull Mufti's son. Praise Allah, what wisdom there is in keeping the sexless ones unburdened with matters of love.

Would we could always remain so uninvolved.

My first duty of the day, then, was to think no more about myself, but to find my young mistress and hear her mind on the matter.

Questioning the first of her maids I discovered in the hall, I learned that she had been up since first prayers, had dragged our old seamstress out of bed, and taken her to the main sitting room where, for all the maid knew, they were at that moment busily working on the young lady's trousseau. For had I not heard the good news? "Our lady is to be married."

This report I found heady with overromanticized nonsense. Our seamstress had once declared aloud and to everyone in general that she would rather make a million sheets and pillowcases herself than have to supervise Gul Ruh in one more stitch, for the girl was hopeless with a needle and it took four times as long to unpick every mistake as to do it oneself.

No one had been more relieved than our little monkey to hear that news and she had danced off declaring herself the happiest girl alive if she should never hear the word *trousseau* again. Obviously the maid had been dreaming her dreams onto another. Nonetheless, I took her at her word and headed off in that direction.

On my way I saw something which made me forget all concerns for the future, both hers and mine. Through a window, my eye chanced to be drawn (although I know now there was very little chance about it) to a figure standing outside in the damp and autumn brown of the garden. It was the figure of an ill-clad dervish.

XLVII

MORE THAN ONCE I had spoken to this same holy man face-to-face without recognition. But I now, in the mystical way of such creatures, knew him at first glance. It was my old, dear friend Husayn—or rather, in his present manifestation, the no less dear but saintly Hajji.

I had known him since childhood. When my family was lost, he had replaced them. He had saved my life on more than one occasion, more than enough to make up for the time I'd saved his, by accident more than design. He had also taken revenge for me, killing the man that had castrated me. In committing this crime, he had willingly given up the comfortable life of a wealthy merchant for the wandering, anonymous asceticism of a dervish.

I had not seen Husayn, I suddenly realized, since leaving Konya, when our girl, old enough now to be a bride, had not even been conceived. And at that first glimpse of my ancient friend, I realized how achingly he had been missing from my life.

My feet shed the years and the steps between us as pitch sheds water. In a moment, I was down in the garden, running towards him and calling, "My friend! My friend! A thousand blessings on your presence here! How my eyes rejoice to see you!"

Hajji stood as stoically as a statue—like a Christian saint instead of a Muslim—and the names of Allah dropped from his fingers (his rosary) like the last of the night's rain from the leafless branches. He did not move to greet me. But when we were close enough to speak, the precipitate form of his words could only be allowed to one totally indifferent to society's rules of polite, flowery greeting. He said no more than this: "Your master, my friend. I have information that there is a plot on his life."

I stood clutching his free hand in both of mine, grinning and panting. He said no more but looked at me steadily until the full import of his words sank in. I swallowed the silliness of my grin away—my teeth were cold beneath my lips—and caught breath to ask soberly, "How? When? Who is it?"

Hajji chose to answer my middle question only, saying, "If he is not warned at once . . . indeed, it may be Allah's will that you are already too late."

"Yes. Yes," I said with a hard but still puzzled nod between each syllable. "I will go. But you must step inside and accept our hospitality until I return."

I found the gatekeeper, the gardener, and the gardener's boy idling by a fire in the gatekeeper's room. It took a bit longer to convince them—I invented more details than I knew in the end. But finally they were willing to stir from their fire. The boy I sent into the garden to find my friend and honor him with hospitality until we came back.

Perhaps this is all foolishness, I thought as the gatekeeper girded himself about with his token weapon—a rusty old sword—and the gardener and I took up sticks to add to my ceremonial dagger. Did not the *chiauses,* real soldiers armed with real weapons, accompany my master as they always did? What good shall we do but cause the laughter of sober citizens as if we were the stragglers of a drunken brawl. It was with these thoughts that I warned my companions not to slow down, but to move with care. My friend had brought this intelligence and I knew he wouldn't lie.

"We do not want to alert the assassin," I explained, "and give him time to evade us."

We made our way quickly to the Second Court—as close to the heart of the palace as I could get using the men's entrance. In spite of my caution, our arrival seemed to be the most excitement that court had seen all day. Because of the weather, the usual crowd of spectators had stayed home from this Divan. Even of the petitioners most, it seemed, had decided their grievances could wait for fairer weather.

A few of the most obnoxious variety of merchants, some craftsmen too indigent to go back to their tools, a eunuch on his mistress's business (so he dared not return empty-handed) and a single, ragged dervish were the only citizens hunkering in the portico. They sat talking quietly to one another or to themselves with the drop of rosary beads. There were no scuffles as adversaries met, no loud cries for justice as a meeting of the Divan could bring forth on a hot, passionate day.

With a rabble of such proportions, the janissaries set to guard the court were at ease—at least they were until we appeared. Three men bursting in flushed with fear and haste brought them up from their gambling to stand at attention. My companions were immediately struck by the peace of the scene and hung back sheepishly, trying to look like common loiterers. This would only arouse more suspicion, I thought, so I took it upon myself to go and speak to one of the guards.

I walked up to one I remembered having seen before: He had a horrible scar from the corner of his left eye to his chin that even left a thin bare gap in his mustache. I had seen him sometimes with Ferhad, the Agha of the Janissaries. Otherwise, men in blue and yellow all look pretty much the same to me and I always mistrust the violence that uniform represents.

The janissary, for his part, let his hand go to his sword and he fingered it nervously as I approached. He didn't recognize me. One eunuch's robe looks like the next in soldier's eyes, I suppose, and they mistrust us all for being secretive.

"How fares the Divan today?" I asked.

"Fine, fine, thanks be to Allah," he said, still mistrusting me.

A few more questions drew these details from him: All the business was done for the day and the meal had already been served.

"The meal!" I thought aloud. "Did the usual poison taster clear it first?"

"Of course."

"And no ill effects?"

"None. Sokolli Pasha is even now enjoying his fill of the pilaf and sweetmeats. By Allah, there are times I envy that man his job."

I was encouraged to see this drop of guard, even though my first suggestion of poison had set the scar atwitch with tension. "This seems awfully early for the meal," I commented. "Why, the noon prayer had not yet been called, has it?"

This, instead of rousing more suspicion, made the man relax further still. "No. Since they've sent Lala Mustafa Pasha off with most of the army to Persia, business has been slack."

"Look here, my friend," I said, lowering my voice. "I'm the Grand Vizier's head eunuch and I've got to——"

In the next moment came the announcement that the Divan was disbanding. "To attention!" A double border of blue and yellow—as neat as if sewn by the finest needle—formed itself along the path through which the dignitaries would pass in reverse order, peeling off from their seats like couples in an old Italian dance. My master was the last to enter the Divan so he received the obeisance of everyone lower. He was the first to leave.

Still inside the Divan, yet where we outside could see him, Sokolli Pasha stopped. He said a friendly word or two to the Agha of the Janissaries. Ferhad took them as graciously as he could, but shame and humility made him awkward. Then Sokolli Pasha left the warmth and light of the Divan and entered the drizzle in the court.

I was shocked by what I saw. For one to whom form gave so much honor, the reality beneath the Divan gave my master little or none today. His look was thin and haggard, one of exhaustion, totally beaten. Even half a day was too much when what was called "deliberation" was merely an exercise to see how many ways of countering him and flattering his enemies could be found. And for no other cause than so they could say in the off hours, "By Allah, didn't I put Sokolli Pasha down today!" No wonder the meeting had been short.

My attention could hardly help but draw his from dark, grey thoughts to me. Life came suddenly to his eyes and to his figure as if I were a live coal and he dry kindling. His smile was not broad, but beautiful, and the hands with which he had been anxiously wringing his robe relaxed. After a moment of what he let the world know was pure delight—I had come to see him, even after our talk last night!—he remembered where he was and his duties. This did not vanquish his smile, however, but filled him with a rash feeling of generosity to the world.

Sokolli Pasha held up his hand for the procession to halt (you could almost hear the grumbling in the ranks behind him) and then made an announcement to our court: "Anyone with a petition—by the will of Allah—he should step forward now."

He would take them all today, and give each his personal attention. He did that for me. The Islamic world knows no greater virtue than magnanimity. Forgetting the cold and damp as well as my scruples, I basked in the sunshine of his honor.

The merchants and craftsmen, too, were moved by the gesture and grew suddenly embarrassed about the pettiness and self-interest of their suits. One even tore his up on the spot and turned away, while the others hung back. Before, had they been accepted for consideration, they would have seen it as a reflection of their own greater worth. "The Grand Vizier took favor on me out of all the others," they would brag at home, "because my presence is more forceful" or "because he knows the greatness of my establishment and had heard my name whispered in the highest courts." Now they could make no such claim for all, from the highest to the lowest, were called forward.

So the eunuch went first: He was on his mistress's business, after all. My master took his petition and slipped it into the coveted velvet bag, not neglecting to murmur some personal compliment to the man. To the janissary, one *khadim* was like the next; not so to my master. This, too, was meant as salutation to me and I took it as such. I murmured a formulaic prayer in thanks for such honor. Then the dervish, being holier than other men and only slightly less holy than women was allowed to approach.

Was there something in the way he moved? Some stiffness in the hip that said he concealed something under his clothes? Or was it only the sight of the dirty felt dervish cap and rope belt fastened with the stones of asceticism which suddenly reminded me of my friend Hajji and of the urgency of his message? Whatever it was, I sensed some few moments before anyone else in the court did (even before the master, who was much closer to the man than I) that these holy robes concealed an assassin.

"Master! Master! Beware for your life!" I called out these words as the counterfeit petition touched the Grand Vizier's hand.

At the first sound of my voice, Sokolli turned ever so slightly in my direction, ever so slightly smiling as if my words were music to his ears. In the next instant, he knew I was in earnest and his hand went to his sword. Waving my dagger, swinging my stick, and followed by the gardener and the gatekeeper, I burst through the line of guards, as yet only dumbfounded. When he did come to life, one of the soldiers took a swipe at the gatekeeper whom in the confusion he took to be part of the attack instead of the rescue. It cost the old man an eye.

But all of these actions were like the pitiful swarmings of an ant hill flooded with water beneath the all-powerful eye and will of Allah. The dervish had pulled out a dagger from beneath his rags and plunged it to the hilt in my master's body.

How protective are manners and robes in normal society! How easily we forget, with these thin screens between us, not only the grosser parts of one another's nature, but even that flesh and pulse are there. The mere hang—with hardly the flexibility for a pleat or the ruffle from a breeze—of the Grand Vizier's rich, heavy fabrics had made him seem impervious. But the assassin's knife cut through the brocade like gauze and the life blood spilled from Sokolli Pasha as if he were no more than one of the hundred common goats the palace butchers dispatch every day.

The assassin gave a wild shout of triumph, but there was some foreign accent on his Turkish so his battle cry did not carry far or bear much weight. I left it to others to constrain him: His deed was suicidal; he did not even attempt to escape. I pushed by him to ease my master's crumple to the ground.

Although too weak to pull it from the scabbard, his right hand still convulsed about the hilt of his own sword. But when I took his left in mine, he let the weapon go in order to grasp my hand in both of his. He smiled at me—like a lover, I thought, when his love had been fulfilled and spent. And though others around will testify his last word was a pious "Allah," I, who was closer, heard my own name, "Abdullah."

I saw him shrink as the life went from him and that which had been truly great dissipated into other realms. Then I was grateful for the forms of religion that diverted the wildness of my grief into a quiet recitation of the Koran's first Sura. I said it, trying to match the very tones Sokolli had used the night before when he had prayed for what he had now received: a martyr's end.

XLVIII

NEVER HAVE I appreciated more the haste with which mortal remains are disposed of in Islam. Sokolli's body was never brought back into our house. Only professional wailers were, so death remained a pure and abstract thing, full of glory and myth to the inmates. I stayed with the body, however, from the Second Court to the graveyard, heedless of impurity. Also, because this transfer happened so quickly, I was able to keep my detached blur of confusion and disbelief. There was never time for horror and revulsion to seize a stranglehold upon my soul.

In spite of the haste, the word—like all news in the city—spread faster than runners could have carried it. By the time the body was washed and ready to leave the mosque, the processional way was thronged with mourners. Every man sought to take his five or six steps beneath the bier and pressed out of his way others who came between him and the honor. I, too, worked my way to touch the wooden slats, the a scrap of white linen showing through. Again and again I attained the relic, though I never felt it have any weight—miraculously, though the miracle is probably explained by the numbers sharing the burden.

The narcotic effect of all this reverence carried me right to the interment. In the cemetery, all the other stones, with the decomposition and sink of soil beneath them, seemed to tilt at angles in obeisance towards the newly turned earth. I had more the impression of rites of pilgrimage at some holy shrine than those of eternal parting.

It was not until the next day in the First Court of the palace again that the myth faded and the reality of grief and lust for vengeance overcame me. I found myself suddenly face-to-face with the assassin.

His punishment had been swift and summary, and now his detached head sat in a little niche at just the height it would have been had it still been supported by a body. This display was meant as a lesson in the awesome justice of the Porte to any others who contemplated similar deeds. It was clearly a lesson in why rapid burial was called for if any sanctity was to remain in the memory of a man. Already the face was sagging with corruption and was clearly well on its way to becoming of the same consistency and revulsion as dog's feces in the swelter of a summer's day.

I had not seen the man closely before. Now I saw —beneath the blood and dirt that bruised his face but turned his dirt-grey cap a royal shade—a face of average appearance. The executioner's blade had neatly cut through a tendency he had to double chins, leaving only a fantasy sight of blackening blood and butcher-shop muscle exposed. He had average black brows, an average mustache, a nose only slightly larger and rounder than the mean. The best distinguishing feature I could see, then, was a round, pudgy chin protruding from a beard only four or five days old (grown as a disguise, perhaps?) pierced dead center by a dimple. His lips, rotting in a bizarre sneer (it wasn't difficult to see what shape they must have had when plans of murder were hissed) exposed one black gap where an incisor was missing.

Who was this man and what were his motives? He must have known his deed was suicide, still it had been worth that price to him. What terrible grudge did he bear my master? A grudge born of ignorance, for surely Sokolli Pasha never knowingly caused it. That rag of a cap still declared him a dervish. But was he indeed? Was that merely a disguise (the few day's beard another clue) that had been adopted with the knowledge that few would suspect or hinder him in such dress?

I questioned the nearby guards, but in their haste to send the vermin to hell, little attempt had been made to identify him. An obvious nickname, Delilo, the madman, was all they'd taken from him for identification. This was one dervish, fortunately, whose death would not make a martyr among the people whether heaven would do so or not. My suggestion, based on what I had heard at the time of the murder, that the man did not speak Turkish as his native language, was a surprise to the fellow I interrogated.

That was all I had to go on as I stood in the court before that head and let its corruption first kindle and then inflame revenge in my heart. Revenge! Against whom? The man was already dead and had made little attempt to save himself from it. But I had such an impression that he had not worked alone, that others, besides my friend Hajji had known about the plot and they had said nothing. Or, more likely, they had known and openly encouraged, promising him the immortality he had bestowed upon my master.

I swore I would, Allah willing, find these people, and I sealed the oath by spitting into the felon's eye. The spittle slipped down one cheek like a slimy tear, leaving a clean trail in the grime. It halted in the mustache and the flies, startled for a moment from their feast, settled down to business once again, which made the mustache seem to twitch as if still alive and the pride and joy of its wearer.

MY BEST LEAD was my friend Hajji. He had at least known enough about the matter to come and give warning. But one quick trip home had been enough to ascertain that he had vanished as soon as his purpose was acquitted. The gardener's boy—very distraught, of course, by both the death of the master and the grievous wounding of his father—was able only to say that he had gone for refreshment for the old dervish and returned to find he'd disappeared. And the boy did not have kind words to say about holy men and their madnesses in general at that moment, so I knew it was useless to ask further there.

But I did ask nearly everywhere else in the city. I asked the donkey boy delivering goods to our door. He admitted to being a novice to a local holy man. I pressed him further, wondering what sort of doctrine he might be learning. His animal shook a cloud of dust and flies from her flank and her master copied her, shrugging carelessly. He was unable to answer even the most basic questions of theology.

"What is it then that your most reverend teacher is good for?" I asked with frustration.

"If I do not pay him his sack of beans and salt once a month," the poor boy confessed, "he grows angry, and his anger is terrible indeed. He can cause all my family to fall ill with a wink of his eye. He has done it before; it's true. If I am careful to pay him, he may deign to visit us on holy days or at a birth or a wedding. Then he may leave an amulet tied in the window to keep away evil and all our business, Allah willing, may then be blessed."

Such leads I pursued no further. The assassin had been unprincipled, no doubt, but in a much more earnest, intelligent and ambitious way than this petty local charlatan. I took much greater heed of the rumors of begging dervishes who appeared suddenly and inexplicably on any street corner. "Such a blessed saint!" I would be told. "His mind Allah has already gathered to Him to sit in Paradise and gaze perpetually at the archetypal Holy Koran. It is only his grosser parts left here below."

So I would go and find the fellow, but my skepticism never allowed me to discover more than a blathering idiot or maniac. I, like so many, others, answered his call: "For the love of Allah! For the love of Allah!" with a small coin and so kept him from being a burden to his family. But I, unlike others, never imagined there was anything either divinely clairvoyant or demonically murderous about this lack of wit.

A visit to every *tekke* in the neighborhood, city, region (my scope expanded as hope dwindled) seemed the next best plan. But Rome has not half so many cloisters as Constantinople has *tekkes*. The place is absolutely honeycombed with these holy establishments. Although a local mosque may support a brotherhood beneath its eaves, the two are not necessarily and always partners. One would need the perspective of Allah to look down on the rooftops of the town and pick out a *tekke* from your average house. Indeed, as the sheikh's family of ten lives on the upper floor, even the All-Seeing One would have to be able to sense holiness through the everyday clutter of drying figs and laundry.

For the poor mortal making his way through the streets, one door slinking with alley cats and mounds of rubbish was too much like the next. And when such camouflage was linked with vows of secrecy among the members, the search was hopeless.

Some *tekkes,* however, were powerful and wealthy enough to have come to the notice not only of neighbors, but also of the tax authorities. Though exempt from dues, the holy men had a constant fight to prove they were indeed religious and not political. Into such establishments I easily gained admittance and almost as easily gained an interview with either the sheikh himself or one of his subordinates.

"Are you a seeker?" It never took long before such questions made me feel the interrogated. "Are you a dervish, one who sits on the doorsill of Enlightenment?"

Even when I learned to answer, "Yes, praise Allah!" more often than not our dialogue was wasted time. Sooner or later the man would drive from me what my true search was. Then, no matter what I had learned of their membership and religious practices, no matter how devout I tried to appear, the answer would always be an abrupt, "When you come seeking the answer to the nagging unfulfillment that is the curse of all humanity, then we may be of help to you. The question you ask may eventually lead you to this search. If it is Allah's will, it might. But until then—I'm sorry."

At one of the smaller houses on the hill just north of the old aqueduct, in an alley shared with a tomb of a long-dead—maybe even Christian—saint, I was quite surprised to find that my contact was none other than Andrea Barbarigo, now called Muslim, the renegade son of the late proveditore of Venice. He was not the sheikh, of course, but of such position that he was trusted as spokesman.

I had not meant my knowledge of his past to interfere with the business at hand but at last I could no longer conceal my astonishment from him. First I had to apologize for our last meeting, in the bazaar by the Jews' shop.

"Your warning was that of a friend," he said, a wave dismissing the dagger cut that had accompanied my words. "I did not take it—but it proved to be true."

"I am surprised" I told him, "by your presence in a *tekke*. Not only that but by the sober knowledge of the Way you've exuded since my arrival."

He spoke laconically. "I can no longer be a Christian, and now that Sokolli Pasha is dead—Allah give him rest—without the particular favor of the Sultan, I am unlikely to advance any further in the navy. It is winter now and I cannot be on the seas anyway. So I come here. Here in the *tekke* I have found friends and new things to strive for. It is simple."

Though we spoke for several hours until a call for prayer interrupted us, nothing further of interest was divulged. This once-compatriot of mine quoted the same mystical poets with the same slick liberality as all the others I had spoken to and seemed only to go round in circles with his speech as the whirling dervishes do in their dance. But this was the first place the name Sokolli Pasha arose without my own conjuring and so, though I did not cease probing into any other *tekke* I came upon, I returned to this one near the aqueduct again and again.

In Constantinople, where they themselves do not reign, the dervishes are not quite the open hosts they are in the holy city of Konya. They cannot afford to be, standing always there in the shadow of the Porte. But as I continued to frequent the place, I found my presence more and more expected, even welcome, though I could not say with truthfulness that I, too, stood on Enlightenment's doorstep. But, with Muslim's and Allah's help, I was able, on occasion, to find myself not too far removed from the feeling of perfect acceptance I'd enjoyed in Konya with my friend Hajji.

I like to say now it was some power of the spirit that kept me coming back. At the time I doubt very much whether I actually felt anything but very lost, confused, and angry. I certainly wasn't conscious of spirit. But eventually that spirit—or mere persistence, the skeptic may say— rewarded me. I joined the *tekke* many nights of that Ramadhan, which began a few weeks later, as I had done in Konya and again I found myself among the brethren on the Night of Power.

We were praying shoulder to shoulder not only because that is the way one always prays in company, for the feeling of unity, but also because the hall was packed. It was always so on this night. Men for whom even Ramadhan is only an excuse for more materialism are religious this one night. They hope the watchful angels who write men's fates for the coming year may be fooled into giving them better than they deserve.

Even though the hall was full, it was still cold and our unified breaths were visible like steam rising from a stew. It made the ranks beginning five or so men away from me on either side seem unreal, like mirror images, or rather, like the fog that condenses on a glass in the bath. One can rub the fog away with the hem of a sleeve. There was great energy there, however, like the intangible sun on gross stones on a summer's day.

So ethereal did the edges of my vision seem that at first I thought nothing of it when one of the figures there took on the appearance of my friend Hajji. One of the angels, I imagined, come among us to observe our mortal faith with a critical eye. I remembered another Night of Power, so many years before, when Hajji had spoken to me, told me truthfully how he had come to be a dervish and what it meant for him. Perhaps this angel, then, was only allowed to be seen at times of crisis

and only on this most holy of nights—and only by those who were worthy.

The clouds of steam I breathed in were full of faith of this sort and
they intoxicated me—my mind seemed to rise to the dome of the roof
with it—and so I humbly lowered my eyes before the vision. My master's murder? It was a little thing in the eternal perspective.

We ate, then danced, and throughout these activities, the image of
my friend appeared and disappeared at the corner of my vision. Like the
reflection of a tree in a slow-moving pond, I thought. And because of
humility and the effervescent nature of the thing, I did not stare or approach but waited upon his will. So as the night progressed, devotion,
spurred on by his presence, came more and more to replace all other
desire in my soul until not only was I content to wait, but it was my own
greatest desire to do so as well.

It was the same hour, the hour of stars, the setting of the moon and
the sharp coolness before dawn. I had taken some food and was now
coaxing down water in a pious, desireless fashion to steel myself against
the rigors of the coming day. My old friend and I found ourselves face
to face and alone in the courtyard. I lowered my eyes to my bowl and
sipped again, waiting on him.

"Peace on you," he said at just the right moment to meet the void of
my desire, after a tantalizing pause. But not too late to lose the dither
of expectancy.

"And on you, peace," I replied. That was enough. I would have been
satisfied then if our speech had never gone any further.

"What do you seek, pilgrim?"

"It." I replied the dervishes' divine *"Hu,"* beyond which there is no
other.

"You shall find It in yourself."

All that followed was afterplay, removed—if not in time or space,
then in true reality—from that which went before. As distant from true
discovery as are the two stars closest to the horizon north and south,
the full arc of the sky from each other. How that vast gap in the fabric
of reality is bridged, in the twinkling of an eye and yet so utterly, is one
of the mysteries a dervish can feel to the very marrow of his bones. Yet
he is unable to describe the mystery but with that one word that is goal
and satisfaction, yearning and striving, all at once: *"Hu."*

Bridge that gap we did, with the sweet nonsense of lovers, lovers of God. And when that was complete, Hajji spoke no more than a score of words from the world. They did not catch up with me until morning. "Purpose came not only from desire, but from within, from the harem. Look well, my friend."

At that moment under the fading stars, we heard the muezzin together as if we had never heard him before. It brought tears to our eyes as if we'd spent all our lives imagining what the glory of that sound might be—the trumpet of the Day of Judgement—and heard it now at last, all our griefs and martyrdoms rewarded in the end. Then we bade goodbye—in silence and without touching. For how long? Another fifteen years? Who could say but the Most Merciful One?

We drifted back into the building to say the prayer at dawn. As I raised my hands to the side of my face, the edge of my sleeve wiped my friend from the mirror of my vision.

XLIX

"FROM WITHIN, FROM the harem. Look well, my friend."

Upon the death of her husband, my lady fell under the protection of her brother. With no man to sit in its *selamlik,* the great house and gardens our master had built were deserted. There was talk of turning the area into a mosque with a pleasure park for the public.

But we moved back into the harem of the main palace. Safiye would hear of no place else, and in apartments right beside her, by Allah! My lady had always been loathe to make a choice between Nur Banu and Safiye. When a firm decision such as this was made for her, however, and larded with protestations of friendship, she was helpless to refuse it. What I saw was that Safiye would find it that much easier now to see that her son, the heir, and his cousin Gul Ruh were brought together.

The move did cut my duties down to almost nothing. I was in favor of dismissing all my seconds, what with the army of eunuchs already employed in the palace. Although the last years of fevered purchase of new girls for the Sultan's delight had filled the harem to overflowing, under such dense conditions, mere guarding took far fewer *khuddam*. But of course one can never look for reason or restraint when the palace is concerned, and somehow my assistants stayed on.

At first I was pleased to be relieved of responsibilities. I was spending all my time trying to track down my master's murderer. But soon I discovered what such 'freedom' did to my power to act for myself. Hours and stations of guard were set in the palace by long tradition. And I was trying to fill old bottles with new wine.

"Hello, *khadim*. What are you doing here?"

"I just thought this corridor seemed unwatched."

"No, no. I'm here. Don't you worry. We've got it all taken care of. Why don't you go run an errand for your mistress into town? Surely there is some new jewelry she needs to get, a new case of sweetmeats . . ."

And the day after the Night of Power my refocused attention made me discover yet another thing the move had taken from me. I had unwittingly, though quite of my own free will, given up the only responsibility I had left—and it was the only one that was of any real meaning. I had neglected my role as confident and comfort to my lady.

Her marriage to Sokolli Pasha had been empty form for years. We all knew that. I had supposed her grief would be but form as well. I don't think she'd even seen her man for over five years. Though they lived in the very same house, their paths never crossed. But I'd forgotten to consider that with this emptiness could come a horrible guilt. And that never seeing him could help create an image of the man in her mind that was worth ten times the mourning the real flesh and blood had been.

She was never a complainer, but on that day just after the end of Ramadhan, Esmikhan herself reproached me. "What have you to do with those men's affairs?" she asked me after I'd stumblingly tried to explain that my negligence had really been in her interest and the interest of Sokolli Pasha's memory. I was seeking revenge, after all.

"Revenge," she said with a wave of her hand, "that is for men. Your place, dear Abdullah, is here with me in the harem."

I knew she spoke truthfully. And how many times had she made similar reproaches but I had been too driven on my course to hear? I heard now and saw besides what two months of lonely grief had done to her. She'd lost weight markedly, and this was not just from the holy month of fasting. Yet the loss of weight seemed no more geared to getting her up off her cushions than the gaining of it had been. The deflated flesh sagged back onto those supports as if it was too weak and lifeless to ever budge again.

This was the woman I'd married. In a mystical, symbolic sense, yes, it was true. She was incomplete without me, and my life had no meaning without her. It had been that way since I'd first knelt at her side and answered her question, "What is he like, this man I must give my body to?"

"There's no man I'd rather be a slave to," had been my reply and with those words, we'd become slaves together, yet together, freer than that man who owned us, who'd never learned how to need another and was now dead.

I knelt beside her once again, oblivious of the crowd in the room with their gossip and needlework. I took her little hand in mine, her stumpy little hand that was now like five little half-stuffed white sausages, and promised her, "No more revenge, by Allah."

"Thank you, Abdullah," she said, and smiled as if it were a rare new practice. She closed her eyes and laid back on her pillow, perhaps to take her first sleep in two months.

I rose to leave her thus, but then stopped to ask after Gul Ruh. "I don't see her in the room."

"No. She doesn't spend much time with us old ladies. You know that."

Yes, I had known that before, at home. But here in the palace, where did she go?

"I don't know. But you'll find her. I know you'll take care of her for me, Abdullah." Esmikhan slept.

I had no idea of all the nooks and crannies, rooftops and cellars the renewed palace might provide for a young woman to hide in. And she'd had two full months in which to find the very best one. My few inquiries were met with either a shrug or (and my heart pounded with sudden fear) "Gul Ruh? Who is she? Is she that short dumpy girl the Lady Safiye has laying out her clothes these days? No, I didn't even know we had a girl called Gul Ruh."

It rapidly became clear that my young mistress had spent very little time with her mother and the others in Safiye's main room since her arrival.

I knew no other plan of action than to start at the farthest kiosk and work my way from top to bottom throughout all the harem looking with the eyes of a child. I had done this once before: I remembered the terrible fire and prayed God might allow me to find her so unharmed as on that first occasion. If she should be found with her cousin Muhammed again, that would have very different implications this time than last. But I knew very few people for whom those implications would be all together bad. Still, some of the horrible panic of that ancient search came back to me and I moved as quickly as I could without, I hoped, jeopardizing any thoroughness.

I entered a part of the palace I'd never been before. A drafty hall ran between slaves' dormitories deserted now in favor of the braziers and blankets in the main rooms downstairs. Then I heard something that made me forget all about Gul Ruh.

I heard a couple murmuring Persian—the language of love—between themselves as a native tongue. Most of it I understood simply because there are words well-known to one even with a cursory knowledge of the love poets.

"No, no. Please, no," she said.

"Why?" asked he.

"He will know."

"He will not know. How should he even guess? There is no danger of children . . ."

"But we can't. You—"

"My love, I have told you before. The cutter was merciful. Most merciful. I can still give us both the greatest of pleasure. Much greater than you've ever known with that old man. The pleasure of the open roses in the gardens of Harun ar-Rashid."

Here I heard her give a little deep-throated groan. I think the word *pleasure* in Persian is so construed of both light and dark sounds that even a stone would find itself constricted at the mere whisper, "pleasure".

"But perhaps the knife was not so merciful after all," he continued, with a note of angry frustration in his voice. "If only you knew what I have endured all these months. So close to you and yet so far."

"My love, my diamond, my jewel. Don't you think I have endured it, too? By Allah, yes. But we must not. It is our Fate. It is not to be. Not yet. Wait until I am free and then . . ."

"You will go back to Persia and I—I will still be here in the belly of the heretic beast."

"No, no. I have wealthy family and friends in Persia. We will raise your ransom."

"And we shall live happily ever after with 'our' children, another man's sons?"

"Yes. That is the bargain my brother bought with his martyr's blood."

"But have you seen her make any move to fulfill her side of the bargain?"

"No, not yet. But she will, I know. When Murad dies. Even she dare not move until Muhammed is safe upon the throne."

"Allah grant it may be tomorrow."

"Hush now. I shall have to be going soon or I shall be missed. Recite just one more verse and then we must say good-bye."

The man obeyed, dropping his voice for the recitation until I could no longer hear the individual words. Still, I guessed it must be that most common of love poems, Khayyam's *Rubiyat*. The couple was clearly far gone in love, needing neither the new nor the turgid to spur them on.

> "With me along the strip of herbage strown
> That just divides the desert from the sown
> Where name of Slave and Sultan is forgot . . .
>
> Look to the blowing Rose about us—'Lo,
> Laughing,' she says, 'into the world I blow,
> At once the silken tassel of my Purse
> Tear and its treasure on the garden throw . . .'"

He did not come to the end of his verse before she interrupted him with their own refrain again.

"No, no. Please, love, no."

"Why? Oh, why?"

"He will know."

"He will not know . . ."

By now I had followed the voices to their source. Setting my ear against the closed door to confirm it, I then quietly lifted the latch and slipped in. Why I did not make my presence known at once and run instead of slip along quietly to stop that thing, I shall never know. Perhaps they were so far gone that the lack of control reached out and strangled me as well. But I must also plead how startled I was—there, in the Sultan's harem! Such a thing had never been seen or even thought before, and both the horror and the unknown of it gave rise to a stumbling confusion.

I was standing in the doorway of a long, dark dormitory, lined on either side by the pallets of the slaves, as regular as janissaries on review. The occupied bed stood out at once, as will a soldier with his bandolier askew. It was about two-thirds down on the left-hand side and I suspect it had been chosen because the clerestory of windows above skipped it with its light. Yet, one could guess how long it had been since the choice had been made, for half the pallet now caught the slant of the midwinter sun.

That weak light was more than enough to allow me to pick out the figure of the woman. She lay on her back and I noticed for the first time a curious, distinctive sort of roundness to her chin, pierced in the center by a dimple. Her caplet was gone and her amber-colored hair was a pillow of fire beneath her head. One elbow was up as that hand luxuriated in that hair. It also served to elongate and emphasize the breast on that side.

The top buttons of her waist-cinching jacket had been undone and the undershirt loosened enough to leave the breasts loose, low mounds rounded by their own weight but with startling peaks of nipple in high contraction. These the dark head of her partner bent from time to time to nuzzle until she groaned aloud and pushed that head away.

Then I could see that the belt of her *shalvar* was loose as well.

All of this I saw in a flash, and in that same flash recognized who the couple were. Although the man had shed his outer, identifying robes and was still in deep shadow, the fact that the woman was Safiye's Mitra meant he could only be one—Nur Banu's Persian eunuch.

In that same moment, he suddenly shed the last of his garments. He did so in a single, rapid movement. But as the man's site of generation still hovered over her shoulders, the young woman gasped to see what existed where only atrophy should be. He was kneeling astride her, but in the half a blink while his garment was still in the air, she managed to work herself free from that straddle with a reflexive shudder. Now his arms were free at last. They caught her *shalvar* and dragged them down about her knees so she could not stand, but stumbled to the ground again. On all fours now, Mitra tried to crawl away down the aisle between the ranks of beds.

Her escape would have been hopeless, but I came alive. I rushed and shouted at them as if they were dogs copulating in the street. And as one rushes at dogs, I picked up a pitcher of ice-cold water on my way. Before any of us knew what had happened, I'd dashed them with it.

The sounds that followed this were as loud as they were inhuman. Nur Banu's eunuch bellowed like a bull. I met him with equally vehement curses, and the woman cried and squealed and caterwauled like a stuck pig.

I must have been almost as startled and dazed as they, for the next thing I realized, the eunuch was coming at me with a heavy brass ewer and murder in his eye. I hedged around until I'd put myself between that threat and the girl, but I could do little more. One blow I deflected with my pitcher, but it was only cheap pottery and it shattered in a thousand sharp-edged pieces all over the beds and the floor around us. Though I raised a now-empty hand against it, the next blow landed square on my right temple and brought me to my knees. The strength of those arms certainly had nothing effeminate about it.

My head seemed to burst with the blare of trumpets and my vision narrowed with popping circles and stars. In all that colliding mass of sensations, there was only space for one image to penetrate. By all

that is in the earth, but it was a bizarre one! His member—on which
indeed there were the scars of a cutter's knife, but very faint and
shallow—let loose at that moment and sent milky ribbons of fertility
floating down on every side. I was grateful for the next blow, brought
down with the anger of orgasm, that blanked me away from my senses
altogether.

I came almost immediately to see again. From my curious perspective on the ground I saw the naked Persian drop his weapon and stagger backwards helplessly. I thought I must be dreaming or that he had
already dealt me the death blow and I had gone beyond, for I could
make no sense of this. Then I saw a great pair of hands about his neck
that were not his own and, as he sank beneath their throttle, the grim,
flattened face of Ghazanfer Agha rose behind him, the very image of
Death.

In a moment, blue blood filled the Persian's face and Ghazanfer Agha
tossed him to the floor, lifeless as a bundle of rags. The Hungarian was
in a quandary then, whether to come to my aid—and masses of blood
from my head made my wounds seem worse than they actually were—
or to do his duty first and go to the sobbing young woman. But by then
the noise had brought most of the rest of the harem running up to see
and there were plenty of arms for both of us. Ghazanfer Agha made his
choice and he chose me, grunting between his teeth as he carried me
to one of the pallets, "I knew we couldn't trust the product of Mu'awiya
the Red's knife."

Quickly my head was stanched and wrapped and a few other cuts I'd
received from falling on the shattered crockery were seen to as well
with uncommon gentleness.

"I'll be all right now," I said, attempting to get up.

"No, you'd better just lie still," said the giant Hungarian.

I protested again. "I can at least make it to my own room and let these
girls straighten up here."

I indicated the hovering slaves who were actually doing more staring and whispering than straightening. They found a loved-on bed a
wonderful anomaly—as if it were a meteorite landed in their midst and
guaranteed to give beauty and fertility. Others were examining the
ewer, fingering its new dents as if by so doing they could inject some
passion into their own dull lives. Ghazanfer looked at them and then

nodded and helped me to my feet, taking most of the weight upon himself.

At the door among the crowd still standing and staring, I saw Gul Ruh. I smiled to reassure her all would be well, then managed to raise my free hand up and lay it on her head.

"What are you doing here, little one?" I asked, trying to laugh. It was, after all, looking for her that I had found myself in this mess. "This is no sight for your young eyes."

She took my hand gratefully in hers and proceeded to walk downstairs beside me. In spite of the fact that if it hadn't been for Ghazanfer Agha, I probably would have gotten myself killed, I was the hero of the hour and she was delighted to be seen with me. But a squeeze of her hand brought other values to my mind. Dear Abdullah, it seemed to say. I know you would do the same or more for me, to save me from a union I do not desire.

L

BEFORE MY PAIN-RACKED body reached my room, the Persian's was in the sea. The rites of Islam were not disgraced by application to him.

Mitra had been helped to her room, too, and was cleaned up a bit. But then she was deserted to wonder about her fate in solitude. She called to see her two little boys, but their nurses would not even allow them to enter the room of one whom the head eunuch might condemn to death at any moment.

Kislar Agha, "the head of the girls," was Nur Banu's creature and should not have hesitated a moment before fetching Mitra out and sending her to join her lover at the bottom of the sea. Indeed, there were few of us who ever doubted that the false eunuch had been acting under the Queen Mother's orders every luring step of his way.

Nur Banu must have told him, "Come, today is the day. I order it. She is over her impurity from the birth of her last son and is attracting the Sultan again. You must disgrace her today or live forever disgraced in my eye."

And perhaps she had even given him a pepper infusion to quicken his blood and rubbed his privates with honey and nettle to coddle and enflame them before he left her that morning. He may not have known how greatly his life was at risk. But Nur Banu knew.

A refined, white Persian eunuch from the knife of Mu'awiya the Red did not come cheaply. Nonetheless, that was a sacrifice the Queen Mother made willingly to rid herself of the greatest threat to her power—that Persian girl of Safiye's. That girl's poetry had won her two sons from the loins of the master and she had been invited back yet again over the most beautiful Circassian the Valide Sultan could muster. So Nur Banu had paid the price of such a eunuch and surely she would do all in her power to see she got what she'd paid for—even after the man was dead.

But Safiye, too, had her means. She must have worked quickly the moment she sensed what was afoot up in the slave's dormitory. Overstepping the head black eunuch, she burst in on the Sultan and several of his companions, her veilless state indicating a grief on the edge of insanity that could not be ignored. But she had the sense to keep the news to herself until the strangers had been excused so the word would get no further than those ears that commanded life and death in all the Empire.

"Our fair Mitra whom you love so dearly, the mother of two of your sons, has been foully attacked in your own harem. She has been attacked by one your own mother dared to introduce to thwart your honor and dignity in the guise of a eunuch. By the merciful will of Allah, one of my most diligent *khuddam* was able to stop and kill the man before the deed was actually done. Come to the room and see for yourself his accursed seed spilled on the floor. There is none, by the mercy of Allah, on her.

"The man has paid with his life as is only well and just, but there are those who would condemn Mitra as well. Lord, think of the love she bears you—and you for her. Think of the two little sons she has given you, bright, healthy boys to carry your name and your glory to the ends of the earth when you—Allah forbid—are gone. Should they be condemned to the shadow of motherlessness at such an early age for no sin on their mother's part at all?

"Finally, think of her poetry, her beautiful voice, that caressing she gives that most romantic of tongues learned at her mother's knee. Could you live with yourself knowing you had denied the world that pleasure?"

No, Murad found in his heart that he could not. Nur Banu was not to be totally unsatisfied, however. Mitra was banished from the imperial presence for one full year. But Murad made the decree as if he himself were to blame and it was penitence laid to his own head.

Safiye could not have been more pleased under the circumstances. She made plans at once for the woman to be sent to the fresh, open air of the palace in Edirne where her sons would grow healthy and strong and all three of them would be far from Nur Banu's intrigue. Safiye also arranged for musicians and poets to accompany the party and for a courier to go up there once a week with word of the latest in literary fashion and the Sultan's personal taste.

Though a year is a terribly long time in the short life of a concubine—her glamour may easily fade in that period—it is not so very long in the life of a reciter of poetry. And, as the separation decree was couched in such terms of personal denial by the Sultan, it was easy to imagine that their reunion would be a passionate and enduring one when it happened—if a weakness in Murad's resolve did not cause it to happen sooner.

All of this Safiye had seen to before she bothered to go and tell Mitra of her reprieve. Relief quite made the poor woman swoon, but as soon as she was brought to her senses, she was on the floor again, on her face in deep gratitude and humility before the mistress who had saved her life.

"How shall I ever be able to thank you?" she asked Safiye.

"Dear child, your life is all the thanks I need," Safiye replied. She smiled and, taking the younger woman's face in her hands, kissed her tenderly on each cheek. "And remember, I still have part of a bargain coming to you—your freedom on the day Murad should die."

"Allah pray that day is years and years away," Mitra said. At the moment, she truly meant it.

"And only then did Mitra go and kiss her own babies," concluded Gul Ruh, whose busy scouting had brought the rest of the report to my sick bed. "And after all those hours when she thought she would never see them again!"

Gul Ruh kept close by my side the two days I spent recuperating and by the time I got up to be myself again, Mitra and her sons were gone.

But it was not three months after this that another horrible tragedy struck. I happened to be sitting with Ghazanfer Agha—to whom I now owed my life—in his usual spot to the side of the central atrium when a sudden movement on one of the balconies across the way attracted our attention. We had time only to focus when what seemed to be a small bundle or a doll passed through the railings and tumbled the full two stories down to the marble paving below.

Both Ghazanfer and I were on our feet in an instant. He ran to the bundle, but I paused only long enough to confirm my worst fears—that it was indeed a child, the little son of one of Safiye's gift-girls to the Sultan. I ran then, taking the stairs three at a time to the place from which we'd seen it fall. The spot was deserted. I ran as far as reasonable in one direction, then the same distance in the other, to no avail. By that time, the shrieks of the nurse followed by those of the mother, then the curses of Safiye and all of her suite brought a confusion and crowd to the entire courtyard. It was useless now to try to sort it out.

I came down the stairs slowly, resisting the earth's pull all the way, then stood racked with disbelief and horror beside Ghazanfer. Having confirmed that the child was dead, my companion stood aside now to make way for the chief mourners.

"I saw no one," I confessed my defeat.

"No," he replied. "I didn't think you would."

"But I saw . . . didn't you see? Or did my eyes just trick me? I thought I saw someone up there at the railing with the boy."

"Your eyes did not trick you. I saw it, too."

"But the guardian, even if she was careless, surely she would not vanish like that."

"I doubt very much it was a 'guardian.' "

"You mean you think the boy was pushed?"

"Nur Banu has gotten her revenge for the death of her false eunuch."

"I can't believe it!"

"Can't you? You lived a sheltered life with the Grand Vizier."

Then I had to admit I could find no other belief to match what I had seen. "A child just learning to walk!" I exclaimed.

"So it looks like an accident and is impossible to prove as anything else."

"But just a child!"

"A child who is the son of the Sultan and will some day grow up to vie with others for the thorne."

"Who would do such a thing? Even Nur Banu——"

"The place is crawling with such people," Ghazanfer Agha assured me. The subject was as distasteful to him as it was to me, but he knew he must continue. "You are just new among us on a permanent basis, else you would realize it happens more often than anyone would confess. On both sides, I hate to admit, but it happens. One must keep the odds even, after all. So far, his virility and hedonistic life, spurred on by both my lady and the Queen Mother, have given the Sultan thirty-five children, of which twenty-one are sons."

"By Allah, I had no idea there were so many!"

"No, few do. The girls are all still alive, but Safiye's Muhammed, Mitra's two, and two to the favorites of Nur Banu——that is all that are left to him now of the sons with the death of this little fellow. Some die to the usual enemies of childhood, disease and weakness, I suppose. But the rate is far too high to be natural. A nurse and her assistants must be awake every moment and even then, as we have just seen, there is danger. Especially when they begin to toddle off on their own . . ."

"Always falls?" I asked, cringing with horror, for I had just caught a glimpse of the broken little boy in his grieving mother's arms.

"I suppose that is the most favored way, for it can happen in an instant when a nurse's back is turned and boys especially at that age——or so I'm told——like to explore and be independent. Alas that those same virtues that would make for the best ruler are the very things that see to it that the boy never gets his chance to rule. Yes, there are all too many falls— one of Nur Banu's camp survived, but he is witless from it, or so the gossips say.

"Falls, but there have been drownings as well, in the fountain, the bath. Strangulation may be seen when the mother or nurse is blamed for rolling on her child in the night. A piece of candy is dropped in a likely place, the child finds it, puts it in his mouth. It is poison. One plate of poisoned halvah was discovered over in Nur Banu's rooms just before you arrived here. It was discovered when some birds that had come to feed from it died. The beekeeper was hung for sell- ing the bakers bad honey, but Allah alone knows how many infant bouts with fever and dysentery, vomiting and colic are natural in this place.

"Then of course there is the evil eye. I myself am skeptical and think, especially in a child so young, that 'evil eye' is just an excuse to cover the doctors' ignorance. But one does begin to wonder when its effects are seen so very, very often."

"It is one thing to see my master killed, a man who had lived a long and useful life," I declared with new vehemence. "But a child?"

"Mitra is lucky to be in Edirne with her boys," was all the comfort Ghazanfer could offer me.

LI

WHILE I WAS still recovering from the Persian's attack (and thinking how curious it was that a man should have his handiwork live so long and painfully after him) Gul Ruh confided in me where she had been when I'd gone looking for her. The word aggravated my headache.

I tried to persuade my young lady against such a position. But when she was not moved, I faithfully kept her confidence until after the death of the little prince—nearly four months and a long time for any secret to be kept in the harem. But eventually one of her spies must have told Safiye, and there was sudden and violent furor—as I had tried to warn Gul Ruh there would be—when it became commonly known. Esmikhan's daughter spent much of her time not in the garden, on the rooftops nor in a hidden corner of the library, but in the company of Nur Banu.

"Whatever do you do there, child?" was the horrified reaction of all and sundry.

"I sew mostly," she replied, which was the truth.

No one had been more surprised than I to see that wild little head bent over a needle and thread with concentration as wild as it was diligent. Nur Banu happened to have a seamstress who may not have been as skillful as the next, but who had twice the patience and did not mind undoing forty rats' nests of a thread a day if rewarded with but the first glimmer of interest. Gul Ruh confessed to me that those knots and tears and crooked seams had driven her to more than a few tantrums. There were days when she would run clear to the end of the garden so fast her lungs ached and there she screamed at the top of her voice like one gone mad. But she refused to quit.

"Why?" I could not refrain from asking.

"Because," she said simply, "I am to be married. What sort of bride will I be if I bring no trousseau of household goods?"

"You could leave it all for the slaves to do. Many another girl in your station would."

"No. I want some at least to be of my own hand. It is only right."

Then I remembered that last night of Sokolli's on earth, how he had called his daughter to him and how, in the morning, I had gone to look for her to promise to find some way out of the match for her. I had forgotten—forgotten because I had not believed and also because of the horrors that had immediately followed—what the slave girl had told me. "She rose at early prayers and called for the seamstress to attend her." I discovered that not only had the maid spoken the truth, but that this passion had continued—indeed, been inflamed—by Sokolli's passing.

I came at length not only to see that this was true, but that this was a reflection on the new Gul Ruh struggling to bloom on the horrible destruction of the old caused by the deaths of first Arab Pasha and then her father. And afterwards I discovered yet another reason she chose to associate with Nur Banu's suite. Nur Banu was the one with whom Umm Kulthum, the Mufti's widow and mother of the Mufti's son, was most familiar. Safiye always declared she could not find room for the woman at her gatherings and no doubt this was because, with the Mufti dead, his widow no longer had anything to recommend her to Baffo's daughter.

"You would still marry the Mufti's son?" I asked my young lady in surprise.

"Of course," Gul Ruh replied.

She said it with such simple faith that if I were to disbelieve it I must be skeptical of the lisped confessions of a million children everywhere echoing the faith they've learned at their parents' knees. The words harked to a time when the world still seems whole and right and, in the end, loving.

"It was the very last wish of my father," she continued, blinking back tears I knew were brought on by an almost tangible remembrance of that last clumsy kiss upon her forehead. "And it was *his* father's last wish, too. Surely it is Allah's will."

In place of His own will in the world of mortals, I read her logic, Allah had created fathers. It was no use my citing the counterexample of an evil, Godless father to confuse her. In her particular case, I felt, as perhaps never in maiden's life before or since, such confidence was well placed. He never spoke of love, but Sokolli Pasha, I knew, would have gladly met that assassin's knife a hundred times over if it could have symbolized the duty and care he felt for this child.

I might have suggested, very tenderly, that perhaps she should wait. The blessings of true love, not just duty and care, might come to her in time. I almost cited to her the case of her own mother and the night in Konya when she had been conceived in love. But in the end I did not—I could not. There was a new and different happiness in Gul Ruh, one I had not sensed in her before nor even, underestimating her as a mere child, perhaps, thought her capable of. But in the end I had to admit it was indeed happiness, or at least the seeds of happiness, and a perpetual and growing contentment with her life as woman she was cultivating here. And far be it from me to try to root it out by force.

Nevertheless, I had to warn her now of reality. Sokolli Pasha had planned to meet with young Abd ar-Rahman's brothers the day of his death to seal the betrothal, but Allah had willed it was not to be. Her guardian was now the Sultan himself. Even so illustrious a family as the Mufti's could hardly conceive approaching the Shadow of Allah with proposals of their own. Nor was Murad likely, even once approached, to give his approval to Abd ar-Rahman over the scores of favorites that must also be clamoring for close ties with the Ottomans.

"And haven't you heard your mother and your Aunt Safiye making plans to break precedent and have you married to your cousin Muhammed? This so you may become a Valide Sultan as powerful as Khurrem Sultan was, the mother of princes. When such glory is held out to you, should you not thank Allah and accept it?"

"I seek to do the will of Allah," she said, unmoved by glory.

I was convinced now of what course would bring her the most joy and I was determined to aid her on it. I watched her with Umm Kulthum, saw the woman's warmth for the girl grow and be returned if not by love then at least by respect. I wanted to nurture that protective relationship. But frankly, I did not see how even the maddest of dervishes could have said mother-in-law, daughter-in-law were relationships forthcoming for them in Allah's will.

Esmikhan and even Safiye had nothing but talk to keep Gul Ruh from crossing the no man's land into Nur Banu's territory. As they remained ignorant of her true motives, certainly of her sincerity, they considered it no more than youth's craving for the dangerous and the forbidden. They left it at that, saying, "Well, you'll keep an eye out and let us know what the old witch is plotting, won't you, Gul Ruh?"

"No, more!" Safiye exclaimed. "You could do the world a favor and take poison to her the next time you go."

"Aunt Safiye, no!" cried Gul Ruh who couldn't be sure if Safiye was joking or not. "I couldn't do that!"

And when Nur Banu replied to the retelling of this tale by saying, if the girl really wanted to make herself useful, yes, she could carry poison, but in the opposite direction, her answer to her step-grandmother was much the same. "Oh, no, lady. No, I couldn't do that!" Gul Ruh remained innocently insensitive to the earnestness beneath both demands.

MEANWHILE, THE AGHA of the Janissaries, Ferhad Pasha, presented the Sultan with a particularly choice bit of booty from the campaigns on the Persian front. It was a history of the life of the Prophet, set in verse and beautifully illustrated and edged in gold leaf. Murad was pleased at the sensitivity of the man's soul. It caused him to weep for joy. Many another commander, he realized, would have thought nothing of tossing the book in when the rest of the rubble was torched. Or melting down the brass clasps for bullets. How to reward this man of obvious charm and even greater sensibility? There was no higher post than Agha of the Janissaries open at the moment.

"Is there some jewel," the Sultan asked, groping, "of which you or your wife is particularly fond?"

"Me? No, sire."

"Your wife?"

"May it please you, sire, I am unmarried."

"Unmarried? Such a romantic soul in one so celibate? What will you be, by Allah, given a chance to taste the feasts of which the poets sing?"

"No less a man, I pray."

The Sultan laughed with pleasure. "No less a man, indeed. Well, we shall not put off the essay any longer. I shall see you married before you ride to the front again. And not to just any of my girls, over twenty-six years old and cast off, by Allah. No, I shall see you have one of the royal Ottoman blood. I'm sure there are one or two appropriate women to choose from. I shall have to ask."

"Gul Ruh" were the first words that came to Ferhad's mind, not particularly because he knew that girl was an Ottoman but because those had become his words meaning "That's impossible!" Of course he did not say this to the Shadow of Allah. He merely bowed and said, "Master, I am your slave."

LII

My master's mausoleum was not as large as it had started out to be (how quickly the world forgets!) and it had a sort of amputated look. But the tile work was of the finest: blue and green forests espaliered against the walls and heavy with blossoms of that rich coral color that was recently born in Iznik and is such a closely guarded secret that it may well die there. Neglect had its benefits, however, for real vegetation promised soon to cover up the rough spots and take the edifice to itself as if it had always been there.

In small depressions in the marblework, rain water collected at which clouds of pigeons drank. Even in death, my master was proving generous. From the roof of plane trees above, herons had slung their nests like saucer lamps, and a recent molt had let a crest of feathers fall down upon the master's cupola like nothing so much as the plume of the imperial turban itself.

A row of cypresses, those emblems of eternity, stood sentinel on either side, draped in ivy like shrouds. They kept back the rude press of staring, lesser monuments. Among these surrounding memorials, the men's were topped with stone turbans in shapes that indicated what station the dead had held in life. Women's stones were carved to end in flowers.

And, whereas in life all had bowed towards Mecca, in death they went every which way, depending on how the body beneath returned to the soil. Instead of the uniformity of death the preachers were always threatening us with——"The impious and heretic shall stand before their Maker and know the errors of their ways"——it seemed rather that life had enforced more compliance. And in death each relaxed into the individuality they had always cherished in their hearts but never dared while living.

Beyond these stones I could not see far: Heavy mist smeared the distance and then swallowed it whole. I shivered in the damp.

He appeared suddenly out of that mist and walked toward the mausoleum at a pace the heart takes when approaching a lovers' tryst: quick, but of uneven rhythm. I remarked at once—he is as handsome and swift as ever. He was early, but I had been earlier, and from my post behind the cypress, I could watch his every move.

Waiting is not much practiced by Aghas of the Janissaries, but Ferhad Pasha had not forgotten the art learned so well by weeks under Sokolli Pasha's roof with the fate of the Empire on his lips. Here he was under the Pasha's roof again, and some of the same thrill was in this waiting, too: the youthful tantalization to be hopelessly, dangerously in love, near and yet so far.

He waited and I waited. I stood until my legs grew numb, cold slowly creeping up them from the mist-dampened grass. For one used to standing and watching most of every day, this was substantial evidence of the passage of time. But Ferhad Pasha still seemed insensible to it. That there was no sun to judge by was perhaps part of the reason, but here was a man with the responsibilities of all the army on his shoulders. Remembering this, I found his patience even more remarkable. It was hard to imagine: what devices he had used to slip from these responsibilities for the day, lingering now into long afternoon. But no call of duty seemed to disturb his waiting, no thought that he would miss something more important.

At last, the call of the muezzin came, seeping its way through the mist like blood through bandages, and Ferhad Pasha started from his heavy reverie. He had arrived just after the last call—a good four hours must have passed. He looked around in a sudden panic. Perhaps he felt himself confronted by Sokolli's presence for the first time, surrounded by the ghosts of the others who slept all around. Perhaps he thought he must have missed something. It put a new focus on his eyes and he saw for the first time the basket set in the shadows just at the entrance to the tomb. He went to it, picked it up, saw it was not something left weeks ago by accident, but fresh, set just that morning.

He leapt down from the tomb in a moment, ran this way and that, calling, "My rose! My fountain! Esmikhan!" The mist swallowed his voice at the edge of sight.

I thought I might now be discovered but a step first to one side and then to the other prevented it. And Ferhad Pasha did not look very hard. His search was more a bodily reflex which all along his mind knew was vain.

The mind soon regained control and brought him slowly back to the steps of the tomb. Now he sat limply on the marble and looked long and hard at the basket's contents. They were all fruit of the end of the present autumn season: a bunch of grapes gone to raisins with a long twig of vine attached, leaves dry and near to dust; an apple, red-cheeked like one sickly but having difficulty breathing; a pomegranate, packed with tears; a quince, the ascetic; almonds still in the husk, tight-lipped and reclusive; and a bouquet of marigold, basil, fenugreek, and forced jasmine. "Petals of the jasmine on fenugreek," the poet says, "are like tears on a yellow face."

Ferhad Pasha fingered the various fruits in turn. Their confused covey of meanings exuded but one tenor.

"Oh, Allah," Ferhad Pasha said when at last he'd made himself understand what he saw. "No! Never, by the All Merciful!" he cried.

He took a handful of the raisins then and bit into them so hard I could hear the seeds crack from where I was. Then he tore into the pomegranate, ate none but left it bleeding over all the rest. At last he made a mad dash for the tree where I hid, and ripping branches from it by the handfuls, he brought them to the basket. The cypress, I remembered, is the symbol for eternity.

But there was nothing more to do than this compounding of symbol on sterile symbol and at last he realized it. In a moment, he had disappeared into the mist from whence he had come.

I waited a breath or two to be sure he'd gone, although I was quite sure he wouldn't give a backward glance. Then I crept forward and retrieved the basket. It still exuded a heavy smell of bruised basil and marigold steeped in pomegranate when I presented it wordlessly to my mistress. She was sitting not a hundred paces away in another part of the cemetery at the tomb of Rahine, daughter of a famous dervish who died, they said, on her wedding night.

Esmikhan acknowledged me and the altered contents of her basket with the twitch of a weary smile that broke through her tear-stained face.

"Thank Allah," she said, "I cannot walk, because more than a dozen times I so wanted to . . ."

Just then a bevy of young girls, chattering maids and grumbling eunuchs arrived at the tomb. Though from all I knew of her history it was difficult to see why, Rahine had become something of a saint to whom girls resorted to pray for husbands. No one in the palace blinked when Esmikhan said she wanted to visit her husband's grave and we had also thought no passerby would find it odd to see a veiled woman sitting—for hours as it turned out—at Rahine's. Still, as the innumerable strips of cloth left by the devotees testified, we were lucky she had not been disturbed before now and Esmikhan instantly took my hand to help her up.

"Let's go," she said.

But as soon as she began to make her labored progress to where her sedan waited, one of the newly arrived girls ran up.

"Auntie! Aunt Esmikhan, is that you?"

She threw back her veil to let us see: it was Safiye's daughter Aysha.

Aysha looked more like her mother than anyone else, but she was her mother watered down ten parts to one. Her hair tried to be blond but the sort of grey-brown of dried oak leaves was the best it could manage. Her eyes were neither a rich brown nor yet a blue but something dully, muddily in between. Bright clothes and jewels, bunches of flowers in the hair or on her breast were things she had to wear just to compete with the meanest serving maid around her. On her they always looked tottering and presumptuous.

Aysha's personality, too, was lackluster, usually mousy, and when it tried to be merry, it generally came out brash and clumsy instead. The girl made just such an attempt now.

"Why, Aunt Esmikhan! Whatever you are doing at Rahine's tomb? You don't need to worry about finding a man."

This discharge, Aysha realized after she'd said it, was tactless. She tried to cover. "Oh, I'm sorry. Of course you should come here. I just keep thinking anyone over thirty-five must be . . ." She found all her struggles did nothing but make her sink deeper and deeper, like one floundering in quicksand.

Esmikhan smiled, wearily, but with indulgence and reached out a hand to rescue the girl. She was, after all, only a child, though growing up seemed to be doing nothing to help the habit of tactlessness.

"So tell me, Aysha," she asked, "what are you doing here? You don't need to worry about finding a man, either."

"Oh, yes I do."

"But your father has offered you to Ferhad Pasha. What more could any girl want?"

"Oh, but the Agha of the Janissaries is perverse and drags his feet. Why he drag his feet, I don't know. Allah knows, he's almost fifty."

"Perhaps he does it out of consideration of your youth," Esmikhan said gently. "You aren't yet ten years old, Allah shield you, after all."

"But the other Aysha, the Prophet's favorite, he married her while she was still playing with dolls. I am much more grown-up than that."

"Indeed. But let me tell you, child, it's not very jolly being married to an old, old man."

"No, but Ferhad Pasha is not like your old Sokolli Pasha. Ferhad is still charming and handsome."

"Yes, yes, he is."

"Why, Auntie! Are you crying?"

"No, no child. Go on now. Make your visit to the Lady Rahine. And I don't mean to try and second-guess Allah's will, but I think it is very likely she may grant you what you wish today."

"Yes, you are. You are crying! Why, Auntie? Tell me."

"It's nothing, child, really. Just . . . just the inscription over Rahine's tomb. It made me sad."

"What does it say?" Aysha squinted at the curved archway. She knew enough to tell there must be writing interwoven with the tendrils of poppies and morning glories there, but she was never very clever at her letters. I suspect her eyes, which appeared muddy from the outside, were muddy to look through, too.

Esmikhan smiled. She had had nearly all day to sit and examine the archway and she recited now without even looking at it the epithet of the young woman who'd died on her wedding night.

"What is fate?
Before half my desires were fulfilled

I was snatched from the world.
That is fate—But Allah will resurrect."

The last line caught on the hoarseness in her voice and she tried it
again. "Allah will resurrect."

LIII

SAFIYE FLUNG HERSELF into the room and onto the divan with heavy
snorts of impatience.

"Why, my dear, what's the matter?" Esmikhan asked.

"It's that Ferhad Pasha."

"What's wrong with him now?

"Here Murad offers him the honor of his own daughter and he hems
and haws. By Allah, he's only a slave after all. He should do as he's
told."

Esmikhan lowered her head and blushed, but she said nothing.

Safiye took that as an excuse to continue. "Allah, what can I do? If I
cannot get Aysha to him, someone in Nur Banu's camp will go. That
man is destined to be Grand Vizier, you mark my words. He's young
enough and clever enough to hold that post for a long, long time. And
if she gains control over him . . ."

"He still won't marry her?" Esmikhan sat up straight and asked with
agitation.

Safiye didn't bother to confirm or deny the question, but forged
ahead with her complaints.

"But he needs a young, strong wife who can give him sons,"
Esmikhan said in utter disbelief.

Safiye ignored the statement and continued to rant and rave as she
always did when nothing else seemed to work. One subject led to an-

other in her stream of frustrations and she was soon on another related problem.

"And what am I to do with that Ali Pasha? He's another powerful man who needs a well-placed wife so I can keep track of him."

"Ali Pasha?"

"Yes, the new governor of Hungary. You know the dangers that go along with such newly conquered lands."

"Yes. My late husband's nephew in Buda. Allah save his soul."

"Well, Ali Pasha has executed the government there quite remarkably. Outgrown that honor, we may say, and is busy looking around for more. He's as dashing as could be. Why it should be so difficult to get him suitably married, I don't know."

"I . . . I would marry Ali Pasha," Esmikhan said. "If you think . . . if you think it would help."

"Help? Oh, my dear, it would be the most wonderful thing that's happened around here in ages. He's a man going somewhere, I tell you. And handsome— But would you really? You know, I'd often thought you must be lonely since Sokolli's death—Allah favor him—but I never dared . . ."

"Yes, I'll marry him," Esmikhan said again.

One thing Safiye forgot to mention to my lady was that Ali Pasha was already married with two sons and a daughter. But it went without saying that for the honor and advancement of marrying into the royal house, he'd divorce her in a minute.

GHAZANFER AGHA WAS present at the divorce as one of the witnesses—the witness who would carry word of the transaction back to the harem, to let Safiye know that all was clear. Ali Pasha, he informed us, was a man of sharp features, slick and sure of his good looks. His brows, like two black daggers, met at the base of his hook of a nose and that nose thrust down to almost meet the black point of a beard that sheathed a dagger of a chin. He had just returned from the frontier and was lean and brown and hard and healthy from the rigors of a soldier's life.

"I felt," Ghazanfer confessed, "like a spark in the tail of a great comet.

As if I should feel myself fortunate to be even remotely associated with such glory."

Then he described how that glory swept in upon the soon-to-be divorcée.

Having once belonged to the palace harem, the woman had both a natural beauty and a fine cultivation of manners and spirit that had been at least considered material for the Sultan's bed. When, at twenty-six, she had seen other, younger girls move in to take her place and her hopes, she was given as a favor to this up-and-coming Pasha.

She had still considered herself fortunate and diligently set about founding a life and an orderly harem of her own to be the backbone of this man and his ambition. Love humbly gave way to respect and even a bit of awe in the look with which she met the return of her husband from the front.

Her three children had had their faces scrubbed until they gleamed like polished brass and wore brand-new outfits to welcome their father home. He had been gone so long that the two youngest could not remember him, but the oldest, in spite of all training in manners and decorum, could not resist springing from his ranks at the first sight and shouting, "Father!"

It was the woman who first realized something was wrong. From Ghazanfer, a eunuch, she feared nothing. But the other witness was both a man and a stranger and she had an instinctive fear of such creatures as cats have of dogs. She instantly threw the edge of her veil over her face and began to back towards the door in confusion. She had made some awful miscalculation, she realized, but what it could be escaped her and she floundered on unfirm ground.

"No, wife. Stay. Just a moment," Ali Pasha said.

She obeyed, but he had not told her to be at ease and she certainly did not take that liberty.

"Gentlemen, witness," Ali Pasha said, unsheathing a smile from the black of his beard. Then, "Woman, I divorce you."

The wife staggered as if she'd been struck.

"I divorce you."

And again, finally, "I divorce you. Be gone from my house and trouble me no more."

As the blows fell, so had the woman's veil, from utter astonishment. What sense she had left by the last pronouncement went to the protection of her children: She grabbed the little girl and pressed one side of her head to her breast, the other with both hands, so her daughter might be spared the world-shattering sound of those words.

The woman tried to move her lips. "Why? What have I done? Oh, husband, forgive it, for surely I never meant it. Why, for the love of Allah?" But nothing would come out. After another brief moment of hopeful disbelief, disbelief vanished. Clutching the little girl so tightly now that the mite was whimpering, and with the younger boy at her heels, she fled back into the harem.

The older boy stood still in his exuberance. Surely his worshipped father's quarrel with his mother could have no effect on him. She was, after all, only a foolish woman. *They* were men.

But, "Off with you, boy." Ali Pasha dashed the child's hopes and sent him to howl in the harem with the rest. "Go stay with your mother. We have grown-up things to discuss now, these gentlemen and I."

"I do not think that divorce will hold up in a court of law if the facts be known," Ghazanfer confided to me after he had finished his tale.

"How so?" I asked, for hadn't he just come from informing Safiye that there was no doubt now that all was legal for her and Esmikhan to proceed with the wedding plans?

"The law requires the presence of two Muslims as witnesses," he answered my question.

"So?"

"I must confess I've never felt less like a Muslim in my life, to have to be a witness to that crime," he said wistfully. "My lady was so quick to save me from my suffering in the Seven Towers, which Allah would have been pleased to end in death sooner rather than later. I cannot understand how she can now use that very same power of hers to cause suffering I doubt even Paradise can heal."

Hours after hearing of the match between Ali Pasha and Esmikhan Sultan, Ferhad Pasha finally agreed to marry Aysha, the daughter of Sultan Murad. As soon as due pomp and display allowed, the formal *nikah* ceremony took place. The actual consummation would be performed sometime later, when the girl was mature, but the *nikah* was binding in every way and could only be broken from either side with great loss of honor. As the girl in this case was an Ottoman, in fact it couldn't be broken at all by anything other than death.

Carried along by the momentum of this match, preparations for the *nikah* and consummation between Esmikhan and Ali Pasha moved on apace. The day before it was scheduled to happen, my lady called me to her and asked if I could arrange an interview for her with the groom. Such a request was rare, but it was not unheard of. It is Islamic law, after all, that the bride must not be married without her consent. A token meeting is always arranged, although granted it usually does not take place until the *nikah* is moments away from finalization. The bride is then usually too shy or frightened to do more than let her guardians speak for her.

No, if a woman doubts her guardians' opinions in the matter, she had better see she uses some other means at her disposal to prevent things from getting so far along.

In a case such as this, however, where the woman was a widow, where the all-important maidenhead was not in the scales and where she was of a much higher class than the groom, arrangements could be made without raising too many eyebrows. I told Esmikhan so and promised I would do my best to make them as soon as possible. I had only two reservations.

The first was that my lady's pale face and agitated manner spoke of something more serious than just a simple concern for compatibility and the chances for conjugal happiness. Second, I wondered why she had suddenly decided to go through me instead of through Safiye and her agents, who had been the only contact with the groom until then.

The greatest delay in bringing about the meeting, however, was caused by the governor of Hungary himself trying to decide which robe to wear to most favorably impress his royal bride.

"Does my lady prefer red or blue?" he asked.

When I told him that she looked best in pink or red, knew it, and always chose those colors for herself in spite of what others might prefer, he did not take the suggestion, but complained, "No, not the red. The blue is by far the most lavish with nearly an asper of silver woven into it and so many fine large pearls."

In the end he opted for ostentation to carry the day rather than any sense of aesthetics. This was my first meeting with the man and I found him to be all that Ghazanfer had described and more. My most difficult task in this new harem, I decided, would be orchestrating the comings and goings of concubines, for a steady stream would be called for to match Ali Pasha's high opinion of himself.

LIV

"A WOMAN CAME to see me today," Esmikhan said to Ali Pasha.

I had been busy serving our guest a tray of five little silver bowls, each with its own tiny spoon and a different jelly or preserve: rose petal, date, apricot, orange, plum, and bright green mint. I noticed he took date—it was the most costly and difficult to make.

I had only half listened to their talk until now. It consisted mostly of Ali Pasha, as carefully as he could without overstepping the bounds of prenuptial modesty, professing the honor he felt by both the proposed marriage and this interview. How beautiful and gracious he knew by all reports this daughter of Selim—Allah favor him—was. She was safely behind the screen so he could say it without a flinch. And he would serve and love her all of his life, with Allah's favor.

These seven words of my lady were the first either of them had spoken out of formula and her first full sentence all together. But it was more than this that made me suddenly jerk up and stare. As it fell on our ears at this far end of the chamber, her tone held something so cold and vaporous that it sent chills down my spine.

Over the years, Esmikhan's bulk had grown and come to consume a greater and greater proportion of my concern: How to move it here and there, how to make it comfortable and so on when it was half again as large as my own. With so much concern for the physical, I suppose I tended to forget the spiritual—what she symbolized not only for me, but even more so for men with both feet placed firmly in the material world such as Ali Pasha. The symbol was brought to me suddenly and with a shock, and I could tell it had come to the governor as well.

Not only did the fact that she sat behind her screen serve to disembody my lady's presence, but an allover dimness and light in irregular and deceptive blotches conspired to do so, too. Her voice seemed to come not from behind the screen particularly but from everywhere at once, to bathe the hearer like the gloom, to be incorporeal and yet very present and very, very tangible all at once. Like the thick fog that sometimes rises off the Danube, it seemed to enter the lungs as if it were water and they a sponge; it entered the brain like wool stuffed a pillow.

And suddenly Ali Pasha knew it would be useless to try and fight this fog with his poor weapons—a sharp appearance and swaggering manners. It would be as useless to fight this as to throw one's dagger and oneself against a Danubian fog for rising unbidden and misleading his troops. Esmikhan's voice was the voice of conscience if not epiphany.

"A woman came to see me today," the voice repeated, having once let us catch our bearings on no ground at all. "I did not remember her, though she had been a serving girl under my stepmother in her youth. Naturally I greeted her as such. She had come to me as the last friend she had in the world. She had no place else to go besides the brothel, being after all a former slave, kin- and defenseless. Of course I said at once that she must stay with me, she and her three children.

" 'But tell me,' I could not refrain from asking, 'how is it you come to be in such a pitiful state? My father, the Sultan of the Faithful, surely he did not leave you so. He would be nothing if not a man of honor and no man with a shred of honor would do such a thing.'

"Then she told me. She told me how her husband, the man to whom my father had trusted her honor and care, had been swollen by ambition to marry another and had cast her off without a backwards glance at the ten years she had served him in perfect faithfulness.

"You would have recognized this woman, Pasha, long before I did. She had to spell it out more clearly before I realized—before I could believe—that she was your wife, Pasha, and that I was the one for whom you so carelessly threw her fair face, supple body, and delicate manners away."

Ali Pasha made some movement to protest that the face and manners of a slave could not compete with those of one of the house of Othman. But he knew full well it was too late and did not get far with his protestations. Esmikhan refuted them all quickly anyway.

"No! How can you think to debase the royal blood of Othman with a nature so lacking in honor and devotion as that! I'm sure you will consider yourself fortunate if I do not call for your death—the usual punishment for treason against the throne—and simply refuse the suit of marriage that has been brought to me. Beyond that, I can hardly wish you peace and good day, Pasha. As Allah lives, I pray He may harrow your soul with guilt even a fraction of what it deserves. That should be enough to make you long for hellfire."

You may be certain Ali Pasha left the palace with her voice licking his heels like flame.

Safiye was furious when she learned what her creature, or so she counted Esmikhan, had done. At first she tried everything from cajolery to cursing to sway the Sultan's daughter, but my lady, still harboring the divorcée and her abandoned children, resisted with the spirit if not the physical force of a lion. Finally Safiye desisted, realizing that any more discussion on a point of view Esmikhan found so clearly immoral would only serve to lose her this important ally.

In the meantime, Nur Banu had sent her emissaries to Ali Pasha with some tempting offers concerning the Ottoman daughters of her slaves . . .

"Ali Pasha refused Nur Banu!" Safiye exclaimed, elated, when she learned the news. "He's refused the old girl. But why? I can't believe I overestimated him."

"No," Esmikhan said with a quiet smile. "I think you underestimated him." And she took the hand of the divorcée who'd sought her protection and who sat dandling her youngest on the divan next to my lady.

There were three months of waiting. The sham marriage to another man, hired for the purpose. And then at last—but not one day later than the minimum the law allowed—Ali Pasha and his wife were reunited and with hardly less joy and passion than I have seen between love matches and virgins. Within another three months, the new bride was with child.

And Ali Pasha, though this business proved to be the end of his ambition, was not totally cut off from all routes to advancement. His wife now had powerful strings to pull in the heart of the imperial harem that she had not had before. The last time I saw the Pasha, I noticed with interest how the bladelike features of his former self had been buried, as it were, in dunes of sand-colored flesh. And though not particularly dashing any longer, one could not say he looked either unbecoming or unhappy.

"What a remarkable mistress you serve" was Ghazanfer's comment on the matter, and I had to agree with him. But he went further. "In many another time and place—less civilized, we might say—a woman who had been so used for no other fault than coming in the way of her man's ambition or his lust, she would have had no recourse. Even the lawyers and jurists in such a situation would be swayed either by the man's wealth or his power, for she had modestly kept herself from all such things. But see, here, that very modesty and, some might say, helplessness won her favor in your lady's eye and thus helped her simple desires. And, I may add, a just and merciful Heaven's will as well. That is how the harem with its all-powerful calls of honor upon the less powerful world of men should work. Your lady understands it well and hence carried the day. If only it were so with my lady! She persists in using the tactics of the *selamlik,* and everything I try to say to her she takes as treason."

Here the great eunuch shrugged and said, "I suppose I only mean to apologize for the cold way my lady has treated yours since these events. Without cause, I believe, and because it is causeless, it cannot last long."

His prophecy was true and the grudge, which hurt my lady deeply, did not last past Ali Pasha's remarriage. But this was not so much because Safiye had learned restraint but because there were other plots afoot. Not the least of these was the marriage of Prince Muhammed and my Gul Ruh.

LV

Safiye was in the midst of paying court to Gul Ruh with a new jeweled caplet and rather-too-intimate caresses on the hair: "Ah! how my son will love these dancing braids."

My young lady replied with the words—one could almost hear the tones—of Nur Banu, "Aunt Safiye, you know full well my cousin Muhammed cannot marry me—or anyone—until he is circumcised and becomes a man."

It angered Safiye to be told so—and in such tones—but she could not deny it was true. No matter how she influenced Turkish taste towards the Venetian in everything from fabric and costume to medicine—for which the Republic should always be financially grateful—this she could not change. Even the Hand of Allah in the form of the terrible fire that had thwarted the first attempt to make her boy into a man could not put it off forever. Muhammed could not rule unless he was a full Muslim and he could not be a Muslim with his foreskin intact.

And every year it was put off meant only a greater danger of serious infection accompanying the operation. In fact, it clearly seemed to be Nur Banu's plan to put off the rite forever so that Muhammed might never rule.

This taunt placed in the mouth of unsuspecting Gul Ruh was enough to call Safiye to her duties as a Turkish rather than a Venetian mother. She proceeded at once to do what she could to circumvent Nur Banu's authority and once more set the preparations in motion. Nonetheless, the planning did take nearly a full year in total. And this was not all on account of Murad's desire to see that his son and heir was circumcised in glory such as the world had never seen before. It was also in part due to Nur Banu's constant and often successful attempts to see that the rite might never be celebrated, with or without glory.

Whenever the flurry of preparation grew white hot, Gul Ruh shied and sulked from it as if it was preparation for her own wedding as, in a way, it was. At such times, even Nur Banu's rooms were hardly far enough away for my young mistress, and I think she was particularly grateful to Umm Kulthum when one day the Mufti's widow invited my young lady to join her and her daughters for a picnic in the country.

❦

EARLY ON FRIDAY morning, the party was ferried up to the end of the Horn where the Sweet Waters of Europe flow through a park to the Sea. The Turks are connoisseurs of waters as Italians are of wine. They know the various qualities of every major spring from Zem-Zem in Mecca northward and will often pay dearly for a flask of some famous source packed in by caravan. Bottled waters, however, are universally declared to be but pale compared to sampling the product on the spot. And within an easy journey of Constantinople, only one or two privately owned springs in the foothills are more desirable than the Sweet Waters of Europe.

At this time of year when the streams were swollen and ice-cold from the melting snow, it was doubted if even the springs could vie. The water, pure from any sediment, was delightfully tasteless in any season. But in spring, when one's mouth was not too numbed by the cold, one could taste something more—the sweetness that gave the waters their name and their fame.

As if the waters were not sufficient in themselves, Umm Kulthum devoted one whole boatload to picnic dainties and sweets. Upon our arrival, the slaves spread these out in dizzy array on carpets on the sward. Sweetmeats and pistachios were unpacked. Dried figs and dates and apricots and raisins, olives and meatballs and balls of rice and ground chickpeas, stuffed pastries sweet and savory, all were heavily spiced and sprigged with fresh-cut mint. The eye could easily confuse the bright colors and intricate detail of the foods on their brass and china platters for the floral patterns on the rugs.

Umm Kulthum and some of her older, matronly friends were content to sit before these mounds and feed like browsing sheep. But eating was not that for which her daughters, their young slaves, and my Gul Ruh had come to the country. One could eat at home.

We had ferried those girls over in tight bundles, wrapped like roses cut in the bud when hardly a shadow peeking out from the green hull hints at the color within. Now, as if those roses had been brought into the heat and stuck in water, they burst into bloom as they played hide-and-seek and catch and danced to improvised music among the great old chestnut and plane trees.

The trees heaved the grass in their shadows up into mounds with their trunks. People turn red when drunk, grass turns but a lusher green and this grass on the banks of the Sweet Waters was far gone. The blades could hardly keep their bleary, heavy heads up. When bruised, they stained with an uncommon vigor. I saw my lady with dark green stains on the knees of her *shalvar* and on both elbows. She had worn her best clothes to honor the occasion, but they would probably have to be given away now, beyond all hope of salvage.

But to see her running and laughing as if she were a child again, and to see the old bloom come back in her cheeks—I hadn't the heart to forbid her. The grown-up sobriety of the last few years was all very well, I thought. Indeed, it was probably necessary. Like the green sheath of a rose, it would be good protection against the sorrows and hardships of life that were bound to fall. But it was heartening to see that in sunlight and pure water, she could still bloom.

Umm Kulthum had had her slaves set up the camp in a broad hollow into which an arm of the waters curled for a moment's privacy before rolling on about its public business. It was the perfect spot because, even by the time it reached our ears—we *khuddam* perched on the surrounding hillocks in a protective cordon—even the most frantic squeal had all but faded. And as no man with any self-respect would take another step towards the first glimpse of a eunuch's robes he saw, the girls' games, delicious like stolen fruit, would always remain our secret.

I regaled in the sight—pitying all mankind for whom it must ever be forbidden—of the beautiful girls more beautiful still in their jewels, their bright yellows and pinks and deep reds, both on *shalvar* and cheeks. Their carefully braided hair now working its way loose like the linen of their undershirts. They flashed into sunlight, vanished into shadows, as if that hollow had a pulse and they were it.

Over their heads, the leaves of both chestnut and plane were as yet fragile and thin, but clouds of the lesser Judas trees in pink-violet bloom were like spun-sugar mist and hid magical worlds of fairy tale. In the rain of their petals, I forgot the myths of my childhood that were beyond redemption. I felt pure joy.

Only when the sun was directly overhead did the muezzin from the nearby Eyüp Mosque call the party to more sober pursuits. A quiet time was something it would be foolish to do without in the heat of the day. But the girls were so exhilarated they would have ignored that need were it not for the all-wise Word of Allah.

Eyüp is the burial place of the standard bearer of the Prophet who died in 672 of the Christian era during the first Muslim attempt to take Constantinople. It is such a sacred place that no man can be considered Sultan until the Sword of his ancestor Othman has been girded on him with those blessed walls.

Eyüp is a popular place for the living to come as pilgrims and for the dead to come and await the Day of Resurrection. Their tombs clustered at the feet of his who first made the ground holy. Some of the girls, my young lady among them, expressed their desire to go and visit the shrine themselves. But that would have to wait for another day. A woman would have to be desperately poor, old, and mad to attempt to jostle with the crowds of men on a Friday. Wealthy young ladies whose griefs could never be allowed a depth to shatter sanity must make other arrangements. The girls knew it was true.

A curious look of satisfaction came to Umm Kulthum when, naturally but regretfully, she had to refuse the request with a "Maybe next month sometime . . ." Although I saw the satisfaction, I soon dismissed and forgot it as no more than a simple woman's delight at all outward shows of piety.

In about two hours, the Friday sermon was over and the mosque emptied itself. Then we *khuddam* made an attempt to shake off our drowsiness. A good number of the males decided, having come so far out in the country, that they would take advantage of the pleasant air and visit the Sweet Waters as well. We ruffled ourselves like threatened cocks and stood to attention so we would be more visible. And all the men did stay removed from our hollow. Why mar newly gained sanctity from the shrine of Eyüp by contact with strange women?

One party, however, did not immediately take the hint. As my colleagues and I moved closer to answer the threat, however, we understood that it was not ignorance on the part of the men but knowledge that drew them. The leader of the small group of young scholars was Umm Kulthum's youngest son Abd ar-Rahman. Soon Umm Kulthum's eunuchs were carrying the remains of our picnic to them. After a while, when the young men were refreshed, Abd ar-Rahman himself came halfway up the hillock and his mother and sisters came halfway down to exchange formal, heavily guarded greetings.

Abd ar-Rahman was full of the day's sermon. The imam he found brilliant and learned. He thanked his mother for the suggestion to come there that day and he would try and do so as often as he could in the future to learn more from the man.

Now his youngest sister Betula, a girl not much older and about the same size as Gul Ruh, stamped her foot angrily, "Oh, Brother, why must you always be so tedious? It's spring! It's a beautiful day and here we are in this park with the birds singing like mad. Can't you for once be just a little romantic?"

"And you are such a silly girl!" her brother retorted with self-righteous indignation. "So brazen in that color. I should be ashamed to give you to any one of my friends to wife. He would blame me and say I gave him a harlot."

The girl blushed, but not with shame. She was rather pleased. Her brother was indignant: She must have succeeded in being truly attractive. And "that color"—pink—must be one he found particularly pleasant for him to raise such a fuss about it. Pleasure always made him uncomfortable. He was so unused to the sensation.

Abd ar-Rahman recited some part of the sermon to his sister, advised her to take heed and sent her back into the hollow in giggles. It was only then that I recognized her dress. It was Gul Ruh who had taken the spill that had seriously stained the right arm, not the Mufti's daughter. It was Gul Ruh who had worn her best pink dress that day. The Mufti's girl had been in green when we left Constantinople. For some reason of girlish vanity I could not fathom (for Gul Ruh looked too sallow for my taste when she wore green), the two had exchanged outer dresses. I had better keep a closer eye on the pair from now on.

Abd ar-Rahman lowered his voice and spoke a few more polite words to his mother and his older sisters, then took formal leave of them, making his way back down through the trees to his companions. His friends must have known where he'd gone—the picnic had not appeared out of the clear blue, of course. But they were a polite and very religious bunch, so they made no more comment than if he had just gone off to answer a basic call of nature. Their thoughts were not driven from the discussion of Holy Law as presented by the sermon for a moment. And Abd ar-Rahman was very glad to escape back into that niche where he felt most at ease.

Suddenly, however, Abd ar-Rahman's Friday afternoon ease was shattered. So was that of everyone else in the park. At first I pretended to ignore the commotion. A chorus of high, shrill voices was shouting and crying, but I assumed it must be a band of rowdy boys. If it was women, as another moment convinced me it must be, it must be a congress of fish mongers' wives fighting over slippers. Surely such hysteria could not be from *our* women in such a public place. But just another moment told me that indeed it was.

A copse of trees and a hillock blocked my view of what was happening. It centered on the fast moving stream. And before I had time to get to my feet, the chaos' focus had drifted past the protection of the hollow and into the open. I thought at first a bough of pink Judas blossom caught my eye. But the splash of color occasionally defied the pull of the water and displayed a mind of its own. And the pink was turning such a dark purple as Judas blossom will take on only after a day of wilt.

My heart suddenly pumped aching fear to every limb—as fine satin will the minute it touches water and begins to soak up deadly weight.

LVI

THE ENTIRE HILLSIDE of eunuchs and women was now running like rainwater down to the lowest level. Abd ar-Rahman, too, was drawn on by that color he recognized from his recent interview with his sister. He reached the water first.

A pair of eunuchs quickly formed a solid chain to the bank lest Abd ar-Rahman, like the log burned light and white with study that he was—be likewise caught in the current. But it was the young man himself who made the rescue. Though he staggered a moment under the unaccustomed physical load, with the strong eunuchs' arms to right him, he insisted on carrying the burden to the safety of the copse. He wanted the personal pleasure of scolding his wanton sister himself.

But it was not his sister. I had suspected the rereversal in clothing all the way down the hill. And as I ran up to the excited rabble that clustered around, hardly giving the drowned soul a taste of precious air, my worst fears were confirmed. She who had become an object of such display was my young lady. That she had nearly drowned was the least of my worries: She'd be better off dead than seen by a hundred men in Friday-after-sermon righteousness.

The same instant I knew the truth, Abd ar-Rahman did, too. Any woman not his close kin was like a jinni to him, something supernatural and as scalding as sparks from heaven. He dropped her none too gently and fled without a word.

Gul Ruh had recovered somewhat, at least enough to recognize her rescuer, likewise a dangerous, awful creature. She was thankful to be dropped, and although part of her stagger was from weakness, it was compounded by a struggle to hide her face.

Gul Ruh's stumble to the ground was padded by many concerned arms and laps, but even if they had not been there, cutting off air, her recovery would have been slowed by her hands. Her cap and veil had been lost in the water. Finding her skirt too water sodden to lift, she covered her face with simple palms instead. And as soon as there was air in her lungs to carry out a sob, the hands became a handkerchief for her grief.

Gul Ruh shook like a leaf. The ice-cold water had aggravated the usual pearly smoothness and pallor of her skin. The veins were visible beneath, a stark blue as they tried to carry normal pulse again. So had Abd ar-Rahman seen her—a fragile thing so in need of comfort and protection. But few of us thought of what the effect of the sight might have had on him. He had seen her, that made our hearts heavy enough.

Now the Mufti's daughter, once more in her own green dress, made her way through the crowd with a warm brew of orchid root. She knelt before Gul Ruh and spoke gently for her friend to take that invigorating drink. But suddenly my lady came to life with a ferocity that startled us all. Were there not so many layers of already-wet skirt on top of them, her legs would have gotten drenched by the potion that spilled as she shoved it away.

"You," she said, tears dragging across the words like flesh over a rusty knife. "By Allah, Betula, you pushed me! Oh, Allah, I am shamed forever. Abd ar-Rahman! I want to die. And it's your fault!"

"It was meant in fun," Betula said in weak self-defense. But every eye on the Mufti's daughter felt that her dowsing with orchid root juice was but easy punishment for what, it now seemed obvious, she had caused.

We quickly bundled my lady first in her veil (which for the first time in her life didn't seem heavy enough) and then in numerous quilts to try and keep her warm. We packed her under the canopy on the boat with the curtains drawn as tightly as possible to hold in the warmth of the day. Then we prepared to sail at once. The sharp wind that often comes up at sunset and was the delightful close of many an outing—teasing the curls and tossing up a wild salt spray to carry on one's face into the harem again—this wind must now be avoided at all costs.

I had hustled the last of our slave girls on board and was about to follow them myself when I saw Umm Kulthum approaching. In one hand she held my lady's bedraggled cap and veil which her son, she explained, had found further downstream. She took the opportunity to apologize for the accident.

"Accident!" I repeated. I was very angry. More than pride was hurt.

Gul Ruh was young, but I wondered if either of us would recover from the events of that day. "This was no accident. Your daughter did it on purpose. She must have plotted it at least as long ago as their first exchange of dresses." Then I quite forgot myself and flared, "In fact, I wouldn't be surprised if you were in on the plot. I wouldn't be at all surprised if this whole outing was planned with no other purpose in mind than to humiliate my lady."

"Not to humiliate her, no," Umm Kulthum said.

To my surprise, that was as far as her refutation went. As soon as the words were out of my mouth, I'd felt ready to apologize for the attack, but now I was glad I'd spoken as I had.

"I only want to see that my dear husband—may Allah favor him—has his last wish fulfilled. I only want to see that Gul Ruh does become my dear, sweet daughter-in-law at last. She shall be the joy of my old age, if only Allah will."

"But Abd ar-Rahman? Now that he—"

"But that's the problem we had to overcome, you see. Every time I bring the question up, he says, 'Oh, Mother. There are a thousand other girls in the Realm of Islam I could marry. Who wants to get mixed up with the royal house when there is a choice? As the old sage Ahnaf bin Qays once said, "Rulers have no friends." Choose, if you must, Mother, though I'm convinced a wife is only a stumbling block to study. And if you must choose, do not choose a Sultan's daughter.'

"Well," Umm Kulthum continued, "as long as he thought like this, he would not ask his brothers to go beg for her hand from her uncle, the Shadow of Allah. And if they would not go, what is the use of me going to her mother? Anyway, his eldest brother is now hatching plans to marry Abd ar-Rahman to the daughter of the present Mufti. Oh, what a scheming, grabbing son my firstborn is, Allah save him! He wants the connection. But the girl? A dull, lifeless thing.

"He's already sent me to interview her mother, and when I saw the girl, I couldn't bring myself to broach the subject. I told him the daughter wants time to consider, for she is but young. Young? She's older than Abd ar-Rahman, Allah shield him. But what my son doesn't know, hidden in the harem, need not come out in the open. Even five fewer years would not make her better favored. Such an ugly dish clout with a voice like the clang of cheap copper vessels. And dull-witted!

"Now your Gul Ruh, Allah bless her, is a scholar. But this girl? You're lucky to get her through her prayers once a day. What would my son and she talk about, I ask you? Betula has had more contact with her and wishes she had less, so my daughter came in on this plot with me rather than see that Mufti's girl brought into our home. If there's anything that would turn Abd ar-Rahman, Allah forbid, into a tedious old scholar with holes in his brain where joy and connubial bliss ought to be—all before he's twenty-five—it would be to marry such a girl.

"He's my favorite, my baby. Can you understand? Though he's foolishly ignorant of the fact, having never seen her until today, Gul Ruh is the only woman who can make him happy and I want him to be happy."

"Lady, I am indeed sorry for you," I said with biting sarcasm. "To be so ignorant of your son, though you say he is your favorite. Abd ar-Rahman is a young man of fierce piety. He would have to be a gypsy or a pagan before he could find shame such as we were forced to display today attractive."

I turned to go with an angry flourish, but I saw that my words had no effect on her. She bade us farewell, her pretty plump shoulders and eyebrows raising in a shrug that did nothing to erase her self-satisfied grin.

LVII

ONE WEEK TO the day later, the palace harem was entertaining Umm Kulthum, the Mufti's widow, again. But this time she headed directly for Esmikhan in Safiye's half of the enclosure instead of along her usual path to Nur Banu's.

She stopped me outside the door. "I told you I knew my own son," she said triumphantly.

I was in a much better mood that day than I had been when I'd left her in the park. Gul Ruh was strong and had caught but a small cold from her adventure and the sniffles were now all but gone. The gossip, too, seemed to have stayed its tongue at least until it could be seen what Abd ar-Rahman meant to do about the matter. In order to be among the first to learn of his reaction, I stopped to hear Umm Kulthum out.

"Betula went to her brother as soon as we got home," she said, "and explained to him that it was all her fault he had had to play hero that afternoon. This only confirmed the impression my son already had that Gul Ruh was the helpless victim.

"You should have heard him! 'So light in my arms,' he said. 'So pale and shaking as if my very touch might kill her.' He saw the accident now not only as Betula's fault but somehow as his own as well. That his sister is wanton is his fault—he's never been stern enough with her. That he had gone splashing into the water, too, that is his fault. He knew there were strange women about. They had their own eunuchs who could have saved her just as well. But he had to make a fool of himself and invade another man's property and a virtuous woman's modesty.

"Well, there is nothing for it now. To recover the honor of our whole family, from Betula up, he must do the honorable thing. He must send his brothers to the Sultan with a request for Gul Ruh's hand."

Umm Kulthum took my elbow and spoke confidentially now. "He talks in brave words like *honor* and *guilt* because he is shy and a coward to mention what he really feels, *love*. That he should go against reason and fall for a girl on no better pretext than that he has seen her face and felt her in his arms—that offends his manhood. He grows red and white at the very thought, stumbles clumsily, then retreats to the safety of his books.

"But I can tell. Soon enough he is back in the *mabein*. He can't read any more, you see. He rails at Betula and threatens to beat her. She simply laughs at him, for she knows it is his excuse to be close to women, a thing he finds himself longing for in spite of his better judgement. A thing he is as yet clumsy at. Oh, they will be so happy!"

And so certain was Umm Khulthum of how her plan must work out that she almost forgot to conclude with *"Inshallah."*

"Allah willing," I added to her wish and then noticed that during our conversation, Gul Ruh had arrived. I don't know how much of our talk she heard, but she was radiant in cloth-of-gold. Her beautiful brown eyes, cleansed by a brief bout with a light fever, sparkled now with crystal-clear health. And perhaps there were tears of excitement there, too.

Unlike her usual manner, Umm Kulthum said nothing to the girl in greeting. She had been announced in Safiye's sitting room and must not delay. But she did pause long enough to produce a sprig of Judas blossom from her bosom which she proceeded to stick fondly into Gul Ruh's hair where it looked lovely against the rich black braids. Nobody said it, but it was plain whose hand had picked that sprig. It looked like his hand in a caress, thin and pale and gentle with timidity.

Gul Rah accepted the flowers gratefully and bowed to kiss Umm Kulthum's hem as a daughter-in-law does to her new mother. Umm Kulthum straightened the sprig once more and then went in to the interview. Gul Ruh and I were left to pace nervously outside the door.

We did not have long to wait. Usually when the proposal has been made, the girl is sent for and given time to dress in her finery before being presented and told the news. I thought Gul Ruh would have to be constrained from springing in too soon and seeming immodestly anxious to be a bride. But as it happened no constraint was necessary. It was not a maidservant who came to the door, but Umm Kulthum herself. She swept by in tears, looking neither right nor left. Gul Ruh and I followed after as close as we dared come to the grief we had seen in that face. It was only when she was safely in the custody of her own eunuchs at the door of her sedan that Umm Kulthum turned to us again.

She did not look at us, but at the gilded and tiled intestinal halls in general as her voice echoed off them. "By Allah, may there come grief to this house to match the grief that they have given to us this day and then I shall be satisfied!"

A man could be killed for uttering such treason. Only a mother bereaved was understood to be so out of her mind that she was forgiven.

"Take your son's suit elsewhere," she had been told briefly and in no uncertain language. Safiye was in the room with Esmikhan and it was Safiye who had done the talking. "In the second month of Rabia, less than two months from now, my son Muhammed will be circumcised. Soothsayers have already chosen the day and preparations are well under way. This time, as Allah is true, the day will not be put off again, for my son is now a man and ready to take on a man's responsibilities. As soon as his manhood has healed, he will take a wife. A wife that is worthy to stand beside a Sultan, not this rabble of slave girls with which we are presently plagued. Before the summer's end, it shall be so. He shall marry his cousin Gul Ruh, as Allah shows favor to the Muslim people."

THE DANCER, SWEATING profusely, kicked off her shoes the better to free herself of the world and enter into the seduction of the music. Her shoulders rolled like sea waves. Over them, with a pair of wooden spoons in each hand, she clattered out a rhythm. The rhythm intercoursed with thrilling shivers amongst the three tantalizing touches on the tenor side of the drum to each heavy grunt on the bass. The shawm squealed, the audience did, too, squealed and blushed and sweated at the suggestion in the merest roll of the dancer's hips. The hips seemed to have a life of their own, a life far removed from that in the stifle of the harem, a life where all desires were satisfied . . .

Nur Banu, watching this, her newest slave, with obvious pride, cracked a pistachio between her strong white teeth.

"You know she killed your father, don't you?"

Nur Banu spat the hull onto the carpet. The dancer was oblivious and danced on it and a spray of others as if on clouds.

"Who did?" Gul Ruh's heart leapt to her throat with fear on the off beat.

"Why, Safiye, of course." Nur Banu picked another nut with care and dealt similarly with it.

Gul Ruh had been ignoring the dancing to vent her grief and anger over the latest happening in Safiye's section to Nur Banu's understanding ears. But this revelation caught my young lady totally unprepared and she could say nothing.

"Oh, she didn't dress up like a dervish and actually do the deed herself. But he was in her pay. Which is the same thing, isn't it?"

"Yes," Gul Ruh admitted. Then she stammered, "But why?"

"To keep you from marrying Abd ar-Rahman. To keep you for herself—and, incidentally, for Muhammed. Do you think it's just coincidence that Sokolli Pasha—Allah favor him—died the same day the sons of the old Mufti were to come and make the marriage plans? No. She had to move fast—and she did."

Gul Ruh was silent, trying to fit the complexity, the duplicity of what she had just heard into the straightforwardness of her mind. Safiye was her mother's closest friend. Yet Safiye had killed her best friend's husband?

Before the tortuous task was half complete, Nur Banu spoke again. "And Arab Pasha, too."

"Brabi?"

"She had him killed on Cyprus. Oh, I know they say they were brigands, but they were brigands as much as that dervish was a holy man— they had the same source for their pay."

Gul Ruh was shaking her head in a dither of disbelief.

"But it's true. And for the same reason. Your aunt Safiye knew only too well what an impediment he was in your heart."

The ancient commandment of blood for blood clamped like manacles about Gul Ruh's hands. She stuttered, "Then . . . then I must take revenge. I must . . ." She could not say it actively and threw it to the safety of the passive: "*She* must be killed."

"It would be nice, yes. But frankly, my dear, I don't know how it is to be done. Allah knows, I've tried. No, she is too closely guarded, she is too strong and clever, even for one like you who may come and go in her presence."

"Allah is merciful to widows and orphans. He cannot let such crimes go unpunished."

"Allah is indeed merciful. Safiye herself may be impregnable, but there are others of her blood who will suit the demands of vengeance just as well—blood for blood—and in fact may cause her more grief than just a moment's twist of the knife."

"Others of her blood?"

"Prince Muhammed, for example. She cannot be with him every minute of every day. It would not be such a difficult thing for you, his dear, trusted cousin, to win his confidence . . ."

"Must I kill Muhammed, then?" Gul Ruh's voice was as weak as milk skimmed of the cream.

"Oh, my goodness, no, my dear! Such a thing for a lady to say! But you might open opportunity . . ."

"Allah! Allah! Allah!" The audience was shouting in an all-consuming rhythm now, clapping their hands with a particularly sharp resonance. A second woman, as if possessed, could not stay on her cushion any longer. She leapt up, tore the scarf off her head and threw it around the first dancer's hips. They danced in a vertigo of waists.

"Praise Allah for our new sister who has freed our souls!" was heard from deep in a hoarse throat.

And from another: "Allah, I will give my right hand to be the one to take her to the baths and wash this sweat from her when at last she drops."

"And ah, to see—to touch!—those hips when the weight of that belt of bells is gone!"

LVIII

SUMMER, THE SECOND month of Rabia and a time the astrologers and fortunetellers labeled laconically "the ascendancy of the household," began on a single day. The Marmara had ironed out its springtime turbulence and lay now like a carpet of honor before the palace enthroned on the Point.

In certain lights, particularly early morning or at sunset, it caught the colors and patterns of Angora wool besides. But then, honor was still in the making, for the caïques and skiffs with their bright holiday banners trailing sped one way and the other like shuttles. On such a day a seven-charge salute sounded from the Tower of the Cannon and the festivities that would make an adult Muslim of Muhammed, the firstborn Prince, began.

For much of this two-week period, I stood in my place at the end of the ranks of eunuchs which in turn were behind the scarlet-robed pages, the blue tutors, the violet lawyers and the green viziers spun out like satin ribbons on the court. The sea of turbans was like a field of mushrooms sprung up in the muggiest of weather. It was easy to leave my insignificant place without causing scandal when I grew weary. I had, indeed, been assigned to do so, to come into the harem and give full reports of all the action at every interval.

I diligently fulfilled this command the first two days, during which Murad received the congratulations of the chief officers, the lords of the tributary states, and the foreign ambassadors. On the third day I described the procession of the guilds of the city to the ladies.

"They certainly vied with one another in both the richness of their gifts and the amusement of their presentation. The sherbet makers' guild came first and presented rare lotus and tamarind concoctions to all present." I paused, hoping someone would ask how I liked these things. I wanted to assure them plain rose or citron was much nicer, but nobody asked.

I continued: "The pastry makers then showered us with sweets. I myself caught two Little Turkish Bonnets." I tried to prod interest from Safiye, but she was not moved. Two other conversations started under me in different corners of the room. I began to speak louder.

"We went from the goldsmiths who presented the master with a filigree bird cage as high as a man, to the jewelers who had encrusted a Koran on every inch of its two-by-two-foot cube, to the animal trainers who presented an ostrich, an elephant, and a giraffe to the palace menagerie. This latter animal, the giraffe, is like a vastly overgrown deer whose neck and legs have been stretched out of all grace." I'd thought long and hard about this description, but nobody seemed to care. In desperation I turned to the little bit of humor I'd prepared.

"By wise programming it was the street sweepers who followed after the animals. They must have feared a display of their simple craft might not be worthy of the occasion although none of us, standing in the wake of the animals, doubted it. Their buffoons and fire-eaters were the most elaborate of all and artfully distracted from the janitorial service that scurried on between them." I was the only one who chuckled— self-consciously.

Now I began to speak at a breakneck speed, just trying to make it to the end. There were maybe five other conversations going now, full of animation. "Even the tanners and thieves' guild was not neglected.

Though out of sight, they have been able to create something that the foreign dignitaries will report back to their governments in wonder. In such a vast congregation of humanity from the highest to the lowest, not a single purse has been cut or pocket picked. One gentleman who, through a faulty clasp and his own carelessness, lost a gold chain in the dust, found it returned to him by a deep blue-black hand. The hand still reeked of tannin and dog dung, but accompanied a gracious salaam and a brief admonition to be more cautious in the future. Even a noble absentmindedness will not be allowed to give the Sultan and his subjects a bad name . . ."

I let my voice fade and no one noticed at all. I began to suspect my assignment was just one of the many superfluous ceremonial ones created for the occasion. I went to the grille on the bandstand built especially for the palace women and saw that they had an eagle's eye view that was better than what I had on the ground. I felt like a fool: Of course Safiye would have many agents she trusted better placed than I to report on things she found more important than fire-eaters and jugglers—a wink passing between vizier and pasha, perhaps. I grew angry. Then I grew afraid. Had I been sent out not for the responsibility, but to have me safely out of the way?

As the celebration progressed, I became more and more convinced that this was the case. I couldn't very well stop attending to stay in the harem and investigate, but I did return as often as I thought possible. There were no results, but I had little interest in the festivities after that.

On the fifth day, for example, for the war games, two great towers had been constructed on the field to be manned by opposing forces, besieged, assaulted, captured, and fired in mock combat. This display so delighted the audience that the engineers worked throughout the night to rebuild them to allow a repeat performance the following day. I was impatient with the show the first time through, however, but could only bite back my anger and mutter: "By Allah, can't we just get on with the business?" There was still more than a week of procession, pomp, and party to go.

During this time nothing was seen of the Prince, in whose honor it all was. But finally, on the fourteenth day, he was brought out of the harem in red- and gold-worked robes, cap, and slippers, and presented to his father. The charity boys, too, were presented to their fathers, but on the other side of the court and seated not under canopies but only on low, simple carpets. The clothes of the charity boys, though doubtless dazzling to eyes used only to grey wool homespun, were of the same colors but of less lavish materials than those of the Prince.

I had not seen the heir for several years, but more recently than his father had. At thirteen years old, he was a son of which even a Sultan could be proud. He had his mother's height and could look his father straight in the eye already. He had neither his father's red nor his mother's blond hair. It was dark, but not quite black, rather dusty, one might say, as that of a wrestler just come up from the heat. It was thin but had a loose, tousled curl, again as if he had just enjoyed an invigorating bout of physical activity.

His skin was his mother's, like cowrie shell, with hot spots of color on the cheek bones from the excitement of the moment. But there was color inherited from another source: that finely formed porcelain was cracked by the blue-black of a scar across his cheek he'd gotten as an infant.

No one else seemed to notice this shadow but me. From the Muslims were echoed exclamations thanking Allah, and even the most hopeful of foreign observers would be forced to write to his sovereign that the Turkish threat was strong for a good many years more.

And perhaps my eyes were swayed by something I saw more clearly than the vagaries of flesh. Around his left wrist, which he flourished self-consciously whenever the opportunity presented itself, Muhammed had tied a white napkin. There would have been nothing so very remarkable in this were it not for the fact that I recognized the rough-trying-to-be-careful stitch along one edge. I had seen Gul Ruh thread her needle to take that stitch. I realized at once just how surely the two weeks of glorious entertainments had distracted me from the most important maneuvers of all—those inside the harem.

The Sultan addressed his son in Persian and then Arabic; in both languages the boy acquitted himself fluently. Then the Shadow of Allah posed several questions on the poets, religion, and finally politics. Only in the latter was the young Prince's response less than perfect. He failed to reflect the results of last year's campaign in an answer concerning the Persian borders. As this displayed more concern with dusty textbooks than with practical knowledge, the teachers were chided. But the boy was not. The father himself put more weight on poetry than on politics.

"After all," the monarch explained, "there are always soldiers around in a hurry to correct you on such matters. But what man has ever seen to the full depth of a poem?"

"And what poem to the depth of a woman's heart?" replied the young Prince in improvised meter and rhyme that delighted all hearers.

The wave of his wrist as he spoke did not delight me. My hand closed reflexively on my dagger. But whom was I supposed to attack?

"Quite so, my boy. Quite so," the Sultan replied with a chuckle and laid a fatherly hand on the lad's shoulder. He seemed ready to say more—perhaps about the boy's own mother—but that would have been indiscreet in company. So, "We shall talk more," the Sultan said instead. "Before you go off to the duties of a man in the *sandjak* of Magnesia, we must talk more."

"Nothing would honor me more, sir," Muhammed said.

I left my station as soon as I dared and hurried back to the bowels of the Serai.

LIX

"WHAT IS THIS sudden change of heart that you now look with such favor on your cousin?"

Gul Ruh met me with a face I could not ruffle with the anger of accusations. Yes, she had seen her cousin several times. Safiye, who always acted as chaperon, had insisted. The boy's courage needed bolstering, she said, to enable him to face this ordeal. Almost nothing could be wrong on the part of either male or female, she recited, that brought another Muslim to the age and strength of fighting for the Faith. I could find no argument to that.

I noticed new jewels on my young lady's neck and wrists. I also no-

ticed she had acquired the same hot spots of color in her cheeks that
Safiye and her son had. But instead of a healthy cavalry riding alert on
the saddle of cheekbones, hers seemed to be the flush of a fever, blotchy
and smeared like bad makeup with tears.

She is intoxicated, I thought, drugged like the foreign ambassadors
by the glory of this show Murad's court can put on. Pray Allah it is not
a permanent addiction and may be slept off as soon as the last of the
bunting is down.

Then I learned that Umm Kulthum had been in the Serai and had
been treated not rudely, but with such decided neglect that she had
found the festivities were better seen from her own home and had not
returned. I bit my tongue in anger and glared hard at Safiye whenever
our paths had to cross. But I said nothing.

I defiantly stayed in the harem after this, but if I wanted to make a
point by self-sacrifice, the point was in vain. Now that the Prince had
been presented, what was left to see was minor.

On the fourteenth day in the morning, Muhammed was brought
into a pavilion heavily hung with brocade and splashing with fountains.
And then, as one hundred holy men recited the Koran for the spectators all at the top of their lungs and all at different paces, the boy was
made a man. The operation was announced, by the grace of Allah, as
clean and successful. Murad celebrated and, incidently, covered up any
wounded wails there might have been (although I am assured there
were none) by calling for two great vases filled with coins. Four men
each were required to carry the vessels and the sovereign dispensed the
contents to the scrambling populace.

The afternoon grew hot. For those still in search of diversion there
were philosophical debates and recitations of the traditions of the
Prophet, but the harem had little taste for such things and preferred to
debate among themselves on more personal topics.

The afternoon grew hotter still—was this heat what the astrologers
had seen when they picked the most auspicious day?—and word was
brought from the circumcision pavilion that the Prince was in fever. His
mother, nurses, and eunuchs had been there from the moment the holy
man with his razor left. But now reinforcements were called for.

Safiye called for Gul Ruh by name. "To comfort her cousin in his distress," were the words. My young lady rose at once to oblige and at first

I let her go without comment because I had never heard of a bride comforting her groom on his circumcision bed. The duties of a bride came later, after the healing. Still, on second thought, I insisted on going with her. She grumbled a bit, but in the end was in too much of a hurry to get downstairs to care just how much extra baggage came along.

The pavilion was as carefully arranged for dramatic effect as had been any of the public entertainments. The crimson, pearl-seeded cap did much to drain every last bit of color from Muhammed's face, pillowed against a great gold-tasseled bolster. Matching coverlets of cloth-of-gold and brocade covered him to the chin, the heavy fabric held away from the tender area by other bolsters.

Besides boxes of exotic dates, the Prince's diversions included a group of musicians playing in the forecourt outside and a reader reading Persian tales of romance and adventure behind a locked screen closet. Several cages of live birds swung from the arches of the pavilion to muffle the boy's moans with happy chirps and in a niche by his head sparkled a small cooling fountain. But no diversion brought quite the relief of an opium draught given just before our arrival.

At the door to the pavilion I stopped to fuss with Gul Ruh's veil until she sighed wearily and stamped her foot as if to say: "Eunuchs! When they cut you, they turn you into neither more nor less than old biddy hens!" She had Nur Banu's very tone—or perhaps Safiye's—and that angered me. But I must confess that that was one time—there have been others—when I looked down at my hands and was both surprised and frustrated to find that they were the big, clumsy hands of a man instead of the small, gentle hands of a mother.

"Even with the musicians and the reader behind screens, you cannot be too careful in such a public place," I chided her. "And I do not want your cousin to see too much, either . . ."

That did seem to subdue her somewhat and we went in together.

The afternoon grew hotter still. The pavilion seemed to work like glass, to magnify and trap the heat within. The deep-sleep breath of the boy seemed to pervade the heat with vapors of opium for everyone. Many of the women who had come to nurse decided that the drugs were doing the job for them and that their time could be better spent in the baths that afternoon.

I tried to suggest this to Gul Ruh. She parted her veil ever so slightly to let some fresh air in and I could see that what was rivulets of sweat on my face turned to steam inside there. But she insisted.

Even when Safiye herself gave up a mother's place, Gul Ruh would not follow. Were it not for the fact that I was convinced the girl was trying to shake me with the longest endurance of misery, I, too, might have succumbed. But at that point I would not leave her all alone in the steamy, fever- and drug-laced room.

Both of us nodded heavy heads. Gul Ruh propped hers up against the wall at the Prince's simple, turbanless cap. I suppose the tiles there were somewhat cooled by the little fountain, for she was able thereby to maintain a watchfulness that had me think of stealing a few breaths of fresh air from outside. I must take such air if only to keep up with her level of alertness. So finally, that's what I did.

I hadn't been out very long before I was brought back in a hurry by a most fearful cry. I found Gul Ruh a limp heap on the floor by the door to the reader's closet, rocking back and forth and keeping time with rhythmic moans of "No! No! Can't! Can't!"

The Prince joined her moans softly, but the drug was too powerful for him to do more, and though at close range it seemed that the agony of her grief could stir the dead, doubtless the fountain and chirping birds were doing their work, for no one else heard or came.

"What is it? What is it, dear heart's oasis?" I asked.

I got no response but that "No! Can't!" to which rhythm she clung as if it were breath itself. I could do no more than wrap her in my arms and rock and rock with her, giving a croon and a prayer for every moan of hers.

"Help me, Abdullah," she mouthed, voiceless as if crying from the bottom of a very deep well. It wasn't much, but for one moment, the horrible spell of her own agitation was broken.

"I will, Allah strengthen me, if you'll but give me some word . . ."

She was back under the spell of her singsong now, but it seemed weaker and came in gasps.

"What is it? Is it the reader? Did he—what? Did he hurt you? Did he try and see more than he should or—?"

She didn't reply, but my pronunciation of the word *reader* had a profound effect on her. I got up and went to try his closet door to see . . .

"No!" Gul Ruh cried, but it was a "No" totally different from any one she'd given before. "Abdullah, don't. He'll kill you." That stopped the singsong short.

"I was . . ." She paused, swallowed, gasped for breath. "I was supposed to let him in."

"To—?"

"Kill—"

"Prince Muhammed?"

"Yes. Oh, Allah, Allah, how could I ever think of such a thing?"

"But you didn't think of it, did you?"

She looked up at me.

"Nur Banu put you up to it, didn't she?"

"She said it would be easy. All I had to do was open the . . ."

"Easy for her, perhaps."

"It was going to look as if just the infection . . ."

"Yes." I nodded, gingerly stepping away from the closet door as if it were infection itself. "I suspect it would have worked, too."

"But I couldn't do it."

"No. Of course you couldn't."

"He's my cousin. We played together when we were little."

"Praise Allah, He made you too good to forget."

"But is it good? Am I not just weak? She killed my father and Brabi. I must take revenge."

Gul Ruh made a half-hearted scramble towards the closet door again, but gave no struggle and actually fell into my arms with relief when I stopped her.

"Who killed them?"

"Aunt Safiye."

"Did Nur Banu tell you that?"

"Yes."

Of course, I thought. Certain things began to fall into place for me immediately, but I didn't say so to my charge. Nor did I indulge in pursuing these things in my own mind right then. Instead I suggested, "Did you ever stop to think it could be a lie?"

"A lie?"

"No, of course not. You are too innocent to go around suspecting lies."

"Do you think it was a lie?"

"I have little doubt." I lied. "You know what bad blood there is between Nur Banu and your aunt. The Valide Sultan would stop at nothing to see that Safiye's power is thwarted."

"She would lie?"

"She would do worse than lie."

"Even . . ."

"Yes, even attempt murder at your guileless hands. Thank Allah we stopped that crime in time."

"Thank Allah . . ."

"Come. If she were guilty of your sainted father's death, do you think Safiye could sit there coolly day after day, looking your mother in the eye?"

Gul Ruh shook her head. What this meant was that she was certain she couldn't do such a thing. She projected the outcome of her contemplated deed into the future with increasing horror.

"So this is what all this recent attention was? Just a ruse to gain the trust of those in Safiye's camp. You haven't really fallen madly in love with your cousin, have you?"

She shook her head in despair. "But what am I to do now?"

"Don't worry. I'll call soldiers to get rid of him," I threw my head in the direction of the closet, "and we won't say another word to anyone about it."

But suddenly Gul Ruh made a lunge for the dagger on my waist and had it unsheathed and on the way to her ribs before I could stop her. Our hands strained, shook. Her lips quivered like those of the thirsty for water. It was the struggle of madness, for under normal conditions she would have been no contest for me. Sanity returned at last and returned her to more than natural weakness. I put my dagger out of reach this time, but then hurried back to her side. She disintegrated into tears in my arms.

"Angel, angel, you didn't really want to die, did you?"

"No, no," she sobbed. "But that should be my punishment for even thinking of such a horrible thing. I should live, marry Muhammed, and live forever among these schemers, never knowing peace or happiness or love again. I deserve it now. Death would be easy compared to that."

It occurred to me that her "Can'ts" and "Nos" had been more shrinking from the possible futures she envisioned than from the murder. She could only ever think of murder in an abstract less real than the future—of that I was certain.

Then, without warning, I began to tell her of my first days as a eunuch. The presence of the newly circumcised brought the memory forcefully to mind. I told her how I'd struggled to accept my fate. At the time any sort of future at all seemed precluded.

"I remember saying 'I can't, I can't'," I told her, "over and over again. But somehow, I was able to. Here I am, thanks be to Allah. And it has not been so bad. It has not been the end of the world as I imagined."

She made an attempt to take comfort from my words, but there was still bitterness in her voice when she said, "Yes, to marry for a woman is what becoming a eunuch is for a man." I didn't tell her how closely her words echoed those of her mother shortly before Esmikhan had been given to Sokolli Pasha.

At that moment Safiye and some of her maids returned.

"By Allah, what's happened?" she asked, looking hastily to make certain her son's breath was still coming deeply and slowly in sleep.

Gul Ruh couldn't answer so I did. "My lady had a scare. She . . . she saw, or thought she saw, someone, a woman . . . a woman in black who sought to . . . who sought to, Allah forbid, harm the Prince."

The maids echoed my prayer that Allah should forbid such a thing. They never doubted my word, for such beings are well known to haunt the pavilions of the newly circumcised, seeking to steal their souls. They have names that are known and incantations by the bookful to which the women immediately fell lest the ghoul return.

Safiye was a bit more skeptical. She looked hard at Gul Ruh and asked, "And you, you stopped this . . . this woman—whatever?"

"She did, thanks be to Allah," I replied, "but you can see it was clearly a trying experience for her."

Then I quickly swept Gul Ruh out of the pavilion.

I was not quick enough, however, to catch the reader-murderer. Having overheard our conversation, he thought it wise to break through the lattice window at the rear of his closet and escape. Since no one I knew admitted to ever having seen his face, he was never apprehended.

Safiye appeared less skeptical of our story later, in spite of the broken lattice. She came up to report that her son's fever seemed to have broken and all, Allah willing, would be well.

Then she said, "It's curious. He woke from that sleep having dreamed a dream. It took a while to convince him it was a dream, it seemed so real. He dreamed that he had died and gone to Paradise where he was waited on by scores and scores of sparkling-eyed houris.

" 'Of all races and types in the world, Mother,' he said. 'Great black Africans like pleasure barges, Russians like pure banks of drifted snow, Circassians like armfuls of apricot blossom in spring. My member,' he said, 'grew from the cutting into a flaming sword with which I cut through their ranks, making them melt before me like butter, sweet, sweet springtime butter I ate and anointed myself with and swam in. It was wonderful. It was Paradise indeed. And was it only a dream?

" 'Mother,' he asked at last, 'why would you marry me to my cousin? Marriages and cousins, they are supposed to last forever. But this dream has taught me that girls are of no use unless they're disposable. I can get fresh every day, every hour, by Allah, every minute if I tire of them. That's the greatest part of their beauty, its fragility, its ability to fade like cream. Like a dream. If there are no limits to it—and, by Allah, a Sultan has so very, very few limits—it is meaningless. Oh, Allah, Mother, how I crave meaning!'

"Who has been teaching my son such things? To what pagan of a tutor should we quickly give the choice: 'Islam or the sword, by Allah!'?

"At first, Gul Ruh," Safiye continued, "when you told me about a woman in black, I thought Nur Banu. I thought . . . well, I didn't believe you. Now? Now I'm not so sure. Something . . . something dark has come over him. Something I am not sure we can control."

I remembered the black scar on his cheek.

"He has grown up, Safiye," Esmikhan suggested quietly. "All you put in him from the beginning—of good and evil—has now come to manhood."

"But he is my son. There must be a way I can control my own son." Esmikhan said nothing.

Safiye paused, then: "All I can say is it will take some hard work and maybe even a little shove through Murad—which I'm not at all sure I can manage right now, since Nur Banu's got that new dancing girl in favor—to bring Muhammed around to this marriage we all want so much. By Allah, control! I need more control . . ."

Her voice unraveled out into a deep musing which maybe never reached but certainly pushed towards the realization: "I need control like my son, Allah spare us, needs meaning. And perhaps, for people like us, neither ever truly exists."

LX

THE MORNING AFTER the final boat race and the final fireworks display, when word came to us that the Prince was recovering well and beginning to walk around a little, Gul Ruh sighed and declared to no one in particular that she longed to become a Christian.

"Allah forbid!" her mother cried, making signs against evil as if she had just wished for her own death. "Whatever makes you say such a thing?"

Gul Ruh's reply showed that she was really too naive of other religions to be taken seriously. The gist of her longing was only that, nun-like, she wished never to marry anyone at all.

As fate would have it, not two hours later we, all three, were commanded to appear before the Sultan himself. Esmikhan had not seen her brother except on formal occasions since his ascension, and for Gul Ruh, the memories of childhood meetings had faded altogether. It was an honor not to be refused and yet one so great as hardly to be borne. Gul Ruh, who thought she could guess its purpose (her aunt Safiye had been busy all morning), clung to me all the way down, as if she were as crippled as her mother.

"Oh, Allah," she kept praying over and over, "I wish I could be a nun."

Murad sat on cushions in the cool of the garden, his legs coiled under him and under a sheet of paper on which he was practicing the art of illumination. The recent festivities, he declared had given him great inspiration.

Esmikhan replied politely that, yes, the festivities had been worthy of his majesty.

"Tell me, Sister," Murad asked, applying color with a brush no more than three hairs wide, "which do you think was the greatest festivity? Your wedding to Sokolli Pasha, may Allah favor him, in that tumbledown town of Inönü, or these most recent events?"

Esmikhan smiled, remembering a similar test question placed before his vizier by her legendary grandfather, Suleiman the Magnificent. "My wedding, of course," she replied, "because you favored it with your presence. And even this most recent circumcision, magnificent as it was, could not boast such an illustrious guest for you were busy being host."

Murad smiled and applied gold leaf with a liberal hand. "And you, my young niece?" he asked. "Did the festivities please you?"

"Indeed, Uncle, majesty, very much," Gul Ruh replied. When pressed to tell her favorite event, she confessed that her mind was a blur but that perhaps the confections made of spun sugar in the shapes of animals and plants suited her fancy most.

"What about the religious debates?" the Sultan asked, looking sidelong up at her from his paper. "Did you enjoy them?"

"The religious debates?" Gul Ruh asked, confused and half fearing she was being led into a trap. Quick calculation told her that while the debates were going on, her mind had been full of her cousin's death. She had been seeing black witches in the circumcision pavilion. Did her uncle wish her to confess something? Something that would make life in Safiye's harem even shorter and more intolerable? Deciding with a deep breath that martyrdom was perhaps the best alternative to the Christian convent Islam had to offer, she concluded the truth would be best to tell in any case.

"I'm sorry, most illustrious uncle. I'm afraid I did not watch any of the debates at all. There were other entertainments, you see . . ."

"No, I don't suppose silly girls' minds find much of interest in the intricacies of Holy Law."

"Actually, I usually find it quite interesting, but I . . ."

"Well, I am glad you found entertainment elsewhere more suited to your sex and nature,"

Gul Ruh wanted to say that the events that had interrupted her at that time had not been at all to her liking, but she remained silent. Her uncle continued without noticing her hesitation.

"Nevertheless, I am sorry you missed this particular round. I'm convinced you would have found much of interest in it."

"I will try and pay more attention next time," Gul Ruh promised.

"Good," Murad said. "I suspect you will find great opportunity to watch the religious banter back and forth to your heart's content in the very near future."

The Sultan blew gently on his miniature to let it dry, then held it up for his audience to admire. They did, as ardently as he could wish. Murad had made a representation of the very debates they had been discussing, with himself an avid listener in the center of the page. To the right was the circumcision pavilion with—edited for history—Muhammed smiling bravely through a window.

"Do you recognize the man debating here?" Murad asked.

Gul Ruh had been struggling so with the emotions the sight of the pavilion brought to her that she hadn't even bothered to look at the left-hand side where the debaters were. But a quick glance failed to enlighten her. Her uncle had striven not so much to render individual characteristics as to meet the miniaturists' traditional criteria for showing handsome pious young manhood. One handsome, pious young man looked pretty much like another. Gul Ruh did not recognize him.

"A remarkable young man." Murad began to describe with words what the picture failed to make plain. "He cannot be much over twenty. Still he defeated many of his elders and betters most brilliantly in a discourse as lucid and learned as it was to the point. The son of the late Mufti, I am told, but the youngest son and with still many, many years of successes ahead of him."

"*He* won the debates?" Gul Ruh exclaimed. She almost pronounced the name "Abd ar-Rahman" aloud but caught herself in time to keep her uncle thinking she did not recognize the man from his descriptions either. "Such a young person, I mean?"

"Yes. Won quite handily. Not only that, but he made me so drunk on his words that I hardly knew what I was saying. As a prize, I offered him anything at all it was in my power to give, even to half of the Realm of the Faithful."

"What did he say?"

" 'Forgive me, O Shadow of Allah,' the young man said, 'but the Realm of the Faithful is not yours to give.' Then he quoted page and verse proving that it was given to me in trust from the Most Merciful and I should not even jest of giving it away, et cetera, et cetera. But finally he came around to saying that there was something it was in my power to give him that he desired more than anything in the world. Can you guess, Gul Ruh, what that might be?"

"Such a modest young man!" Esmikhan exclaimed.

"No, I cannot guess," Gul Ruh said, feeling her heart pounding in her throat.

"Modest, Sister, maybe. But he is not above demanding for riches when they fall near his hand. He has asked me to give you to him, Gul Ruh, in marriage. What do you think of that?"

Gul Ruh could say nothing, but dropped her head and pretended to examine her hands. I do not doubt that if I, too, had examined them I would have found them wet with tears.

It was Esmikhan who had to reply, "What did you tell the young man, Brother?"

"I asked him to look in his books and see if there isn't a commandment not to give women in marriage against their will. 'Even a sultan is bound by this,' I told him. 'I must ask the young lady's will in this matter before I make promises like that.'

"Ah, it was gratifying! To beat the winner on his own ground! Hurry and anxiety, those are two things a debater must avoid at all cost and that young man let them get the better of him in this case. I think I could have been something of a legist if only . . .

"Still, I gave him my word to ask the young lady and do what I could to sway her opinion if it could be swayed. What am I to tell him? That she looks sullen and says nothing? I fear the young man is to be disappointed and I shall have to give him half the Realm of the Faithful after all, to mollify him."

"Oh, no, Uncle, please!" Gul Ruh exclaimed, then sank into modesty and tears again.

Murad laughed and repeated " 'Oh, no, Uncle, please'? It sounds as if she has turned him down, does it not?"

Gul Ruh managed to catch her mother's hand with ferocity and this prompted Esmikhan to say, "Now, Brother. Don't be a tease. You may tell the young man to make his preparations for—for the earliest day at his convenience."

"It will be my pleasure," Murad said. "And though the treasury is already broken by this circumcision, I think we can find enough to get together a wedding at least to match yours, Sister. And there will be an Ottoman heir or two to grace it, besides."

Gul Ruh quickly kissed her uncle's hem in gratitude.

"My only worry now is . . ." Murad folded his hands and looked sharply at Gul Ruh over them. "Just how these two young people came to be of such a common mind. I fear a leak in the security of my harem and that, *khadim,* is your department."

The sharp, dark eyes of the Shadow of Allah fell on me. I could feel them, but I couldn't meet them, and that must declare my guilt. The entire world must be guilty in his presence.

The Sultan laughed. "Still, if you will assure me my honor has nothing to fear by this match—"

I assured him quickly.

"Then be off with you, girl," the Sultan said, planting a quick kiss on each of his niece's eyes, "and may you be as happy a wife as you are a bride."

So Abd ar-Rahman and Gul Ruh were married before the summer reached its peak, and my young lady went off with a whole train of slaves and eunuchs to be her own mistress—under Umm Kulthum, of course. Had she not been so overjoyed by the prospects for her future, she might have spent more time rejoicing at what a relief it was to escape the Serai.

Safiye had the good grace to realize when she had been defeated fairly and honestly. I think her only consternation was that it should have been innocence and virtue that defeated her instead of more devious machinations.

For my part, I had my faith restored in the possibility of a present-day princess living happily ever after.

LXI

IT WAS PROBABLY in a mad attempt to revenge herself for the failure of her plot against Muhammed during his circumcision that Nur Banu infiltrated the ranks of the eunuchs with another product of the knife of Mu'awiya the Red. This fellow was caught and disposed of long before he got as far as the Persian, but word of it came to Murad, and the Sultan took steps to see that neither party took his honor so lightly again.

By imperial decree the whole household was reorganized. Instead of white and black eunuchs in charge of the women together, from now on it would be blacks only who, in the heart of Africa, are cut off right at the belly and hence can prove no threat at all. Or if they did, by accident or design, avoid this fate, it was assumed their race would render them less attractive even in desperate eyes.

Ghazanfer Agha, myself, and a few of the other more trusted white eunuchs were spared immediate shift to the outer household. It would take years to build up the necessary black population—only one in three or four survives the severity of that operation—and the change could happen but slowly. White *khuddam* glutted the market and suffered such a drop in price that, in spite of myself, it preyed heavily on my self-esteem.

Then, after a few months of dreadful uncertainty we were finally promised our positions for life.

"Which may not be long, under the circumstances," Ghazanfer mused pessimistically.

"What do you mean?" I asked. Although as Esmikhan's particular slave, the word would have to come directly from her before I faced transfer, nonetheless I had felt great relief at the announcement and did not want to be bothered with clouds that day.

"Just look," Ghazanfer Agha told me, and called my attention to the fact that Safiye seemed, in but this short time, to have accumulated far more than her share of the black attendants. "She knew this decree was coming before the Sultan made it," Ghazanfer explained. "She'd been buying up every black *khadim* the moment he hit Cairo for months. And if you don't think there are the ambitious among them . . . but enough about us. I think it's clear who has won the upper hand in this harem now."

And indeed it was. Almost as if buying that second Mu'awiya eunuch were a final act of desperation, Nur Banu seemed to have signed her own death warrant with it. She retreated to the small private garden palace she owned in her own right near the Edirne Gate and was reported to be ill.

"Ill? The witch? Nonsense!" Safiye declared.

But when a fortnight brought no news of improvement, my lady began to worry, particularly when rumors of "poison" began to fly.

I found poison difficult to believe. "Nur Banu Kadin has always been too careful of such things," I assured my lady. "She will eat nothing that has not sat upon her celadon plates, and that green ware will turn black in warning at the first touch of anything unwholesome. She is always vigilant against mercury, monkshood, scorpions—all the usual methods."

I thought, but not aloud, that Nur Banu would not be poisoned because she herself was mistress of the art and continued, "Besides, if it were poison, wouldn't we have heard—Allah forbid—of her death by now? Safiye would not do such a job halfway."

"Abdullah, you should not say so."

"Or we should have heard of her recovery, now that she is in her own palace with only her own slaves about her."

"I mean you should not suggest Safiye could have a hand in poison. It is some secret witch, some infidel enemy, not Safiye."

I sighed. Esmikhan would never believe the worst of which I knew her friend was capable. My lady had known she could not befriend both sides of the conflict. She had come to live on Safiye's side of the demarcation line only after a long struggle with her heart. The deciding factor had been the thought that Nur Banu was Valide Sultan, therefore Safiye was the weaker. Still she refused to credit more than a slight jarring of personalities to the fray: "It is the same with mothers- and daughters-in-law the world over." I knew it was useless to try to shove a darker sin than simple liveliness and a strong desire for her own way upon my lady's best friend.

Still, Nur Banu was my lady's stepmother, as close a being to mother as she could remember, although *nurse* had the more tender connotations in her mind. When Nur Banu's retreat had extended more than a month, Esmikhan knew she must make the effort to cross Constantinople to pay a call.

Safiye did not thwart her. "Yes. Please go and find out what the old scorpion is up to."

"Safiye!" Esmikhan pleaded compassion.

Safiye was unrepentant. "I've no doubt it's some sort of witchcraft of her own and we must be warned."

Safiye even lent the new carriage she had as a lavish gift of friendship from England's Queen Elizabeth. I'm not certain how the Fair One juggled this relationship at the same time as her continuing one with Catherine de' Medici, who was more powerful in France than ever. I can only imagine that Catherine and Safiye shared secrets like Italian schoolgirls at the end of the garden when the nuns are elsewhere. And where was the room for a third in this? What fates were decided between the three women will never be known. But I am sure no life from the Sea of Marmara to La Manche was unaffected.

I would have thought close ties with France would preclude them across the Channel. But then, the unfogged eyes of power know no love of country, no boundaries. Safiye's correspondence with England's Elizabeth was a little more public if for no other reason than that it had to go through the dragomans for translation. Elizabeth's letters spoke of a Muslim East and Protestant West crushing the idolatry of Catholicism between them.

"Perhaps so," I heard Safiye reply aloud and offhandedly. Religion—anybody's—had never been of overriding concern to her. "But if England had not thrown out Latin with the Church, I could have done more for Elizabeth. She and I could have communicated better." It is my suspicion that Safiye never did take Elizabeth's envoys more seriously

than their persistence demanded. "In that northern climate," she insisted, "people have no time for culture. They are too busy trying to
keep warm."

But Elizabeth had sent a carriage.

It had taken some doing to find Turkish horses who could pull the
thing, not to mention the reassembly required after two months at sea.
In the meantime the plain wood paneling and salt-spray-stiffened
leather seats had been ripped out, replaced by silken brocade divans and
mother-of-pearl in a dozen intricate patterns. Shutters and curtains
went to the windows. The final result was more in harmony with eastern taste.

And now, wherever Safiye rode, something was always threatened
with being crushed. If not idolatry, certainly local Muslim pedestrians.
The question was raised whether the attention the carriage's passing ig-
nited were in keeping with eastern taste. Certainly the harem's reserve
and dignity must suffer. Others had a more basic complaint: the filth the
horses left behind them in the streets.

"They'll get used to it," Safiye said to any and all objections.

And in friendship Esmikhan could not refuse the offer to take the
carriage to Nur Banu's.

The ride was a good deal rougher than that provided by well-trained
sedan bearers over Constantinople's streets. The streets had been paved
within the last century but not with such contrivances in mind. Still, I
had to admit a carriage was faster—it could quite take the breath away.
It got us out to the Edirne Gate with a remarkable amount of time to
spare between the two morning prayers.

And a eunuch could ride as well instead of trotting alongside. Safiye's
guardians—except Ghazanfer—rode up on top with the driver. But
when there was only one woman passenger—and she congenial—
there was room within the cab. I enjoyed that and told myself firmly we
must not do this too often. Only by walking had I managed to escape
that curse of many in my condition: a mind-numbing obesity.

The carriage was faster, but Esmikhan required the extra time before
the prayer call to recover her equilibrium after such a ride. And where
the horses were taken to recoup I cannot imagine: Few palaces were
provided with such accommodations in those days. But the edge of

town was not far off. No doubt the driver just took the patient beasts out the gate and hobbled them among the grazing sheep beyond the walls.

In time, we went in.

The smell of Nur Banu's rooms, even halfway down the hall, was not that of poison but the vinegar, moldy lemon rind of a malignant cancer.

LXII

HOW LONG, I wondered, had this dreaded disease been coming on? And the Valide Sultan refused to call retreat?

The shutters of the room into which we were ushered were draped and drawn. The Valide Sultan could no longer bear light upon her face. The chamber was close and stifling hot, kept that way by half a dozen braziers whose constant stoking with pungent sandalwood was the full-time and single-minded task of one maid. The odors of hot healing herbs—southernwood, jasmine oil—added to the dense, murky atmosphere. But they could not camouflage the stale, sour smell of sweating attendants in health nor that of the patient, her opium, and her nausea.

Before we could could fill our lungs enough to catch our breaths, the heat of this air had us in a sweat, as it did everyone else in the room save Nur Banu. Nur Banu's torso, stripped to the *shalvar,* betrayed, even in the half light, the wasting of her flesh. She had shrunk down to the most basic harsh angles and jutting joints. These caught what light there was in sharp sheen and shadows, like naked bone, with no softening curve in between.

This wasting was not the work of but a week or two. The Valide Sultan must have hidden her condition from Safiye's camp for months under heavier and heavier garments. And Safiye might have interpreted the change, if she considered it at all, as simply more and more greed for finery.

How ironic, that the final assault should come not from an outside enemy, but by betrayal of Nur Banu's own body, that body whose very curves had been the route to power in the first place.

In the flurry of our arrival, a plump yellow cat jumped up among sample silks spread by a seamstress on one of the low tables covering a brazier. The fire-stoking maid shooed him off.

Nur Banu smiled wryly, patient with a beast's liveliness when she had so little herself. "That is a sign it will snow." She gave the usual superstitious interpretation of such an omen. The dull grey haze in her once-remarkable black eyes belied her hope. Personally, I doubted that she had such a thing as a future to divine.

As if new clothes were a guarantee against death until they could be worn at least once, Nur Banu was in the process of ordering yet more lengths of yet heavier silk worked with yet more gold and gemstones. All this when her doctoring required that she be naked to the waist much of the time.

The Fig was there, leeching. She shot me a tyrant's glance, but went about her business wordlessly.

"I enjoyed a two-week respite." Nur Banu smiled crookedly at my lady in an attempt at bravery, but hadn't the vigor to talk of anything but her treatment. "She would not leech as long as the moon was waxing."

Nur Banu looked weakly at the Fig for at least the strength of surgeon's confirmation. The Fig must have given it, but I saw no such return glance.

"During the waxing of the moon," Nur Banu found energy to go on, "my blood would be increasing. Good, new, healthy blood which might flow too vigorously, might not clot soon enough if bled. But now that the month is waning . . ."

Nur Banu shrugged one hollowed, bony shoulder apologetically. The Fig pressed that shoulder back into the cushions to give herself an undisturbed plane of operations. Nur Banu waved the seamstress around to the front of her to continue her selections. Esmikhan followed, I think to escape the sight I continued to endure.

The Fig began applying the leeches, the best Anatolian leeches, starved to voracity. She scooped them quickly out of a Chinese porcelain jar and pressed their little heads down to give them the idea, precise spaces apart on the bony white back. In the half light I imagined the creatures could be slithering slabs of the Fig's own blue-black flesh. She was layering them upon her patient in an attempt to transfer strength and corpulence.

The Fig periodically sought out her patient's pulse throughout the treatment until at last the fat worms began to drop off of their own accord, sated. Then the Fig hissed quietly through the gap in her teeth. The little trickles of blood that wormed down the pallid skin after their makers were likewise red-black. More bleeding would be necessary until the healthy blood flowed, with a healthy golden sheen as its basis instead of choking bitumen—like rubies mined during the moon's waxing. The patient may at least weaken, I thought, until mercifully death takes her.

Nur Banu found Esmikhan insufficient as distraction, once the new costumes were ordered. My lady, I suspected, found the proximity of death took her tongue into its grasp. Nur Banu called for a storyteller instead. This large, waistless woman was ordered to "Tell the same again."

"The same" was, incongruously I thought at first, an adventure of Alexander the Great. How, "in the time before, when the sieve was in the straw, the camel was a street crier, and I was rocking my father's cradle," the ancient king marched his army to the very center of the world. At the center of the world is the Mountain of Kaf, which holds up the sky and which "offers only space enough for a man to crawl beneath its pinnacle and the base of heaven."

Alexander sent one of his bravest up to this mountaintop to see what he might see. The man came down quite shaken. All he could report was that at the top he had met, coming up from the other side, "one just like me in every way." From among his uniform, disciplined ranks, Alexander chose another, then another to attempt the same mission. In the end the king decided he must go up himself.

And what he met on the summit was something he never expected: another Alexander. He who thought himself unique was confronted by his twin, identical in pride, inimicability, and peerlessness.

"So Alexander returned," the tale concluded, "much humbled, having learned there are worlds upon worlds, generations upon generations, and only Allah is One. Three apples fell from the sky," ran the traditional "happy ever after," "one went to the one who told the story, the second to the one who wasted her breath, and the third to the one who listened to her tale. As each heart finds its own happiness, may Allah grant each of you find your true love in this narrow world."

As soon as she could politely do so after this, my lady took her leave. She offered profuse wishes for her stepmother's recovery and promises that she would soon return. But I could tell that in spite of her natural charity, Esmikhan longed for the carriage's confines as the more comfortable surroundings. She would curse herself every day she left those promises unfulfilled. But sometimes charity requires more bravery than my lady had been given to go along with the rest of her nature.

As I climbed into the cushions beside her, Esmikhan took out a linen handkerchief and began to weep. "It is too bad, too bad, *mashallah!* Nur Banu Kadin admits defeat." I think it was my lady herself who admitted defeat. The sudden lurch of the horses compounded her heartache.

That is another drawback of a carriage: It cut down on intimacy in voice quality if nothing else. Above the head-splitting noise of the ride, I begged Esmikhan not to grieve.

"To fight against the will of Allah—as the Valide Sultan's death seems clearly to be—is to deny His mercy and to draw out our own pain. She should not try to fight heaven's will, Nur Banu Kadin should not. It will only draw out her agony—and that of those who love her." I took my lady's trembling hand and she pressed mine in return and gratitude.

"At least I can report back to Topkapi that there is no poison, no witchcraft here."

"Poison would be easier," I murmured, hoping again that the Fig might at least hasten her patient's demise.

And yet I found myself dreading the Valide Sultan's death not so much for the sake of the woman herself but for the counterweight she had always been to keep Safiye's ambition in check. Now—but I didn't want to consider that *now* through the ear-numbing clatter of Safiye's carriage. The noise totally engulfed us, offered no escape, and seemed ominous indeed. Who should counter that malignancy now, if only with malignancy of her own?

No one, drummed the horses' shoes in answer. And virtue, like the little pat of cream of a hand I held, was no defense against such evil. Like the tallest minaret, perfect virtue probably only attracted the destructive glance of lightning.

Such thoughts brought tears of fear, of empathy to my own eyes. And though a weeping eunuch is not so extraordinary as a weeping man—our natures allow, nay, demand it—I fought desperately to change the subject. For my lady's sake, I must change my emotion.

"I read an interesting series of poems the other day," I told her, "written by a countrywoman of mine. Only one of the verses sticks in my mind. But shall I recite it?"

A poetess is not such an anomaly in the harem as it is in the West. Indeed, most of the new poems Esmikhan had ever heard had, naturally enough, been written and published within the harem. The writer's sex did not impress her as much as it did me.

But she, too, seemed grateful for the distraction and jumped at it. "Please do."

I did:

> "I am safe now.
> But I remember the danger
> When through your eyes
> And handsome face
> Love held out to me
> His burning torch.
> And intent on wounding me
> In a thousand ways
> He had gathered the flames of my fire
> Even from the river of your eloquence . . ."

I faltered, remembering too late why the verse had had an impact. But the little hand in mine gave me a squeeze, lent me courage to go on.

"I transform my mad love
Into friendship now
And, thinking of your immeasurable gifts,
I reshape my soul to emulate you."

And cool friendship eased the carriage's jarring way.

LXIII

NUR BANU DIED without seeing another snowstorm, on Wednesday, the twenty-second day of Dhu'l Ka'da, the seventh of December in the year of our Lord 1583. Her son Murad put on black in mourning, the first time a sultan had ever done such a thing for his mother. Guilt makes people—even sultans—do unusual things.

Murad helped to carry the bier as well, out of the garden palace and through the twisting streets to the mausoleum at Aya Sophia. Here Nur Banu would rest eternally next to her lord Selim and the five little princes who had died in order to raise her son to the throne.

None of the deceased's new dresses went with her: One goes naked to the grave in Islam. Over the simple shroud of seamless white silk rested Nur Banu's headscarf, a few favorite hair ornaments, the braids of silk she had added to eke out her own hair as it had thinned towards the end. That was all. And she was gone.

Now Safiye was alone in her kingdom.

On the surface, this seemed not so bad. Miraculously, the sudden deaths of little princes stopped. The household multiplied at a rate unprecedented—Murad even became a father twice in a single night. The most serious conflicts were over whose infant should rock in the hammered-gold, jewel-encrusted cradle of the Ottomans. And Safiye's word never failed to settle the matter.

So sure of her power was Baffo's daughter now that she said nothing when Muhammed was called away from under her wing to begin his training to rule in the *sandjak* of Magnesia. She saw him settled with a sweet, beautiful, malleable little Greek girl and then kissed him quickly good-bye. The Kira was waiting, Ghazanfer Agha was waiting. There was business to attend to, and only time and Allah would bring the fullness of her power as Queen Mother to fruition.

Yet these eleven years as favorite and Mother of the Heir were Safiye's most powerful. Now that there was peace in the harem—the peace of tyranny—she could turn her full attentions elsewhere.

Safiye and England's Elizabeth wrote one another as "dear sister majesty." Elizabeth followed the gift of the carriage with a magnificent thousand-pipe organ. Safiye herself did not care for the instrument. It reminded her a little too much of the sound that pervaded the convent gardens every Sunday, that most oppressive of days in her childhood week. But it was such a novelty and obviously such a fine piece of crafts-manship that, like a rare cabinet or rug, it was allowed in the harem on those merits alone. And one or two of the girls, not the most musical, but the most fun-loving, were allowed to take lessons from the in-stallers. They learned a few simple-minded hymns which they insisted on playing over and over again. When more accomplished musicians tried their hands at it, they found that the one-key-one-solid-note sys-tem hampered their usually elaborate Eastern modulations and trills. Eventually the organ was forgotten and gathered dust—like nothing more than a very large and empty inlaid chest.

Safiye was gracious enough, however, to return gift for gift. Exquis-ite jewels and fabrics were sent off to that distant island and something Elizabeth craved even more was arranged there on the shores of the Golden Horn—trading privileges which equalled or excelled those of any other Christian nation.

Safiye corresponded with most other sovereigns of the East and West at one time or another as it suited her needs. But since they were all men, to those in the East she went through the harems, whose power she trusted more anyway. The West frustrated her, and she spent hours agonizing over the powerlessness of a woman in those countries, not even excluding Catherine and Elizabeth. Any communication she un-dertook with those princes had to be through agents. Fortunately, they were usually servants of the Grand Viziers who, with Sokolli gone, more and more came to be her own creatures, picked, groomed, and elevated to this office by her own hand.

Under Safiye, the realm of the Ottomans reached greater extent than it had had even under Murad's grandfather, the great Suleiman. Successful expeditions pushed into Moldavia, Poland, the Crimea, Daghistan, Transcaucasia, Georgia, Persia. There were setbacks— rebellions in Egypt and Syria—as there must be when the head of power is unable to move swiftly to trouble spots on her own. Her agents moved quickly and decisively enough, however.

The Druses in their mountain fastness, for example, were put down—with unparalleled severity, I understand—by Safiye's Ibrahim Pasha. Though until the matter found its way into the memoirs of re-tired soldiers, we, safe in Constantinople, safe in the harem, knew nothing of it.

Closer to home, the janissaries rebelled in April 1589, the *spahis* three years later. We did know of that: No one could escape the clatter of their overturned cooking pots and rattling weapons, the choking smoke of their campfires turned to torches and firebrands and arson, the threatening growl of their hunger up through the Third Court to the very gates of the harem. I stood with other eunuchs at the gate, arms crossed on our chests, trying not to flinch at the threat of what the wave of angry, armed men could do to us if they chose. In the end, the mys-tique of sexlessness turned them—though I never felt power in myself, even a coarse and bloodthirsty mob felt it in me. My crossed chest was as far as either party got and decided then to take terms.

My chest was, in fact, the very core of their complaint. Both mutinies were against "interference in our affairs by the harem," as well they might be. Sometimes I rue that I ever stood sentinel with my back pressed to the gates' silver studs. Perhaps I should have taken the first man in the press, spitting venom beneath his wild mustache. I should have taken him quietly by the arm and led him straight to Safiye's rooms. I could have let him cut one throat to spare tens of thousands in the years to come.

But Esmikhan was also cowering behind those silver studs. I could never be certain the man and his fellows, leaping with impotent rage as they were, would leave just so quietly afterwards. I could risk no guarantee they would not stop in every other room of the palace to do all the other things soldiers do. For Esmikhan's sake, I stood and crossed my arms in the troops' hot breath and did not flinch.

Safiye, the euphemistic harem, survived by our flimsy protection and by judiciously cutting her losses, making certain "necessary sacrifices." For instance, she let the janissaries have her Kira. Esperanza Malchi, who'd become a plump and very well-to-do widow, was not protected by harem walls. She was dragged from her house along with one of her helpless grown sons and torn to pieces by the soldiers' bare hands. Another son barely managed to escape and fled into exile.

The thousandth year of the Muslim era occurred during this time and was preceded by much end-of-the-world fanaticism. Christian and Jewish minorities suffered greatly and the government did little to stop the more radical elements. Here again Safiye cut her losses, gave the rebellious a vent for their emotions. The vent in fact came nowhere near touching the true cause. And the true cause, though couched in pious Suras, was of course that, as they waited for judgement day, pious Muslims must suffer a Christian—and worse, a woman—to rule over them. But the fanatic, once he has larded his purpose with loftiness, can rarely see his satisfaction clearly, either.

Safiye allowed a number of churches within the capital to be converted into mosques, churches the Conqueror himself had promised might remain Christian. This, though the Greek Patriarch hovered about outside the harem door for days on end. *She* was born and raised a Christian. *She* must show mercy. Like a bedraggled raven he was, fasting until he had to be carried away for weakness. To no avail. It was his church that first had the icons smashed and the minaret foundation dug.

So did Safiye deal with those who had been most faithful to her. But I had always known that was her style.

Safe within the harem, Esmikhan and I ignored all this in the world. Safiye wanted nothing more from us, my two ladies and me, so she left us in peace. And Allah—all praise to Him—sent us a great distraction from her.

Not too many months after her grandmother Nur Banu died, Gul Ruh gave birth to her first child, a son. Two years did not pass afterwards that she did not birth another, strong, healthy child: two girls and three boys in the end. It was always Esmikhan's wonder that Gul Ruh suffered very little to gain her progeny. Indeed, each new blossom seemed to make her bloom all the more herself.

Esmikhan and I spent a great deal of time at the old Mufti's house on the Golden Horn. It was always a delightful bit of instruction to me to arrive there and see all the things a harem was *not,* things most in the West insist that it is. The raven Patriarch himself seemed to have imagined his enemy to be like these wild rumors. And maybe he was closer to being right, in Safiye's case, where the world of men intruded. But not in Gul Ruh's.

The silent, somber, somnolent world stifled with boredom and frustration is a better description of Abd ar-Rahman and his brothers' *selamlik* than the harem. In the *selamlik* in dusty, crinkly tones, the scholars and legists pursued their endless discussions. Their topics might have something distantly to do with the wars and mutinies of more active men. But to assure judicial detachment, they always carefully reduced the cases to flat pages of black and white, to some theoretical man named a generic Amr or Zeyd, to a woman named Hind or Zeyneb. All was strained to the clearest broth without the least pother lump into which to sink an emotional tooth. And in this state they dissected unpassionately, weighing all against the immutable Word of Allah, and filed appropriately for future reference.

How unlike the world that burst upon us when we finally reached the harem doors! The *selamlik* was like the somber black veils of a woman, to slip quietly by, a phantom. But when she removed them, she was revealed to be in her holiday best, blinding with silks and gems and fragrance and larklike trills of laughter. The *selamlik* was the rough, dirty grey-green rind of a melon, thwarting the hungry. Opening revealed the sole purpose such things were grown in the first place: the brilliant burst of orange, sun-warmed flesh, swathing the nose with sweetness and juice.

Entering Gul Ruh's harem was like opening a melon, hungry, thirsty, on a hot day. Every day was crammed with events which, while none was earth-shattering enough ever to gain a place in the historians' annals, were certainly always thrill and worry and joy, the recurring joy, enough for my life to contain. They were all the new wonders of budding teeth, first steps, first spelled word. The little disasters of a skinned

knee. A fever. A family tiff. These events for all Gul Ruh's lively bunch
as well as for her brothers-in-law's wives, children, nurses, pets, and
friends.

"Why don't you come and live with us permanently, Esmikhan Sultan?" Umm Khulthum asked every time we arrived, every time we left.

I wondered the same myself, even though my lady gave the ritual response over and over: "A woman belongs in her brother's harem if she
cannot have her husband's. Or her father's."

We'd stay for weeks on end, sometimes the whole month of Ramadhan. But in the end we always returned under Murad's roof. Under
Safiye's. I'll confess I sometimes ached to return to the imperial harem
for the quiet. But that was water stilled by terror. In truth, I would
never trade that quiet for the rowdy joy.

I know for a fact that Abd ar-Rahman could hardly keep away, obliged
to run his hands all day over the dull, unyielding rind of the melon.
Every day when his work was done, he would run almost like a school-
boy, even as the passing years made him stout. He would run to reviv-
ify himself in that happy chaos. Would Gul Ruh have had so many
children? Or bloomed so happily with each one if it had been otherwise? No guilt festered in her singing heart. No regret. No neglect. No
unfulfilled ambition.

But I think I need say no more of that. It is a private joy. In fact, it
is *haram,* prohibited, sacred. To allow men's eyes to pry, to reduce
to black-and-white chronicles, has been an evil I gave my manhood—
and my life—to guard against. To expose it further would allow the
blood-soaked ills of the outer world to intrude. And I, who had to
straddle both worlds, appreciated as perhaps no harem denizen could,
that sanctuary was a hallowed privilege, a great blessing of the One
Creator.

So—this brings us to the Sultan. In fact, many may wonder that I
have not mentioned Murad before. But was Murad actually Sultan at all?
I have certainly suggested otherwise. And the chroniclers suggest it,
too, when they call this era euphemistically "The Reign of the Favored
Women".

Murad, in fits of pique whenever he discovered his own weakness,
would sometimes insist on flexing what was left of his power by de-

posing or beheading one Grand Vizier after another. But Safiye was always careful to have another man waiting in the wings, a flatterer to the Sultan long enough to get in, her man entirely the moment the clouds seemed to have lifted and Murad had retreated again to his artists and his poets.

The Sultan went from illuminating to composing poetry to playing the oud. His was a nature weaned on opium and convinced that the arts were the only truth in the world. Yet ever and again he found that truth to be as illusive as a desert mirage. And no matter what joy it gave him, sooner or later art would turn to politics in his—as he sometimes called them in a fury—"leprous Ottoman hands." Sooner or later a music instructor would begin asking other favors—for his nephew, his cousin. The poet came to have something else besides ethereal images on his mind and weighted his verse with flattery and untruth.

"But a poet, too, must eat!"

I remember the last time I saw Sultan Murad alive. Unexpected as the sighting was, yet unlike the case of Nur Banu his mother, the sovereign gave no indication of his approaching fate.

LXIV

IT WAS ON the Night of Power and I can imagine how upset Safiye was that Murad would not spend it with some hand-picked virgin of hers. But Murad had come to take the dervishes' view: Union with the Almighty was more auspicious.

I'd been watching the faces in the *tekke* that night with more than usual interest. I don't suppose I really expected my friend Hajji to put in an appearance. He had not done so for many years now. I was told he'd gone on a pilgrimage to the land of the Afghans and had not been seen since. But if he would deign to visit—or to send someone in his place—this, of all nights of the year, would be the one.

The circle of faces whirled around, losing their natural solidity and individuality, sending off sparks like fireworks, sparks that did not soar and burn out, but continued to glow as they fused with neighbors and then rose to fuse with Infinity. Still, with its last shred of individuality I recognized one of the faces. I recognized it with a start, and my first reflex was to think it was my friend. Only Hajji's face would have seemed more startling there because I had given up all hope of ever seeing it again.

Second glance assured me it was not Hajji. It was the face of none other than Murad, the Sultan of all the Faithful. The Grand Turk was neither getting heirs that night, as was his legal right, to capture fortune for his people, nor eating and drinking in royal style. Rather, here he was in the *tekke,* allowing, inviting, profane hands to touch his person—gestures that might be met with death if attempted elsewhere—and losing his royal self in the greater Self.

How many of the other brethren also recognized him I do not know. None gave a flicker of profane recognition although they took him in wholly as one of those who seeks, souls who recognize one another the world over.

With the whirl of the dance we were brought side by side. I took his hand, stripped of gold and gems for the night, and forgot eternal love for a moment. Not only did I think, This hand has power of life and death over me and everyone else in this room. But I also remembered a night when this hand had sought to destroy me in a very personal wrath, in an individual jealous rage over my singular relationship with what he took to be his own.

Time had been when such feelings had made me stumble in the dance when I took our sheikh's hand, too. Our present sheikh had once been called Andrea Barbarigo and had pulled down a nobleman's mask to stare at me with scorn.

In both cases I recovered my steps, however, by the power and mercy of God. Murad and I became no longer sovereign and subject nor rivals for a mundane affection that had limits and conditions. Our feet moved as one, our hands melded. We were equals, partners, at peace before the One.

Later I overheard this conversation:

"And what made you a Seeker, Brother?"

"Another search, a profane search, was consuming all my life away. It brought me eventually to this Search, the Good Search, the Search which is the archetype of all others."

"Yes. It is even so with me."

The two speakers were none other than the Sultan and Andrea Barbarigo, talking together as if they were no more than two strangers in beggars' clothes, meeting one another for the first time on some deserted back road. Before the night was over, even I forgot to have that little ache in the back of my neck, that knot of tension that reminded me the Caliph of all the Faithful and my particular master was present. I did not think of it nor wonder again until the midst of the next day's fast when the weight of material creation was heavy upon me.

※

MUSLIM, FORMERLY ANDREA Barbarigo, was the last to leave the *tekke* that night. He had stayed long hours listening to the sheikh expound on the mysteries. Others grumbled that the old man just liked to hear himself talk. But Andrea stayed. It was true: He never did get to express himself. But here was someone who cared if he came or went.

He should have accepted the invitation to stay overnight, he chided himself. What was at home? A tiny room in the corner of a poor shopkeeper's home. The shopkeeper's colicky kids at night, shrewish wife by day . . .

He entered the empty street with dread, but that dread suddenly exploded into a terror. A huge figure came upon him out of the deep shadows like a blow to the head. He thought for an instant that he was going to die. Another instant would have resigned him to the fact.

But then he recognized the figure. Not that it was any less frightening then: the huge, tortured figure of Sofia Baffo's head eunuch. By Allah, it had been years since he'd seen the creature!

A salaam. Stiff. But maybe it was only from waiting in the cold. Then no word, but one fur-cuffed arm motioned for him to follow.

"I have business, *khadim*——" Andrea began, then stopped himself.

Idiocy! Ghazanfer could break his neck right there in a moment if he wanted to. Best do as he asks.

Around a corner, down a blind alley. Then Andrea stopped short. So would any other Muslim have done, finding himself confronted by a woman's sedan chair. Still the eunuch waved him on. He took one tentative step toward the vehicle and jumped when a ghost-white hand appeared from the deep shadows, sliding the grille to one side.

"Hello, Andrea."

It was Italian. But of course he had guessed it would be. Knotted around that hand and its wrist—creepers around a ruin of old Roman statuary—was the chain of his mother's mosaic locket.

"Do you sometimes find it hard to sleep, Andrea?" the voice asked.

Andrea was still having difficulty imagining the sedan as holding a live person. It was like a jewelry box and now he found it had some wonderful mechanism that could make it talk. No more.

But she took his silence as an affirmative. "I do, too.

"Perhaps," the voice said then. "Perhaps we can help one another."

The grille slid shut, the hand disappeared. Bearers were called from their huddle at the end of the alley. He was not quite sure how, but Andrea knew he had been given orders to follow. He did, up one street and down another and finally in through a courtyard door to a place he'd never been before, nor did he think he could find it again. There was a strangely familiar smell, however. Fish, was it?

DAWN HUNG IN the sky like panels of mother-of-pearl. Andrea found himself in the street again and he stopped short. Had he dreamed it all then? A night vision sent by the Evil One to make him think he had come to the end of the Search? No, there was that smell again. It was too real. He also remembered now where he had smelled it before. In the brothel where he'd gotten the welt on his face so long ago.

Thoughtfully fingering the scar a well-tended beard usually covered, Andrea turned around to look back at the door. But he found the great monster of a eunuch standing there, dour as ever. He turned at once to leave, but just to show he was not too terribly intimidated by this symbol of Muslim virtue, he began to whistle. It was an old Italian song. He and Sofia had sung it together, quite astounding one another with how well they remembered the words after all those years. It was called "Come to the Budding Grove, My Love."

GHAZANFER WATCHED THE man go. He thought: He thinks I am angry. Well, what has he given my mistress this night, after all? He thinks it is himself. It always does that. Inflates one's self worth when most one should be humbled, at least before the majesty of Allah. No, fellow. Whistle on your way. It's not you. You are but a minor character. This—this is between me. Me and her.

LXV

WE SHOULD THANK Allah that in his last days Sultan Murad found comfort in the art that seeks not praise in this world, but in the world to come. They say, indeed, that this man began to prefer that the girls in his orchestra should sing the words of the mystic:

> "I feel myself sick of languor.
> Come, o Death, come lie this night next to me."

Death, so unexpected, came in the midst of these very verses, they say, as Murad lay contemplating the flight of clouds through the windows of his kiosk. A loud salute of cannon in his honor from two Egyptian ships shattered the glass in a skylight and sent it in a rain down to his feet. Now, many a salute had sounded before without ill effect and many a time he had listened to those verses. But this coincidence of events he took as an omen, an answer at last from the mystics' Beloved, and that night he closed his eyes for the last time and dutifully responded to the call.

We, of course, were kept ignorant of the death until Safiye and her lackey, the Grand Vizier, should have time to bring the heir Muhammed from Magnesia. I was not one of them, but still there were those whose sixth sense told them what was afoot. They began to try and consolidate their positions.

※

I REMEMBER ONE day in particular on which, had I been able to read such things, the very air should have told me something. Ghazanfer and I were walking through the inner harem when, for no reason we could name, we paused in one of the smaller courts. No wider than two men laid foot to foot, and yet three stories high, the court was very like a well, and this was added to by the fact that there had been rain in the morning that left the walls and flags in the floor grey and slick with moisture.

A clematis not yet brought to bloom in that shadowy place clung to the wall like moss. Pigeons fluttered through the blue so far overhead, and somewhere on the third story a girl—scrubbing floors, perhaps— let her youthful exuberance out in a song. It seemed disembodied and far away as if it came from the next field, the next hillside, and was the product of wind on stone.

More real to us at the bottom of that pit came a heavy sound, like a drone, the sound of someone weeping. We set out to find the source of that sound and it took us longer than one might imagine. It was coming from the last place either of us thought to look—the little room where only months before one of the girls had died in childbirth. Until that episode could be forgotten, the place would be avoided as too rife with evil spirits.

"Mitra!" Ghazanfer cried when our eyes adjusted to the gloom and the sight. "Allah spare you, but you should not be here in your condition." Mitra was just beginning to show her third pregnancy, brought on by her great skill at reciting Persian mystic poems. "Allah forbid, but might not the brokenhearted soul of our dead sister, Allah have mercy on her, seek to infect you here?"

Mitra looked up, her face swollen and grey as death from the weeping. "And what if she should? We are dead anyway, all of us: me and my sons and this little one I carry. To go at her phantom hand would be more merciful than at . . ." Here her voice dropped to a whisper and she turned her head to the wall again so I had to guess that she finished the sentence with the name "Safiye."

It was then that I got the first inkling of what might be afoot in the rooms of the Sultan.

Ghazanfer tried to allay her fears, but she protested, "No, he is dead. I know he is dead. Three days now, four, I have not been called to his side to recite."

"You know he is disturbed to see women with child," I soothed her. There was only one person anyone meant by "he" in the harem.

"But that's never stopped us before. I can recite from behind a screen."

"He is sick," I suggested, "and Allah may grant him a rapid recovery."

"No, no, it is always in sickness that he loves my voice best. Nay, he is very sick, beyond hearing. He is dead. And so . . . so am I."

I tried to think of more comfort and turned to Ghazanfer for aid. But Ghazanfer was one of those who already knew or guessed. He could offer no comfort. And that was more comforting to Mitra, somehow, than all my vain words. She turned to him now, full of hope.

"You know," she said to him desperately. "You know, don't you? You know that once her Muhammed is on the throne, my sons and I are useless to her. Worse than useless. Dangerous, for who knows what sort of rebellion might form around my little boys? I swear by Allah we have no such interest in power, but such vows are of no use here. By Allah, all we want is to live in peace. All I ever wanted, from the time I was a child, was to live in peace. And she made a bargain with us. You know, Agha, the bargain she made with us. 'When Murad is dead . . .' she said. She said she would free me and I could return to Persia, to my home, with my babies. And my brother, he fulfilled our part of the bargain. He killed the man. But they killed him and now I have no one to speak for me. I fooled myself all along into thinking— But now I know I was a fool. She'll never keep her half of the bargain."

Mitra's words would not stop, a torrent. "She has the right—nay, the obligation according to the ancient law of the Ottomans—to kill all brothers to the heir, whether living or yet unborn, in order for peace to reign in the Empire. What is the peace of one little slave girl compared to peace in the Empire? And she will do it, too. I have seen it in her eyes. Those eyes I thought had picked me out with favor, raised me to the imperial bed. All the time that glint of cold steel was there.

"Once I took it to be true affection, but as I've watched my sons grow—the oldest is eleven now and already a comely young man, Allah bless him—I've come to know it is something else. I know it is the gleam of someone who has found something truly useful, complaisant to her will—and dispensable."

I murmured some condolence or other which, under the circumstances, could be no more than an appeal to Allah's mercy. Out of the corner of my eye, I was watching Ghazanfer. What was his reaction to this? Did he confirm with a glint of green, a shift of his shoulder, that all Mitra suspected was true? Could he offer some hope? Or would he report the woman's faithlessness back to their mistress?

"I'm sorry. I cannot help you," I said.

"No, but you can," she exclaimed, suddenly animated. "You, *khuddam,* can help me escape. Help us escape, me and my boys. To Persia, that would be best. Persia, if it is Allah's will. But somewhere, anywhere. It doesn't matter to me if I spend the rest of my days in a fisherman's hovel, so long as it is away from here."

Ghazanfer Agha looked up—to the door. Did he merely check that we were not overheard? Or did he look towards her he would tell?

My heart raced at the threat. Though we were counted friends, Ghazanfer and I, I often felt friendship was on the surface. It was an adjunct of the fact that we were the only two white eunuchs left with the women from the days before the reorganization. Yes, something was wrong with the Sultan. I could read that in my fellow eunuch now. But I hadn't before. And he hadn't been the one to tell me.

And I still could not read that stoic *khadim*'s loyalties.

I knew no aid for this poor woman weeping before us. But stopping such betrayal as his eyes might be seeking at the door would have to be a first step. I couldn't delude myself. There was no way, either physically or by suggestion of loyalty, that I could counter the monstrous Hungarian on my own.

Presently the *kapu aghasi* turned back to us—to my surprise but gratitude—with vague words of hope. "I will think on it," he said.

Mitra was surprised, too. She was surprised enough, at least, to let us bring her out of that ill-omened room. And to cease—for another week or so at least—her terrifying plaint that Murad the Sultan was dead. When she did weep again, her voice joined that of all the palace, indeed, of the Empire from one end to the other.

LXVI

Muhammed returned from Magnesia a stronger figure than any of us remembered him going. There were several hectic days of funeral and investiture and reception of obeisance from the outside world first. But when he did at last make his triumphant entry into the harem—"like a bridegroom into the bedroom"—he had only rested from the hard forced ride from the *sandjak*. He had not yet lost any of the burnished bronze of his skin to the pampering of gold-fringed canopies.

That bronze was set with rubies like a masterpiece of the jeweler's art. A ruby the size of a quail's egg dangled from one ear. On the pure white silk of his turban was fastened a second stone like a pool of blood caught in the palm of the hand and clotted there. That gem held heron plumes aloft and radiated three strings of diamonds to either side. His fingers were jeweled as if to cut off circulation, and the Sword of Othman, strapped at his waist, had received new gems to its hilt for the occasion.

Dazzled by the jewelry, few can have noticed the robe. It was cream silk of the highest grade with an unusually dainty floral pattern worked in a peach-colored velvet. Yet it, too, had effect. "Under this power and pomp," that cream and peach seemed to say, "is a man of pure and gentle motives, whose love would be worth the price of twenty gems, if only it can be won." It was womenfolk who heard this message most clearly. How it made the hearts of the harem sing!

Only a slight scar on Muhammed's cheek seemed to mar the picture of a merciful new sovereign.

Throughout his residence at Magnesia, Safiye had seen to it that her son's needs were satisfied by a single plain but very complaisant Greek. His eunuchs, over whom Safiye had complete control, were under strict orders to get nothing from the slave market on their own unless it was women of proven barrenness, and indeed, their allowance permitted nothing else.

But Muhammed was still young. At twenty-four, ardor comes hot and swiftly enough that one does not stop to consider the shortcomings of one's partners. Nor does it occur that failing passion is the very shadow of death, to be beaten back with all means possible. The Greek was obedient and willing enough and had presented her master with two sons. If Muhammed ever thought more could be asked for, he thought it must only be an opium dream.

Now Safiye had once explained to the girl how one could keep pregnancies from occurring. The girl was complaisant. But those two sons indicated that she was too complaisant to try and thwart the will of Allah, too simple to practice even the rudiments of the apothecaries' art.

Safiye had hoped to put off the day when there would be a new woman in the harem with solid claim to power in the world of men. This had made her harder on the Greek girl than she had need to be.

But now the unavoidable day had come. No more than let him appear on the throne in rough wool could Safiye let her son go without the further trappings fit for the world's most powerful ruler. The flood gates must be opened, but she was careful to see that she was the one to open them.

Yes, one could see in the face of Baffo's daughter that she would rather have scattered the Golden Way with a few old laundresses and two or three girls with heavily poxed faces that day. But Muhammed was Sultan now. If she would wield power through him, it would not do to try and curtail his power in any way. It would not do to try and keep him content with a little Greek girl when his hand—and through it, his mother's—reached from the Danube to the Indian Ocean.

But Safiye had had many years in the harem on her own to prepare for this day. She trusted that every one of the maidens that lined his triumphal way into the inner sanctum was not only the most beautiful the Empire had to offer, but also totally dependant upon her will. The will of the new Valide Sultan.

There were two hundred of Safiye's girls, a material recreation of the dream Prince Muhammed had once dreamed of Paradise. There were blondes and brunettes, blue eyes, brown eyes, and green, the svelte and agile, the cushiony and comfortable, all blushing in the perfect bloom of youth. The presence of a man brought them to their peak, like roses with dew. For some of them this was the first man they'd seen since their seclusion and careful training began as toddlers. For all of them, this was their man, the only man they would ever know, if Allah were favorable.

And Muhammed strode between them with an equal glow. In his cream-peach robes he walked and scattered a handful of coins from the tray borne by the coffee-colored eunuch behind him. The coins were a mere pretense of generosity, as the earlier ritual of placing their hennaed hands under his mother's foot had been pretense of sudden submission. The girls hardly bothered to scramble for the money, except as a scramble might better show a cleavage or an ankle. Those who thought modesty or long lashes were their best features did not move at all but blushed and giggled.

Studded with rubies, the Sultan was twenty-four years old and come at last to his own.

I saw no more of this ritual than that. For Ghazanfer had contrived to get Mitra there among those scrambling—or not scrambling—in the Golden Way.

She was heavily disguised and veiled, of course. Had Muhammed actually laid eyes on her, his father's concubine, it would have been rank incest. The even greater threat was that Safiye might see. Or guess.

Still, it had to be risked, under the celebratory confusion. The Golden Way was but a few steps from the antechamber where Ghazanfer had a sedan chair waiting. To what safety he meant to carry her, I never learned. My job was only to see that she got out the back door and into that sedan before Muhammed passed, before Safiye noticed she was gone. It was safer that I knew no more.

I was, in fact, grateful that the monstrous Hungarian seemed intent on protecting me as well as the girl. I did my job without a hitch. We slipped out of the stale, overused air of the harem's bowels and into the fresh winter chill.

But only my part of the plot was ever fulfilled.

"Where . . . where are my sons?" Mitra turned to me from the cavernously empty sedan.

"Ghazanfer Agha has them safe somewhere," I said quickly, perhaps too quickly. In fact I had no idea what he had in mind for the boys. "Get in now, lady."

"No. I will not go without my sons."

"They are safe, I am sure. Come now. Let me give you a hand."

Still she hesitated. I did not know how much longer the giggles and shrieks in the Golden Way would cover us.

"Will you swear by the Most Merciful they are all right?"

"Allah is merciful," I said. "They are in His hands."

"It's curious." She sat down on the edge of the chair but would not yet swing her feet up into the box so we could close the door and be on our way. "That is just the line Mustafa, my eldest, wrote in a little poem last night. You know he's quite a poet. Already! At his age, Allah shield him."

"Well, with such artistic parents . . ." I said, trying anxiously to humor her.

She smiled gently. It seemed all the long afternoons she had sat in the cool of a kiosk reciting to our dead master passed across her face like a breeze from the Bosphorus on one of those afternoons . . .

She took a scrap of paper out of her bosom and unfolded it. Then she read the poem aloud. But I could tell, with her gift of memory, she had already committed it to heart, and needed the paper only as the physical evidence of one whose round, youthful hand had so lately touched it.

The hand was childish, but the words seemed those of a stoic old man who has looked Death in the face and smiled in recognition and welcome. "We are in His hands." She finished the verse and there was a silence neither of us could break for a long time, a dangerously long time.

Then she said, "I am sorry, Abdullah. Forgive me."

"There is nothing to forgive," I said. "Or, rather, you should forgive me that I can't do more for you."

"No," she said. "You don't understand. It was I. Well, my brother and I. In my desire to be free and to live, I killed him. Your master, Sokolli Pasha. I killed him."

"Nonsense," I said. "I was there. It was a dervish."

"A dervish who was my brother," she said. "You see, she promised . . ."

Her chin quivered. And I saw that it was the same round chin I'd seen on the executioner's stand, pierced by the same round dimple.

Just then came the flurried entrance of Ghazanfer Agha.

"Make haste!" he hissed in a whisper. "There is no time. You should be gone!"

Mitra collected herself as she collected the folds of the little scrap of paper. "I will not go without my sons."

Ghazanfer's face could not hide the truth when it was demanded of him like that. He was unable to save the boys. Only Mitra herself and that offspring she cradled under her heart.

"Pray it may be a girl," he said fiercely, "then Safiye may forget your threat and not spend the rest of her days pursuing you."

Mitra stood up firmly from the sedan. "I will not go without my sons," she said one more time.

"Your sons are the next to greet the new Sultan," Ghazanfer said. "Muhammed has decreed he wants them and all the young princes circumcised today."

"But that is nonsense." Mitra smiled, stretching the dimple out of her chin. "Princes are not circumcised without a party, a celebration . . ."

"Yes." Ghazanfer said no more. There was no need for more.

It was not a religious man with a razor, but the deaf mutes with the silken cords that met the young princes in the circumcision pavilion. There were twenty in all who survived their father. The nineteen youngest were buried next to him in miniature little mounds by the mosque before the soil of his own grave had lost its clammy moistness.

As for Mitra, she did not have long either to mourn or regret. On the chance that their children might be male and threats to the throne, she and six other members of the harem in various stages of the same condition were rowed out to sea by night. Here they were stuffed in weighted sacks and sent to the bottom whence divers retrieved tales for years to come, tales of seven sacks waving like seaweed in the current: this one trailing an amber curl, this one a hand the late Sultan had kissed so fondly and decked with an emerald ring.

Her sisters went down cursing the she-devil whom they had trusted as their guardian and mistress and a thousand bargains broken. Mitra, I was told, recited poetry. Her final bubbles formed the shape of Allah's all-encompassing hand. And sometimes, they said, the current moaned in the tones of a Persian poem.

That evening after he'd wept over his brothers' corpses, laid out in size and age from Mitra's eldest to the youngest infant but three months old, Muhammed took to his bed a pair of the girls from the Golden Way. They were the two who had been most coy and artfully hid their faces to catch his fancy. The next night it was . . .

But I forget them all after that. And it doesn't really matter. To the outside world, a new reign had begun. But within, we still had Safiye.

LXVII

As HIS GRAND Vizier, at the suggestion of his mother and his sister, Allah chose Ferhad Pasha. My lady Esmikhan made the supreme effort on one occasion to be carried and hauled up the narrow stairs to join Safiye in the Eye of the Sultan to see her beloved at work in the Divan. After that she protested that affairs of state had no interest for her and that she was uncomfortable to be so close to the world of men.

I suspect these were just catchphrases anyone would accept to hide the real cause of her refusals. And the real cause was that peering down on the man through the Sultan's Eye was too reminiscent of the first day she'd seen him, wet and exhausted from his three days' ride. It was similar, and yet too different.

For she was no longer the young woman she had been to bloom like a rose at the first touch of the sun. And he was a man married to someone else. There was grey now beneath his beard, a dignified carriage and a caution brought on by weariness, perhaps. There was a definite and deep weariness in his eyes that had never been there before.

Safiye was his mother-in-law.

Then, too, the masculine form that had given Esmikhan the most exquisite of joys now wore the green robes of a grand vizier. It was the same costume she had seen so often on Sokolli Pasha. To look upon that costume was almost to look upon a second cuckolding. And now that she, too, wore streaks of grey, the all-justifying passion of youth seemed but an uncomfortable foolishness. She didn't like to think of her love in such terms, so she never went again.

In spring, when word came that the snow had cleared from the mountain passes, Ferhad Pasha left at the head of the army to war in Hungary against a coalition of Austrians and Germans. Ibrahim Pasha was temporarily elevated to take his place in the Divan.

And then it was heard that, hardly at the borders of Bulgaria, the janissaries had revolted.

Among the measures Ferhad Pasha took in the field to put down the rebellion was to exile two of the army's leaders whom he felt were responsible. This move infuriated Safiye, for those men were her protégés, sure to do her will even when Ferhad would not. One of them, in fact, she had been grooming for the post of Grand Vizier when Ferhad should become dispensable. I suspect the man had grown tired of waiting, as ambitious men will.

But other news grieved my own lady more. It was said that in his wrath, Ferhad cursed the unruly troops and swore by Allah that no janissary should ever have the virility to get a child again until the Judgment Day. Whether the report was true or not, Esmikhan took the words to heart and rode them up and down through all possible double meanings meant just for her.

Ferhad wished that he, too, as a young soldier had never gotten a child. Or he wished to berate Sokolli, dead and in his grave, for ever allowing the men to marry. Esmikhan thought this unworthy of the man she loved. My lady and this man had not spoken to one another for a quarter of a century, and yet his words still had such power to move her.

In the Divan, this report was also taken seriously. The janissaries, even in rebellion, were the might and power of the Empire, the right hand of Allah. The power of their arm was equal to the power of their other parts and to curse either was tantamount to cursing the future of the Empire and Islam as a whole. It was treason; worse, it was blasphemy. Ibrahim Pasha was immediately sent with a contingent to find out if the rumor was true. Ibrahim assumed from the first that it was and would find what he looked for. What Safiye promised he might find. He went to depose Ferhad and to claim the post of Grand Vizier for himself.

Only my constant trips from my lady to Safiye and then of Safiye's eunuchs to the Sultan's private apartments finally got the precious firmen written and sent. Ferhad was under no circumstances to be killed.

When the message was received on the front lines, Ferhad Pasha and a few of his faithful troops were holed up in a manor that was his personal property. The smell of blood had brought most of the janissaries in line—behind Ibrahim—and they had Ferhad Pasha totally encircled. Grudgingly, Ibrahim complied with the firmen. And that was the last word we had.

SOME FEW NIGHTS later I was awakened. Darkness was thick and heavy everywhere I looked, but what had disturbed my sleep I could not tell. All I could hear were the sounds of my colleagues asleep in the little cubicles around me. Their snores and sighs drifted in and out of the open windows like moths in search of light in which to immolate themselves.

Suddenly, something knocked against the edge of my bed. It knocked again and then would not stop, shaking things with such a violence that the corners of the earth seemed to roar.

"Who is it? What do you want? Stop it!" I wanted to cry, but by the time the words had formed, I realized it was no mortal hand and no attack against me personally, but the hand of Allah shaking all the earth as if it were no more than a feather bolster and He a housewife giving a thorough cleaning.

I did not move from where I was. It would be useless in any case, for if I did manage once to get to my feet, the earth would drop from beneath them between steps. And where should I go if I could walk? The violence attacked the palace from sea wall to sea wall and from the dungeons to the highest minaret.

My colleagues were all awake now. I could hear some of them trying to murmur prayers, but the rest were silent, holding their breath, closing their eyes tight. We began to hear things now, the crashing of crockery. Something fell from the ledge three stories up and shattered in the courtyard just outside my door. The collision of other possessions was as if a thief were rummaging through an old trunk, careless of what he would leave behind, seeking only in a mad rush that which was of the most mundane value. Children cried and a woman or two screamed, but that was all. The rest of us held our breaths and waited.

At last the earth twitched itself like a dog come from copulating, turned on its tail one more time, and settled down to sleep without a further spasm of guilt for its rash deed. I lay and listened to the returned stillness with more amazement than to the earthquake itself. Then I heard some of my colleagues out in the court wondering in low whispers. I got up and joined them, nodding in agreement at their formulaic comments on the power and mercy of Allah which is about all one can really say at a time like that.

We did not think much about the women. There were eunuchs on duty in their quarters who could come and tell us if anything more serious than lost sleep and frazzled nerves had happened. One *khadim* began to tell us how in his village in the mountains they had suffered such an earthquake when he was a boy that the . . . It was as formulaic as praising Allah, but I moved nearer to lend a polite ear. As I did, I stepped on whatever bit of crockery it was that had fallen from the top floor.

"By Allah, that I should come through the quake alive and have this happen afterwards!" I exclaimed as the other *khuddam* laughed in relief more than mockery and hastened, some to help stop the bleeding, others to pick up the pieces.

In the midst of this, one of my lady's maids came running in, white as milk spilled on anthracite. I was needed at once in our lady's rooms, she said.

With my foot still bleeding onto the rags, I was in no condition to be chasing off through the harem, so I put her off for a while. Had she never been in an earthquake before? Thank Allah, we were all alive. Trying to get back to sleep again would be the best for all concerned.

So I stalled. I stalled so long and so unforgivably that I gave my mistress time to get herself to the eunuch's quarters. Then I knew it was no common terror that stirred her. Never in all our years together had she come to see me. It was always the other way around.

I hobbled up on one and a half feet and gave my bed for her maids to ease her onto. There she sat, speechless with tears, wringing a handkerchief and looking at me with eyes like saucers filled to the brim by a host of lavish generosity. That look stirred me enough to wave the anxious girls and eunuchs from the room.

The instant they were gone, her grief exploded. "He is dead!"

"He? Who is he?" The Sultan, it occurred to me, but I banished the thought from my mind with an "Allah forbid." Fratricide on ascension made for a rule free from pretenders, but it did nothing to protect the Empire from the upheavals the minority of a three-year-old boy would cause.

"He," she said, her voice quavering on the syllable like that of a dervish on the Name of his Goal. But she mixed it with such anguish, I knew she could only mean Ferhad Pasha.

"It is just a dream the quake caused," I said. "Ferhad Pasha is far from here. Perhaps where he is they didn't even feel the shocks." I comforted her with such things. "It is Allah's will. You do not know but what this is only an evil spirit come to haunt you this dark night."

But I could convince myself no more than I could convince her. The reverberations of that "He" had sent chills down my spine. By the eery lamp light I saw my lady as if she were a corpse. I also saw the vein of a new crack in the plaster of the ceiling over the bed's head that had not been there when I finally closed the book I was reading and blew out the flame that night. Allah only knew how close any of us was to death at any time. Perhaps one more shake would have sent the two upper stories down on me, on Esmikhan . . .

I shivered again, held her and prayed until she slept. Not long after that the muezzin called the dawn prayer with renewed vitality and meaning. He called people from the rubble of their houses in the poorer sections, called to people who had not ceased to pray since the earth had shaken them to their knees several hours earlier.

And word came in hushed, fatidic tones later that afternoon, ridden hard and fast from the troops on the border. Ferhad Pasha was dead. Some persons unknown had crept into his manor by night and murdered him. His head was cut off. Some said, afraid that the very words might set the earth shaking again, that men close to Ibrahim had tossed and kicked that head like a ball around their campfires.

I don't think anyone ever gave my lady those details. She was feverish enough without when she woke from her sleep. Because she was spared such details, I hoped she might recover in a week or two.

But she never did again rise from her bed. The earthquake, some said. Running around that night and catching cold. They were people who had not heard her say that "He," like a dervish calling on his God. "He," It, which is neither a young man in *spahi's* garb, nor a grand vizier, but something which encompasses all the earth and yet dwells in so little space as the heart of a gnat.

That same strength with which she brought forth her daughter against all odds of physical endurance stood with her again throughout that winter, but in the spring, when the army was making ready to march once more, I knew her time could be numbered in hours. Her daughter and grandchildren and those of us who loved her were already there, sleeping and taking our meals in the presence of Death to ease the way into Paradise and remind ourselves that our times too, would come. But when she began to fade back into a time when they were carefree girls together and called on the name of Safiye, I thought I should go and see if the daughter of Baffo would not come now. Surely, for this old, dear friend, she could not refuse.

I was told the Queen Mother had retired for the night. Because even sleep cannot forestall death, I pursued her further. I was surprised to find the doors to the Queen Mother's apartment's unguarded past the first courtyard. The door to her main chamber was even ajar. I took courage and let myself inside. The room was deserted. Lamps had never been lit there that evening, nor had the bolsters and cushions been unfolded.

So in this final wish I disappointed my lady. I returned to her side and held her hand until she died, peacefully in her sleep. Perhaps she was convinced her friend was with her all the time. But in my heart I hoped I was sufficient. I had had to be, time and time again in life.

I, at least, was not disappointed. There was no blessing of life my lady had not given me. And now she gave me the sorrow, the gift of her death.

LXVIII

AFTER HER MOTHER'S death, Gul Ruh insisted that I come and live with her. It seemed the best plan, although she already had a full hierarchy of eunuchs and I would be living in the honor, yet the inactivity of semiretirement. I agreed to that, nonetheless—for what should I do in the palace?—and prepared to relinquish my cubicle to one of the black *khuddam* who now, except for Ghazanfer, were all the staff.

Ghazanfer came to say good-bye and, though I had vague recollections that he had taken time during our bereavement to offer comfort, my grief had been too deep to recall any but this interview in detail. For some reason I mentioned my nighttime search for his mistress and how distressed I was that I hadn't been able to find her in time for her to sit at Esmikhan's side.

"Safiye avoids deathbeds," Ghazanfer said.

"Yes, I know. But you'd think for such a good old friend . . ."

"Friend? Does my mistress have friends, I wonder? Who do you suppose will be at her deathbed, eh?"

"Allah postpone the day."

Ghazanfer did not amen me, but went on. "Your mistress was one of the sweetest and gentlest of Allah's creatures, and yet Safiye saw that sweetness and gentleness as shortcomings, things to be exploited for her own use. That is *her* shortcoming. She feels herself immortal as if daily consumption of power and worldly wealth were an elixir for eternal youth. Others take time to die. Others die because through some personal failure they let the zenith of their powers pass, because they are not smart enough or strong enough to avoid poisoners, palace accidents, or merely the throes of daily life."

I had never heard Ghazanfer speak so harshly, nor yet so truly against his mistress and I wondered at it. He was a changed man since his failure to rescue Mitra. But I wondered more at the words that followed.

"Safiye has passed her zenith now. Not that she isn't as physically strong as ever, but time never waits and always brings up other generations in one's stead. I see this. She sees it, too, though she is loathe to admit it, even to herself. She will fight it—even the mere admission—to the end. She is the Queen Mother, yet she dare not sleep in the Queen Mother's chambers. One night she sleeps here, another night there, taking only her most trusted maids with her, telling no one beforehand where to find her. Is that a woman at the zenith of her power?"

"So that is why I couldn't find her that night?"

"Of course. I do happen to know she wasn't sleeping anywhere that night—that night when your lady's passing took the last of what was good and gentle from this place and left us all the weaker for it. That was when the Sultan had just announced he planned to go into battle in Hungary himself this year instead of trusting the army to Ibrahim Pasha alone. That front, as you know, was left a shambles by last year's rebellion and neglect. Your late master, may he rest in peace, was wont to say, 'Grand Viziers may turn and flee, but when the Padishah himself leads Allah's armies, there is no turning back nor defeat.' "

"The presence of a powerful head is, of course, what this Empire needs," I suggested.

"Yes, needs, oh, so painfully. And yet Safiye is loathe to let her son go. On the frontier, she thinks, too many hearts and hands can come between Muhammed and herself. She must stay behind in the harem, and too much policy may be decided without her.

"Our young Sultan, you may know, is much enamored of his position, both of its pomp and of its duties. He would not be swayed this time. And so she determined on a plot to make him see how much he was needed here at home. She sent troops devoted to her throughout the Empire with orders to massacre all Christians."

"The Christians!" I exclaimed. "But she . . ."

"Yes, she herself was raised as one and has often taken their part in the past. But such devotions are merely the pawns of power to her. Even were she not a Christian born, is it not women's place, in their own weakness, to protect other underlings? Fortunately for all of us, Muslims and Christians alike, the mother of the Crown Prince got wind of this plot. And she did not forget her Greek upbringing, much less her own humanity. Her pleas and tears, though outward signs of weakness, were strong enough to turn our Sultan's heart against his mother. He thwarted Safiye by sending warning of his own to all the Christian communities, prohibiting Christians from entering places where the assassins were, until the threat should pass. He has also sent out a firmen that any man in his pay found guilty of such atrocities against a minority will surely be put to death. Well, as you can see, the massacre never took place and Muhammed has marched north with the armies as planned.

"The upshot of all of this is that Safiye has realized that though she rules the harem as a general his army, there are some things terror and might have no strength over. She fears poison and the dagger and so she sleeps here and there like a gypsy within her own walls. But that is only because those are methods she uses. She has not yet learned even to put a name to the devices that in the end will be her defeat. They will defeat her because she thinks they are harmless. And I wonder who will be at her bedside when they come."

The green eyes grew cloudy and looked away. "Somehow," Ghazanfer said, "I fear I may be the only one."

LXIX

I SAW GHAZANFER one more time. I had been living with Gul Ruh
for several years and had endured the hospitality but uselessness as long
as I could. I'd found ever more occupation for the long hours with the
dervishes, but that year it occurred to me that rather than sitting and
waiting for my friend Hajji to appear, I should go in search of him myself. I determined, with that Rajab's march, to join the rest of the pilgrims on the road to Mecca. Ghazanfer Agha had heard of my plans and
came to wish me Allah's good favor.

"It is in my power as *kapu aghasi,*" he suggested, "to have you assigned to the brotherhood of *khuddam* guarding the holy places. That
place of greatest honor in the world."

"Thank you, but I am not certain yet I will want to stay in Mecca or
Medina."

A burst of childish laughter came from the harem. Ghazanfer turned
his green eyes towards the sound. "Yes," he said. "I can see there is
much to draw you back again."

"And I have never been what one could call a truly converted
Muslim."

"No. It is Allah's will that you are a Seeker. But just in case . . ."

Without further word he drew a thick legal parchment from his
bosom. Curious, I unfolded it. I discerned quickly the formal seals of
Sultan and *kapu aghasi,* then read enough below them of praise connected with my own name to blur my eyes with tears. I folded the
paper and placed it in my own bosom. It still held the warmth of Ghazanfer's very feminine breasts.

I was speechless, dumb for words to express my gratitude. At length
I stammered the most generous thing I could think of: "You . . . you
could come with me. I would like it better if I wasn't a total stranger."

"Not this year. I can't. I have—one more bit of business to do."

"What is that?"

But he wouldn't tell me right away.

Instead, he gave me a small purse of gold that I might carry, along with his name, to the House of Allah. There was such a sense of resolution and new beginning about him. This sense seemed so similar to what I myself had been feeling in recent days that this purse, this physical declaration that he would not be joining the caravan quite took me by surprise.

It was a day in early spring of glorious sun. The old bones seemed young again and thrilled as if it were several months later in the year. Ghazanfer and I sat in the doorway to the courtyard. We took more interest in the pattern of sunlight tossed through the swelling buds of the fig tree outside than in the sherbets and pistachios between us. The conversation, too, seemed to hold little interest although Ghazanfer pursued it—a tale of one further palace intrigue—because it was what little common ground lay between us now.

The Sultan's third-born son was a little fellow his mother had named Muhammed in an attempt to flatter attention away from the Greek girl's two older boys.

"When that did not work," Ghazanfer said, "she turned to magic instead."

"Ah, magic again," I nodded wearily. "That vile thing."

"This woman found a dervish who, upon seeing her son on a horse for the first time was moved to prophecy, 'By Allah, give that child the head of the Islamic army and he will bring the failing Empire back to the ascendancy we knew during the time of Suleiman.' Of course the nature of our master is such that he will hear such things and believe them. Safiye had to act swiftly. Before Muhammed the Sultan could consult with the Divan on the matter, she had the child, his mother and the prophetic dervish . . . well taken care of."

Ghazanfer coughed and hid his final words in a sip of sherbet for which he really had no desire. Then I saw that this was because my young lady's littlest son had joined us in the garden. The boy was supposed to be memorizing his lessons for tomorrow and, considering his age, was doing quite well with the obscure Arabic of the Koranic passage. His tutors said he would be like his father and grandfather before him, a great scholar, and have the Book memorized very shortly.

But the child did like a break from time to time—he could hardly resist the weather. He came and ask us what we were doing, and when our only, boring reply was "just visiting," he clambered on my knees and helped himself to pistachios. He made fighting galleys from the shells— whole ones Turkish, broken ones the "heathen Christians"—and played at sea battles for a while. And when he got too loud, I scolded him to study once again.

When the boy trotted off again, Ghazanfer smiled and said, only half aloud, "Perhaps that was one day she had mercy. The day that boy was born. If so, Allah bless her for it, for He can bless her for nothing else."

I asked what he meant, but Ghazanfer at first refused to explain. I pressed him and at last he said:

"A son of the Blood. That lad is a threat to the throne. Even if a very distant one, there are some who might see in him a way to wrench the crested turban from Safiye's Muhammed. At least I'm sure such a chance is not lost in her mind."

His tone sent my mind back past the last little diversion of pistachio sea battles to the dervish-prophesied and condemned prince and I shuddered. "But thank Allah she never meddled with such distant princes."

"Didn't she?"

"I mean, not with any outside the palace harem itself."

"Didn't she?" Ghazanfer said again. "I mean, wasn't it obvious?"

"I don't know what you mean, my friend." I laughed nervously.

He took another sip of sherbet and frowned darkly.

"Well, I will tell you," he said, "as it is clear you never guessed. I will tell you because it will ease my blackened soul. Like confession to our village priest did when I was a boy. And because where I go from here, it will be better if people understand. At least people whose good opinion I cherish."

"My friend, what are you talking about?" I laughed again at his riddles.

"I mean the little sons of Esmikhan," he hissed as if spitting out poison.

"It was Allah's will," I said, shrugging, "that they should all be born dead."

"None of them was born dead. Three full-term lads and none of them should live? The girl alone should live? Surely you have a low opinion of your late mistress's ability to bear children."

"What do you mean?" My blood ran cold. "The midwife . . ."

"Yes, the midwife. The old Quince."

"Safiye told you this?" My clumsy eunuch's voice betrayed me in a squeak.

"She did not, not even me, her faithful Ghazanfer." He spoke his own name and its faithfulness with bitter scorn. "But I began to guess. Especially after the case of Mitra . . ."

The great eunuch's voice faded for a moment. When he recovered, he continued, "Then one day last summer I went to the infirmary."

"I thought the Quince was dead."

"No. The new midwife. The Fig. I asked her point-blank what she knew of the matter.

" 'I'm not sure,' was her reply.

" 'But you have suspicions?' I pressed her.

" 'Things the Quince, my dear, dead lover, said when the fit was on her.'

"I pressed for details. Nothing very clear.

" 'But I know how we can find out,' she said finally. 'If you're willing.'

"I was willing."

Ghazanfer paused in his tale, sipped his drink, and rested his sight with unguarded pleasure on a bed of crimson and white tulips. Sometime later I would wonder at the uncharacteristic effusion he displayed then. All I can say is that it was a very uncharacteristic experience he had to describe. Whenever I wondered, How could he do such things, this taciturn, unemotional *khadim?* the simple thought that he did this for me, so I would know, kept me listening. Listening with deep appreciation.

"I was no longer quite so willing as at first," Ghazanfer said, "when I made my way as directed to a house tucked in beside the aqueduct later that evening. Bizarre, barbaric sights and sounds greeted me before I reached the door.

"The fanatics at the *medrese* must hear this, I thought, and hesitated to enter. You know, as a work of charity, I have established a religious school in the neighborhood of the aqueduct. I am ashamed to say that some of my scholars were among the most vicious to Jews and Christians during the recent disturbances. I cut funding to the most disruptive, but I can't have rooted them all out. They were barbaric to the People of the Book. I could imagine what they'd do to such an assembly as this was, even before I knocked at the door.

"But then I thought, Well, if I'm in the lodge, instead of here, outside, I may be able to save some lives when the mob comes, just by being recognized. And I suppose I must have been recognized by the sullen doorkeeper or spoken for by the Fig, for I was admitted without question.

"Every African in Constantinople must have been there. And I, a minority of one. A minority not only in color but in soul. A pair of our like from the black eunuch's college were flailing on waist-high drums. At least these are colleagues, I thought. But they were not.

"These *khuddam* had stripped to the hips, and without the camouflage of long fur robes, the tortures a man's body suffers without its male parts was grotesquely evident on them: the sunken barrel chest, overlong arms like those who've been stretched on a rack—and somehow survived. Together and in turns they beat out the rhythm with hands so bony and twisted they couldn't lay them flat. When such a deformity overcomes a *khadim,* he orders the sleeves of his robes cut longer and tucks those hands up under the sable cuffs.

"But I can hardly say these men were our colleagues. They had no impulse to hide. Their talons flew like birds of prey over the untanned hides of their painted drums. They beat with such vigor! I began to suspect that every man who'd ever hurt them from the first moment of their capture in the bosom of their mother Africa until their last bastinado was getting his just deserts under those twisted hands.

"The beat was so heavy I could feel each reverberation in the core of my sternum. It twitched in my joints. I could hardly keep from leaping to my feet and dancing myself. None of the others in the room made any attempt to resist such impulses at all.

"Chickens were brought in to the midst of the dance, black capons, squawking, fanning with their feathers. Their throats were quickly cut, and presently the smell of cooking birds mingled with that of pine smoke, raw blood, and sweat on hot, black bodies. The bodies of porter and scullery maid, laundress and many, many eunuchs seemed to swell in that environment like purple grapes in the sun. They acquired a luscious, sweet juiciness. For here was a mingling of the sexes that would have turned the beard on any *medrese* student a premature grey. A mingling, charged with bestiality. And yet somehow totally innocent at the same time. Even the *khuddam* were affected by the spirit—by the throbbing virility.

"There is nothing for me here, I was convinced. It's too wild, too strange, nothing to do with my world. The mob from the *medrese* may come if they must and do their worst. Against this strangeness I cannot, will not stop them.

"But as if she had been watching me, as if she read my thoughts, the moment I turned to leave, the Fig made her entrance into the assembly from a curtained inner door. And then I couldn't leave. You know how buffoonish the midwife usually looks in her Turkish dress, how overdone, how ostentatious. Well, suddenly I saw what clothes Allah had created her to wear.

"Simple lengths of brilliant fabric in unusual patterns skirted from her hips. Great, simple golden hoops in her ears, feathers of the sacrificed chickens sticking with a little blood but mostly of their own accord in the round, wiry black pincushion of her hair. Her neck was draped in strings of gems, but also other things that seemed more precious: shells. The severed, spurred legs of cocks, talons flexed. Claws. Bones. Between these ornaments and the first roll of cloth at her waist, there was nothing. Only smooth, blue-black skin, smooth, black, purple-tipped breasts that swung slightly with each step as if tossing out a challenge to the world.

"I thought, Did the Quince ever see the Fig thus? Did the Quince ever come to the lodge, looking for new cures, perhaps? If she did, I no longer question the rumors that they were lovers. Indeed, I found myself envying the Quince her fortune.

"The Fig moved in and out of the crowd, greeting everyone by name, accepting kisses to her hands, her hem, her feet, accepting gifts and offerings. We exchanged nods, no more.

"Then the drummers who had seemed to be fading somewhat with exhaustion, suddenly leapt with new life. A new rhythm sprang off the young, tight drumskins. And almost in the same instant I saw—I actually saw the rhythm enter the Fig. Something like a pulsing sheen, just below the black hull of her skin.

"She moved, but the movement was no longer hers. At first another jerked her joints, sometimes at impossible angles, as if she were no more than a puppet on strings. But then the puppeteer slipped down the strings and molded the midwife's limbs to her own.

"It took no more than an indrawn breath for the audience to fall back and give the Fig room. The out-breath mouthed the name, 'Yavrube, Yavrube!' This, I knew, was the name of their demon goddess. And now—the name of their priestess as well.

"Before, the Fig had moved with confidence, as she always does. But how much more so now! She whirled, she twirled, she hopped, she dropped, she rolled, she heaved, she rippled, every space of flesh like small wavelets passing on a dark, moonlit water.

"Such energy! I have only seen children with such energy before, naughty children, and then the little ones soon drop with exhaustion. But on and on the possessed Fig went. The irises of her eyes had rolled out of sight, a twitch of her head as she passed rained me with sweat. Others crowded together to receive such rain, considering it a blessing. Constricting to the drums, you could hear her breath, nearing the point where mortality must burst, dragging in and out of fraying lungs like an anchor chain in and out of the hold."

Can this have been as much like the dance of the dervishes as it sounds? I asked myself. Where every man accepts the divine, not just a leader. Ghazanfer had never been to a *tekke* or he might have made the connection. But I said nothing, letting him continue.

"And then—the strings were cut. The bones seemed to fly from the Fig as she melted to the ground, bitumen on a hot day. Some went to roll her gently over, but the eyes were still unflawed mother-of-pearl set in her ebony face, unseeing. Yavrube still animated her limbs. The people stepped back, in awe.

"And then, the voice came. I recognized the voice, but it was not the Fig's. It was the Quince's."

"The dead Quince?"

"Syllable for syllable. As the words shuddered from her, Yavrube moved like a woman under her lover. It was obscene. But somehow, not so in that company, with those drums. And I could not look away.

"And the voice said: 'Babies'."

LXX

I COULDN'T HELP but interrupt Ghazanfer at this point by repeating, "Babies?"

The great Hungarian nodded. " 'Babies. Their insides all bled out.' "

"In the Quince's voice?"

"Exactly. It gave me such a start to hear it coming out of those full black lips instead of the Quince's thin, tart ones."

"I, too, have heard the Quince say those precise words. When she saw my little lady. But what does it mean?"

"The voice went on to say this. At every lying in of Esmikhan, the Quince, under Safiye's orders—because she loved Safiye beyond all reason—"

"She is not the first to have done so," I murmured.

"At every lying in, the Quince was to see if the child was male or female."

"So she did. So does every midwife."

"And only then was she to cut the cord."

"She ties the cord off and then cuts it. I was at the lying in when Gul Ruh was born. I know how such things are done."

"Ah, but only if it were a girl child was she to tie the cord. If it was a male child, one who because of his mother's blood and the high name of his father Sokolli Pasha might prove a threat to Safiye's son's throne, then the cord was to be left untied."

A shiver crept up my back and spread across my shoulders. I remembered something Esmikhan had begun to say as she watched this business of the Quince's hand, something she found odd, new, at the birth of her daughter after three tiny sons. But I had not listened. And Esmikhan had been too weak to find the words.

"Such a tiny little mistake," Ghazanfer was continuing. "But in a matter of minutes, never more than an hour, the strongest child must succumb. 'He was weak from birth,' they say. 'He was never meant to live.' "

Now my mind went blank with the horror. There had been inklings, perhaps, but I had always blanked them out, too. Now could it be true? Our lives, all of our lives had revolved around a truth of a different nature. Much of my lady's undying love for Ferhad was because he had given her the one thing Sokolli had been unable to. Sokolli had gone to his grave, thinking himself a lesser man, content to be a cuckold. Esmikhan's crippling—she might have recovered had she not been so convinced her sins deserved a punishment. I had allowed that adultery because all the while I thought . . . and who could say but what Gul Ruh was the perfect sort of child she was for no other reason than that from her very first day she had sensed . . . ?

"Can this be true? All of our lives . . ." I exclaimed aloud. "Are they nothing? Built on a horrible black deed like that, madness as great as that of the old Quince?"

"That's what turned her mad in the end, not so much the drug to which she retreated for comfort when Safiye denied her love."

"Allah, Allah," I mourned. "Tiny, innocent babies."

Ghazanfer did not understand all I had been thinking, but I had been silent long enough to make him guess he understood. He offered some word of sympathy which I was as yet too horror-stricken to accept with much grace.

"But Esmikhan was her best friend!" I protested.

"What does friendship mean to the Fair One before power?" he asked. "All her life she has confused the Sofia she was born to—that the Christians call wisdom—and Safiye—that the Mulsims call fair. She has confused the virtues and in the confusion, perverted the power of each, supreme intelligence as well as supreme beauty.

"And ask yourself this: Why was Esmikhan Safiye's best friend? Because she could be used. By Allah, don't you see? She does the same thing to her own daughter."

"Aysha?"

"Yes, Aysha. Aysha could not get a child from Ferhad Pasha when Esmikhan could?"

"By Allah, would Safiye really do such a thing? To her own grand-children?"

"By Allah, she has already done it. And Aysha herself was spared when Ferhad died, spared to be passed on to Ibrahim Pasha. And the next Grand Vizier. And the next."

"Nothing is sacred."

"Nothing," Ghazanfer agreed, "to her."

I suddenly looked at the *khadim* and realized what he had been say-ing. "You knew about Ferhad then?"

"I knew."

"Safiye knows?"

"Perhaps not. What I guessed—in this matter—I never told her."

"That's some blessing. I suppose I'm not as clever at these subterfuges as I tried to be."

"You were a faithful guardian to your faithful women, that is what is most important. You have brought it to this peaceful, happy pass," he said, gesturing towards another burst of laughter from within.

"Sofia Baffo," I hissed.

Ghazanfer nodded. "Yes. She is the destruction of the heart of the harem, I fear, the very heart. This reign of the favored women is the end, mark my words, of the harem's power. And with it goes the power of the Empire. The very thing Safiye seeks but cannot grasp—like the sunlight through these branches."

He paused a moment and seemed to consider his next words. Per-haps he was only using the time to make certain we were alone and that Gul Ruh's son was far off, well engrossed in his chanting.

"Aysha, Allah spare her, is but a simple girl who tries to do her mother's will. One may well expect such a creature to be trampled in the fierceness of this press. Yet I myself will probably not be exempt from the coming purge. I who have, I hope to Allah, always tried to keep my wits about me, who understands the system so well from my good teachers in the torture chambers of the Seven Towers. I, who knew from the start that I was her creature altogether, that my life lay best in being but her right hand, silent, mute as the tongueless ones who pull the silken cord. I—I must bring the midwives to the lying in of virtuous women, knowing full well what they will do, and yet I say nothing. I must open the doors to poisoners, look the other way when the dagger strikes. Yes, I will tell you something else you probably didn't know. The dervish that struck down your master—he, too, was in Safiye's pay."

"That I knew," I said.

"You did?"

"At least in part. After all, it had been my consuming search for months after the death. Until one Night of Power. But then Mitra told me, poor girl, before she died."

"Ah, yes. I see."

"But by then, it didn't seem so important after all. Revenge?" I shrugged.

Ghazanfer nodded. "You are most fortunate to be able to shrug off revenge."

"But I have never understood why Sokolli had to die—Allah favor him. Nur Banu told my young lady it was to prevent her marriage to Abd ar-Rahman, but that never seemed reason enough."

"No, that was but a small part of the reason."

"Nur Banu was the one who, along with Uweis and Lala Mustafa Pasha, was most firmly against Sokolli. My master was powerful and, I would have thought, useful to Safiye in many ways against them."

Ghazanfer shrugged. "Sokolli had come to the end of his usefulness. Particularly with the death of Michael Cantacuzenos the Greek."

"No more than that?"

"No more. But as I was saying, about myself. I am her right hand, have been for years, and yet now even I see the knife lowering. I have been forced to take too many positions that have gangrened me. She knows it. I know it. She knows some day the infection will become too severe because she has fed it with too much wealth, too much power. I will be cut off, allowed not even a show of begging for mercy. When the day comes—and it comes soon—I will be better cut off. Better for her to come out whole and clean and strong one more time.

"Indeed, I can see this so well that I know just how it will be. I have seen so many of her victims, any one of them might have had my face. I think she will save the sword for me. A swift stroke, and I shall be face-less, anonymous. This body I take for granted, with which I served her with all of its strength—it will twitch once or twice while the janis-saries cheer and the Sultan salutes them . . . by Allah, I've dreamed it so often, it'll almost be a relief to have it happen once and for all, and then no more."

There was sweat like a frontlet of pearls strung from every pore on his great, flat face. He continued, now in a quieter vein. "But I have an-other vision too. It is one of those we eunuchs hate to have, for it sug-gests to us that it is possible to gain our manhood back. Even for myself, who asked for the knife, that thought is sometimes so painful that I may go mad from it, like one who may scratch out his own eyes when they have offended his with too much horror . . .

"I asked for Mu'awiya the Red's knife, yet in this dream I find my-self in my lady's room, alone, with her, at night. There is but a single lamp, burning low, and by its light, she smiles at me. Her hair is as golden as the burning oil, her skin like alabaster, like egg white, and split from the brown shell of her jacket open to her waist. Her smile broad-ens. She reaches for me. How she trusts me. How she longs for me . . ."

I made a sign that he should stop. Such a confession wasn't necessary. It would be unendurable to both of us. But he was determined.

"No, let me continue," he said. "Such was my dream all the first years in her service, and I, as you would, always stopped it at that point by force, by a quick plunge in ice-crusted waters, by twisting my own fingers so hard that the memory of the Seven Towers came back strong enough to turn my thoughts to other things.

"But these last few months, chased by the demons of that first dream—that of my own death—and by the revelations of the black goddess—I have no longer had the will to stop this vision. And so I have seen how it continues.

"She reaches for me, trusting, longing . . . what she longs for neither of us knows. Or rather, we think we know, but we are fooled by the images of love the world has wanted us to believe all our lives. Slowly, as I touch the golden flame of her hair, I realize that she has had all the mere beastly copulation a woman could ask for. Yes, but it is love she seeks, love she ever sought when she sought power and wealth. It is a different kind of love than that the world will sell her for her golden hair and her golden coffers, however. It is a love that will finally, finally let her rest.

"As my hand runs down the alabaster of her body, gently begins to knead those breasts, I feel it so strongly beneath the coolness of her exterior. It is a heat that has all but consumed itself, a lamp that sputters and longs to be extinguished quickly and not be left to die a long drawn-out death of more and more the same. So I reach over her to the niche and catch the wick between two love-wet fingers. Then, while my hand is behind her head I reach in the darkness for one of the pillows. Gently, slowly, like a caress, I draw it up and over her face. I press down. I hold it there.

"And you know, she doesn't struggle. Her hand is on my arm until the last and she doesn't once sink her nails into me, as she could so easily do. Not even in pain do they clench me. But they continue to caress me as in gratitude, growing weaker and weaker until peace is hers at last.

"That is the love of a eunuch—that peace at last. Perhaps there is no greater love. . . . Anyway, that is what I've dreamed. And every day, every hour, it seems more real . . ."

The light coming through the tree had gained a red tint now, as if the light of spirit had gained blood and needed only that elusive quality of flesh to make it material. Ghazanfer rose, wished me luck and blessings with my pilgrimage, and I returned the wish. Then he was gone; business in the belly of the palace called him. And suddenly I knew, too, that what had begun so long ago in a convent garden, a glimmer of lust for power, was about to be snuffed out.

I sat a long time beneath that tree, looking at the shapes of light upon the ground. Then I followed the branches up and saw how low and strong and inviting to climb are the limbs of a fig. Before I half knew what I was doing, I had answered that invitation and found myself seated in a crotch some five or six feet off the ground. It was not a climb such as I had once made many years before when rigging was my home and long robes only for old men's ceremony. But I was well reminded of that day I first saw her, the convent garden, the golden hair wanton from her coif. The bawdy song she whistled came once more to my lips.

But instead of the little chapel and the refectory, through the trees, over the wall now I saw a street of weavers. And I saw they were making were the trappings for the pilgrims' caravan, the heavy brocade for the two lead camels, the new black curtains broidered with gold for the Ka'ba. They worked furiously and their work was nearly finished. Soon it would be time for us to go. I gently touched the parchment now inside my robe.

I sat in the tree and remembered and thought. I thought about all Ghazanfer had told me and wondered what Allah's—or God's—will would be in all of this. I thought of that one mistake in trusting judgement that had so ruled all our lives. I wondered how often such things happen—perhaps every day—and then I wondered if it really mattered in the end where there were truths and where lies. Other things were more important. Other things caused more joy and life.

Finally I turned all this wondering upon myself and said, "You lived your life convinced what the knife had done to you was the greatest of evils and that you could never recover from it and know joy. But was that a mistaken judgement after all? Was it mistaken, meant by God to be mistaken because otherwise you would have been too careless with those good times He did give you and always be waiting for the better?"

I thought some more and wondered until I heard a little voice from beneath me. *"Ustadh? Ustadh?* What are you doing up in that tree?" And the little boy laughed aloud.

I climbed down rather sheepishly, and to hide that sheepishness, I turned sternly to him and demanded to hear what he had been learning. He would not let me get the better of him here and recited most plainly:

> "In the Name of Allah, the Compassionate, the Merciful:
> Verily, man is insolent
> Because he sees himself possessed of riches.
> Verily, to your Lord is the return of all.
> Adore and draw nigh to Allah . . ."

I poked him fondly in the belly (that belly that the grace of God had spared the midwife's hand) and gave him the end of my sherbet and some more pistachios as a reward.

Then, as I took him by the hand and entered the house, I called him "Biricchino." That was my special pet name for him. It is Italian. It is what my old nurse used to call me.

GLOSSARY

Agha—A term of respect meaning lord.

Akçe—A small Turkish coin.

Altena—In Venice, an upper-story patio or flat roof.

Awqaf—Plural of *waqf,* see below.

Baraka—Great holy power or blessing.

Chiaus—An imperial bodyguard.

Fatiha—The first and shortest Sura of the Koran, commonly used as a prayer.

Ghrush—A large Turkish coin.

Habibi—A term of endearment.

Haram—The Arabic root from which our word *harem* comes. It means many things, but in particular something forbidden and sacred.

Haremlik—Simply the Arabic *harem,* ending with the Turkish *lik,* or place, to make it parallel with *selamlik.*

Inshallah—"If Allah wills."

Kadin—A lady, one who has borne the Sultan or his heir a son.

Kapu aghasi—A high position in the Ottoman government that included control of the sanctuaries in Mecca and Medina.

Khadim—Arabic for "servant," used euphemistically in Turkish for "eunuch."

Khuddam—Plural of *khadim,* see above.

Lufer—A fish that seasonally migrates between the Black Sea and the Mediterranean.

Mabein—From the Arabic for "between"; a portion of a Turkish house between the *haremlik* and *selamlik* where a man may meet with his women without disturbing the rest of the harem.

Mashallah—An exclamation usually of wonder meaning "What Allah hath wrought!"

Medrese—An Islamic religious college.

Minhal—A camel litter.

Muderisler—Professor in a *medrese*.

Nikah—A betrothal ceremony where the marriage contract is drawn up.

Oda—A room or chamber, base of the English word odalisque.

Proveditore—A high official in the Venetian Republic, advisor to the commander of a military force.

Razzia—A raid.

Sandjak—A Turkish province. The word comes literally from the Turkish word for horsetail "standard" or "banner," harking back to the Turks' wild days on the steppes of Asia, which the *sandjak bey* would have carried before him.

Selamlik—The men's portion of a Turkish house. It is a hybrid word containing the Arabic *selam* (like salaam, literally peace, a greeting, hence this is the place where guests are greeted) and the Turkish suffix *lik,* which means "place of."

Shalvar—Turkish trousers worn by men and women.

Spahi—There are two types of *spahis.* I use the word only in its rarer form, to refer to an elite cavalry troop chosen from the ranks of Palace School as a bodyguard for the Sultan. The more common *spahis* were freemen awarded lands for services rendered to the throne and who were required to present themselves, horsed and armored, when called upon, something like feudal knights.

Sug—A bazaar.

Tekke—A Turkish monastery for dervishes.

Tughra—A highly stylized signature with the letters twisted together in an artistic fashion used for formal documents.

Ustadh—Turkish, from the Arabic, with the sense of "master" or "teacher"; used to address eunuchs respectfully.

Valide Sultan—The mother of the Sultan, the highest feminine position in the harem.

Waqf—Turkish word, taken from the Arabic, which refers to a pious charitable foundation or trust.

Yelek—A floor-length jacket buttoned down the front and worn as part of a Turkish woman's costume.